Love Always, Damian

d. Nichole King

Love Always, Damian

Limitless Publishing, LLC
Kailua, HI 96734
www.limitlesspublishing.com

Formatting: Limitless Publishing

ISBN-13: 978-1-68058-148-5
ISBN-10: 1-68058-148-1

Dedication

For Virginia Pierce,
a wonderful CP, writer, and person,
who lost her battle with cancer on August 9, 2014.
Until we meet again, my friend.

Chapter 1

Damian

The box under my bed taunts me. I ignore it. This year, I won't succumb to its cries.

"Fuck this shit." I roll off my bed and search the dresser for my keys. Not there.

Where the hell did I put them?

I yank the door open and round the corner into the bathroom. Nothing but the usual.

Out in the living room, I throw the cushions off the sofa and check the chair and the coffee table. A handful of loose change, a couple of empty condom wrappers, three McDonald's French fries, and a ten-dollar bill, which I pocket. No keys.

"Goddammit!"

I stomp into the kitchen and grab Dylan's motorcycle keys from the drawer. Dude never misplaces anything. Predictable bastard.

Apparently he heard me because when I get back to the living room, he's standing there.

I glance at him on my way past. "Borrowing

your motorcycle."

"What are you doing, Damian?"

Turning around, I dangle the keys in front his face. "Borrowing. Your. Motorcycle." I repeat it slowly, enunciating every word so maybe he gets it the second time.

"That's not what I mean," Dylan says, but I already know that. Each May is the same, and he's got my MO down by now.

"I'm not asking your permission."

"Last day of finals is tomorrow." My roommate is annoyed. "Look, bro, it's been four years since Ka—"

Suddenly, I have Dylan pinned to the wall, my hand around his throat. I squeeze hard enough to make him understand. "You're my best friend, man, but I don't need your psychobabble bullshit again. Not today."

Dylan sighs and nods as best he can.

I take a step back, letting go of him. He rubs his neck and a pang of guilt zips through me. Dude means well.

"I can't deal with this right now." I flip the keys into my palm and walk out the door.

I love the sound of Dylan's motorcycle when I rev it up. The noise drowns out everything, especially the shit in my head. Her memory hasn't faded, not even a little.

Speeding down the street, I don't think. The route is on autopilot in my brain.

I park in my usual spot and stuff the keys in my pocket. It's Tuesday night, so the lot is almost empty. Good thing, too, because tonight I want to be alone.

Loud music assaults me as soon as I walk in. I don't even look around to see who's there. No need; everything I want is behind the counter.

"What'll it be, Damian?" Max asks.

"Tequila. Straight up," I say, pounding my fist twice on the wood.

"Sure thing, man."

I don't sit on a stool, and I don't wait. On my way to a booth in the corner, I shoot a passing glance at the guys playing pool. I recognize a couple of them from school. For them, tonight is about relaxing. For me, it's about forgetting.

I slide in, running my fingers through my hair. The way her dark eyes still pierce through my mind guts me to the core. They'll always haunt me.

"Damian, my love, my final wish is for you to let me go."

I can't do it.

"Two tequila shots."

I almost jump out of my seat at the sound, but when I stare at the waitress, I realize the voice didn't belong to *her*. Of course she would never have said that. She hated me drinking.

I give the new girl a quick nod. She turns, and I down the first shot, watching the way her ass sways as she walks away.

Flipping the glass over, I send a wave to Max then knock back the other one. He usually cuts me off at ten, and tonight, that won't take long. It won't be enough to drown her out of my head, but it might be enough to make the images fuzzy.

"Are you happy, Damian?"

3

I squeeze my eyes shut. What the fuck kind of question is that? A knife stabs me through the heart and I want to vomit.

I hear two more glasses hit the table in front of me, forcing my eyes open. My gaze darts to the nametag on the waitress's t-shirt, barely above her left nipple that's poking hard into the cotton. I lick my lips.

Cameron.

I guess she'll do.

"Another round," I say.

As I wait, my mind takes me back to that morning and how Kate waited until sunrise to leave me. Maybe it was her way of reminding me.

"It's amazing, isn't it? No matter how dark it gets, the sun always rises and starts a new day. The darkness is forgotten."

God, I miss her so much. Everything about her.

Cameron sets two more shots on the table, and I don't look at her this time. I'm gonna need more alcohol for that.

I rub my face with my palms.

"I'll always be with you."

Fuck, no!

I jab my fists into the seat, pain racing through my knuckles. She fucking left me all alone! She's gone and I'm here. It's not fucking fair.

The sting of tears threatens, so I kill the shots, one right after the other. I slam the last glass on the table too hard, but I don't care.

When Cameron comes back over, she sets two more in front of me and says, "Rough night?"

I huff and down the first one. "You could say

4

that."

Her bare thigh is so close to me. I can't wait to feel it up later.

"Bring me two more if you would," I say.

She bites her lip. "Um, I don't know. Max…"

"Just bring me the fucking shots. Max and I have an agreement."

Cameron peers over her shoulder at the bartender. Getting confirmation from Max, she swings around. "I'll be right back.".

I lean back, rubbing a finger over my lip, the alcohol finally kicking in.

"You have a whole life in front of you. Don't waste it. Don't dwell on the past."

Cameron saunters over with a tray of my last two shots of the night. I stare at her thighs, already imagining what they taste like. *I'm moving on, baby. Just like you told me to.*

"Thanks," I say as she sets them down. "When are you off?"

She hesitates. "Um, like, now. My boyfriend is picking me up."

Well, shit.

I down the last two and go up to pay my tab. My buzz is decent but not enough. It's never enough anymore.

"Thanks, Max."

"See ya, man."

Stuffing my hands in my pockets, I take my time walking across the parking lot to Dylan's motorcycle. I pull out the keys and rev the engine. Her face isn't gone, but it's barely recognizable now. Exactly how I want it.

5

Slowly, I back out and notice Cameron standing against the side of the bar, hugging her arms from the chill.

Stood up. Sweet.

I pull up next to her. "Need a lift?"

"Uh, no. Toby should be here any minute."

Toby Stanton, maybe? If so, Cameron might be a great lay.

"Toby should have been here by now," I say, reaching out to her. "Come on. I'll take you home."

She bites her lip again, and I hope to know what that feels like in about ten minutes.

Cameron sighs and takes my hand. "I live on campus—Frederiksen Court."

I help her up behind me, her arms slipping around my waist. Smirking, I say, "Hang on."

We peel out into traffic, the wind slamming against my face. Cameron nestles her head into my back and holds me tighter. She says something, but I can't hear her.

On the way back to mine and Dylan's apartment—off-campus—I take a shortcut. By now, I just need to get Cameron naked. Fuck everything else.

I park beside my BMW and cut the engine.

"I said Frederiksen Court," Cameron says, confused.

I climb off, then back on, facing her. "I said I'd take you home. This is where I live."

"Toby—"

"—is off fucking someone else and forgot about you." My hands find her knees and begin to slide up her thighs. Damn, they feel as good as they look.

6

She frowns, but doesn't say anything. I'm right and she knows it.

Taking in every inch of her skin, I run my palms up her inner thighs as what I said sinks in. To let it go deeper, I kiss her neck, sucking on the flesh. She'll cave. They always do.

"He's probably working out late at the gym," she says, trying to convince herself.

"Yeah, probably not." I switch sides, and she tilts her head, letting me continue. Down below, I move her panties to the side to massage her. She stiffens a little, gasping.

"Toby...he's a...a National Champion boxer. He—uh—" She pauses, her breaths becoming shallow, just how I like it.

Yep. Toby Stanton. This is gonna be good.

She swallows. "He works out a lot."

I grunt. "I bet he does."

I know *he does.*

She nods. "He does."

Her hips slowly move against the pressure I'm putting on her, and I crush my lips onto hers. I'm not surprised when she returns the kiss with fervor. Toby only dates the feisty ones.

My fingers start to slip over her, and I can't take it anymore. I have to get my mouth on that.

When I let go, a disappointed gasp escapes her. I help her off the bike and lead her inside to my room.

My shirt is over my head before I have the door closed behind me. Kicking it, it slams closed. I don't take the time to lock it.

Cameron fumbles with my belt. Fuck that. I pull

her close, slide my hands under the waistband of her skirt, touching every inch of the smooth skin hiding beneath. Walking her backwards to my bed, I lean into her until she sits and I can finish the job, tossing the skirt and her panties across the room.

I undo my belt and jeans, stepping out of them. Toby is clearly out of her thoughts now. She moans in excitement. Now to get the rest of her clothes off.

Gliding my palms up her thighs, I take a short detour between them.

"Oh, yes!" she cries out as I slip inside of her. I finger her until she's on the verge of coming.

Pulling out, I chuckle, knowing it's about to get a whole lot better real quick. She frowns, giving me puppy-dog eyes.

"Don't worry. I'll be back," I whisper in her ear.

She throws her head back with a smile on her face.

I grab the bottom of her shirt and begin to lift it, but it won't move past her chest. She's pinned her nametag to her bra.

"Oh, Cameron," I groan. I hate that I have to take the extra time to undo the damn thing.

"Sorry," she says, panting. Music to my ears. "Here, let me." She turns the top of her shirt inside out, unhooking the pin. "There. Oh, and this is my friend's nametag. I forgot mine. My name is Katey."

Someone just punched me in the stomach.

"Don't leave me, Katie. I'm gonna fuck up, but don't leave me."

"Get. The fuck. Out," I breathe.

Her brows furrow. "Excuse me?"

8

"Get the fuck. Out of here." I gather up her clothes and shove them in her chest, knocking her backwards a little. "Now."

The pathetic expression on her face doesn't faze me. She means absolutely nothing to me.

I throw the door open and don't look at her as she shuffles out, undressed from the waist down.

"How am I supposed to get home?"

"I don't give a damn," I say and slam the door in her face.

A stunned second later, she screams, "You're a fucking asshole!" from the other side.

I collapse on the bed, my face buried in the blankets.

Yeah, Kate, I know. I know.

Chapter 2

Damian

"Come on, man, and get your ass out of bed. We're gonna be late."

Dylan banging on my door rips me from my sleep. Awesome, numb, drunken sleep, where even Kate is absent from my mind.

Fucking bastard.

I roll onto my back and something crunches beneath me. As I shift to dig it out, the empty bottle of Templeton Rye drops off the bed and clinks against the other empty bottle on the floor. My fingers close around the object, and I pull it out.

The small black notebook with a red rose on the cover stares at me. It's Kate's diary.

Suddenly, last night is no longer a fuzzy mass of shit I don't remember. The anniversary of the day I watched her take her last breath is the worst goddamn day of the year. Actually, this whole week is an annual painfest. It's an unnecessary reminder of her leaving me. That she tore my heart out and

10

took it with her to the grave.

I don't want it back. It belongs to her.

I scan over her letter to me again—her last entry. Her beautiful, hopeful words promising me I'd be okay. What the hell did she know? She's gone, and I'm left here with all the fucking memories she dumped on me.

My last wish, Damian, is that once you've read my diary, you'll put it in a box. Place it in the attic somewhere and leave it there. Let it collect dust.

That's not all, though. You have a whole life in front of you. Don't waste it. Don't dwell on the past. Move forward.

Life isn't about merely surviving. It's about living.

Damian, my love, my final wish is for you to let me go.

Love Always, Kate

How the hell am I supposed to forget her? Move on? She has no freaking clue what she did to me.

Fuck!

I'm losing it. Breaking down again now that I'm no longer numb.

She shouldn't have left me. She should have taken the stupid drug then I could have saved her. My blood. My blood was a match to hers, and I would have given it all to her if she held on a little longer.

My stomach hurts. Hell, my whole body hurts. I

can't breathe as the same thoughts plague me year after year, never letting me forget.

I glance at the empty whiskey bottles on the floor. I'm still the same bastard I was four years ago. The only difference is now I don't have my brother's girlfriend to fuck when I need the extra release alcohol can't give me.

No, Ellie high-tailed it out of my life the morning of Kate's funeral. One last roll in the sack to deaden my pain, and then she moved to Florida. Something about studying marine biology or some shit like that.

I haven't heard from her since. Whatever. Easy lays aren't hard to find here.

"Damian!" *Bang, bang, bang.* "Dude, we gotta go!"

Philosophy final. Shit.

"Yeah, man. Give me a minute," I yell, throwing on the first t-shirt I see. I grab a pair of jeans off the floor and tuck my phone in the pocket.

"About time," Dylan says, tossing me a set of keys. "Found 'em."

I swipe a protein bar out of the cupboard. "Yeah? Where?"

"Right there, on the counter." He sounds annoyed. Dude's a perfectionist, and sometimes I think his decision to room with me is his idea of community service. Dylan's had my back since junior high though, and he's the only person I consider a friend.

"Thanks," I say. "So, are we going yet? I don't want to be late."

Dylan shakes his head at my irresponsibility and

follows me out to my BMW. Philosophy is the one class we share this semester, and parking is a bitch, so we're riding together. But I have plans after this final, and Dylan isn't part of them. Hopefully he has another ride home, 'cause I'm not waiting for his slow ass to finish the exam before I leave.

Sure enough, an hour and a half later, I'm done and Dylan is still scribbling out his answers. There's a good ninety minutes left of class, and my roommate will use each and every one of them before he walks out. No way in hell am I staying that long.

"Hey, I'm leaving, man," I whisper to him.

"Seriously? You're finished already?"

"Uh, yeah."

He's annoyed because while he's been pulling all-nighters for a week, I've cracked a book for maybe two hours. If I don't know the shit by now, no amount of poring over the material again is going to do any good. Besides, this week I have other things on my mind.

"Fine. Go," he says.

"Later."

I gather my stuff and head up front to the prof. His eyes lift over the rim of his glasses to study me. I'm the first one to hand in my final, and he probably thinks I've done a half-assed job.

I didn't, though. When he checks it, he'll find every answer as flawlessly correct as usual. I'm a Lowell, and for the last six years I haven't been living up to that. Until now. Because of the deal I cut with the Good Doctor.

I've held onto an almost perfect 4.0 GPA for the

last five semesters.

Finally, the prof nods at me and I walk out of class, leaving my junior year of college behind.

~*~

It takes me an hour to get to the cemetery. After Mom and Liam died, I never stepped foot here. Not until Kate convinced me to come. It had been one of her five wishes. One through three I'd done because she was with me. Because I loved her. I promised her number four, so I followed through. Number five, though?

Number five is impossible.

I come here often now—day, night, whenever I need to be close to her. Even in death, Kate draws me in. To this place where she'd only trodden once when she was alive.

I grab the three bouquets of flowers from the passenger seat and swing the door open. When Kate brought me here four years ago, I barely managed to get out of the car. Now it's easy.

Too fucking easy.

I don't even think about coming anymore. It's automatic. Routine, like my nightly shots of whiskey.

It shouldn't be like this. In three short years I lost the three people I loved most. Death sucks, and I've had my fill.

I slam the door closed and tread over the grass. The three identical stones jut up from the ground, and even when I'm here after dark, I don't have a problem seeing them. They're etched into my memory.

The idea to have Kate buried here beside my mother and brother was entirely mine and entirely selfish. The Browdys had asked me to help with her funeral arrangements, and other than the time of the graveside service, this had been my only request. This way she'd be close to me.

Shade from the elder tree casts a shadow over them. I stand inside its cover from the sun, facing the cold memorials. These pieces of granite have no real connection with the people they were.

Hell, they didn't even pick them out. Didn't see them, yet their names, dates of birth and death are etched into them as if they'd been owned by those they claim to represent.

Cemeteries—these stones—aren't for the dead.

No, they're for the living.

My gaze trails over the Celtic symbols engraved at the center of each one. Identical to the tattoos inked into my body. Faith. Brotherhood. Hope.

My eyes linger on Kate's as they usually do, and the memory of when I'd given her the trinity heart necklace pours over me.

"It's the Celtic symbol for hope. Now you'll always know where to find it," I'd told her.

Damn. I'd given it to her so she'd think of me whenever she needed me, but really, it was I who needed her.

I take a deep breath to hold myself together. I lost everything the day Kate died.

I rake a hand through my hair and shut my eyes. Out here, away from everyone, I don't have to pretend that I have a fucking clue how to live without her.

Out here, it's just me.

In front of Kate's gravestone, I lower myself to the ground, dropping the flowers at my side. My chest is empty, yet somehow, it hurts. It's the same damn thing year after year—aching to see her smile at me just one more time. One more and I'd be satisfied, I tell myself.

I know it's a lie because one more smile from her would never be enough. I need to touch her, run my fingers over her warm skin and protect the hell out of her.

But I'm a failure. I had the power within me, in my blood, to save her, and I failed.

I can barely see the inches in front of me as I break down. Four years ago, my father sat here with me and told me the pain would never go away, but it would lessen over time.

What a load of bullshit; the pain has only grown.

"I miss you so damn much, Katie," I say even though she can't hear me. And that thought kicks me in the gut as much as anything. No matter what I say to her now, she'll never know any of it.

I slide my fingertips over her name: Kathryn "Katie" Browdy. Seventeen short years on this earth and I only had her last months. They were the best months of my life.

I sit with her until the sun begins to send streaks of gold over the horizon. Even though Kate would be disappointed, I need to pick up more liquor before I head home. I have to have something to get me through this pain.

A gust of wind rustles the dead flowers I left on

their graves last week. I scoop them up and replace them with the fresh ones I brought. Daisies for my mother, some generic flowers he wouldn't give a shit about for Liam, and red roses for Kate.

Always red roses for my Katie.

"Love you, Mom," I murmur, fanning out the daisies in the vase beside her headstone.

Then I move onto Liam's. "Take care of my girl, man," I tell him, then I remember how I'd taken care of his. "But if you touch her, I'll fucking kill you."

I squat down and lay Kate's roses at the base of her stone. There's nothing I could say to her that I haven't already said a million times. So I settle for the words I couldn't say until just before she died. "I love you, baby. I'll always love you."

~*~

My liquor cabinet is now well stocked, and I grab a bottle of tequila. I knock back a swig. Damn good shit right there. I pound down another on my way to the living room.

Dylan's probably at The Underground, grinding against the chicks who only order sex on the beach because of the name, and have had one too many. Or two too many.

But what the hell. Finals are over, and The Underground is the place to be tonight. I might head over later after I've got enough of a buzz going to forget what this week means to me.

Either way, at the end of the night my plan is to be passed out in bed, gloriously numb to the hole in my chest. I really don't give a shit how I end up there.

I collapse on the sofa and swing my feet up on the coffee table. Gulping down another drink of tequila, I hear my phone go off in the back pocket of my jeans. Without setting down the bottle, I twist and dig it out.

"Hello?" I answer.

"Damian?"

The familiar voice smashes into my ear, and for a second, I'm paralyzed.

Fuck. Me.

Chapter 3

Elizabeth

"Damian, are you there?" I repeat since he hasn't said anything. "It's me, Ellie," I say, because he won't recognize my new Florida cell phone number. I wanted a fresh start when I left Iowa, and that included seven new digits with an 850 area code.

A lot has changed in the last four years, and I wasn't sure he'd remember my voice.

"Uh, yeah. I'm here," he finally says, and in the background, I hear the clunk of glass hitting a table.

Inwardly, I cringe. I guess some things don't change.

Just hang up, Ellie. This is a stupid idea.

I tuck my legs up under me, the wicker loveseat creaking. I should take my own advice, tell him this was a mistake, and figure something else out. Damian wasn't the only reason I had to get away, but he was the biggest one.

"How've you been, Elle?" he asks.

He's the only person who ever called me Elle.

Liam started calling me Ellie when we began to date, but I was Elizabeth to everyone else. Even now, after all this time, a flood of chills sweeps up my spine as he says it.

I swallow, giving myself a second to reply. "I'm doing okay. You?"

Small talk is worthless. I should either end this call or get to the point. No use allowing these tiny ripples of emotion to make themselves at home in my stomach after I've worked so hard to keep them at bay. Destroying them by moving fifteen hundred miles away and immersing myself in my studies didn't work, so this is the next best thing. Really, it's all I can do to pretend they don't exist. I can't let them control me again.

"Yeah, I'm good. I'm good," he says without conviction.

He's not doing good. I can hear it in his voice. I also know the timing of this phone call sucks, but I won't be in Iowa much longer, and I need to get this over with sooner rather than later. I've waited as long as I could, and now I'm cutting it super close.

The problem is I'm still debating whether or not to go through with my plans. Unfortunately, I've run out of options, and Damian is my absolute last choice since my friend Kerri had a family emergency and flew home to Canada last week. My plane leaves in two days, and if I don't have something lined up, I can kiss this spectacular opportunity goodbye. Great Barrier Reef projects of this magnitude don't come along every day. I *need* this to complete my thesis.

I only wish it hadn't come down to asking

20

Damian a favor. Of all things, that's what I'm left with.

"Well, um, the reason I'm calling is that I'm in Iowa for a couple of days, and I was wondering if maybe we could…uh…meet up tomorrow morning?" I say against my better judgment. Then I hold my breath, half hoping he'll tell me he never wants to see me again. Honestly, that would be best for both of us.

"Tomorrow morning?" he repeats. "Yeah, sure. We can do that."

Dammit.

"Great. Um…"

"I have a place up in Ames, close to campus. I can text you the address."

His place? I'd been hoping for somewhere a little more…public. But before I can suggest a change in venue, the flutters rippling under my skin make their way to my mouth. "Okay."

I'm a glutton for punishment. So stupid.

We don't have to stay at his house, though, right? I mean, when I arrive there tomorrow, I'll suggest we go out for breakfast or something. The last thing I need is to be alone with him again. The last time I let my guard down with him…well, it's the reason I'm meeting with him in the morning.

I've got to get myself under control before then. I'm twenty-four years old now, for God's sake. I can handle this.

I straighten my back, sitting up taller for my own encouragement, and take a deep breath. "I'll see you tomorrow, Damian."

"Bye, Elle."

Shit. That name again.

"Bye," I breathe out and hang up before my heart rate doubles again. I lift my head to the porch ceiling, and suddenly I regret the whole conversation. I'm such an idiot! I shouldn't have called him. I should have...I don't know.

I don't have another choice unless I call my professor and say "Screw the trip." If I did, I'd be out a ton of money that took me over a year to save up, but hell. Maybe that's worth not having to face Damian.

I mean, can he even handle it?

I peer into the backyard of my childhood home. So much has changed, yet so much has stayed the same. The old swing set my dad built for me still sits in the exact same spot it has for twenty years. Unused for the bulk of those years until the other day.

It's nice to see my parents again in the flesh instead of over Skype. I haven't been back since I left. Plane tickets are expensive, and between school, work, and everything else, I've never made the time to make it up. They did make it down to Florida once though, since I moved. Christmas, three years ago. Before Dad got too bad to travel.

This isn't how I had envisioned my life. These aren't the plans Liam and I made. Not even close.

As soon as we graduated from college, we were going to get married. Liam should be at Harvard Law right now while I teach kindergarteners how to read and write. Maybe we'd even be discussing when to start our own little family.

I take a drink of lemonade and set it back on the

end table as I shake off the life I was never meant to have. The life Liam took with him when he died.

It's been six years since I said goodbye to him. The first two after his death were the most difficult, but at least I had Damian to comfort me, numb me. And at first, that's all our relationship had been about.

Then…then something shifted. For me, anyway. I can't pinpoint when it happened exactly, I just know that when Kate Browdy entered his life, it tore mine apart for the second time. I have nothing against Kate; I never even met her.

But it was because of her I realized somewhere during those two years, I developed feelings for Damian. Feelings I tried hard to bury because they created a swell of guilt within me. I'd been Liam's girlfriend, and now that he was gone, I was falling for his brother.

So, as soon as I finished the semester at Drake, I transferred to Florida State. I had to get away. Away from Liam. From the guilt and from the man who didn't love me back.

And now, tomorrow morning, I have to ask that man a huge favor. A favor he knows absolutely nothing about, because I had to distance myself from him.

I have my life on track now. I have a goal for my future, and it doesn't include Damian Lowell.

Hopefully, four years is enough time for my heart to forget how much I loved him.

Chapter 4

Damian

What. The fuck. Was that?

Four years. Four goddamn years I haven't heard from her, and now, *now*, she calls to tell me she's back and wants to see me? What the hell!

Surely she's not wanting a quick roll in the sack. Not that I wouldn't oblige since "Cameron" left me blue, but judging by the sound of her voice, it's something else. God knows what, though. Something tells me her coming tomorrow won't be a jovial chit-chat after how I left things with her.

Five to seven nights a week she appeared in my bedroom, craving a way to extinguish the memories that haunted her. That is, until Kate.

I didn't let go of Ellie quickly, but when I did, I never looked back. Nightly visits from her became nonexistent, and I didn't once check on her to make sure she was okay.

I have no idea what other way there would be for her to cope. She rarely drinks and snagging herself another fuck buddy is way outside of who she is. Before she ran off to Florida, she'd only been with my brother and me, and it took her almost four years to let Liam inside her. I know this because one night, a week after Liam's death, she broke down and told me. I doubt she'd suddenly be okay hooking up with some stranger after she left.

I hunch forward on my knees, staring down the bottle of tequila. Along with thoughts of Kate, what Ellie wants mixes with them, and suddenly I don't want to be alone with my demons any longer.

I don't want to deal with this shit. I don't even want to think about this shit.

Leaving the bottle of tequila on the coffee table, I stand up, swipe the keys to my BMW off the counter, and head out. Max's Place is too low key for what I'm craving tonight.

Loud music. Sweaty, pumping bodies grinding on the dance floor. Never-ending shots. And as a bonus, the Kappas give celebratory after-finals blow jobs in the men's bathroom of The Underground.

That's where I go.

When I arrive, I flash my ID to the bouncer at the door. The place is packed, and the guy studies my license meticulously before he gives me the all clear with a nod of his head.

Inside, I beeline for the bar. Weave my way through the throng of students without seeing them. I'll have plenty of time for that after I clear my mind.

"Damian, what's up, man?" Chris yells over the music as I lean up against the counter.

"Same as everyone else," I tell him. "Four

Horsemen."

"You got it." He flips over a shot glass and starts to mix my drink. "Philosophy final was a bitch."

I chuckle to myself. It was a fucking sophomore level class, and I've wiped my ass with paper harder than that shit. "Sure was."

"Here you go," Chris says, setting the shot in front of me.

I knock it back and ask for another.

Chris quirks a brow. "Damn, dude."

I survey the dance floor. Fog machines pump out smoke from all four corners, making individual people difficult to see. The flashing lights move to the beat and bounce off the old school disco ball on the ceiling. Dancers congregate in the middle, squeezed together in a tight mass of skin. A couple more shots and I think I'll join them.

A few Four Horsemen later, the thoughts from earlier grow fuzzy. Good. A sexy little thing slides up next to me, wearing one of those open back shirts that shows nothing but skin with no bra. Damn, that's hot.

She orders a Long Island Iced Tea, and from my experience, that means the girl is out to get plastered and laid.

And tonight, that's what I came for.

"What else can I get you, Damian?" Chris asks while someone else mixes hottie's drink.

"Heineken."

Chris is fast with this order, and I'm taking the first drink in under twenty seconds. My gaze never wanders from the brunette beside me.

The girl twists toward me, her long brown hair

falling over her shoulders. She gathers it up and sweeps it all to one side. A silver Kappa charm on a chain hangs around her pretty neck. Oh hell yes. These sorority girls lay it all out after finals. This will be easy.

"Hey." I cock my head once at her and she smiles.

"Hey," she answers, then tucks half of her bottom lip between her teeth in a flirty grin.

The bartender puts her drink on the counter so it touches her fingertips. She glances at it, then picks it up to take a sip, keeping her eyes locked on me.

I move closer. Hook an arm around her waist and pull her against me. She giggles, and I can smell the remains of her last Long Island on her breath. The girl is already drunk. I dip my head low, my lips grazing her ear as I talk to her.

"Are you having a good time tonight?" I ask.

"For now." She presses herself further into me. Her hips slowly sway to the beat of the music, rubbing me in all the right places.

I shamelessly peer down the canal between her breasts. "So, what happens later?"

"Why don't you come dance with me and find out?"

She swivels, positioning herself in front of me and wiggles that little ass against my dick, which is already throbbing. How can I say no to that?

"Let's go." I take one last swig of beer, ready to discard it still half full, and reach for her hand.

"Wait," she says, stopping me. Then, with a sexy little smile, the girl sucks down the rest of her drink, leaving nothing but ice in the glass. "Can't let that go to waste."

I'm hard. So hard.

She entwines her fingers with mine and leads me to the dance floor. This is a girl who knows what she wants. At least, when she's drunk. And with the way she wobbles when she walks, she's one drink away from being completely sloshed.

Fuck.

Yeah, I probably shouldn't go through with the afterhours plans I have for her. A better idea would be to find another girl who will remember what she agreed to in the morning. But that means leaving this Kappa girl to fend for herself, and I know the guys here and what they look for when they're on the hunt—girls who are piss drunk who will agree to anything. A few have already been charged with rape.

I'm left with two choices: bring her home with me anyway because I'll be gentler than the next guy, or be noble and take her back to the sorority house and let her sisters take it from there.

Suddenly I remember this is why I hate post-finals parties at The Underground.

We're on the dance floor now, though barely. The building has got to be maxed out, but more people are filtering through the front door.

I decide not to think about what I'll do with the girl later. I have time to consider my options. Maybe I can steer her clear of the bar for a couple of hours. Keep her dancing. 'Cause either way, I don't want to be scrubbing puke out of my car tomorrow.

She faces me and digs her fingers into my hips,

drawing me to her. I don't object. Actually, it's fucking hot. She rubs and moves against me, lost in the bass slamming into the air. I like it because this doesn't remind me of Kate or Ellie, and I can concentrate on how this girl is arching her back and pressing her breasts into my chest. How my hands slither over her bare back and dip just under the waistband of her tight, black skirt.

The music pounds into my body, and I grind against her, feeling her up. Wanting to strip this hottie down and get more of that sweet, sweaty skin on me.

My intentions to be noble are fading real fast.

She rotates in my arms, tosses all of her hair over one shoulder, and shoves her ass into me. Now that's nice. I hold onto her hips, helping her twist them to the rhythm of the club song playing. Her new position offers me the perfect view of her cleavage. Braless breasts jiggle as she dances. It doesn't get better than that.

Song after song plays, and I'm not tired of this girl's gyrating body bouncing against me. In fact, this is the easiest form of foreplay. I'm dying to see if it's working for her too.

The only shitty part is that I'm beginning to feel the effects of my buzz slow. I could use another couple of rounds, but Kappa girl sure as hell doesn't. She's still tipsy, though better than before.

This is dilemma number two of the night: me or the girl.

I glance at the bar, then back at the boobs I've grown very fond of. And I make my decision.

She'd better be good.

As if reading my mind, she lifts herself up on her tip-toes and wraps her arms around my neck. "I need another drink," she says.

I smooth my palms over her shoulders. "I got a better idea. How about we skip the drink and get the hell out of here?"

She puffs out her lower lip. "I can't. I, uh"—she curls her mouth in a seductive grin—"have bathroom duty in twenty minutes. But you can join me in there if you want."

Oh. I want, all right.

What I don't want, however, is to have to wait until she finishes her sorority shift to get her in my bed. I need to wipe this day from my memory as soon as possible, and this girl's body is going to help me do it.

"Twenty minutes?" I repeat.

"Yep."

I wonder what her sorority sisters would think of her making an appearance, then me sweeping her out of there for an even better time. Giving guys head all night without reciprocation can't be that much fun.

"Let's go grab a couple of beers, and I'll be your first appointment." If all goes well, I'll be her *only* appointment, and then I'll have her sprawled over my mattress, panting until she can't take anymore.

"Lead the way," she says.

I order her a Smirnoff, low alcohol and fruity— basically Kool-Aid for adults. I half expect her to whine a little when I give it to her—it's no Long Island Ice Tea—but she smiles and downs half the bottle. For myself, I order another Heineken and a shot. Easy to get down fast and I'm on my way to a mind-blowing good time in less than twenty minutes.

The kind of time that makes you forget about everything. About Kate. About my shithole life without her.

About Ellie.

Damn, I need to move this night along.

I wait until my hottie finishes her girly drink before I lead her to the men's bathroom. With her on my arm, I won't have to wait in line this time.

One of the walls is lined with urinals, the other has a couple of sinks, and there are two stalls in the back. That's where we're headed.

A couple of Kappa chicks man the line of hard-ons waiting their turn. I figure the senior members are awarded the less messy job of directing traffic. As one guy leaves a stall, another goes in. It's a pretty simple concept, and the event usually runs rather smoothly. Guys are more willing to behave themselves if they're getting rewarded with free head.

"Hey, Shayla," one of the girls says, nodding at us.

Ah, that's her name.

Whatever. I won't remember it tomorrow.

"You can relieve Rianna in the last stall when she's done."

Shayla twists her hair behind her head and wraps a rubber band in it. "Okay. I brought a warm up."

The girl's gaze glides down me and lands on my crotch. Real subtle. Then she grins at my bulge. "Have fun with that, Shay."

31

I've seen some of the girls take in their boyfriends first—a nice perk, I guess—so no one objects when Shayla has me follow her in, cutting in front of the five guys already in line. Like I said, free head is free head.

Shayla reaches around me and locks the door. Her eyes travel over me the way they did earlier at the bar when I first noticed her. She places her palms on my chest, and I watch her every move. How her hands slowly slide down my body, pushing into my abs some. Then they lower more, and she works to unbutton my jeans. Unzipping them, she flashes her green stare up at me, and I inhale with anticipation.

This isn't normal protocol for this event. Normally the girls simply go for the gold, no bullshit, and I have to undo my own pants. I keep my arms at my sides, though, letting her lower my jeans and boxers to my ankles. As she does, she sits on her knees, on the black yoga mat beneath her.

I'm ready for her. So ready for this.

Leaning my head back against the cold metal wall, I close my eyes, awaiting the warmth and wetness of her mouth. The caress of her tongue. The grip of her fingers.

I'm not disappointed.

She takes me in deep right from the start. Fuck, it's amazing. And the best part is that it doesn't remind me of Kate. Hell, it doesn't remind me of Ellie, either, so it's perfect.

Shayla's tongue flicks over the underside of my dick, moving up and down the length. Once. Twice. Three times before she engulfs it again, her lips clamping down around me.

I'm in it, losing myself to the sensation. My hands wind around her ponytail, and I gently push her into me, commanding the rhythm.

She lets out a little moan with a breathy giggle, and Kate's face flashes in my mind. My eyes fly open, searching the space in front of me for what won't be there. The voice didn't belong to my Katie, even though it sounded like her.

No, it belonged to the girl on her knees, doing what I can no longer feel.

I'm done with this. It's gonna take more than a couple beers and a blow job to vanquish the demons whispering in my ear.

I ease her head away from me, then gently help her to her feet.

She narrows her eyes at me. "What? Did you not like it?"

I pull up my pants, shoving my dick back inside. "Oh, I liked it. I just want more." I lower my head and suckle on the skin at her neck. "I want to be inside you."

Her breath falters at my words, and she shivers. "I'm not supposed to leave yet."

"What if I don't give you a choice?"

"What do you mean?"

I grasp her earlobe between my teeth. "Do you want to come with me?"

She shivers again and slowly nods her head. "Yes."

"Good," I murmur, tilting her face toward me so I can taste those lips. "Then let's go."

I pick her up. Reach to unlock the door and

sweep her out of the bathroom to the confused looks of her sorority sisters and the guys who'll have to wait a little longer to get theirs now. Outside the bathroom, I put Shayla down, and we make for the exit.

She laughs as she scurries beside me in the parking lot. "That was so cool!"

I open the passenger side door for her, and she falls in, still laughing. "Sure," I say, unamused. I only care about tapping this girl and being done for the night.

On the way back to my place, she straightens her skirt and clears her throat. "My name is Shayla, by the way."

"Yeah, I gathered that."

She cocks her head to the side, her brows narrowed in confusion. "Have I already told you?"

"No, babe, the girl in the bathroom said your name."

"Oh, yeah. Right." She sits in silence for a full thirty seconds before adding, "So, what's yours?"

"Damian."

"Damian. Da-me-on," she sounds out with a slur. "Hmm, I've never met a Damian before."

"Then you've been missing out," I tell her, taking a quick peek at her cleavage again to convince myself not to do a U-turn to take her back to the Kappa house. She and a few more shots of tequila are my ticket to mental numbness tonight.

I park my car, noting how Dylan's motorcycle is here. If I'm lucky, he'll be in bed. If not, he'll grab his cane and top hat to play his version of Jiminy Cricket. I'm not in the mood.

He knows how torn up I still am over Kate, and he doesn't approve of how I handle the pain. He's right, though. What I do doesn't work because I'll be in even more pain when I wake up.

But the temporary fix, the short time that I don't hurt, is what I long for.

Quietly, I open the back door that leads into the kitchen. I don't hear the TV on, so I figure I'm in the clear. I guide Shayla toward the living room, only to be caught by the stare of my nerdy roommate who desperately needs to get laid. Plus, he's sober, even after spending the last five hours at The Underground.

The dude is playing video games with his damn headphones on.

His gaze shifts to my evening playmate. Taking the headphones off, he frowns.

"'Night, Dylan," I say curtly before he has the chance to interject, and I pull Shayla behind me to my bedroom.

Now, I can concentrate on what I came here to do.

"Your roommate doesn't look happy about—" Shayla starts.

"I don't give a fuck. Come here." The first thing I do is unhook the halter around her neck, letting it fall forward so I can see the tits that have taunted me all evening. They're nice and round with dark nipples bubbling out from the centers.

I bend down and suck one into my mouth. Shayla gasps as I roll the other one between my thumb and forefinger. She wobbles a little, so I grab her ass to steady her before walking her backward to my bed.

I position myself between her legs and lower her onto the mattress. She lies back like a good girl, wetting her lips with her tongue. Even though her eyes are bloodshot, pupils dilated, I'm in too deep to stop now. I realize this makes me an asshole, but that's nothing new.

Kate was the one who made me want to be better. Without her, there's no point.

I lift her skirt up over her hips, revealing black satin panties, which I slide down her legs, then toss on the floor.

I'm not concerned with foreplay. We had enough of that at The Underground.

I strip down and roll on a condom, ready to dive inside her. First, though, I flip her onto her stomach. Face to face sex is too personal. I don't like to look into her eyes or have her look into mine. It's easier this way.

Shayla obliges, and I fill my palms with ass cheeks before I position myself over her. I slip a finger inside her to make sure she's ready. I'd like to tell myself that I care about her experience, but right now I don't. This is for me.

She's wet enough, so I thrust into her. Her muscles immediately tighten around me, and it feels so fucking good. Better than her mouth.

I hold off, pumping harder, faster. Drowning my mind in the tension of my own body. My orgasm climbs, and I can't think about anything except how goddamn amazing it is.

This is it. The top of the hill where my pain melts away. Where Kate is absent, and the thought of Ellie showing up tomorrow is nonexistent—as if her call never even happened.

This, right here, is where I go numb.

I think Shayla is coming, but I barely hear her cries.

Harder. Faster.

Harder. Faster.

Harder. Faster.

And then I lose control, groaning out my relief and what's left of all that's haunting me—if only for a little while.

~*~

Two hours later, the booze is leaving my bloodstream, and the pain I spent all night trying to wash away is returning. Full force, louder and louder.

Sara, Sahara, Sharna, whatever her name is, is sound asleep beside me, the sheet only half covering her partially naked body. Usually I have no problem convincing myself to use women for my own satisfaction. But these nights, the ones where the memory of what Kate and I shared crushes me to the bone, I'm reminded of who I am and how I never deserved her.

I work to push it away because Kate's gone and she's not coming back. I'll never love someone the way I loved her, so it doesn't matter who's in my bed.

If I'm being honest though, what I feel right now is my own personal brand of punishment. The hangover that leaves me in shambles and more pain than when I set out.

This moment I crave more than the sex.

I suck in a deep breath, raking both my hands through my hair, and stare at the ceiling. I'd woken up to the sound of Kate's voice in my head, softly reiterating her third wish.

"I wanna see the sun rise with you every morning for the rest of my life," she'd said.

"That's a whole lot of sunrises," I told her. *"Are you sure you can put up with me for that long?"*

"That and longer. For always."

The ghost of her face appears in front of me, her brown eyes so beautiful and tender, gazing at me like she's actually here. The corner of her mouth pulls up into a grin. I reach out to touch her phantom cheek, and she closes her eyes to feel me.

"Always isn't long enough," I say into the darkness.

And then she fades away in the shadows of my memory.

Chapter 5

Ellie

My palms are sweating.

I grip the steering wheel tighter and take a deep breath. This is such a stupid idea. I mean, this is two whole months I'm talking about. Eight full weeks. Can I trust Damian for that amount of time?

After Liam and Nora—his mom—died in the car accident, Damian started to do some really stupid shit. His once straight-A report card filled up with D's, and he took his anger out on windows, buildings, and cars. He began smoking to piss off his dad. Alcohol drowned his pain, and later, so did a steady stream of girls when I wasn't available.

I never said anything, though. I used him as much as he used me, filling the unbearable emptiness inside with him night after night because it was easier than admitting Liam was gone. With Damian, I could pretend that a piece of him hadn't left me. That somehow I could still touch him.

The difference now is that I've moved on with

my life. I let go.

Sure, Damian's relationship with Kate helped speed up that process for me, but at this point, Damian's had plenty of time to mourn his losses and do the same. The fact that I'm pretty sure he was drinking last night when I called makes me wonder though.

God, if he's still up to his old tricks, there's no way I can go on this trip to Australia. No. Freaking. Way.

With my mind on the fritz, I pull up to the house. I check Damian's text on my phone again to make sure I have the right address. The place seems safe enough. A one-story beige and brick ranch-style home with a two-car garage. It's also a decent distance away from Iowa State University campus. Not bad digs for a college student. Then again, I don't expect anything less from a member of the Lowell family.

It's not Damian's housing conditions that concern me, anyway. It's what happens inside the walls that worries me.

My phone rings, and I half hope it's Damian calling to cancel. Glancing at the number on the screen, the hope dissipates. I guess our morning meeting is still on.

"Hi Blake," I answer.

"Hey babe. What's the verdict?"

Three dates and a handful of kisses don't exactly qualify for him to call me "babe," but I don't protest. We've been friends since I enrolled in the marine biology undergrad program at Florida State, and now we're both working on master's degrees.

Blake is doing the Australia study too. And he wants me there.

"I don't have one yet," I say.

"Have you talked to him?" he asks.

"That's what I'm about to do. I don't know, though, Blake. What if he can't handle it?"

"Then you'll be on the first flight out of Cairns. It's gonna be okay, Elizabeth."

"You don't know Damian," I mutter.

"And neither do you anymore, right? Give the guy a chance. He might surprise you."

I tap my nails on the steering wheel. Blake's right. Damian deserves a shot to prove himself, and maybe I'm not giving him enough credit. Maybe he has changed.

Only one way to find out.

I sigh into the phone.

"I'll call you later," I tell him, peering up at the house again.

"He deserves to hear it from you," he assures me. "You're doing the right thing."

"I hope so. Bye, Blake."

I press end and take a deep, cleansing breath, keeping my gaze focused on the front door. Damian is expecting me, and I'm technically five minutes late. Even so, I sit in my car a little longer, debating with myself again.

What if…

In the back of my mind, I'm convinced I should turn around and go back to my parents' house. Call my professor and see if there's another study I can participate in closer to Tallahassee. Even Miami would work.

41

Yeah, that's totally what I *should* do.

But…

Three words: Great. Barrier. Reef.

I sigh for the millionth time. Let's just see how the morning goes.

~*~

I hike the strap of my purse over my shoulder and cross the yard to the front porch. After four years away, the prospect of seeing the man I fell in love with has my heart thumping wildly in my chest. I'd like to say it's nerves over what we need to discuss—if it gets to that—but I've always been a terrible liar.

It's more than that.

I should have checked my makeup and hair in the car before I got out. Now, my only option is to comb through it with my fingers and hope for the best. For the most part, I look the same as I did the last time we saw each other. Same long, blonde hair that I curl with the fattest curling iron available. Same arched eyebrows, thick lashes, and pale blue eyes. The biggest difference is in my hips, boobs, and thighs. They've filled out since then, and I find myself worrying what Damian will think.

Ridiculous, yet…ugh.

Here goes nothing.

I raise my hand and press the doorbell. Taking a step back, I stare at the door, wondering if my heart will ever slow down.

And then it opens.

Standing there in a t-shirt and mesh basketball

pants is…*Dylan Aoki*? Damn, I haven't seen him in forever. Well, since Liam's funeral.

Dude hasn't changed much. Dark almond shaped eyes and pitch black hair that sticks up on top. He used to tip the ends, but not so much anymore.

"Elizabeth? Elizabeth Van Zee?" he says, smiling.

I nod. "Yeah. How've you been?"

He opens the screen door for me and ushers me inside. "Good. What're you doing here?"

"I, uh, I'm supposed to be meeting with Damian this morning. Does he—" I scan the living room for traces of leftover immaturity—"live here?"

Dylan breathes out a laugh. "We're roommates."

Ah, that makes sense. Like Liam with Dylan's older brother, Damian and Dylan had been best friends before the accident. I'm glad they seem to have reconnected after Kate's funeral.

Then, suddenly, Dylan frowns. "Um, he was expecting you?"

"Yeah, I mean, that's what I thought from our phone conversation yesterday. Is he not home?"

Dylan scratches his head while twisting around to look behind him. "Uh…" He drops his hand and turns back to me. "Yeah, he's home. I'll go get him. You can sit if you like," he says, motioning to the sofa before rounding the corner into the hallway beside it.

O—kay.

I sit on the edge of the cushion and hear Dylan knocking on a door.

"Hey man," he says. "Elizabeth Van Zee is here to see you."

There's some inaudible grumbling and quick shuffling around. Then I hear the soft click of the door as it opens, and Damian's voice filters into the living room even though he's speaking low to Dylan.

"Shit, man. I'll be right out. Keep her busy or something."

Not a good sign. What little hope I had is rapidly diminishing.

Dylan comes back in, and I smile at him as if I'd heard nothing.

"He'll be out in a minute. Can I get you something to drink?" he asks.

"Oh, no thanks. I'm fine."

Dylan takes a seat in an armchair. "I heard you moved to, like, Florida or somewhere."

"Yep. I'm studying marine biology down there."

"Impressive."

"How about you?" I say, making small talk.

"Pre-med, same as Damian."

Well, that's interesting.

"Damian's doing pre-med, huh?"

"Yeah, some sort of compromise he had with the doctor. Three years later, he's never bothered to switch to anything else."

"Three years? He's not a senior?"

"Nah." Dylan shakes his head. "After Kate died, he didn't do much. Months later, his dad convinced him to enroll fall semester. Dr. Lowell bought this house and asked if I'd room with him. Not a bad offer."

"Not at all," I agree, and as I say it, someone steps out of the hallway, but it's not Damian.

I shouldn't care. Really, I shouldn't. I have no right to care. So, why can't I breathe at the sight of her doing an obvious walk of shame?

Booze. Girls. Nothing has changed with him.

I make up my mind then and there. I'm not telling him. I'm not going to Australia.

The girl, who is barely able to hold herself up, is a tiny thing, probably only a freshman or sophomore. Not legally old enough to be as hung over as I can tell she is. Her hair is a ratted mess, half in a ponytail, half strung out everywhere else. And last night's party clothes are scarcely covering her frame. Her top is on inside out, the zipper of her skirt off-center, and she's carrying her underwear instead of wearing them.

That's fantastic.

I glance away when I see the embarrassment flash across her face, her cheeks reddening as she takes in her audience. Quietly, I clear my throat and stare in front of me, wishing I'd stayed home like my gut told me to.

The sound of Damian's voice reaches low into my abdomen, and I hate how it still has that sort of power over me.

"I'll be right back, Elle," he says softly from the hallway.

I feel his gaze pinned on me, but I don't meet it. Instead, I force a smile and nod. "That's fine."

"No, dude," Dylan says, standing. "I'll take her home. Elizabeth came to talk with you, so you should do that."

From the corner of my eye, I see Dylan help the girl as she wobbles into the kitchen. Damian has no idea how I feel about him, and especially after what I just witnessed, I really need to pull myself together and pretend his behavior doesn't bother me. Because it shouldn't. Because I shouldn't still be in love him.

He walks around the furniture, and his socks come into my line of sight. "Sorry about that. I overslept."

I gather my strength and lift my head. "No problem. It's"—I swallow—"good to see you."

Too good. Damn, if it's possible, he's more attractive now than when I last saw him. Not as skinny and more…sturdy, I guess. Like he's spent more time in the gym or playing basketball, which he used to do a lot before he gave that up too.

But what really catches me are those sapphire eyes of his, darker than mine and oh so powerful. I'm glad he doesn't know I see those beautiful blue irises every single day, and maybe that's part of the reason I can't get him out of my head.

"It's good to see you too, Elle."

Damn my heart.

I inhale, the air not fully filling my lungs. I can't let him do this to me. Not when this will be the last time I ever see him. I'm leaving to go home to Florida tomorrow, and I'm not looking back. Out of sight, out of mind…sort of. As much as it can be.

"You hungry? I thought we could grab some breakfast somewhere," I suggest. No way can I stay here, on his turf. At this point, I want to eat, say goodbye, and forget I even considered asking him for this favor.

"Famished," he replies. "There's a little diner

down the street that serves the best sausage gravy. Almost better than my mom's."

His mention of Nora like that makes me smile. Maybe he's at least moved into a better place with regard to her death.

"Sounds promising," I say.

I'm not hungry, but if I up and leave, he might figure something's going on, and I definitely do *not* want him swinging by my parents' house to find out. I need to be smooth, calm, and collected.

Then get the hell away from him and these condemning palpitations in my chest.

"Come on, my car is in the garage," he offers, the corner of his mouth tugging up and showing off a dimple.

Liam had them too. In fact, they're what made me talk to Liam in the first place. Unlike Liam, Damian's are far from innocent, yet the dimples give that impression, though, and they, like his eyes, his voice, have the power to pull me in.

I can't ride with him.

"I should drive separately. I don't have much time today."

Damian crosses his arms. His gaze washes over me, and the sexy grin falls from his face. He takes a few seconds to respond. When he does, it reminds me that I've known him too long, and he knows me too well. "You didn't drive all this way to spend a thirty-minute meal with me. What's going on?"

My palms are clammy. I have no explanation to give him, so I agree to his riding arrangements. "Nothing. We can take your car." I stand up, wipe my hands on my jeans, and grab my purse off the sofa. "Lead the way."

He eyes me skeptically. He doesn't buy my response, but he walks to the kitchen. I follow him out the back door that leads into the garage, and I'm surprised to see he still has the same black BMW he's had since his sixteenth birthday—a gift from his father.

He opens the passenger door for me, and I thank him. Nora made sure to teach her sons chivalry because, she once told me, "real gentlemen are rare treasures." I doubt she'd be pleased with how Damian uses her advice.

Damian backs out of the driveway, and as he glances over his shoulder, I see the wheels turning in his head. The muscles in his jaw tense, and there's a heavy glint in his eye. My being here is probably as awkward for him as it is for me, though for different reasons.

Because he never loved me.

"How are your folks?" he asks when we're on the road.

My parents are older, and four and a half years ago, my dad had a massive stroke. He lost the ability to walk, even talk for a while. Physical therapy has helped some, and he can use a walker around the house, but it exhausts him. Damian was there for me when it all happened, and for that I'm thankful.

"They're okay, I guess. Mom's tired, and she had to hire a part-time in-home nurse to help take care of Dad."

Damian nods. "I'm sorry, Elle. That sucks."

"It's life," I say, and as soon as I do, silence

drops over us like a wave. I break the surface first. "How about your dad? Things good between the two of you?"

I ask because after Liam and Nora died, Damian and Jackson were constantly at each other's throats. Instead of mourning their loss together, they grew further apart. But from what I understand, Kate Browdy helped bridge the gap.

"We meet for dinner at Hickory Park every Thursday night."

I smile at that. "That's awesome."

We're at the diner now, and we both order coffee. Damian gets sausage gravy over their advertised made-this-morning-fresh buttermilk biscuits, while I settle for a waffle with fruit.

It's a little tense between us, and since I'm not going to ask him the favor I originally planned on, I don't have much to say. He waits for me, though, sipping at his coffee with two creams and twice the tablespoons of sugar.

I unzip my purse and pull out a package of natural sweetener. I sprinkle it in and leave out the cream.

"That's different," he says, noticing. "You used to dump so much shit in your coffee that it ceased to be coffee."

I snicker because it's true. I probably single-handedly paid someone's yearly wage at Coffee-Mate. "I guess I got used to the taste of the coffee itself."

A few moments of silence passes again before Damian breaks it. "You gonna tell me why you wanted to see me?"

No.

I shrug. "I was in town and thought—"

"You'd drop by and feed me a line of bullshit?" His eyebrows quirk up when he says it, his blue stare holding me in place and trapping me there. He won't let go until I fess up.

"I...I had some plans but they got cancelled at the last minute, so what I came here to talk about doesn't matter anymore."

Nothing but truth.

Unfortunately, he's not dropping it.

"How did your plans involve me in the first place?"

"They...didn't. I mean, not completely. I mean..." I'm flustered. I don't have an answer, and I am not—*not*—telling him what I originally wanted. "It was stupid, so..." I take a drink to avoid answering.

Thankfully, our food arrives before he can respond.

"Can I get you anything else?" our server asks, and I shake my head.

"We're good, thanks," Damian says.

"Enjoy your meal."

"I think I'm gonna go wash my hands," I say. I need a minute to reorganize my thoughts and figure out how the hell I'm going to get out of his interrogation.

I begin to slide out of the booth, Damian's gaze hard on me. Believe me, I understand how weird this must be to him. Four years of nothing, then *BAM*! I show up because I want to ask how he's been? I wouldn't buy that story, either.

When I reach the end of the booth, my purse falls to the floor. It's still open from when I pulled out my packet of herbal sweetener, and now the contents are spread out on the linoleum. Damian scoots over to pick up the items beside him. He hands me stuff: old receipts, lip balm, two pens, a data stick.

And…

"What's this?" he asks, picking the picture up off the floor.

No. No, no, no, no.

Horrified, my cheeks burn red. He studies it, recognition creeping into his face. His lips separate, and his eyebrows pinch together.

Shit, shit, shit. I shouldn't have come here today. This, *this* is exactly what I didn't want him to find out.

He flips the photo around so it faces me.

Bright blue eyes stare back at me, the exact same hue as Damian's. Long, blonde hair that frames her face falls around her shoulders, and her smile, that sweeter than sugar smile, pushes her cheekbones up so high she squints. I love this picture of Lia—taken only last month when we went to the beach in search of seashells.

I'm caught.

I swallow. "My daughter."

Chapter 6

Damian

Daughter?

I'm in shock. Ellie's face softens as she waits for me to piece it together, but deep down, I've already guessed. I'm just not ready to admit it to myself.

My gaze lowers to the age written on the back: three and a half years old. I turn the picture back over in my palm. She's Ellie's daughter all right: same blonde hair, same heart-shaped face, same small nose.

But I don't see Ellie in this little girl.

No, I see my mother.

After Mom died, I spent countless hours flipping through the picture albums she kept. Photos of Liam and me growing up. Her and Dad's wedding day. Her childhood. I'd done it because I never wanted to forget.

And this picture in my hand...is her.

I'm transfixed as I do the math in my head. The visual confirmation isn't quite enough, even with my own eyes staring back at me.

Nine months plus three and a half years puts Ellie and me together the night before Kate's burial. May—exactly four years ago.

Holy. Fucking. Shit.

Ellie studies me, blinking. She's hoping I won't figure it out. Or refuse to believe it. And hell, part of me doesn't. This is too damn big to wrap my mind around.

"What's her name?" I ask.

Ellie sits back down in the booth, her trip to the bathroom no longer a priority. "Lia."

"After Liam?"

"Yeah." She drops her head, and under her breath she mumbles something I don't catch. "What was that, Elle?" I ask.

She hesitates before she glances up at me. "I said I also named her after Kate. Because…"

I lean back against the booth. She doesn't have to pick up where she trailed off. The name is because of when and why Lia had been conceived. Finally, we're getting to the point of Ellie's visit. This *little* matter she hid from me. What the hell?

I return my focus to the picture as Ellie finishes, "Lia Kathryn is her full name."

"Lia Kathryn what?" I doubt our daughter has *my* last name.

And I'm right.

"Van Zee," she answers. Then she lets out a giggle. "I call her Lia-Kat, though."

I glare at her, and not only because it's a stupid nickname. This whole conversation is sinking in and getting too damn real. "Like a house pet?"

"No. Like, short for Kathryn, Damian." Ellie's shoulders rise and fall in a sigh. "I guess I thought it fit, considering…"

I don't want to delve into where this is heading. I understand why she doesn't straight-up call her Lia, but Lia-*Kat*? Why not gut me all the way through and call her Kate? It's not like Ellie ever knew her.

I'm getting irritated, and I'm pretty sure that's why Ellie wanted to go out for breakfast. She figures I'm less likely to blow up here, though I'm close to the edge.

"I thought you were taking birth control, Elle. How'd this happen?"

"It's not fool-proof, Damian. And with everything going on with my parents and planning out the details of my transfer, I had a lot on my mind. I guess I wasn't consistent in taking them. Plus, since we weren't, you know…well, I didn't think I needed them anymore."

Inhale. Exhale.

My eyes dart around the room as I work to rein in my anger. I realize she had other shit to deal with, but why the hell didn't she say anything before she let me fuck her? She knows I keep a stash of condoms in my room.

"Dammit, Ellie," I say, my focus landing back on her. "What did you think would happen?"

"I don't know, Damian. I…the idea of getting pregnant never crossed my mind."

"That's all you got? It didn't cross your mind."

She bows her head before her eyes lock on me again. "What do you want me to say?"

Not good enough.

"And then what? After you left, you were too busy living it up in Florida, you just forgot to tell me you had my child?" Hell yeah, I'm pissed. This isn't something you fucking hide for four years.

Color drains from Ellie's face. She sucks her lips between her teeth while she averts her gaze, and one of her biggest tells spawns the realization—her nostrils flare. And I get it.

"You never intended to tell me, did you?" I say.

Her pale blue irises flick up to me, and the regret I see in them does nothing for me. "I started a new life, Damian. One with no connections to this place. When I found out I was pregnant with Lia, the last thing I wanted was to drag her into my past. And you..." She pauses. "You were going through enough."

"Shit, Ellie." My appetite is gone. I cover my eyes with a hand and squeeze. What the fuck am I supposed to do with this? And why is she laying this on me *now*? I drop my hand. "So, what do you want? Child support?"

She's quick to answer. "No, Damian. Nothing. I don't want anything from you."

"Then why are you telling me now, after all this time?"

She shakes her head in fast, small movements. "I had no intention of telling you. You found the picture, remember?"

"Well damn. I feel so much better now." My voice is raising, and it's caught the attention of some people at the counter.

Ellie sees them too. "Can we go back to your place and talk about this?" she suggests quietly.

I pull a twenty from my wallet and toss it on the table next to our untouched food. Without a word to Ellie, I slip the picture of Lia in my back pocket and slide out of the booth. Heading out the door, my head is spinning. This was definitely not the bomb I thought Ellie would drop.

This one is nuclear.

I get in my car and Ellie joins me two seconds later. She doesn't say anything to me on the short trip to my house, and it's a relief because I need to think.

I have a kid—a daughter. I don't know anything about kids. I mean, other than Brennan, the little boy with cancer who befriended Kate at the hospital, I have no experience with them. And Lia's like, a toddler. Basically a baby, right?

What do you do with one of those?

Ellie didn't want me to know about her, so does Lia even know about me? What does she think when Ellie takes her to the park where other kids' daddies are pushing them on the swing? Or…

Fuck.

Maybe my little girl does have a father in her life in the form of Ellie's boyfriend. I can't help glancing over to Ellie's fingers in search of a ring. There isn't one. Even so, the thought of some guy being with Lia when I didn't even know she existed shoots a fresh stab of anger into my chest. How could Ellie have kept her from me?

Then again, what would I have done had I known?

I don't have an answer for that. In fact, I'm so fucking out of answers that I'm desperate for a drink to clear my mind.

Talk about messed up.

In the garage, I park my car, but I don't make a move to get out. Beside me, I can hear Ellie's soft breaths, and like me, she's not reaching for the door. I focus through the windshield at the empty wall in front of me.

I squeeze the steering wheel, holding my breath until my lungs are on fire. I'm trying so fucking hard to hold it together right now.

I shake my head and throw the door open. Get out then slam it shut. I don't give a rat's ass what Ellie thinks, I'm pouring myself a drink. Or two.

Hell, this calls for a whole bottle of something strong.

I grab one of those small juice glasses from the cupboard Dylan pours his OJ into each morning, toss in a couple of ice cubes, and top it off with Captain Morgan. The liquid goes down easy, but I'll need a hell of a lot more to work through this "I'm a father" thing.

I lean against the counter, the glass in front of me, when I hear Ellie enter the kitchen. I'm on my second glass of rum now, and I still don't have a fucking clue what to say to her.

"Alcohol doesn't solve all the problems of the world, Damian," Ellie says from behind me.

"No, but it helps deal with them."

Ellie's beside me now, giving me one of the too-wise onceovers she learned from my brother. "It only gives you something to hide behind."

I chuckle at her little philosophy lesson. She should talk. "Like hiding the fact that I have a kid so you wouldn't have to deal with it?" I rattle the ice in the glass and shoot her a wink. "Sounds the same to me."

I go to take another drink, but Ellie swipes the rum away from me. "What the fuck, Elle?" I say, stunned that she had the gall.

Her eyes burn into me. I've seen her like this before, but I've never been on the receiving end of it. "You want to know why I didn't tell you?" She dumps the alcohol down the drain. "This is why. You'd rather wallow in your self-pity and pain than let anyone in."

Oh, I don't think so.

I'm pissed as fuck now. "What the hell would you know about letting anyone in? In case you've forgotten, I *did* let someone in and she fucking died, Ellie. But you? You ran away. So, don't give me any of your bullshit. You didn't tell me because you—*you*—wanted a new life, one that didn't involve any connections to Liam."

Her bottom lip trembles as she glares at me, and I know I've hit the motherlode. Good. She doesn't get to come here, lay all this shit on me, then blame me for it. I didn't ask to be a dad, or for Ellie to return in the first place. I'm beginning to think she should've kept her fucking secret to herself and stayed in Florida where she belongs.

I don't need this shit.

I turn away from her and start toward the living room. As I do, I dig the picture of Lia out of my back pocket. Her small, happy face peers up at me, and I instantly realize I'm wrong. No matter what the circumstances are, this is something I should know about.

Now, I gotta figure out what to do with it.

I hear Ellie enter behind me, but I don't face her when I speak. "Why did you come here if you didn't want to tell me about her? Why now?"

"Because I *was* going to tell you about her," she says, the anger filtering out of her tone.

"What changed your mind?"

When Ellie doesn't respond, I swing around to look at her. Her eyes are glassy, her lips curved inward like she's trying not to cry.

"What changed your mind, Ellie?" I repeat.

She stares at the floor when she answers. "You. That girl who was here. The rum." Her gaze rises to meet mine. "I came to ask you a favor. I, uh, was accepted to a research team to the Great Barrier Reef this summer—a big one. Tagging sharks. The friends I trust in Florida all have internships or other projects and couldn't take Lia for that amount of time. And you know my parents can't, not with Dad's medical issues, so…so my plan was to ask you."

She's not really asking me right now. No, she's simply reiterating out loud that my life isn't stable enough for a child. She's not wrong. But it still doesn't give her a right to withhold my daughter from me.

Even so, I can't be a father. I don't have an answer for the question she didn't ask. Hell, I'm not doing so good at taking care of myself. The words still spill out before I can stop them. "I want to see her."

~*~

Ellie

I'm weak.

Damian doesn't get it, and I'm not going to enlighten him. My feelings for him, not Liam, were the reason I left. I've always known he didn't love me, and for a while, I was okay with that. But then, after Liam died, after I realized I'd fallen for the other Lowell brother, I hung onto the hope that maybe he would someday.

Someday was definitely not today. I've got to quit thinking that it will ever happen. It's way past time to move on.

And after this morning, after seeing his flimsy one-night stand, his beeline for the liquor cabinet, I know I can't leave Lia with him. Damian is not cut out to be a father, not now anyway.

So now, as I'm driving back to my parents' house, I'm kicking myself for agreeing to let him see her tonight. I couldn't say no to him, though. I'd expected his surprise, but the utter betrayal behind those blues I love so much? Nothing had prepared me for that.

One-handed, I fumble around in my purse, searching for my phone while keeping my eyes on the road. I find it, pull it out, and tap Blake's picture. It's best to tell him I'm not going to Australia sooner rather than later. I doubt he'll be happy, but Blake's a good guy, and he'll understand. He's been a reliable friend every step of the way since Lia was born.

"So what's the verdict?" he answers.

I puff out a sigh into the phone. "Negative."

"He won't watch her, huh? I'm sorry, Elizabeth." The disappointment in his voice rings out loud and clear. Heck, it's in my own voice too. This trip was huge.

"I didn't ask, but I can't leave her with him. He hasn't changed. When I arrived there this morning, some super hungover girl emerged barely dressed from his bedroom. Then, after I told him about Lia, he went straight for the booze."

Blake's quiet for few seconds before he murmurs, "Did he want to see her?"

"Yes, but—"

"Elizabeth," he says, and he has that take-my-advice tone. He knows what I'm thinking. "He's her father, and he needs to be able see his daughter. At least give him that before you make this decision, okay? Kids have a way of bringing out the best in people."

"At what cost, Blake? I can't put Lia through hell for Damian's sake."

"You are taking her to meet him, though, right?"

"Yeah. Later tonight."

Blake's level-headedness is what drew me to him four years ago when I chose him as a lab partner. We connected from day one, but I always held him at arm's length when it came to having a relationship beyond friendship. Like always, he has the right thing to say.

"Remember, you just dumped something huge in his lap today. Maybe it will work, maybe it won't, but go and see what happens tonight, babe. I know what it's like to grow up not knowing your father, Elizabeth, and I don't want that for Lia. Who knows, maybe this visit will be life-changing—in a good way—for her. Possibly for Damian too."

"Maybe," I mutter.

"See how it goes, all right? Then call me."

"Yeah, sure."

I hang up and turn into my parents' driveway. Lia's inside waiting for me. What am I going to tell her?

Chapter 7

Ellie

"Is this a good idea, Elizabeth?" my mother asks as I zip up Lia's jacket.

My mother knows some about my "relationship" with Damian. Not all of it since she disapproves of what little there actually is. She supported my decision to keep Lia a secret from him, and that was encouraging at first, especially when I wanted so badly to cave, run back to Iowa, and tell him everything—about Lia and how I feel about him. Even though she doesn't know the last tidbit, she'd been vital to my not returning back then.

"What good would it do?" she'd asked, and I had no reply.

I never worried about the information leaking. My family and Damian's family aren't exactly involved in the same social groups.

It's better this way, because the longer I've been gone, the less I've thought about him.

"You knew it might come to this," I tell her. "I

63

haven't decided what to do yet, but either way, he deserves to meet her. She's half his."

"Maybe you could take her with you?" Mom suggests.

"To Cairns? And do what with her? I'll be out on the ocean for twelve to fifteen hours a day. The whole lower deck is a laboratory. Really, Mom, it's not suitable for children. Besides, I doubt the head researcher would be completely cool with it," I add.

"They have day cares in Australia," Mom points out.

"And who's going to pay for that?" I face my mom, one hand on my hip. "I get it, okay? But if I want to go on this trip, Damian is the only option I have left. Kerri fell through last minute, you and Dad can't take her, so if you have a better idea, I'm all ears."

Mom's quiet for a moment. "Listen, Elizabeth. Damian has been through more than anyone should at his age. Just..." She places a hand on my shoulder. "Just remember that."

I stare at her, confused with her sudden one-eighty. "Are you defending him now?"

"No, sweetie." She purses her lips before she continues. "I want you to think about the implications of putting Lia into his life, only to take her back to Florida with you when this is over. You can't give the two of them this time, then rip it away and expect him to be okay with that."

Damn.

~*~

64

"Where are we, Mommy?" my sweet Lia-Kat asks from the backseat.

I'd told her we were going out for dinner, which was true. On the way, I stopped and bought her a chicken nugget Happy Meal with sweet and sour sauce, apple juice, and the latest in McDonald's top of the line kids' toys.

I unbuckle my belt and twist in my seat. She's stroking the My Little Pony's purple mane as she peers up at me with her father's sapphire eyes and long lashes.

"Do you remember when I told you that Blake wasn't your daddy? That your daddy lived in the same state as Grandma and Grandpa?"

She bobs her little head, blinking like she understands what's happening. And the fact is, she probably does.

"Well, this is your daddy's house. Would you like to meet him?" I ask.

For a second, she says nothing, then a small smile begins to appear on her face, and the dimples she inherited from Damian pinch inward. "Okay."

I love that at this moment she's not a jaded adult who has seen the worst in people and what they're capable of. No, my Lia is as innocent as they come, trusting and loving to a fault. She sees only the good in people, and that's what daddies are to her—good.

I hope Damian doesn't ruin that outlook for her.

I get out of the car, walk around, and unbuckle her, then we head up to the house the same way I had this morning. Damian said Dylan would be working all day, so we'd have the evening to ourselves. He better be sober.

And alone.

Seeing his latest lay leave this morning was more than enough. I won't be able to handle a second round.

I take Lia's hand and ring the doorbell with the other. Damian opens the door almost immediately. He's wearing jeans that hug his hips and a t-shirt that fits him well in all the right places. I hate that my breath catches at the sight of him.

Get a hold of yourself, Ellie.

His gaze hinges on mine for a split moment before it slowly slides down to the little girl at my side.

Lia takes a step closer to me, her body half behind my left leg. Her eyes go wide at the man in front of her. Damian's frozen in place, mouth slightly parted, so I squat down to Lia's level and smooth her hair to break the tension.

"Lia, baby, this is Damian. Your daddy," I say.

She slinks into me, and I wrap an arm around her. "Hi," she breathes out to him, her dimples appearing as her cheeks move.

I glance up at Damian. It could be the reflection of the porch light, but his eyes seem to glisten with extra moisture. As if Lia's greeting brings him to his senses, he crouches down and extends his hand.

"Hi, Lia," he says.

She puts her hand in his, and he shakes it lightly. Then Damian flicks his attention up at me. "Why don't you come inside?"

"Sure."

Damian steps inside, holding the door for us. Lia

stays close to me, but her eyes remain fixed on Damian, and Damian's on her. I take the opportunity to do a quick scan of the living room for any traces of Damian's latest sexcapade. I see nothing though, which is a huge relief.

I sit on the sofa and help Lia with her jacket. Damian takes a seat in the armchair beside us, watching my every move with our daughter. When I'm done, Lia positions herself between my legs. This is her shy way of wanting me to pick her up and set her on my lap, which I do.

Damian nods at Lia's toy. "What's that you have?"

She plays with the pony's tail, twisting it around her fingers. "A My Little Pony."

Damian only had one older brother, so he might not have a clue what a My Little Pony is. Still, he smiles like he does. "Do you like My Little Ponies?"

Lia glances at me then back at her father. "Twilight Sparkle is my favorite. She's a princess."

"Oh," Damian says, his brow furrowing as he tries to understand. Honestly, it's really cute. "Like Cinderella?" he asks.

Lia giggles and shakes her head. "No. Cinderella is a person. Twilight Sparkle is a pony."

"Right. Of course."

"Do you want to see her?" Lia offers, and now it's my turn to smile. This is going better than I thought.

"Yeah," Damian says.

Lia slips off my lap and walks over to him. She holds out her favorite pony, the one I had to specifically ask the McDonald's people for. The one she has ten of at home—though not from McDonald's, and strangely enough, don't seem to get lost—and two at my parents' house. The girl is obsessed, I swear.

Damian accepts the girly toy. "Thank you."

This makes Lia smile again, and she points at the pony's hind end. "That's her cutie mark, and she's a unicorn, so she can do magic. And these?" she says, showing him the protruding plastic, "these are her wings."

"She can fly too?" Damian asks, intrigued. "That's cool."

Lia puffs her chest out. "Yep. With her wings."

"Wow. Well, I can see why she's your favorite. Can she be my favorite pony too?"

She swings her attention to me like she's asking permission, and I grin back. "Um, okay," she finally says. "If she's your favorite now, you can have this one. I have lots of her at home."

For a second, Damian is speechless, and I can't help falling in love with him all over again. The way he is with Lia, the way he looks at her with adoration, makes me want to forget all his faults and all the reasons why I couldn't allow Lia to stay with him even if he offers.

He hugs the toy to his chest. "Thank you, Lia."

Damian

This little girl had me mesmerized at my first

glimpse. I can't get over how much she looks like me—like my mother.

Watching Ellie with her—wow! She's a good mother, definitely cut out for this. Patient, loving, kind—

Which is why I decide on the spot that I can't keep Lia this summer if Ellie asks. Since Ellie left this morning, the idea of having my daughter with me for eight weeks is the only thing I've been able to think about. But Ellie built a life for herself and her daughter in Florida, and by what I see right now, it's a good life. One that doesn't need me to come in and fuck it up. Yeah, they're better off without me.

Besides, being close to someone isn't worth the shit that comes after they're gone. Daughter or not, the best thing I can do for either of them is to stay the fuck away.

"She's beautiful, Elle," I say after I scoop Lia a bowl of ice cream I bought specifically for tonight. Because kids love ice cream.

"Well, she takes after you more than me in that department." Ellie blushes, her pale blue irises peeking through her long lashes. Lashes that mimic Lia's, I notice. "Hey, Damian, I'm sorry that I came in and blew all this on you. It wasn't fair."

I clear my throat, and flash a sideways glance at Lia. She's sticking another mountain of pink ice cream into her mouth. "So now what? You going back home?"

Ellie nods. Like me, she knows leaving Lia here with me is a stupid idea. "Our plane leaves tomorrow evening at six."

Part of me wants to ask her if I'll ever see them again, but I'm not sure if I want to. Clean breaks are better than drawn-out ones, and it seems Ellie had the right idea to stay away for so long. Suddenly, I kind of wish she'd stayed gone longer.

"What about the research trip?" I ask.

Shrugging, Ellie adjusts herself on the dining table chair. "Something else will probably come up. Something closer, where I can be home with Lia every night."

"Yeah," I agree. "That would be good."

Ellie's got it figured out.

"Oh, here." I pull out the picture of Lia from my back pocket, the one I picked up off the diner floor.

Ellie shakes her head and holds up a hand. "No, you should keep it."

I flick the edge, wondering if that's really a good idea. Not exactly the clean break I had in mind. "Thanks," I say and slide it back in my pocket.

"Mommy?" Lia asks, ice cream all over her face. It reminds me of this photo of Liam Mom kept on the mantel of his second birthday.

Ellie laughs when she sees her. "Yeah, sweetie?"

"Can I have some milk, please?"

"I'll get it," I offer. I open the fridge and grab the gallon of milk. If it weren't for Dylan and his six glasses a day, we wouldn't even buy the stuff. Then I grab a glass from the cupboard and turn to Ellie. "Um, I don't have sippy cups or bottles or anything."

She suppresses a grin. "She can drink from a glass."

I fill it and consider handing it to Ellie to give to

her. For some reason, though, I bypass her and set it on the table in front of Lia. She lifts her big, blue eyes to me and I can't help the jolt that passes through me. "Thank you," she says in her tiny, sweet voice.

"Sure, whatever," I answer, because the goosebumps spreading over my skin remind me to steer clear. Keep my distance.

I don't sit back down. Instead, I stand behind the kitchen peninsula. Now, a milk mustache replaces the strawberry ice cream one Lia sported earlier, and I feel a grin tugging at the corner of my mouth.

I can't let this little girl draw me in. She may be my own flesh and blood, but disconnecting myself from her is the best way I know of to protect her.

"It's getting late, Damian," Ellie says after she wipes Lia's face with a paper towel. "We should go."

"Yeah, sure. Thanks for coming over, Elle." As much as I shouldn't be in their lives, I mean it. Even if it's only this once, I'm glad to have seen my daughter.

"At Grandma's and Grandpa's house, I get to sleep in bed with Mommy," Lia quips, proud. She slides off the chair that's too big for her, and she pushes her hair from her face. The action isn't gentle and now her hair's even more of a mess.

Why does she have to be so fucking cute?

"You like that, huh?" I ask.

When she smiles at me, I notice the tiny gap between her two front teeth. "Yep."

"Why don't you go get your jacket, sweetie?" Ellie says, directing her toward the living room.

"Okay," she answers.

This may be the first and last time I ever see her. Lia bounces away, and I can't help the lump rising in my throat.

It's for the best, I remind myself.

The lump only grows at the thought.

Ellie stands beside me, almost touching me. "Again, Damian, I'm sorry for not telling you about her."

From the kitchen, I watch as Lia pulls her pink jacket off the sofa cushion. She studies it, flips it around, and starts to put her arm through while the coat is upside down. She spins in a circle trying to insert her other arm. When she can't make it work, she looks at me—not Ellie—and frowns. Her eyebrows lower as she pleads with me from across the room.

"You need to go, Elle," I murmur, because I'm close to doing something stupid. I have to do for Lia what I couldn't do for Kate and walk away. Still, I can't take my eyes off her.

"I can send pictures or something, if you want," Ellie offers.

I shake my head. "Just go."

Ellie obeys, walking toward our daughter. She squats down to help Lia with her coat, zipping it up.

"Thanks, Mommy," I hear Lia say, her tiny voice carrying across the room to me.

Ellie takes her hand and leads her to the door. Yeah, I'm letting them leave. I can't be anyone's father. That little girl deserves so much better than me.

Besides, I gave my heart to Kate four years ago,

and she took it with her to the grave. I have nothing left to offer anyone.

As Ellie opens the front door, Lia spins around, eyes piercing into me. Then she smiles and waves her tiny hand at me. "See you tomorrow, Daddy."

Chapter 8

Damian

Goddammit!
Shit!
FUCK!

I can barely see through the blur of fury as I speed down the interstate. I fucking can't do this. Dammit, Ellie!

Because I have to maintain some control over the situation, I think about how this is Ellie's fault. All she had to do was take the damn birth control pill. Why did she even have to be in Liam's room that night? She knew I'd be broken. She fucking knew what I'd want from her!

I can't breathe.

Lia's innocent little voice repeats in my head, louder and louder. *"See you tomorrow, Daddy."*

God-fucking-damn-it!

The tires skid over the pavement as I spin into the cemetery, my personal sanctuary. The only place I truly belong.

I cut off the engine and leave the keys in the

ignition. It's dark outside, but I don't need light to know where I'm going. I bypass the three headstones that usually give me the solace I crave. Right now, I need to punch something. Pound on it until this fucking ache ripping through me leaves me the hell alone.

The elder tree protecting my loved ones serves as my relief. I've used it before, so it knows what to expect. My fists do too, which is why I come here instead beating the snot out of a bag at the gym. Here, the bark rips into my knuckles with each hit. It hurts like fucking hell, and I beat into the trunk harder and harder until blood I can't see slides into my palms and mixes with the sweat pooling inside my fists. Still, I don't stop.

I can't.

I have to fucking undo this mess I've created.

Voices and images filter into my mind. The pain and regret in Ellie's eyes. The sweetness in Lia's smile.

And Kate. There's always Kate.

"It'll be okay. I promise," she'd told me.

"Don't make promises you can't keep," my own shaky voice echoes back at me.

"I won't."

It's only when I no longer feel the pain that I drop to my knees and cover my face with my bloody palms. I never should have asked to see her. What the fuck was I thinking?

I stare at the three tombstones peering back me. Nora Lowell. Liam Lowell. Kate Browdy. The three people I've loved more than anything in this world. I came here for this reminder tonight.

Because of me, they're dead. I never want to forget that.

And I won't—*I won't* add Lia to this list.

Ellie is gone, and she took Lia with her. That's what was supposed to happen. They're safer far away from me. I won't go after them, won't call them. Ever.

My gaze lands on the red roses on Kate's grave. Then, slowly, it rises to her name. Kathryn "Katie" Browdy. I slide my focus over to the marble stone beside Kate's—to Liam's.

"Lia Kathryn," I whisper into the chilled air. I barely get the words out. Lia-Kat is such a stupid name to call her. She's not fucking named after a pet. No, she was named for two of the most amazing people to ever set foot on this godforsaken earth. Two people who deserve to still be here.

"You should see her," I say. "Mom, she's the spitting image of you when you were young. Big blue eyes, long blonde hair, and a smile that will make you melt. Liam, your girlfriend is a natural as a mother, but I'll bet you already knew she would be. You probably figured she'd have your kid instead of mine." I snicker. "Hell, I did too."

I pause when I come to Kate. What do I say to her? The question I always ask myself rears again: how do I tell her how bad I fucked up after she died?

I spent so much time apologizing to her when she was alive, though. I guess that hasn't changed. "I'm sorry, Katie. I have no excuse other than I'm an asshole. But Ellie named her after you if that's any consolation." I pause and run a hand through my hair. "God, Kate, I wish you were here. I don't know what to do, and I can't fuck things up even more."

I wait in silence for an answer that won't come. Even so, I brush a bloodstained finger over her name again, begging for a reply. "Please, Katie. Tell me how to fix this."

~*~

It's sometime after midnight when I get back home. Dylan is lounging out on the sofa, nursing a beer and watching some crappy sci-fi movie.

"Hey dude," he says. When I don't answer right away, he glances up at me. "Damn, man. You look like shit."

I don't have to examine myself to know what he sees. Dried blood coats my hands and clothes. I probably have it smeared on my face too.

"Please don't tell me you got into another bar fight," he says.

"I wish." I nod at his drink. "Any more of that?"

"In the fridge. Help yourself."

Unlike me, Dylan usually sticks to the lighter stuff. Tonight, I'll drink his cheap beer, though. I want to stay sober to remind myself that I'm making the right choice in letting Lia go. I can't run off and do something I'll regret because I'm drunk.

I don't wash the blood off me before I yank two bottles from the refrigerator, pop the top on one, and sink down in the armchair. This whole scene is unusual for me, which is why Dylan eyes me instead of going back to his movie. I down half the beer in one swig, and Dylan's eyebrows quirk upward.

"What happened tonight?" he asks.

Dylan and I don't do the heart-to-heart thing. However, tonight I make an exception. I blame it on Dylan's shitty beer.

"Ellie came by to tell me we have a kid together," I say, then top off the beer.

Dylan's eyes widen. "A kid?"

I open the second bottle. "Yep. She's three and a half."

"Holy shit, dude," Dylan says, sitting up.

"That's what I said."

"Wait." Dylan's brows furrow. "Three and a half?"

My roommate is stellar when it comes to repeating what I've told him.

"Three and a fucking half," I confirm.

I wait while he puts it together. Dude's smart. Won't take him long.

He shakes his head. "After Kate."

Dylan knew about my "relationship" with Ellie. He never approved, but he kept his mouth shut, which I appreciated.

"Yeah. After Kate," I verify.

"Okay then, what're you going to do?"

I take a long drink, then shake my head. "Nothing."

"Nothing? You serious?"

"One hundred percent. They're both better off without me."

Dylan takes a second to digest what I said. "So, Ellie just came here to tell you she had your kid three plus years ago, and that's it? She didn't ask for help or child support or anything?"

"No. She earned herself a spot on some big research project in the Great Barrier Reef for two months and needed someone to watch Lia during that time."

"Lia as in *Liam*?"

"Lia *Kathryn* to be exact."

"Fuck, man."

"Tell me about it." I suck down more beer.

"And you don't want Lia while she's gone?"

The whole evening replays before me, and I have no regrets. Slowly, I shake my head again.

"Why the hell not, man?" Dylan asks, his voice raising some. I understand why. Dylan's dad bailed on his family before he was even born. Tough stuff to deal with. "She's your daughter."

"Because I'll make a shitty-ass father, that's why," I tell him as I finish off the bottle.

"So you're just gonna let them leave and never see her again."

"That's the plan. They fly out tomorrow, back to the sunny skies of Florida where they belong. Far, far away from me."

Dylan pauses for a moment, incredulous. "Let me give this to you straight, man." He leans forward. "You are a fucking coward, Damian. A selfish, fucking coward. You have the opportunity to get to know your own daughter, and you're going to squander it for what? So you can spend the summer drunk off your ass, scoring with a bunch of chicks who don't give a damn?" He shakes his head, pissed off at me. "You think if you let her go now you won't lose her, but dude, from where I'm standing, it looks like you already have."

When I wake up the next morning, my hands are unrecognizable. Still covered in blood with strips of skin hanging off them, they resemble raw hamburger. I shower and let the soap slither under what's left of my skin. It stings, but I can't go to the hospital on my first day with knuckles like this.

Working for my dad should be something I never want to do again, yet other than at the cemetery, it's the only other place I feel close to Kate. It's where we first met, so I spend my summers on the oncology floor of Methodist Hospital in Des Moines.

I wrap my hands in bandages the best I can. I'll see if one of the nurses will help me out when I get there. Someone who won't ask for an explanation. Yeah, right.

Dylan's not up when I leave. After his lecture last night, I finished off the rest of his nasty beer and went to bed. I don't give a fuck if the dude's studying to be a psychiatrist; he's got to stop analyzing me. I know what the fuck I'm doing.

At least, I did last night.

This morning, though, I'm not so sure.

They're better off without me, I repeat for the thousandth time to fend off my growing impulse to keep Lia this summer.

As I pass the counter to swipe my keys off it, a familiar swell of emotion fills my chest. The purple pony Lia gave me stands on the edge of the peninsula, and her calling me daddy rings loud and clear in my head again.

Before I can stop myself, I stride over and pick up the toy. I can't remember what she called these things, but this one is special to her. Because she's a princess. The silky purple hair has a streak of pink in it. Damn horse is so fucking girly that it makes me smile thinking about Lia playing with a whole hoard of these things.

I push the thought out of my head. Lia's gone, and she's not coming back, thank God. That little girl deserves more than I can ever offer. I need to get her out of my memory before I change my mind.

On the way out to my car, I dump the toy into the garbage.

~*~

"From the gym?" Leslie, Kate's favorite nurse, asks. It's clear she doesn't believe me.

"Finals week was tough," I answer. "I had to take it out on something."

"A cement block?"

I puff out a laugh. Leslie and I have a like/hate relationship. The only thing we ever agreed on was Katie. Somewhere along the way, though, I won Leslie over, and I can't figure out how. After all the crap I did, I was never good enough for Kate.

"Let's clean it up and I'll ask your dad to write up an antibiotic script for you."

"I appreciate it, Leslie."

After I'm wrapped up, Leslie, who acts as my supervisor of sorts, gives me the rundown for the day. I'm limited in what the hospital will allow me to do, but I work my ass off and do what I'm asked. Completely unlike how things were before Kate.

Before, I didn't give a flying fuck and the hospital was the last place I wanted to be. That fact was clear to everyone here. I was an asshole, destroying hospital property, creating more work for the nurses, and doing what I could to make their lives hell. Until Kate, I never gave a patient a backward glance. It was Kate who changed that.

Now, the patients are my biggest reason for coming. None of them deserve to be here fighting for their lives like this. Cancer is the devil, an evil monster that destroys everything in its path.

And all the kids in here have looked him square in the mother-fucking eye and said, "I won't let you win."

When I'm finished with what Leslie gave me, I make my way into The Commons for some down time. The room is like a large rec room with sofas, tables, and chairs, a ping-pong table, a seventy-inch television with a Blu-ray, Wii U, and X-box. Windows line one whole side and the adjacent wall has been painted by the kids who've spent time here. Anything they wanted to paint or write in whatever colors they choose. It's a memorial, an inspiration, and a reminder to keep fighting. The patients call it the Hope Wall.

I've searched the wall high and low, and I've never found Kate's. I guess she died before she got the chance.

There are two bald little boys playing *Mario Kart*, faces contorted into competitive mode. Brennan crosses my mind and how I let him win the tournament at his remission party over four years ago. Leslie tells me he's doing great with a head full of dirty blond hair and has only been back for check-ups.

As I scan the room, I realize the boys aren't alone. In the far corner, sitting on a pink beanbag and reading a book, is a girl. What strikes me is the long, blonde hair that falls in her face the same way Lia's did last night. In fact, this girl can't be more than a few years older than Lia.

I don't want to approach her, but my feet move toward her anyway. She looks up and studies me.

"Are you a doctor?" she asks, frowning.

I shake my head. "Maybe someday. My dad's a doctor, though."

"Is the doctor here your dad?"

"Maybe. There's a few doctors on this floor."

She blinks, contemplating my answer. Something stole this child's joy, and I'm pretty sure I know what since she's sitting here, in the pediatric oncology ward.

Tears spring in her eyes as she extends an arm to show me the inside of her elbow. Other than the medical tape and cotton balls, I don't see anything, but I know what she's going to say next.

"He took a lot of my blood because there might be something wrong with me. I don't want to be sick for always," she sobs, her lower lip trembling. "I don't want to lose my hair."

Footfalls close behind me make me turn my

head. My father stands inside the doorway watching us. I nod at him to let him know I'll be right there, then I return to the girl.

"Hey, it'll be okay. Just because your blood might not be all right doesn't mean there's something wrong with *you*. I used to know this girl who was the most beautiful girl inside and out. Even when she lost all her hair. She spent a lot of time in this very room, and you know what she did almost every day?"

The girl shakes her head.

"She wrote in a diary. It was her secret place where she could say anything she wanted, any time she wanted."

"I'm not very good at writing. Except my name."

I reach behind her, grab a piece of paper and a box of crayons, and hand them to her. "No, but you can draw, right?"

A small smile forms on her lips. "I like to color."

"Good. Tomorrow, I'll bring you your own book and your own crayons, and you can draw pictures about anything you want."

Her eyes brighten at my offer. "You're going to make a good doctor someday," she says.

~*~

The clock in my dad's office reads four-thirty. Ellie's and Lia's plane leaves at six, and they'll be on their way home, safely away from me.

"What's her name and what's wrong with her?" I ask my dad, and he knows I'm referring to the little girl in The Commons.

"You know I can't—"

"Hypothetically."

He laughs and takes off his glasses. "Hypothetically, huh?"

"Yeah, tell me a story."

Dad rubs his chin. "All right, once upon a time there was a six-year-old girl named Olivia. Her parents kept taking her to the doctor for chronic bronchitis. Olivia seemed to be sick more often than she was well. Then she began to complain about frequent stomachaches and that she couldn't breathe. She lost weight, and when her parents noticed swelling on her belly and under her arms, they rushed her back to clinic. Their family doctor referred the girl to another doctor who specializes in blood cancers. That doctor is keeping her for testing."

"What does that doctor think is wrong with her?"

"He needs to run a couple more tests, but he's fairly confident it's Non-Hodgkin's Lymphoma."

"Cancer," I mumble.

"Cancer."

I sigh. "What's her prognosis?"

"I think we caught it early, so good. Very good."

I lean back against the chair, thinking about how Olivia is only three years older than Lia. How it would kill me if Lia ended up here. They're so young, only kids. Kids should be—I don't know—not here.

I stand up and walk over to Dad's bookshelf. Medical journals line most of the shelves, all except the top two. Those are reserved for old family pictures. There's one of Liam holding me after I was born. One of Mom and Dad ringing in the new year two years before she died. One of Dad, Liam, and me playing basketball in our driveway.

I don't reach for any of those though. Instead, I grab the collage of Liam when he volunteered here. It's littered with pictures of my brother and little bald-headed patients. He's grinning like an idiot in all of them, but so are the kids. Yeah, my brother's joy was in helping people.

I'm not ready to tell my father about Lia. Or about Ellie's return. Still, I've always been compared to my saint of a brother, and I need to know if I'm out of my mind.

"We both know that Liam would've made a great dad, but do you think I could handle it?" I ask.

"Where did this come from?" Dad asks.

I shrug. "Olivia, I guess."

Dad gets up and joins me at the bookcase. He peers over my shoulder at the pictures I'm holding.

"Your brother put his heart and soul into everything he did," he says.

"That's not helping, Dad."

"Hear me out. Liam always gave a hundred and ten percent. When he got passionate about something, he drove everything he had into it. And Damian, he was passionate about a lot of stuff. You, however—"

"Am passionate about nothing."

"No. You're pickier because giving a hundred and ten percent isn't enough for you. You see, whereas Liam put his heart and soul into what he did, you wanted to put in more. You'd lay your very life down for that one thing, that one person who

86

was worthy of your love and attention."

"What if I never find that one thing again?" I ask.

"You found it once, son. You'll find it again. That's what Kate wanted for you, right? To live for something."

~*~

I have no destination in mind. I just drive, letting the last twenty-four hours roll through my mind.

Ellie.

My daughter.

The whole situation has me tripping. Where did this all come from? Two days ago my life wasn't complicated. Shitty, yeah, but not complicated. I had school, booze, girls, the cemetery—and guilt and pain.

Now, though? Now it's like I don't know who I am.

I hang a left, heading toward the interstate. The city buzzes by as I drive west out of town.

Dylan thinks I'm a coward, and he's right. I'm scared to death. There's no way out now that I know Lia exists.

So, what the hell am I supposed to do with that?

I can't even wrap my mind around the fact that Ellie's reappeared in my life. And since we have this kid together, where does that put us?

I spent two years with Ellie, doing what I promised Liam—taking care of her. Even though it wasn't how he would have wanted.

God, this is fucked up.

I think about Olivia. What's ahead of her after Dad gives her a diagnosis. How young she is, and how easily that could be Lia.

I'm sick to my stomach.

Then I consider what Dad said about me, about Kate, and what she would have wanted. I wonder if getting to know my daughter, letting Ellie go on that once-in-a-lifetime research trip, might be what she would have wanted.

Actually, I know it is. Kate wouldn't have hesitated.

I know what I have to do.

Chapter 9

Ellie

Lia is wheeling her miniature pink suitcase behind her, and she doesn't want to hold my hand. The Des Moines airport isn't busy like Tallahassee, still I'd feel better if I were touching her instead of simply walking beside her.

"At least until we're in line," I insist.

Groaning, she juts out her hand. The girl is three and a half going on sixteen. Oh boy am I in trouble.

"Thank you," I say as she sulks next to me.

My dad and I said our goodbyes at home, and Mom dropped us off at the airport. Dad's taking a nap and she has to be back before he wakes, so she doesn't come inside to see us off.

Last night's conversation with Blake continues to run circles in my mind. His offer sounds good, but...

I don't know. Lia has never met his sister. Hell, I haven't, either. I'm sure she's as great as Blake says—responsible with two kids of her own—but I just don't think I can leave her with a stranger like that. Besides, the group is leaving for Australia in two days. That's not enough time for me to drive Lia to Alabama, get to know Blake's sister on an I-trust-you-with-my-kid-for-two-months level, drive back to Florida, and board a plane across the world.

Granted, until yesterday Lia had never met Damian, either. But he's her father, for heaven's sake. That counts for a whole lot more in my opinion.

Plus, I know Damian in both good and bad ways, and I know he'd never purposely do anything to hurt Lia.

Ah. It doesn't matter. Damian is too irresponsible to take her, and after our visit, I don't think he wants to even if I did ask. I of all people know how much a child can change your life, and Damian's lifestyle isn't exactly childproof.

I'm making the right decision to stay home and find something smaller, closer to home.

The sliding glass doors open, and Lia and I walk through, heading for the American Airlines line to collect our boarding passes and check our luggage—our one extra bag for the both of us that, in hindsight, we could have done without.

Lia tugs her hand out of mine hard. "We're in line now," she sasses. She takes a side step away from me too.

There are four people in front of us, and now is not the time for her to make a scene. I crouch down and lower my voice as I speak to her. "What's wrong, Lia-Kat? We're going home, back to your friends."

She puffs out her lip and rolls her pretty blues the way one of my classmates taught her. Great.

"Why isn't Daddy coming with us?" she retorts.

Not this again. I spent most of the afternoon explaining that we weren't seeing Damian today, and that he has to stay in Iowa because he goes to school here. She didn't like my answer, proven by her stomping her feet and storming off.

"He can't, sweetie. His home is here."

"But why? Addy's daddy lives with her. So does Lanie's daddy," she says, referring to two of the girls in day care.

I massage my temples in a fruitless attempt to dissuade the oncoming headache. This is not the easiest conversation to have with a three-year-old.

"Addy and Lanie's mommy and daddy are married, so they live together. Damian and I aren't."

"Why not?"

Oh geez.

"Um, well…because…we don't love each other that way."

Lia frowns. "Why not?"

This is *not* a fun game.

"Sweetie, we just don't."

"Do you love Blake that way?"

Lia is too bright for her age, though I shouldn't be surprised. She is Damian's daughter. I smooth through her hair and tap her little nose. "No, but maybe someday I will."

She scrunches her face up. "Blake's okay, I guess."

I laugh. "I'll let him know you approve."

We finally check our one bag, and I slip our

boarding passes in my purse. Everything is set. The airport is a little busier since we arrived, and when I take Lia's hand this time, she doesn't protest.

She points ahead of us. "Escataters!" she cries out, and I'm glad the earlier conversation seems to have been forgotten.

I giggle because my mom once told me I used to call them "alligators." At least Lia's word is closer than mine.

I check my watch. We have forty-five minutes till boarding. At the top of the "escataters" is security, and who knows how long that will take.

"We'd better get moving because the escalators won't wait forever," I say, and Lia grins big. "We're only going up, though. Not up and down and up and down like at the mall."

Lia heaves a sigh. "Fiiiiiiiine."

We're almost there when I hear my name from behind.

"Ellie, wait."

Anywhere else I wouldn't have given a thought to it because whoever was calling out probably didn't want *me*. But only one person's voice has the power to rip through me in pain and pleasure, and that's the one I hear. I turn around.

Seeing him jog toward us doesn't register. I'm probably hallucinating. It's the only logical conclusion my brain can come up with. I mean, why else would Damian Lowell be *here*, at the airport, waving us down after how adamant he was that we leave?

I still don't believe it, and he's standing directly in front of me now. Beside me, Lia is beaming at him.

He grins back at her, the dimples in both cheeks reaching the same intensity as his daughter's.

His expression changes to more serious when he addresses me, though. "Elle, can we talk?"

I suck in a breath and shoot a glance over my shoulder. If we're going to make our flight, this needs to be a short talk.

"Uh, yeah. For a minute."

Damian cocks his head to the side, wanting us to follow him. The three of us move out of the flow of ticket-holders surrounding us. Between us, Lia leans her back against the wall, peering up at Damian in awe.

"I know the timing is shitty, Elle, but I want to keep Lia for the summer. You can go on your research project."

What the hell? Is he serious? One look into his deep blue eyes says he is. It's just—

"Have you been drinking?" I ask, because it's the only explanation to this sudden change I can think of.

"What? Elle, no. Look, I've thought about this since you two left last night. Just hear me out, okay?"

I study him for a moment, part of me dying to know what's in his head and the other part too scared of what he'll say. And then my emotions will take control of my brain, and I'll do something stupid—

Which is what happens.

"Fine," I agree. "Talk."

"I understand why you did what you did, Elle.

I'm not saying it was right, but I get it. I've messed up a million times over, I don't deserve this, and I want to make it up to you."

"To me?"

Damian hesitates, then he nods. "Yeah, to you." He rolls the tip of his tongue over his bottom lip and stares at the floor. "And Mom. And Liam...and Kate."

"Damian, don't," I say when I realize where this is going. I want to tell him no one blames him—*I* don't blame him—but that opens a whole mess of crap I don't want to discuss in the middle of an airport.

His gaze lifts to mine. "I'd like to get to know my daughter, Elle."

The way he says it blows me away. I've seen this same quiet, pleading, determination in his eyes before. It's what happens when he breaks through the pain and becomes the man I fell in love with.

My resolve is beginning to waver.

"Damian, I don't know. Are you sure you can handle this? I mean, eight weeks is a long time, and Lia can be a handful. What would you do with her while you're at the hospital?"

Really, this is the least of my concerns. However, if he doesn't have the little stuff figured out, it saves me the trouble of having to discuss the real issues I have with leaving Lia with him.

"She can come with me, Elle, play with the other kids in The Commons. I'll have an eye on her all day long."

I swallow and shift uncomfortably against the wall. "Where's she going to sleep?"

"I'll buy one of those girly princess beds and put it in my room."

My eyes go wide. I open my mouth to object to this, but Damian cuts in, his voice low enough that Lia can't hear. "No sleepovers with other girls, I swear. I want to make this work."

"The alcohol?" I ask, my voice as low as his.

"Give me this one chance, Ellie. I won't fuck it up."

Now what? God, I want to trust him. I want to soak up everything he says, believe it, wrap my arms around him and kiss him.

I'm such an idiot.

I'm silent long enough for him to reach out and skim his fingers over my cheek. "Please, Elle," he murmurs, and shivers race down my spine, making my whole body tremble at his touch, his words. For an instant, I can't breathe. Can't think.

I can't say no to this man. And, Lia *is* his daughter. This is what I came here for, right?

I'm running out of time. I need to either catch this flight or see if I can get a later one so I can think.

My gaze lowers to Lia, and a sliver of doubt creeps in. But then I think about Blake. He had a point when he said I could be on the red-eye, flying right back here if anything—*anything*—goes wrong.

"We already checked our luggage, and she only has her blanket and a few toys in her carry-on," I hear myself say. Am I really doing this?

"That's okay. Girls like to shop, right?"

"Um…" I say, buying myself some time. I flick my eyes down to Lia again, and I wonder if I'm doing the right thing. Once I'm on that plane, it'll be the farthest I've ever been from my daughter.

I crouch down like I always do when we have to talk about something important. My Lia-Kat will always be my first priority, and before I make a decision on this, I need to know where she stands.

She faces me, her eyebrows high in expectation. I take one of her hands in mine and squeeze. She's my miracle, perfect and precious. The light of my life.

"Sweetheart," I start. "What would you like to do? Do you want to stay here in Iowa with your dad?"

"What will you do?" she asks, and it's so sweet the way she says it. Like she's taking care of me instead of the other way around.

"Go with Blake to study in the ocean," I say.

"That shark thing?"

I laugh. "Yeah, the shark thing."

"Will you be okay without me?"

I grin. Tuck her hair behind her ear. "I'll manage."

Lia glances up at Damian, and I swear her smile reaches her ears. "Did you hear that?" she asks him, and my heart does a little flutter. In good and bad ways. Because it knows I'm letting her go and because of how happy she is right now. "I get to live with you, Daddy!"

Damian squats down with us, his knee grazing mine. "Yes, you do, Lia." Then his eyes cut to me. They sparkle with a delight I don't recall seeing in them before, and I'm glad to have given that to him. "Thank you, Elle. I promise I'll take care of her."

"I know you will."

~*~

I'm crying. Tears falling down my cheeks. Thankfully, I have a window seat I can stare out of so no one sees me.

I checked all possible avenues, but I couldn't book a later flight that would get me back to Florida in time to catch the plane to Cairns. I'm cutting this close as it is.

I wish I didn't have to leave her so quickly.

I've been in the air for less than twenty minutes, and already I want to call Damian and make sure everything is okay. I'm going to be such a mess in Australia. I'll end up on anxiety medication if I can't control this. I have to trust Damian at his word. Easier said than done, I'm sure.

I rub my arms with my palms in an attempt to tame the goosebumps prickling over them. They're not there because I'm cold. No, they're there because I'm scared.

Oh God, I hope I'm not making a mistake.

Chapter 10

Damian

I guess I'm doing this.

I put Lia's pink booster seat Ellie gave me in the back of my BMW. I have no clue how this thing works. Where the hell do the straps go?

Lia pokes her head around me. "I can buckle myself," she informs me, then squeezes by and sits down. Her short legs dangle off the seat. She twists and grabs the seatbelt while I watch her work. Using a couple of pulls, she finally has enough length, and sure enough, I hear the click. "See?"

That's it?

"Uh, good work," I congratulate her. First day on the job, and I'm completely lost.

"Blake taught me."

"Oh yeah? Who's Blake?" I ask, swinging her carry-on luggage around her and into the next seat.

It shouldn't matter who Blake is, but he's obviously spent more time with my daughter than I have, and for some reason that doesn't sit right with me. That and Ellie never mentioned him, which could mean anything.

"Mommy's friend," she says.

I don't know much about kids, especially kids this age, but I do know they're honest. Brutally, sometimes. I get the feeling my daughter is no exception.

"Is he a good friend?"

Lia shrugs. "He comes over a lot. One night, I saw them kissing. Gross!" She makes a face and shudders.

A weight dips in my stomach at the thought then disappears just as quickly.

"He's going to Australia with her," Lia offers.

"That's nice," I say and slam Lia's door harder than I intended. Through the tinted window, I see her jump and snap her head in my direction.

"Sorry," I mouth.

I walk around the back of the car. I'm happy for Ellie. She deserves someone as awesome as my brother, and I convince myself the only reason this protective instinct is kicking in has to do with Lia. Because, why wouldn't it? We were never together.

By the time I'm behind the wheel and driving out of the airport, Ellie and this Blake guy are nothing but a whisper in the back of my mind. By tonight they'll be completely gone. Ellie's relationships are none of my business, like mine aren't hers.

"I guess our first stop should be the store, huh? Because you need clothes and shit," I say, checking on Lia from the rearview mirror.

She cocks her head to the side. "I need clothes,

but what's 'shit?'"

Oh damn.

"Uh, it's nothing. Bad word, sorry. I meant stuff, like a toothbrush and"—fuck, do I have to change diapers?—"other stuff."

Lia frowns, her lower lip jutting out. "My favorite jammies are on the airplane with Mommy. I can't sleep without them."

Jammies? What the hell are jammies?

"We'll buy you new jammies, okay?"

"My Little Pony jammies?" she asks, her pretty blue eyes pleading with me, and right then and there I vow to myself that I'll find her My Little Pony jammies if I have to go into every goddamn store in Des Moines to get them. My daughter already has me whipped.

This will either be a very long or a very short eight weeks. I'm not sure which I'm hoping for.

I turn into the Target parking lot on Mills Civic Drive. Target is an easy choice because it was Kate's favorite store. I swear, she bought everything here.

Lia gallops to the clothing section like she lives there. Goes straight for the pajamas and squeals in delight.

"Eeek! Lookie!" She rips something off the hanger, spins around, and hugs it to her chest.

"Jammies?" I ask because I have no fucking clue.

"Duh, Dad." She rolls those gorgeous blues, and either that's a girl thing they learn from a very early age or she inherited the move from her mother. But I'd never tell Ellie that.

"Your mom said you wear a size four," I say as I rummage through the rack and pull out an identical nightgown in the correct size. "How's this?"

"Can we get two?"

"Of the same thing?"

She bobs her head quickly, eyes wide and hopeful.

Oh, why the hell not.

I grab another size four and drop it into the cart. The term "wrapped around her finger" comes to mind.

After loading the cart with most of the clothes in the little girls section, shoes, panties—not diapers, thank God—a toddler bed and girly comforter, I wonder where the hell I'm going to put all this stuff.

"Toys!" Lia cheers, pointing to her left.

I check our overflowing cart. "Toys, too?" I ask.

"All of mine are in Florida," she reminds me.

"Right." I do a quick reorganization to find more space. "Okay, on to the toy department."

Lia leads the way. She cleans out the My Little Pony shelves, and as she does, I shoot Dylan a text to retrieve the purple horse from the garbage in the kitchen.

"That's all you want?" I ask, surprised there's nothing except pony shit in the cart. No Barbie dolls, baby dolls, Disney princesses.

"This is good," she replies.

I lead her to the educational toys anyway, because, well, because. She picks out a couple of things, and as we swing by the electronics, I toss in some pink video games since *Resident Evil* and *Slaughterhouse* are probably not appropriate. Then I dump in a few books, and we're ready to go.

So far, this fathering thing isn't too bad.

Ellie

Blake is waiting for me in baggage claim. His gaze narrows as soon as he catches sight of me. Then he tilts his head to the side in question. The way his dark hair sweeps over his forehead when he does it is adorable.

I force half a grin at his expression. Over the years, this guy has become my best friend. He knows how to make me laugh without trying. Whether or not he sees it on my face, Lia's obviously not with me, and Blake understands how much it hurts to leave her behind.

I pick up my pace until I reach him, tears forming again behind my eyelids. He doesn't greet me with words. Instead, he circles his arms around me and brings me into him. His chin rests on my head. One hand smoothes my hair in the same manner I had with Lia's before I left.

I let go of Blake and wipe my eyes. "I'm sorry," I apologize unnecessarily.

"She with Damian, huh?" he asks, taking the handle of my carry-on so all I have is my purse.

"Yeah. She, uh, wanted to stay with him."

Blake pushes loose strands of hair out of my face. "It'll be good for both of them, Elizabeth. And for you too."

I nod as if I agree with him.

It's strange to think that when he dropped us off, there'd been two of us. Now, he's only picking up one.

"You hungry?" Blake asks as he pulls into traffic.

"Um, no." I shake my head and dig out my phone. I can't think about food until after I talk with Lia.

I feel Blake's gaze on me, then his hand as it slides onto my thigh to stop it from bouncing.

"I'll order pizza," he decides.

I barely hear him, though, since I've already dialed Damian's cell and it's ringing.

"Hey, Elle," Damian answers softly, and my stupid brain takes me back to his bedroom when he used to moan out my name in that same hushed voice. I squeeze my thighs together.

I glance over at Blake, and he grins back at me, winking his encouragement.

"How's Lia?" I ask.

"She's fine. In fact, she fell asleep about ten minutes ago," Damian says.

"Oh…"

"I tried to keep her up. But we shopped all evening, ate Chinese, and then she reiterated our entire day to Dylan as soon as he got back from work." Damian laughs. "She talks like she's spent her life around graduate students, Elle. What the fuck did you do to my daughter?"

That makes me giggle because I can totally see it. She started talking early and hasn't stopped. It's one of the reasons she's the unofficial mascot of the marine biology grad department.

103

"I finally got her settled down with a My Little Pony movie," he continues, "and she was out two minutes in."

"And you're still watching it, aren't you?" I guess, grinning, because I've been there, done that.

"Damn, this shit is addicting, Ellie. So, Twilight Sparkle apparently wasn't born with wings, huh?"

"No, Princess Celestia gives them to her later."

"The pony with the crazy, windblown hair?" he asks after a moment's hesitation. I can just imagine his expression. God, I wish I was there.

"That's the one."

"I can hardly contain my excitement," he says, and I laugh. On the other end, I hear him laugh too, and I realize that we haven't laughed together in such a long time. It's so good to hear that sound from him.

"Tell her I love her, okay?" I ask, referring to my Lia-Kat.

"I will, Elle. Talk to you tomorrow."

"Good night."

A second passes before he replies. "Good night."

~*~

I can breathe again. In more ways than one.

"She's okay?" Blake asks. I'd been so caught up in the conversation with Damian, I completely forgot he was there.

"Yeah, she's all tuckered out. Fell asleep a little while ago."

Blake smiles. "Good."

When we arrive at my apartment building two

blocks from campus, Blake helps me with my stuff. I bummed my mom's washing machine so all our clothes are clean. Blake joins me in my bedroom after calling in our pizza.

"Twenty minutes," he says.

"Ham and pineapple?"

"On your half."

"And boring ol' sausage on yours," I drawl out in my best Alabama accent. It's horrible in comparison to his native one.

He shoots me a sideways smirk for my effort. "Don't knock it until you try it, babe."

"Repeat: boring ol' sausage." I nod this time as I deepen my fake accent to drive home my point.

Blake's face goes slack, clearly not amused. He saunters toward me and hooks an arm around my waist, pulling me into him. Finally, he cracks a half-smile and leans in. Like the handful of kisses I've received from him, this one is light and slow. He takes his time with me. I've been straight with him from the beginning: I'm not looking for a relationship. With school and Lia, I don't have the time.

What I left out were my ever-present feelings for Damian.

Blake sucks my lower lip between his teeth before he lets go. His eyes search mine as if asking if what he did was okay. He's respectful like that, which is one of the reasons I think Blake and I could work—if we take things slow.

He's like Liam—the complete opposite of Damian.

I grin back at him to let him know I enjoyed it.

"I figured I'd better do that now. You know, before you have ham and pineapple breath," he teases, and I gently push him away.

"Here," I say, handing him a stack of Lia's clothes. "Go make yourself useful."

Blake's here a lot, so he knows the ins and outs of this apartment. In fact, he put together Lia's bed and furniture, helped me paint her walls, and decorated her room.

Blake kisses me again. "I thought I already did."

"You wish."

He waggles his brows at me as he backs out of my room. Then he winks and disappears into Lia's adjacent one.

We finish putting everything away, and as soon as we're done, our pizza arrives. I grab the parmesan cheese, and Blake sets the box on the coffee table.

"Pop?" I ask him.

"What about my dad?" he says, teasing me again. There are some words that are ingrained in my brain and always will be no matter where I live.

I roll my eyes before I can stop myself. Lia does this enough for both of us, but she's not here to see my slip-up.

"Coke?" I clarify.

"Dr. Pepper, please."

"Stocked just for you," I say. I hate the stuff and keep it around for Blake.

I hand him the can and settle down on the sofa with him. He already has a comedy picked out on Netflix.

Twenty minutes in, we're both done eating, and

Blake puts an arm around me, tugging me against him. This is new for us, but I let it happen. It's nice, and with Blake, I know I'm safe. Unlike Damian, Blake's not a wild card. He's solid, has his life put together, and his future planned out.

Safe.

When the movie is over, Blake kisses my forehead and holds me closer. It's warm in his arms. So incredibly warm, and I feel my body responding to it.

His palms glide down my arms then back up until his fingers tilt my chin up to him. I'm nervous, not knowing how far he intends to go. I'm not ready. I mean, I'll tell him no if I have to, but I'd like to not have to go there, even if the rest of me is screaming yes.

Blake brushes his lips over mine, and I like it. Really like it. So much that I want a little more. I roll into him so we're now both lying on our sides, facing each other.

Blake threads his fingers through my hair. "I love spending time with you, Elizabeth."

"Me too," I murmur.

Shivers race under my skin. My nipples are rock hard, aching beneath my bra. Blake leans his forehead against mine before he kisses me again. I cup the back of his neck.

Oh God, this is good.

Blake's tongue caresses my lips, tasting them before he separates them and lets himself in. A moan slips out of me and Blake responds by hiking my leg over his hip. He pushes me into him, his erection rubbing against my center.

This is too much. No matter how much I'm enjoying what he's doing, how much my body is crying out for it, I can't. I'm a mother now, and I have to be responsible. And the responsible thing is to not lead this man on. I've only been this intimate with two men my whole life. One I was in love with. The other was a mistake.

And I can't make another mistake.

I break away from Blake's kisses to catch my breath. "Blake…"

He's panting too, but he doesn't stop roaming over my face, my hair. "Too fast?"

"I'm sorry."

He holds my chin with his forefinger and thumb and presses his lips on my forehead. "Don't be. I promised you we'd move at your pace." Even though his words are sincere, there's disappointment laced through his chocolate irises.

I force a smile. "It's late."

"Yeah, I'd better go."

I roll off the sofa and intentionally turn my back to him so he'll have a minute of privacy. Then his hands are on my shoulders and he's spinning me to face him.

Blake's fingertips glide over the side of my face. "You sure you're gonna be all right? I can crash on the sofa."

"I'll be fine, but thanks."

"Okay, I'll see you tomorrow."

"I just got back from one trip, Blake. I have so much to do tomorrow before we fly to Australia, and I could use a day to myself."

He nods, understanding. "If you need anything,

you call me?"

"Of course, Sir Lancelot."

"Prince Charming," he corrects, and I giggle.

"Fine. Okay, Prince Charming."

I close the door behind him and lean against it. Without Lia here, the apartment is too quiet. But having Blake stay here wouldn't make me feel any better, especially not after the make-out session I ended a minute ago.

I flip off all the lights as I walk through. Then I open the door to Lia's room, taking in how empty it is. I miss her so much. I forgo my own room, and with my clothes on, I curl up and fall asleep in Lia's bed.

Chapter 11

Damian

Lia's coming with me to the hospital today. After hanging up with Ellie, I carried Lia to her bed in the corner of my room and called my dad.

"Dad?" I say for the fifteenth time. I wonder if I should drive over and check on him. "Dad?"

He still doesn't answer. The stunned silence thing is understandable, but come on! Give me *something*.

"Wow," he finally says.

"That's all you've got?"

He blows into the phone again. "And she never told you?"

"No. If it weren't for this research project, I'm not sure she ever would have."

"Wow," he repeats, and for a man whose job it is to talk to people, he pretty much sucks at it.

I glance over at Lia. She's lying on her side so all I can see is her mass of hair assaulting the pillow.

110

"I know she just arrived, but do you have plans tomorrow night?"

"Kinda looks like I don't have plans for the next eight weeks, Dad."

He laughs. "All right, well, why don't you come over for dinner after work? She can play in the pool."

So those are the plans for our first whole day together. Lia joining me at work, then dinner with her grandpa.

I can't help smiling as I get the two of us ready to leave in the morning. Talking with Ellie last night put me in a good mood. It's been a long time since I laughed like that, even longer since I heard *her* laugh like that. God, she sounded amazing. Like the Ellie I remember from when Liam was alive. When she practically lived at our house.

"My grandpa is a doctor?" Lia asks, scooping another spoonful of Lucky Charms in her mouth. I'll buy Dylan another box later. Dude and his freaking kids' cereal.

"He's an oncologist," I specify.

"What's that?"

"It means he helps people who have cancer."

Lia pushes her hair out of her face. I tried to brush through the mass, but she kept whining that it hurt, so I gave up. I have no idea what to do with it.

"What's cancer?" she asks.

"A horrible, horrible disease," I answer, downing the last of my coffee. "You ready?"

"Yep." Lia slides off the chair and grabs one of the Twilight Sparkles I said she could bring along.

I open the back door of my car, and she hops in

and buckles herself. I'm not the one who taught her, yet I'm proud. It's strange.

Lia stays close to me as we walk through the double doors and ride the elevator to the third floor.

"I've never been in a hospital before," she informs me. "Except when I was born."

"Good. Let's hope you never have to be admitted into one."

The elevator doors open, and sitting on the bench right outside of them is my father. His gaze pins on Lia, and his jaw slackens. Seeing that she's an exact replica of Mom must be even more shocking for him than it was for me.

"Dad, this is Lia Kathryn. Lia, this is your Grandpa Lowell." Lia stands half behind me, holding onto my leg like she did with Ellie when she first met me.

"Hey there, Lia," Dad greets her.

"Hi," she quips, and I bend down to pick her up. Her little arms wrap around me as she leans in.

He grins. "She looks like your mother, Damian."

"I know," I say, squeezing her. "She's Mom all over again."

"Well, so were you and your brother."

"I wish Mom was here to see her," I say, and as I do, I realize that if Mom were alive, Liam would be as well, and this little girl in my arms wouldn't be mine. She'd be his.

A couple of days ago I wouldn't have cared. Today, I'm not sure.

"Lia, it's a pleasure to meet you," Dad says, smiling at her. "Now, I think there're some kids in The Commons who'd love to play with you."

Lia's eyes brighten. I carry her down the hall because I'm not ready to put her down yet. We pass the nurses' station, and I suppress the laugh bubbling in my chest. Mouths hanging open, the nurses gawk as we pass. They all remember my mother, and it's not hard to put two and two together—especially with them. The news of who Lia is will spread fast now.

The Commons is at the far end of the hall, next to the chemo room. Dad was right. There are several kids already here, playing and receiving treatments. In the corner where I saw her yesterday sits Olivia. She has some crayons out and doesn't seem to have a care in the world.

"Lia," I say, "there's someone I'd like for you to meet."

I lead my daughter over to the table and lower myself on my haunches. Olivia glances up and breaks into a smile as she recognizes me.

"Hi, Olivia," I say. I unzip my bag and pull out a My Little Pony notebook Lia picked out and a large box of crayons. "These are for you."

Her smile widens. "Wow. Thank you."

"I'd also like to introduce you to my daughter, Lia."

"Hi," Lia says, waving even though the girls are only a foot away from each other.

"Hi," Olivia answers, waving back.

"I'm going to leave you two to play, okay?" I say, looking back and forth between the two. I linger on Lia.

They both nod.

"If you need anything, Lia, you can ask Olivia or

one of the nurses. They come in frequently. I'll be back to check in soon."

"Okay," she says.

At the door, I twist around. Already the girls are giggling with each other and breaking in the new crayons. I watch for a second longer before I slip out.

~*~

On my break, Leslie teaches me how to brush Lia's hair. I'm catching on—until she braids it. Then I'm completely lost.

"Can you braid Twilight Sparkle's tail?" she asks Leslie, holding up her pony.

"Sure, sweetheart. Now, pay attention, Damian." Leslie splits the hair in three pieces. So far, I get it. But when she starts to move the three strands, they all blur together, and suddenly I have a headache.

"Uh, I'll YouTube it," I say when she asks if I've got it.

Leslie laughs. "You do that."

"Thanks, Miss Leslie!" Lia quips and runs off.

"She's beautiful, Damian," Leslie says.

"She is," I agree as I watch Lia show off her braid to Olivia.

"Kate would be proud."

The wind is knocked out of me at Leslie's sentiment. She means well, but I doubt Kate would be proud of me knocking up Ellie the night before her burial.

Lia's blues flash in our direction. She points at Leslie, and Olivia claps her hands in excitement

114

before they start toward us.

"Looks like you have another customer," I say, happy for the quick change in subject. I stand up and take off before I have to sit through another hair-braiding lesson.

~*~

Dinner at Dad's went great, and now Lia's on the phone with her mom, dishing out her entire day. Word. For. Word.

She's definitely Ellie's daughter.

"He has a swimming pool inside his house!" she squeals into the phone. "Daddy says we can go swimming there again. Maybe tomorrow."

"I didn't say that," I interject even though she's not listening.

Lia frowns. "But Mom, it's *inside his house!*"

I can assume what Ellie is saying. It's summer, so Lia should swim in an outdoor pool with other kids. Dad told her the same thing. Frankly, I couldn't care less.

"Yeah, he's right here," Lia says with a corresponding eye roll. "Okay. I love you too, Mommy."

She gives me the phone after making a kissy noise into the receiver.

"Hey, Elle," I say, and last night's conversation slips into my memory.

"She sounds happy," Ellie says, and I can hear the smile in her voice.

"We're doing all right," I tell her. "You fly out tomorrow?"

"Yes, so we'll have to deal with the time difference after I land."

"We'll figure it out," I say, my gaze flitting to Lia playing on the floor. "Be safe, okay?"

My comment carries weight, and we both know it. Ellie and I know too well what it's like to lose someone, and I'll be damned if Lia has to go through that. Hell, *I* can't go through that.

"I will, Damian," she says, and I catch a quiet sniffle.

"What's wrong, Elle?"

She hesitates. "Nothing. It's just hard to be this far away from her, you know?"

"I'm not going to let anything happen to her," I assure her, and I wish I could look her in the eye as I say it. It's how I'm used to comforting her. Over the phone makes it sound like a shallow promise. To lighten the mood, I laugh. "Besides, you're going to the Great Barrier Reef to poke needles in sharks, Elle. The last thing you should have to worry about is what's going on here. So tell me, how well did they test that shark-bite suit of yours?"

That earns me a giggle, and I smile, imagining the corners of her lips curved up and the way she bats her eyelashes at the same time.

"Yeah," she agrees. "I'll call you as soon as I land."

"Please do."

"I will. Good night, Damian."

I pause for a moment to prolong the call. "Good night, Elle."

~*~

I read Lia a bedtime story and tuck her in. She's wearing those My Little Pony pajamas she picked out, and I'm glad I bought two because I'll have to wash this one eventually. She rolls onto her side, holding her favorite blanket in one hand and sucking the thumb of her other. Damn, that's adorable.

"Sleep tight, little Lia," I say, smoothing her hair.

I take a final glance at her before closing the door. Two days with her, and I think I have this dad-thing down. Maybe I won't fuck this up.

I grab a beer from the fridge and plop down on the sofa with Dylan. He tosses me an Xbox remote.

"You're a natural, man," he says.

I shrug. "Well, I'm not gonna brag, but I have played all the other *Grand Theft Auto* games. This one's a breeze."

"I meant with Lia."

I knew what he meant.

"Yeah, well, Ellie needed to go on that research trip and there was no one else." I pop the top off the bottle and take a swig.

"Sure, man. Whatever you say."

"Don't worry, dude. I have eight full weeks to mess this shit up." I'm half teasing, half not. I know what I'm capable of. This summer is my chance to prove I'm not the selfish bastard I think I am.

Dylan grins because he understands. Then he turns serious. "Well, just remember, if you fuck up, you not only hurt yourself, you hurt that little girl and her mother too. This isn't only about you, Damian."

"How much do I owe for that, Dr. Laura?" I joke, even though it's not funny. Both of us have been on the receiving end of his statement.

He shrugs. "Bill's in the mail."

"Go to hell."

I knock back the rest of my beer and shoot a look at my closed bedroom door. Dylan's right. But I won't let that happen. I will fight for her. I owe Kate that much. Because when I could have saved her—fought for her—

I didn't.

I won't make that mistake again.

Chapter 12

Damian

Lia's antsy, waiting for Ellie to call. She's sitting at the table, her palms plastered against her cheeks, and her too short legs swinging under the chair. It's been two days since we heard from Ellie, and I don't expect my phone to ring for another couple of hours. Her plane is scheduled to land in Cairns at 11:26 a.m. their time, which is over half a day ahead of ours.

Dylan's read Lia two princess stories, I've sat through a few episodes of *Friendship is Magic,* and neither have distracted her. Maybe some food will.

"Let's go out for pizza," I suggest. It's been McDonald's Happy Meals since she arrived, and I could use a change.

Lia's head snaps in my direction, and she sits up taller. "Really?"

"Yeah. What kind do you like?"

"Ham and pineapple!" she exclaims, the anticipated call pushed aside.

I grimace. "Sure. Fine. Whatever."

Damn you, Ellie.

"Come on, Dylan." Lia yanks on my roommate's arm.

"Nah, you two go ahead," he says.

Lia's face slackens, and she bats her lashes like a pro. "Please?" *Bat, bat, bat.*

He's a goner.

He avoids direct eye contact with my three-year-old teenager, cutting his gaze to me instead.

I shrug. "Everyone's gotta eat," I tell him.

"Dude, we walk in a pizza joint together with a little girl, people are either going to stare at us or erupt in applause," he says, reaching for a way to get out of this.

"True. So, let's not wear those matching rainbow outfits we'd planned on then, huh?" I slug him in the shoulder. "It's just pizza. We can talk wedding invitations tomorrow."

Dylan huffs. "You're paying."

"Of course, sweetpea. And you can return the favor later." I wink and shoot him the sexy smirk the girls at The Underground cream themselves over.

"Fucktard," he mutters.

"Dickhead," I return.

By the time we arrive, Lia's less jittery, and I'm thinking I should earn Dad of the Year for my awesome anxiety-soothing idea.

"Two adults, and she's three," I tell the lady at the register.

"Okay," she says. "Anything specific you want on the buffet tonight?"

"Ham and pineapple!" Lia exclaims with the same enthusiasm as earlier. Girl loves her pizza.

The lady smiles. "I'll put that right in."

We seat ourselves, Lia beside me and Dylan across from us, his back to most of the dining room. From where I sit, I can see the whole place. Most of the tables are taken, and I recognize a few students who are staying in town for the summer.

"Do you want something while we wait on your ham and pineapple?" I ask.

"Hmm…chocolate milk," she decides.

"One chocolate milk coming right up." I slide out from the booth and head across the room to the buffet. I load up a plate for myself before I fill up a glass with chocolate milk for Lia.

On my way back, I catch a steroid-induced guy glaring at me. Dude looks familiar, but I'm not sure why. I ignore him and head back to our booth.

I sit down, giving Dylan the go-ahead to grab himself some grub.

"Want a cheese stick?" I ask Lia after she sips on her drink.

"What's on it?"

"Uh, cheese. And bread."

She makes a face where her nose scrunches up. "Ew, no thanks."

"So, it's only ham and pineapple for you?"

"Yep-yep!" she sings and sucks down more chocolate milk.

I make a mental note to talk with Ellie about expanding our daughter's limited pizza palate. Preferably something not puke-worthy like her current favorite.

I'm too busy with Lia to see someone approach us. Not until he clutches my shirt and rips me off the bench.

"Come here, you little fuck," he growls, slamming my back against the wall.

My head hits the brick, and the wind is knocked out of me. It takes a second for my eyes to refocus. When they do, I realize this is the same guy who was eyeing me earlier.

"I think you got the wrong guy," I say. Whoever he is, he has me pinned flat so I can't move.

"You Damian?" The vein in his too-thick neck pops out in anger.

"Yeah. Who the fuck are you?"

He loosens his grip for a split second, then smacks me into the wall again. My gaze cranks over to Lia in the booth right next to me. She's backed up into the corner, eyes wide with fear, lips quivering. The way this guy has me, I can't break free to get to her.

"Lia," I say. "Lia—"

"Shut up," the guy demands. To back up his point, he punches me in the stomach.

I can't breathe.

"You finger-fucked my girl, you motherfucker," he growls.

"I've finger-fucked a lot of girls, asshole, you're going to need to be more specific," I cough out.

That vein of his is pulsing now. I don't see his right hook until he sends it barreling into my face. I immediately feel the burn, and I can barely make out Dylan directly behind the son of a bitch.

"Get Lia, and get her out of here," I order him,

so he doesn't consider helping me.

The guy is in my face again, blocking my view of my daughter, his breath steaming hot over where he punched me. "Katey."

Oh shit.

I remember Katey. I didn't nail her after she told me her name. In fact, I sent her away completely unfulfilled and pissed off.

My eye is swelling shut, but through the other, I see Dylan with Lia in his arms, running outside. Good.

"If you were a real man, she wouldn't have come home with me in the first place," I spit out.

A couple of days ago, when I found out Katey's boyfriend was Toby Stanton, the NCAA national champion boxer, I'd expected this confrontation. Hell, I wanted it, which is why the thought of banging his girl that night had appealed to me— other than the actual banging, of course.

Booze and sex alone don't cut it for me anymore. No one touches Toby Stanton's chicks, so pissing him off is a great way to remind myself of who I am.

Now, though, I have Lia. And for the first time in years, I have someone in my life who means more to me than my pain.

Toby thrusts his fist deep into my stomach. Once. Twice. Three times.

I double over, but Toby doesn't loosen his grip like I'd hoped. No, the dude holds on tighter. Fucking A.

"You lay an eye on her again, I swear I'll rip your fucking dick off and shove it up your ass. You understand?" he growls. For emphasis, he jabs his knee in my crotch.

Holy hell!

I see stars. Real fucking stars.

I'm on the floor, but I don't remember how I got there. A foot kicks into me over and over again, making contact with my head a couple of times before everything finally stops.

"Hey, you okay?" someone asks, and all I can think about is how much I hurt. How the voice speaking to me sounds all fuzzy.

I groan. "Yeah. Yeah, I'm good."

I'm not good. I just had the shit kicked out of me in front of a room full of people.

"You're bleeding," the person says.

My hand automatically flies to my head. Sure enough blood is pouring from above my swollen-shut eye.

"That doesn't look good, man," he says.

"I'll be fine. Got a towel or something?"

He gives me a wad of napkins, and I press them against my head.

"We called the police," the kid informs me, "but the guy ran out of here. If you know him, you can press charges."

I shake my head. "Nah. I—"

I'm dizzy. The room is spinning, and I might puke. I have to push through this though; I have to make sure Lia's okay.

"I'm good," I finish. "Sorry about all this."

Every eye is on me as I struggle to stand up. Mine, however, are on the door. I walk Quasimodo style toward it, ignoring the whispers from behind

124

me.

Dylan has my car parked right outside. I see Lia through the tinted back window, and I let out my relief. I doubt she was in danger, but dammit, shit could have gone downhill fast, and I couldn't get to her.

I grab for the door and collapse in the seat.

"Dude…" Dylan says, studying me. "What the hell was that about?"

"Me being an idiot," I reply.

"Daddy?" Lia's voice travels up to me, worried and small. "Daddy, are you okay?"

I twist around. Her eyes are glistening with tears, and I'd give anything for them not to fall. "Yeah, Lia, I'm okay."

"Yo, man," Dylan says, causing me to turn back around. "That is one nasty cut."

I flip down the visor, remove the napkins, and examine my head in the mirror. He's right. The wound is gaping open and hasn't stopped bleeding.

"Hospital?" my roommate suggests.

"No. I'll call Dad. Let's get Lia home."

~*~

I'm lying on the sofa in my living room. Dad took the lampshade off the lamp, and Dylan holds the light above my head, blinding me. Real smooth operation we have going here.

"Son, you can't go looking for trouble. Lia could have been—"

"Yeah, Dad, I know," I reply. I don't need my father rubbing in my mistakes. Karma's a bitch, and

I just got served.

Dad sets the empty vial on the floor. I've had stitches before, and I know what's coming. God, I hate needles and this is gonna sting like a mother.

I hold my breath as he drizzles the local anesthetic over the cut. The idea is for the medicine to kick in before he jabs the needle into the wound. For the record, that's a load of bull—the topical swash of Lidocaine doesn't do a damn thing.

"Damian, relax your face," the doc says.

"Fuck you," I answer, and he pokes into me again.

Lia's supposed to be in the kitchen coloring. After what she witnessed today, she shouldn't have to see this too, but it wouldn't surprise me if she's at the doorway, peeking out.

Dad grins. "All done."

"Thanks for going easy on me, Dad."

He shrugs and goes straight for the curved needle and thread. "A little closer, Dylan," he instructs. My roommate is good at following orders. Unlike me.

My sure-handed father slips the needle into me. I know because I feel the tugging, not the pain anymore.

Then my phone rings.

"Shit. Ellie," I say, recognizing the ring tone. "Dylan?"

My phone is on the end table he's sitting on. Knowing Ellie, if I don't answer, she'll worry something has happened, especially since we haven't spoken in two days. I'd really rather her *not* find out about what happened today.

I reach my arm above my head, which earns me

sideways glare from the man with the needle. He can wait. I assume Dylan will give me my phone. He doesn't, though. He freaking answers it.

"Hello?...Yeah, this is Damian's phone...Oh, hi Elizabeth."

I'm an idiot. Dylan answering my cell is like calling Ellie myself to say, "Hey, guess what? I royally screwed up today."

"He's here. He's, uh, preoccupied?" He says it like it's a question, and for a smart dude, my roommate is a complete moron.

"Give me the phone," I demand.

"Don't move, son," my dad warns me.

"Yeah," Dylan continues with Ellie as if he didn't hear me. "He'll only be a couple more minutes. How was your trip?"

"So help me, Dylan, give me the phone," I try again, louder this time.

"Hold the light steady, Dylan," Dad says, and I can sense the irritation in his voice. That's typical, though, when I'm the patient.

"Whoa, wait. Was that Dr. Lowell? Why is Dr. Lowell there?" Ellie's voice filters out from the phone. Her high-pitched, worried voice.

Terrific.

"Lia's fine," my idiot roommate spouts off.

"Shut up, Dylan. Shut. Up. Now," I growl.

"One more stitch," Dad says, but it's not because he's being nice and informative. "Don't move, or I'll make it two."

"Dylan, tell me what's going on!" Ellie yells.

"I swear to you, Elizabeth, everything is fine. Lia is in the other room coloring, completely unharmed, and—"

"*Unharmed*? What's that supposed to mean?"

"Is that my mommy?" Lia bounces into the room.

Oh shit.

"Let me talk to Lia," Ellie demands.

"No," I clip out at the same time I hear Lia answer, "Hi Mommy!"

"You gave her the phone, Dylan? You ass," I say.

I'm dead.

"Grandpa's sewing Daddy up. Some big guy at the pizza place beat him up. It was super scary, and he was saying fuck a lot. You know, that word you said is really, really bad," Lia rattles off.

Great.

"No, I'm okay. He only hurt Daddy," she tells Ellie.

"I'm finished," Dad says, and I spring up off the sofa. Kneel down beside Lia. "Can I speak with Ellie, please?" I ask her.

She frowns. "But I'm not done yet."

"Real quick. Then I'll give it back, I promise," I say.

She studies me for a second, and I can't tell if she's examining her grandfather's handiwork or if she's trying to decide if I'm lying. Either way, she hands over the phone. "Fine."

"Ellie? Hi," I say like today is another average day. It's important for her to know I have everything under control, which I do.

"Damian! What the hell is going on there?" She's screaming. Loud, anxiety-ridden screaming.

"Calm down. It's not a big deal, Elle. A misunderstanding, but everything is perfectly fine. How was your flight?" I redirect her.

"No way. You do not get off the hook that easy."

I stand up and duck into my bedroom for some privacy, even though I can hear Lia outside my door. I explain the gist of the situation, enough to pacify Ellie and make it believable. No reason to give her more than that.

"Do I need to come back?" she asks point blank.

I lower my voice. "No, Elle, of course not. I have everything under control. You stay there and kick some shark ass."

She breathes into the receiver, extending the silence between us.

"Ellie, you gotta trust me," I beg. Yeah, I've resorted to that because after today, I don't have much dignity left. "I'll never let anything or anyone hurt Lia."

Finally, she sighs. "So, are you okay?"

I smile at the concern in her voice. "Yes, Elle. I'm okay. One stitch, that's all that was required," I lie. I'm pretty sure there are five or six.

Again, I have to wait for her to answer. "Good," she says, relief tinting her tone. "I'm glad."

"Talk tomorrow?" I ask, and I'm already looking forward to it.

"Kiss Lia for me, please?"

I glance at Lia's empty bed. "I will."

"Bye, Damian."

"Good night, Elle," I say, then sink down on the edge of my bed, remembering how we never used to say that before we fell asleep in my bed.

~*~

We have to call Ellie back because I forgot to let Lia talk with her again. She's on the phone for fifteen minutes before she begins to run out of things to say. After they hang up, I usher Lia to the bathroom to get ready for bed.

"Mommy gives me baths every night," Lia says when I tell her to brush her teeth.

Right. A bath.

"Uh...okay. I'll fill up the tub." I stick the plug in the drain and run the faucet.

"I like bubbles," Lia tells me.

I did buy some of that no tears baby wash for her. I dump half of it in the water and make a mental note to pick up some bubble bath.

Lia comes up behind me and taps me on the shoulder. "Can I play with my ponies in the tub?"

She holds up Twilight Sparkle and two others I haven't caught the names of. Her eyebrows perch high on her forehead as she begs me with her cuteness.

"I don't see why not," I reply.

"Yes!" she squeals. "Mommy never lets me."

Ah, shit.

She starts to undress and is almost naked by the time I stand up and notice.

"Whoa. Um, let me get out of here first." I close my eyes and slide around her.

"Mommy stays in here with me. And if you leave, who's going to wash my hair?"

Her hair?

"You can't do that yourself?" I ask, keeping my

focus on the door.

"No."

I wipe a palm down my face. "Okay, uh, go put a swimming suit on."

"Seriously?" she drawls out, sounding more like a sixteen-year-old than a three-year-old.

I turn around. She has her hands on her hips, one foot forward, one hip popped to the side. Her expression is priceless, and I immediately think about her mother in the exact same pose. This little girl may look like me, but she's got Ellie written all over her.

"Yes, seriously. Go," I instruct, and she sulks off to dress.

When she returns, she climbs in the tub and immediately lies down and makes a water angel. She's laughing, and it's the cutest thing I've ever seen. She rolls onto her stomach, sticks her face in the water, and wiggles.

"I'm a mermaid," she says after blowing water out of her mouth fountain-style.

I let her play and splash, and after the bathroom floor has more water than the bathtub, I wash her hair.

"Okay, you're done. Hop out," I say.

"I don't want to be done, yet. I'm not all pruny."

I scratch my head. Check the clock and relent. "Ten more minutes."

"Yay!"

Ten minutes later, while she's putting on her jammies, I soak up the water on the floor. Ellie does this every night?

Lia jumps in her bed and brings her blankets up

to her chin. Then she peers at me with puppy-dog eyes.

"Will you read me a story again?" she asks, her mouth doing that pouty thing she's so good at.

I slide out a plastic tote from under her bed. "Which one?"

"Hmmm." She examines each and every one before she finally settles on the one we read last night. My mom used to call that "stalling" when I was a kid, and it probably is, but I don't care tonight.

"My Little Pony, huh?" Shocker. I sit down on the floor beside her bed. "Okay, here we go."

She hangs onto every word, clutching her stuffed version of Twilight Sparkle in her arms. "Look, Twilight, there's you!" she exclaims each time the pony shows up in the book—which is nearly every page.

"The end," I say and close the book. "Bedtime."

I half expect a retort, but when I get up to tuck her in, her eyes are already drooping. They flutter briefly, and Lia smiles. "Thank you, Daddy."

"You're welcome." I lean over her and press my lips against her forehead. "The kiss is from your mom."

Lia yawns, gathers her favorite blanket in her tiny hand, and sticks her thumb in her mouth.

I chuckle to myself, the sassy image of her in the bathroom flashing through my mind again. Lia's leaving her mark on me. Single-handed and easily, she drew me in. Filled a hole. And I don't want to imagine my life without her now.

"Good night, my babygirl."

Chapter 13

Ellie

I'm checked into my room at the Cairns facility. It's more like a hotel room than an apartment. One room with a bed, a loveseat, desk, dresser, and television. Along the west wall is a tiny stove and dorm-sized refrigerator. And of course there's a bathroom, but that's it.

My home for the next eight weeks.

I don't unpack. Instead, I sit in the middle of the bed, legs crossed. I'm still thinking about the phone call with Damian. My first response was panic. Fear because this is why I hadn't wanted to leave Lia with him in the first place. What was I thinking? Damian has no idea how to be a parent and all the position entails. My little Lia-Kat requires two eyes on her at all times.

Drunk guy with a steroid problem? Damian's explanation *is* believable.

The kicker is I wanted to be there. Not for Lia. For Damian.

133

I fall back onto the pillows. I have to stop thinking about him. Stop wanting to comfort him. Those years are gone, and it's time to concentrate on something else.

Seeing him back in Iowa, though, brought all the feelings I'd tucked away to the surface again. I need to get a grip. Keep our daily phone calls about Lia and Lia alone.

And short. Super, super short.

Because while I'm in Cairns, my head stays in my work. It's what I came here to do, and I've got to focus.

Deep breath in.

Let it out.

Orientation is in the morning, and Blake and I have a dinner date tonight. Who knows? If I can manage to remove Damian from my heart, maybe something can happen with Blake.

Lia adores him. He's been so good to us. The guy definitely deserves a chance. So, tonight, I'm one hundred percent committed to giving it a shot.

Being here in Australia without Lia and with Damian halfway around the world may be exactly what I need to get my love life back on track.

"Right this way," the waiter says, directing Blake and me onto the portico.

It's breezy, but the view of the ocean is spectacular. Water laps over the sand below us, and the golden rays of the setting sun sparkle on the waves like glitter.

Blake pulls a chair out for me and glides a hand over my bare shoulders as he scoots me in. He's quite debonair in his white button-up and black suit.

The waiter pours us each a glass of champagne before he leaves.

Blake holds his glass up. "A toast."

"All right," I say, mirroring him.

His eyes twinkle as the flicker of the candle on our table reflects off them. "To eight weeks of pure awesomeness in the land down under with the most amazing girl I've ever met. Elizabeth Van Zee, to you."

I feel the blush coming on before it hits my face. "Cheers."

Our glasses clink in the middle. With gazes locked, we take our sips. I set my champagne down. The part mischievous, part delighted grin Blake has stirs a flutter in my stomach. It's been there for a while, patiently waiting, and I'm finally ready to unleash it and see what happens.

"This place is beautiful," I say, flicking a glance out to sea again.

"I made these reservations months ago. If you had decided not to come, this would have been a very lonely dinner. So thank you."

I slide my attention back to him. "Months ago? You sound like you were pretty sure of yourself."

He gives a cocky shrug that makes him seem more adorable than arrogant. "And here you are."

"You made it easy."

Blake sips at his champagne. "Elizabeth, I meant what I said. You really are the most amazing girl I've ever met. You're strong, resilient, and the way you take care of Lia is remarkable. Look at all you've accomplished since you left the Midwest. You made a whole new life for yourself, and I respect that.

"But I gotta be honest, Elizabeth, I want in. I want to be a part of that life you're building with Lia, and not as just a friend. I understand why you've kept me at arms' length, and I've been okay with that, but I want more. We're here for two months without Lia, so if it doesn't work out, she won't get hurt."

Blake reaches across the table and takes both of my hands in his, rubbing his thumb over the backs.

"Can you give us a shot, Elizabeth?" he asks, his eyes searching mine.

Suddenly, I'm cold. Goosebumps racing over my arms and shoulders. I'd been expecting this. Heck, I even had my answer ready. Even so, I'm caught off guard because I didn't anticipate this conversation to happen so soon into the trip.

I gaze out over the water to gather my thoughts. I could put this off for a few days, and Blake would be his patient, understanding self about it. So different from Damian.

More like Liam.

I suck in a lungful of ocean air, hold it, then let it out slowly. My mind runs circles around my earlier decision and the doubts that accompany it. Still, the fact that Lia isn't here makes it easier.

Blake and I will either return to Florida as friends like before, because that's how Blake is, or we'd return as a couple, in it for the long haul.

Those are my choices, and even though they both

136

look good on the outside, life has taught me that one will always be a mistake. Like running to Damian after Liam died.

My eyes wander back to Blake's. Dark and considerate, they wait for my answer.

If I'm going to take the plunge, now's the time.

I smile and squeeze his hands. "Yes, Blake. I can do that."

~*~

Blake walks me to my apartment door. My hand hasn't left his since the restaurant, and it's a strange feeling. This never happened between Damian and me because we were never a couple. Before Blake, the only other man I did this with was Liam.

Until now, I didn't realize how much I missed the intimacy of it. I actually don't want him to let go.

"Where did they put you?" I ask.

"One building over, across the courtyard." He gestures with a tilt of his head.

"Um..." I shift my weight, wondering if it's a good idea to ask him in. Even though I'm in this relationship one hundred percent, I don't want to rush into it head first...which is kind of stupid if I think about it. I've known Blake for almost four years.

Blake hooks an arm around my waist, drawing me in. His fingers slide down a strand of hair I left out of my updo. Leaning in, his palms glide over my arms, leaving a trail of warmth on my skin.

"Pick you up in the morning?" His breath wafts

over my mouth, steamy and cool at the same time. "For orientation," he adds unnecessarily.

"Yeah, sure."

His lips brush over mine in a light kiss. "Good," he says, and lowers his head to suck at my neck.

Desire courses through my veins and dives deep into the pit of my abdomen, and suddenly I'm back in Tallahassee on my sofa with him. The same urges cloud my mind.

Inviting him in is on the tip of my tongue when he pulls away, no longer touching me at all. My body goes into shock at his absence. I'm cold and left wanting more.

Blake flashes me that seductive half grin, his long dark eyelashes partly concealing mocha irises. Maybe it's how easily he turned me on and let go that has me realizing how attractive he is in a not-just-friends sort of way. With black hair accenting creamy, soft skin, Blake is totally drool-worthy, and I wonder why it's taken me this long to notice.

My nipples are rock hard and stabbing into my unlined bra. As if on cue, Blake's eyes dip low for a second, and by the way his half grin widens to a full-on smile, I have no doubt that he can see them.

"See you in the morning, Elizabeth," Blake says. He gives me another quick onceover, and saunters down the hallway.

"In the morning," I repeat to myself, thinking how a cold shower is long overdue.

~*~

Due to my newfound relationship with Blake, I

give myself a pep talk before I make my daily phone call to Lia. I'll have to talk with Damian too, and I could use the extra courage to not fall prey to his voice.

I sit on the edge of my bed, staring at my reflection in the mirror. I've left my blonde hair straight and down today but slipped a scrunchie over my wrist for later. My makeup is done like always, yet it doesn't conceal the nerves flushing my face.

"You can do this, Ellie," I encourage myself. "No small talk. Simply ask for Lia and be done."

I take a deep breath before I hit the call button. It's evening there—yesterday, which is weird to wrap my mind around.

It only rings once before Damian picks up.

"Hey, Elle," he says, and I can hear the smile in his voice even though his tone is low.

Crap. Stick to the plan.

I straighten my back, flip my hair off my shoulder. "Hi, Damian. Is Lia right there?" I'm matter-of-fact, no emotion. The complete opposite of all the conversations before.

A second too long of silence engulfs us, and I'm fighting to cave in. He clears his throat. "Uh, yeah. Hang on."

"Mommy!" Lia cries into the phone, and I've successfully evaded Damian. I *can* do this.

"Hey, sweetie! How was your day?"

"Daddy took me to the hospital with him, and I have a new friend there. Her name is Olivia, and she likes Fluttershy," my little Lia-Kat informs me, talking about the yellow pony with pink hair who

139

loves animals.

"Oh, very nice," I say. "I like Fluttershy too."

"But Mommy," Lia continues, ignoring me. "Olivia is sick. Daddy says she'll lose all of her hair soon, but...but...she's going to go home tomorrow, and I'll only see her two days a week." She sighs heavy into the receiver, and I can imagine the cute expression on her face. She's so melodramatic sometimes. I fear her teenage years.

"Well, sweetie, two days a week is better than no days a week."

"Moooooom!" She drawls it out as if I don't understand. "She's sick! She should stay in the hospital."

"Would you rather be in a cold, lonely hospital when you're sick or at home in your nice warm bed?" I wait for an answer. On the other end, I hear her muffled voice as she discusses this conundrum with Damian.

"At home, I guess," she finally decides.

"I'll bet she'd be happier being sick at home too."

"Fine," she relents, a hint of huffiness in her tone.

"Everything else okay?"

"Mmm-hmm. We're all good here. I miss you, though."

"Sweetie, I miss you too."

"Is Blake with you? Can I say hi?"

"No, he's not, but I'll tell him hi for you when he gets here."

"All right. I love you, Mommy. Here's Daddy back."

"No, wait!" I call out.

She doesn't hear me, and the next thing I know, Damian's voice filters into my ear again. "She's full of energy. So, what about you? Ready for your first day today?"

Him asking about me throws me off my game. "Uh, yeah, I think so. It's just orientation, though. The fun stuff begins tomorrow."

As I say it, I peer at myself in the mirror. My eyes seem brighter and more content. All signs of anxiety are gone.

"You're going to do great, Elle," he encourages me, and I avert my gaze to the wall because I can't be the person in that mirror. The one who melts into goo at the sound of his voice and whose heart pitter-patters against her chest like a lovesick junior high kid.

No, I can't go there. Not again. Not anymore.

I switch the phone to my other ear to give myself a moment to regain my composure. "Thank you. I should go, though. Tell Lia I'll talk to her tomorrow. Goodbye."

I say the last part too fast and hang up immediately afterward. That last word hurts enough as it is, and the truth is, I hate when he says it back to me.

Chapter 14

Ellie

Three days out on the ocean and training is officially over. We're in for the good stuff now, doing the tagging ourselves. Unfortunately, the first dropline was empty. Blake sits on the bench, his sunglasses on and a goofy grin on his face.

"It's going to be a good day," he tells me, waggling his brows.

"And you can tell that how?"

He looks at me like I'm crazy. "First of all, you're with me. Secondly—out here, doing what we're doing—this is freaking awesome, babe! We're gonna tag a dozen today."

"Oh yeah?" I'm skeptical because the most we've done so far in a day is half that number. But we did prep more droplines for today, so he might be right. I *hope* he's right. This is what I came out here for.

"Yep. Big ones too."

I roll my eyes because I know what's coming

next. It was all he talked about for the two weeks leading up to this trip. "You're eager for that nineteen-foot hammer, aren't you?"

Hammerheads are Blake's favorite, while I like anything in the carcharhinidea family—requiem sharks: grey reefs, blacktips, whitetips, lemons, and tigers. However, everyone here would give a limb—maybe even literally—to go on a great white expedition.

"I'd die a happy man."

I laugh at his swooning expression.

"Damn, can you imagine pulling one of those gorgeous beasts up from the water?" he continues.

"That would be pretty sweet," I admit.

"*Pretty* sweet? A nineteen-foot hammer is better than 'pretty sweet.'"

"All right, Blake," Dr. Hannah Marsh, the lead on our team, hollers. "We're coming up on that second dropline. Get ready."

Blake dips the hook into the water. He pulls up the orange buoy and hands it off to one of the team members behind him, who slowly begins to roll the wire.

"Whoa," he says. "This one's tight. I think we got something."

The first hook is empty. Blake passes it off and keeps going, the grin on his face widening. He sees it in the water before I do, and God, is it beautiful! I will never tire of seeing these gorgeous animals. The black tip on its first dorsal fin gives him away immediately.

"Nice one!" Hannah shouts out. "I'll bring him up nice and slow. Elizabeth, Marcus, help Blake get that beauty onto the net."

Hannah lowers the bed, and Blake guides the shark to it. The blacktip does some tail slaps against the water. Beside me, Marcus has the salt water pump flowing. I'm between him and Blake, holding a towel with my jaw hanging down to my chest. If this piece of exquisiteness is the only one we manage to tag today, Blake will still be right. Good day, indeed.

The shark thrashes as Hannah brings him up. Blake hands off the wire to me and takes Blackie's tail.

"Come on, buddy," Blake says. "Marcus, the pump."

"Working on it, man. Elizabeth, turn out his lights."

I lean over the rail and drape the beach towel over the shark's eyes to calm him down. It works well enough for Marcus to shove the water pump into its throat. Immediately, our first catch of the day abates.

Blake laughs, and I swear the guy is glowing. I know *I* am. This blacktip reef shark is our first one together.

"The line's still tight," Blake says. "I think there's another one on here."

"He'll be fine out there. Let's get this one tagged first," Hannah instructs.

I grab the tape measure. Marcus holds it at the tip of the nose, and I extend it out to the tail. "Five-point-one-feet."

"I'll convert that later," Hannah says. "Get a fin clipping."

I do what she asks as Marcus obtains the blood sample, and Blake clamps the ID tag onto the dorsal fin.

"Tag number is Y61107," Blake says exactly the way I'd imagine him calling out his first set—professional and elated at the same time.

"Satellite tag?" Hannah asks.

"It's going on next," Blake answers. "You want to do it, Elizabeth?"

I don't hesitate. "Yeah!"

"Clamp it on the—"

"Seriously?" I shoot back.

Blake chuckles. "Sorry."

I lift the transmitter from the box and pass off the empty box to Hannah, who writes down the serial number. Marcus checks the water pump, and Blake's hand roams over the shark's back like he's petting a cat. I have to admit, I'm a little jealous of that.

"All right, Blackie. I'll make this quick," I say, placing the transmitter at the top of the first dorsal fin. Then I clamp it in place. "Finished."

"Great," Hannah says. "Let's get the hook out and get him back in the water."

Marcus cuts the hook off, then holding onto the shark's head, he pulls the water pump. Blackie is still fairly docile as Hannah lowers the bed back down into the water. The blacktip is revitalized and swims off to a round of whooping cheers from everyone on the boat.

"Pull in the next one, Blake. This entire line is yours," Hannah instructs.

Blake winks at me. "Round two?"

"My fingers are crossed for your giant hammer."

We don't get one, though. Instead, Blake's dropline has caught two makos, which we tag, and a turtle that we set free.

My dropline, however, yields nada. By the end of the day, though, we tag thirteen sharks, and neither Blake nor I can wipe the stupid happy grins off our faces.

This trip is so worth it.

~*~

Damian

On Wednesday, I leave Lia at home with Dylan so I can go to the cemetery. Armed with three fresh bouquets of flowers, I weave my way between the other headstones until I'm peering at the ones I came here for.

I didn't tell Lia what I was doing when she asked. Instead, I told her I had a meeting and she had to stay with Dylan for a few hours. She shocked me by stomping her feet and retreating to my bedroom, slamming the door behind her.

"You got that, right?" I asked Dylan since I was halfway out the door. Plus, I have no clue what the hell that was about.

He shook his head, daring me to leave. "No way, man. She's your daughter."

I gave him a nod and a "thanks, dude" before I left.

Ellie warned me about the little miss's attitude, but today was my first experience with the tantrum

146

aspect. I'll have to take care of it later for sure, because even I know not to let that shit slide. No way is my daughter going to be one of *those* girls.

"Oh, Mom," I say, then I chuckle. "Wow, I could use some advice. Lia's, well—she's a girl. So far things have been good, but earlier today, it was like she didn't want me to leave." I rub a hand across the stubble on my chin. "I'm not sure what to do about that.

"God, Mom, you'd love her. She has such a big heart. You should see her with Olivia at the hospital. She gets it from you, you know. Always thinking about others before herself. You and Liam. Damn. The two of you could have changed the world."

I sit down as if she was here, ready to indulge me and my problems and give me that motherly advice she was always so good at.

"I know I'm not cut out to be a father. And I know somewhere down the line I'm going to fuck up. Hell, I already did," I say, thinking about the fight with Toby. "But I, uh, I care about her, Mom." I pick at the grass, tear some out by the roots. "It scares the living shit out of me too. Because caring for someone this much"—I pause to steal a glance at the headstone two doors down—"means eventually you have to give them up. No one stays around forever."

I toss the grass and pull up more. "I don't know what I was thinking when I told Ellie to let her stay. I guess I wanted to prove to myself that I'm not a coward. But now I realize this isn't about me. A week with my daughter, and I *am* a fucking coward.

I never asked to be a father, yet here she is, and I never want her to leave. At the same time, I do, before I get any closer. I have seven weeks left with her and then what? Ellie takes her back to Florida, and I'm left here alone.

"What should I do? I won't be able to take it when she leaves."

I wait for her to answer me. She never does, of course, but I long to hear her voice regardless.

I hunch down to her headstone and place a hand over her name. "I miss you, Mom," I say. Then I back up, adjust the arrangement of lilies I brought, and move on to Liam.

"Cubbies won." I tell him about his favorite baseball team to start us off. "Beat the Padres two-zip last night. They play again on Saturday. Also, I need to talk to you about Ellie."

Even though my brother is gone, talking to him about his girlfriend who's now the mother of my child toes the line of awkward. "At first, I chalked up her behavior to first day nerves, but it's been the same thing every day this week when she calls. 'Hey, is Lia around?'" I mimic. "I pass off the phone, and when Lia's done, Ellie gives me a clipped, 'Goodbye, Damian,' and hangs up. Does this sound like her to you?"

I wait a second before I go on. "I don't know, man, after the whole fight thing, she seemed genuinely concerned about me, and it felt good. Really good.

"I wonder if it has to do with this Blake guy she's down there with, you think? Lia's talked about him, and she says they're friends, but fuck, dude. She's three. What does she know?" I rake a hand through my hair as I realize what I'm saying. Then I chuckle. "Yeah, you're right, man. It's none of my business. Ellie is out of our hands."

Even as I say the words, it doesn't sit right with me. I hate the thought that she might be with that guy.

Lastly, I move on to Kate. My Katie.

I do this in part to torture myself. Lay it all out there in case God changes His mind and takes me instead of her. Because that's what should have happened. I should have been long gone before I ever entered Kathryn Browdy's life.

"Hey, baby. Did you miss me?" I ask, sinking down on the grass.

I tell her about Olivia at the hospital, how Dad's releasing her to go home and she'll come in for chemo treatments two days a week. I figure Kate heard my rants to Mom and Liam, so I don't repeat myself.

An hour passes, and it's getting late. I should head back home to Lia, but I don't want to leave. I'm safe here with the people I still mourn. Out there, among the living, that's where their ghosts haunt me. Where my fears are real. Where the pain constantly pounds on me.

And I let it. Because it's easier to be broken and feel nothing than allow the guilt and hurt to overtake me.

"I'd better go, Katie." I stand up and brush grass off my jeans. Stepping toward the granite, I press two fingers to my lips. I place them on top of her stone. "See you next week, baby. I love you. I'll always love you."

~*~

I'm home before Ellie calls. I don't know why, but I miss hearing her voice. The one that wasn't hard and clipped and stubborn. Hopefully, tonight won't be like that.

When I walk through the door, I expect blonde hair and big, blue irises to race toward me, happy I'm back. Then I remember her attitude before I left and disappointment plunges into my gut as I'm greeted with dead silence. Not even the sound of the television pours out.

I toss my keys on the counter and round the corner into the living room. Dylan's there, on the sofa, with his laptop and headphones on. Lia is—

Nowhere to be seen.

"Yo, dude," I say loudly even though I'm standing next to him.

He slides the headphones off and fucking *glares* at me.

"Where's Lia?" I ask.

He doesn't answer right away. Instead, my babysitter takes his sweet-ass time putting his laptop aside and takes a drink of beer. Then he sits back and kicks his feet up on the coffee table.

"Where is Lia?" I demand this time. His silence is beginning to piss me off.

"See these?" he asks, holding up his headphones. "I put them on over two hours ago because she wouldn't stop screaming after you left. From inside *your* bedroom."

"She's not screaming now, man. Have you checked on her?"

"Yeah. She cried herself to sleep thirty minutes ago. But let me warn you, dude, your room is destroyed."

"Destroyed? What do you mean?"

The asshole has the gall to smirk at me. "Go see for yourself," he says, and puts his headphones back on, effectively drowning me out.

"Shithead," I mutter.

I make my way to my bedroom. In case Dylan is right and Lia is asleep, I open the door quietly and stick my head inside. The pony nightlight beside her bed is on, but it's not necessary to see her. It's still dusk outside, and small beams of sunlight filter through the curtains and land on her.

Curled up in the very middle of my bed is my daughter, sound asleep. Holding her blanket and sucking her thumb. She has one of my dirty t-shirts draped over her like a sheet with her tiny bare feet sticking out of the bottom. My heart thuds at the sight of her.

Around me, I see what Dylan warned me about. Lia's books and toys are everywhere, scattered about like confetti. My clothes are on the floor too, but I can't remember if I left them there or if this is Lia's handiwork as well.

The clothes I don't care about; the shit that was sitting on top of my dresser, however, I do. None of it is there. Not even the little Twilight Sparkle Lia gave me.

But the missing pony isn't what's causing flames to erupt behind my ribs.

Anger burns in my chest, and I start to lose it. I'm breathing hard, rolling my fingers inward and tightening them.

I've got to find it.

I drop to my knees to search behind the dresser. Under the bed. I rummage through the clothing on the floor, tossing shirts, jeans, and socks as I go.

I don't see it anywhere.

Shit.

I squeeze my eyes closed for a second so I can gain some control. The last thing I want to do is flip out on Lia, even though every cell in my body wants to.

I unclench my fists and open my eyes. Stand over the bed.

A ray of sunlight catches something in Lia's hand. The gleam bounces off, and the piece of jewelry sparkles, revealing itself. Instant relief rushes in.

Gently, I pry Lia's fingers open. The diamond trinity heart is clutched inside her tiny hand, the silver chain wrapped around her wrist so I can't get to it. She stirs, and an eyelid pops open. Her lips curve downward as she gazes up at me. Those blues glisten with fresh tears, and suddenly Lia's eyebrows pinch together and her lips pucker.

"You were not supposed to leave me. Ever!" she cries.

The outburst surprises me, but I don't flinch. "Lia, I was only gone for a few hours. I was coming back."

She shakes her head, tears spilling over her lashes and down her cheeks. "I didn't have a daddy before you, and you can't go away!"

What clicks from this admission is that until Ellie introduced us, Lia never knew she had a father. She met me that one night, and I told Ellie to leave. The next day, they went to board a plane and had I not showed up, Lia would have been fatherless again. To Lia, my absence tonight struck fear into her little heart that I might be gone for good.

I sit on the edge of the bed and gather her into my arms. "It's okay, Lia. I promise you, I'll never leave you and not come back. Never, ever," I say, and I mean it.

"Promise, promise?" she asks, her lower lip trembling.

I hug her against me. "I promise, promise."

~*~

Ellie's due to call any minute now. She'd said she preferred to call us instead of the other way around. At least until her schedule was set.

The phone is on my bed, and I'm helping Lia pick up her mess. I toss my dirty clothes in the basket in the closet. Lia collects her books, puts them in her tote, and slides it under her bed.

She gave me the necklace, which I laid in the velvet box where it belongs. Then I set it back on top of my dresser along with the rest of the stuff Lia hid under my pillows.

"What's the necklace for?" she asks, studying me.

"It belonged to a very special girl."

153

Lia points to the picture on the nightstand beside my bed of Kate and me at prom. "Is it that girl? The one with no hair?"

I nod. "Yeah, it's that girl."

"She's wearing the necklace in the picture."

"She wore it all the time."

"She doesn't have hair like Olivia won't have hair," Lia muses.

I sit on the edge of the bed. "Like Olivia, Kate had cancer and the medicine made her hair fall out."

"Where is she now?"

I swallow and bow my head, unsure of whether or not to tell Lia the truth. Olivia's prognosis is good, and I don't want to scare my daughter. But I also don't know what else to tell her. "She died."

Lia frowns. Her eyes dart to the picture then up at me. "Will Olivia die?"

"No, babygirl. Your grandpa is going to help Olivia and make her as good as new."

Lia doesn't respond, puckering her lips as if she's letting what I said sink in. She glances up at my dresser and points to another picture sitting there. "Who's that boy with Mickey Mouse?"

I slide my palms down my thighs and stand up. I grab the blue frame, staring at the face beaming back at me. At Kate's funeral, I'd asked Brennan to send me a photo of him and Mickey Mouse. He and his mother went on the trip to Disney World that I'd originally bought for Kate and myself.

I show Lia the photo. "This is Brennan. He had cancer too, but your grandpa is a good doctor, and Brennan doesn't have cancer anymore."

"Like Olivia won't," Lia says matter-of-factly,

accepting what I said.

"Right. Like Olivia won't."

Lia nods, happy, and resumes picking up her toys. Two minutes later, my cell rings, and she drops what's in her arms. "Mommy!"

I hold up a finger to silence her before I answer. "Hey, Elle."

"Hi, Damian. Can I talk with Lia?"

It's the same thing she's said for days. She calls in the morning before she heads out on her study. I strain to hear something in the background, something that tells me she's not alone.

Why? I have no fucking idea.

There's nothing, though, and that rubs me the wrong way. It should make me relieved, but it doesn't. Maybe if I knew Blake stayed all night with her, I'd have a reason for her nonchalance when she "talks" to me.

Or maybe it'd give me reason to fly to Australia and beat the guy's face in. Either way.

"Yeah. Hang on," I say like I always do and hand the phone off to Lia.

Lia bounces around the room, talking Ellie's ear off. Ellie calls every twenty-four hours without fail, yet Lia always finds a ton of stuff to say.

"Daddy had a meeting tonight and left me with Dylan," she tells her mom. Funny how she leaves out the parts about her screaming and throwing shit all over my bedroom. She pauses and cocks her head to the side. "What do you mean 'what does Damian smell like?'"

I have to admit, I find that amusing. Ellie must think I left Lia to go boozing. Probably picked up a girl while I'm at it.

"Yes, Mommy, he came back home alone."

Bingo.

She doesn't trust me. I don't blame her, but it still stings to hear.

"Okay. I love you too, Mommy." She sends Ellie a kissy noise before she gives the phone back to me.

"Hi, Elle," I say again, expecting her usual clipped "Same time tomorrow. Goodbye, Damian" routine. Instead, she says, "You left her with Dylan?" There's an accusation in her tone and because I feel the need to prove myself, I want to keep calm.

"I was gone for three hours, Ellie. That's it," I reply.

"And you couldn't have taken her with you?"

"Do you take her everywhere you go? To class?"

"No, I take her to a licensed day care right next to campus. Does Dylan know CPR?"

I laugh inwardly. "Yeah, actually he does."

Silence.

"Oh," she finally answers.

"Ellie, relax. Dylan's a good guy, and I trust him. Lia was perfectly safe."

I hear the muffled noise as she heaves a sigh into the receiver. She seems to do this often. Then she clears her throat. "You had a meeting, huh? At the hospital?"

I grin. This is kind of cute, her wanting to know. It's also kind of cute that I know she knows I didn't have a meeting.

I stand up and move out of Lia's earshot. "I went to the cemetery. Like I do every Wednesday."

156

"You still go there?"

I let the question hang for a second, not sure I want to answer. "I have stuff I need to make up for."

She doesn't answer right away. "Nowhere else?" Her voice cracks a little as she says it, and I have the sudden urge to hold her in my arms.

"No, Elle. Just there."

"Good. Um, I guess I'll call again tomorrow. Goodb—"

"Stop," I interrupt her, and I hope like hell she won't hang up. "How are you?"

Silence assaults my ear. I'm about to give up because I assume she hung up already and I missed my chance.

"Everything's great," she answers.

I'm not sure I believe her. There's doubt in her voice. Doubt I've heard a million times and recognize, apparently, from halfway across the globe. After Liam died, everything she said sounded like she does now.

"You tagging a bunch of sharks?" I ask. I want to keep her talking, even if it's only for another minute.

She laughs. "I did a hammerhead by myself yesterday."

"That's cool."

"Yeah, it was a small one, but it was so awesome."

"I'm proud of you, Elle." Even though the words slipped out, I mean them. She's been through the same shit I have and look at her. She's pushed through.

"Thank you. Um, I'd better go. I have fifteen minutes before the boat leaves without me."

"Okay. Talk to you tomorrow," I say. Then I cringe at what comes next.

"Sure. Good bye, Damian."

A lump I didn't count on forms in my throat. I can't get rid of it. "Bye, Elle," I say, but the line is already dead.

I toss the phone on my bed and clench my jaw. Lia peers up me, and all I can see is Ellie in her expression.

"What's wrong, Daddy?"

I force a smile so she won't worry. "Nothing," I say.

Because I don't know the answer myself.

Chapter 15

Ellie

I love being out on the boat, the wind sweeping through my hair, the idea of millions upon millions of creatures beneath us in a vast, under-researched ecosystem. The ocean, bigger and more powerful than any of us can imagine, around us.

But—

I'm distracted.

My head is not in the game today. I can't breathe.

Since I hung up with Damian this morning, I haven't been able to get him out of my mind. My emotions are all over the place, teetering between relief, jealousy, pain, pride, and wanting to ditch this project and Blake, fly back to Iowa, tell Damian how I feel about him, and hope for the best.

I'm lame. So incredibly lame.

Here I am in this beautiful place. I'm doing exactly what I want to be doing. With this amazing man. And all I think about is Damian.

What is wrong with this picture?

I run through the list of reasons why I should give Damian up. It's a mile long, and one by one, I tick them off.

Our similarities are on another list. One I keep locked away in the darkest of corners of my mind. There's no reason to review it because it's so much shorter than this one.

The negatives far outweigh anything on the positives list.

I reach for a box of vials and knock over a test tube filled with blood I collected from a reef shark. The tube hits the floor and shatters. Glass shards litter the floor under my feet.

"Shit," I mutter.

Blake, who's working at the station beside me, rushes over. "It's okay, baby. You collected two, right?"

I grab a cloth and the bottle of bleach water from under the sink in the corner of the lab.

"Yeah, I did," I say, bending down and spraying the blood.

I scrub hard, bits of hair spilling out of the knot I secured on top of my head. I hate that I can't tame my emotions enough to curb stupid mistakes.

Blake's hand rests on my arm. "Hey, let me get this."

I lean back on my knees and wipe the hair from my face with my forearm.

Again, I think about the difference between Blake and Damian. When I packed up my life and moved to Florida, Damian did nothing. Not even a phone call.

But Blake? Blake's with me in Australia.

This should be the world's easiest decision. So why isn't it?

Why do I continue to hang on to a man who will never reciprocate my love?

This is ridiculous. Even more so that I promised Blake I'd give us a shot.

I need to get my head back where it belongs—on Blake's chest as we cuddle up together.

"Hey, Blake?" I say.

"Yeah?"

"We've gone out every night this week. Let's stay in and rent a movie tonight, instead," I say.

Blake's gaze floats over me. "You thinking chick-flick or something decent? 'Cause if we're doing chick-flick, I'm bringing Indian food."

Did he seriously say that?

My eyes meet his, and yep. He's totally serious. Until a sexy lopsided grin appears on his face. I puff out a laugh, shaking my head at his amusement.

A hand brushes over my cheek, his coffee-colored irises softening. "There's that smile I've been dying to see all day."

Heat rushes to my face, and I bow my head to hide the blush threatening to give me away. "Sorry. I…" I trail off because I'm not mentioning the real reasons behind my distraction today.

"Thinking about Lia?" he finishes for me, and I nod, even though it's only partially true.

Okay, so it's mostly untrue. I talk with my Lia-Kat every day, and from her voice she's perfectly happy with Damian. If she weren't, I'd be dead from anxiety. And Damian probably would be too.

161

She may only be three, but she has the vocal cords of fighting raccoons when she's upset. They're lethal.

I jump to the most believable story I can think of, and I sound like a broken record. "I've never gone this long without seeing her."

"You talked with her this morning, right?" he asks, his hand cupping my chin.

"Yeah, she's good. She really is. I'm"—I breathe out a nervous laugh—"being a pathetic, worry-freak mom."

"Elizabeth, you are a great mother. You're entitled to worry about her. But she's fine, and she's safe. And you're here, so *be* here." His thumb glides over my chin, and with a gentle tug, he eases me toward him. Forms his lips over mine for a few seconds then lets go.

I inhale and open my eyelids in slow motion. Blake's there, caressing my cheek. Grinning at me like I'm special.

Trapped in his stare, I forget about Damian. And I do what Blake asks.

I'm simply *here.*

"So, what are you in the mood for tonight?" Sprawled out on my bed, Blake flips through the Pay-Per-View options while I throw away the little cardboard boxes from our Chinese take-out. "We have...ugh. Chick-flick city."

"Is it just me or have movie titles gotten less creative? I mean, Chick-Flick City sounds so obvious." I pour myself a glass of wine and pop the top off a Four X Australian beer for Blake.

Blake shrugs, not missing a beat. "It's probably a crappy *Sex in the City* remake. Without the sex."

"And with little yellow birds waddling around," I joke.

Blake snorts out a laugh. It's an embarrassed laugh though, as he covers his face with a palm. "The first pun was decent, but I can't let that one slide, babe. That was horrible."

I hand him the beer, which he immediately sets on the nightstand next to him. My glass is in my hand, and I attempt to gracefully climb onto the mattress. Blake's eyes teeter back and forth between me and the wine sloshing around, sliding close to the rim.

"You can put that down, you know," he says.

He's lying on the bed on his side, his head propped up on a hand. Dressed in a pair of dark blue jeans and a white t-shirt, Blake resembles a Calvin Klein model with clothing on. The five o'clock shadow that pokes out perfectly from his tanned skin makes me shiver. He definitely rivals Damian in the looks department.

Stop it, I scold myself. I'm done comparing the two of them. I've made my choice, and I'm not going back.

I shoot him a flirty smirk. "Nope. I can see that mischievous glint in your eye. I'm safer with the wine."

Blake's half-grin widens. It's adorable and so incredibly sexy. Slowly, he tucks his knees under himself and straightens up. He takes the glass from me, his gaze drifting over me before he reaches around my waist. His body presses against mine, and heat pools low in my abdomen.

Damn, his lips are so close, but they don't touch me. I hear the soft clink as he puts my glass on the nightstand behind me. Then his hand is on my hip.

A voice in the back of my mind says I shouldn't feel like this. Like I want him to kiss me and lower me to the mattress. I'm more responsible than that. I can't lose myself to another man, and Blake and I have technically only been dating for a week.

I have to think about Lia. My life no longer belongs only to me, and my actions—even though I'm far from her—have repercussions.

Heck, she was made from a stupid split-second decision when I let my guard down that night. And I secretly loved the man who gave her to me.

I don't love Blake.

Not yet, anyway.

But four years of no sex—let's face it, I'm horny. My entire body is flashing the green light. Heat flows free, egging me on to lose control. Yeah, my hormones are going haywire, and I'm not sure if I can reel them in. Nor do I know if I want to.

I caress the side of his face just to touch his skin. He feels amazing, and I can only imagine the rest of him is even better. To test my theory, I allow my fingers to glide down his neck and tease the collar of his shirt. God, I was right. Wow.

Desire is coursing through my veins, warming me and telling me how much I need to let go of my pent-up energy. And, man, the release would be incredible.

Yet the voice in my head screams louder to put on the brakes. To not do something reckless that I might regret…again.

Blake sinks a hand into my hair. He eases me forward until my forehead touches his, his breath slow and steady on my mouth. His tongue slips out, grazes over my lower lip, and I wonder how much more I can take before what's left of my willpower crashes down.

Before my brain shuts up.

My nipples poke out full force and rub against Blake's chest as he sucks on the lip he just tasted. His fingers trail the elastic of my yoga pants, brushing over bare skin. I'm wavering. I shouldn't give in, because I think…

I think…

I can't think.

Blake's tongue massages mine now, and it feels so, so good. He's slow, gentle, and knows exactly what he's doing to me.

"I've waited a long time for this, Elizabeth," Blake murmurs in my ear.

Suddenly, Lia's big blue eyes flash through mind. She gives Damian her Twilight Sparkle, and identical blue eyes smile back at her. I'm slung back into reality.

Lia.

Damian.

"Blake," I breathe out.

"Mmm?" Blake hums as he nibbles on my earlobe.

"We should slow down," I say, even though my hands betray me by grabbing a hold of the hem of his shirt and tugging upward. I catch the warmth of skin under my fingertips and force myself to let go. "I can't. I'm sorry."

Keeping his grip on the back of my head, Blake leans backward a little to peer at me. His thumb roams over my jaw. "Lia's not here, if that's what you're thinking."

"No, it's…not that. It's—"

Blake kisses me again, and I squirm under the pressure of his lips.

"It's too soon, Blake. I'm not ready."

He stares at me for a moment. Bowing his head, he breaks our connection and completely lets go of me.

"Okay, I don't want to rush anything you're not ready for," he says, exhaling.

I nod, feeling small and stupid. How can he be so nice while I lead him on one minute and push him away the next? I seriously need to get my act together.

He kisses me one last time. "Come on. Let's find a movie."

Again, I nod. My mind wanders to the conversation I had with Damian this morning. How easily my barrier shatters by the mere sound of his voice.

I take a sip of wine and settle down beside Blake. He smiles, putting his arm out to invite me in. He must be uncomfortable and would probably rather be under a cold shower right now, but instead he cocks his head to the side and shoots me that sexy grin of his.

Conceding, I slide up beside him and lay my

head on his chest. His arm circles around me, his lips pressing against my head.

Maybe I should just sleep with him, if only to get Damian out of my head.

No, I remind myself. *You've tried that trick before when you first jumped into Damian's bed to get over Liam.*

My brain needs to shut up now. Thankfully, Blake's on top of that for me.

"On second thought, let's steer clear of the chick flicks tonight," he says, scrolling through our options.

"Yeah, okay."

"That leaves us with all of the Bourne movies, *Cinderella: The Musical*, a documentary on the Civil War, and *When Harry Did Sally*." He waggles his brows.

I lift myself up and huff at him. His eyes are still smoldering, but there's laughter in them too. "*When Harry Did Sally* has my vote."

"Bourne movie," I say with a firmness that's half a giggle.

"You sure? 'Cause Harry and Sally sound like they're having a great time."

I point to my eyes. "See the daggers? Hmm?"

"All righty, then. Jason Bourne it is, since your vote counts for two."

"Damn right it does. And don't you forget it."

Laughing, Blake squeezes me closer. I cuddle up to him and I'm asleep before the movie is over.

~*~

The first thing I notice when I rouse is the lingering scent of Blake's deodorant on the sheets. Blake has always smelled so good, and the reminder of him on my bed last night elicits a sigh from me. Under me, material shifts as something moves. Then it moans.

My eyes snap open and I see a chest—Blake's chest. Wearing the same t-shirt as the night before.

I unwrap my arm from around his torso and glance at him. He's awake, chocolate irises meeting mine.

"Good morning, beautiful," he says, and my breath hitches at the sound. It's deep and dives straight into my stomach.

"You stayed all night?" I ask unnecessarily. Of course he did, that's why he's still here.

Blake's eyes sparkle as the corner of his mouth curves up. "I didn't want to wake you."

"Don't you usually go to the gym in the mornings?" I ask, catching the time on my alarm clock that's due to go off in three minutes. Then we have to get ready for another glorious day on the Reef.

"No way would I miss an opportunity to wake up beside you." He reaches down and brushes hair out of my face. "I'd like to do this every morning."

I don't know what to say to that. I resisted him last night but barely. If he's in my bed on a nightly basis, I doubt my resistance will hold for long.

Blake tips my chin up and presses a kiss against my lips. "When you're ready," he says.

"One day at a time." I don't ask because it's not a question. There is no other option for me.

Not until I can get Damian out of my heart and be fair to Blake.

Chapter 16

Damian

Olivia has a chemo treatment today. Lia's sitting on the floor outside the chemo room, waiting for her friend to arrive. Her elbows sit on her knees, and her chin rests on the tops of her fists.

I shuffle through patient files at the nurses' station, searching for the one I need. From the corner of my eye, I see Olivia round the corner. Lia sees her too and jumps to her feet. Olivia breaks into a huge grin, and the girls squeal out their delight. It's been a whole four days since they saw each other last.

"I got you something," Lia says, holding out the pink gift bag.

"For me?"

"Open it! Open it!" Lia bounces up and down.

Olivia rips the tape at the top and reaches in. Her eyes light up when she pulls out what's inside—five over-the-top girly headbands.

"Do you like them?" my daughter asks.

Yesterday at Target, she'd screamed when she saw them, and right away she knew "Olivia *must* have these, Daddy! She must! Pleeeeease?" Then she'd batted her eyes at me.

"Toss 'em in the cart," I'd said.

"They're so pretty," Olivia says, examining each one. "Oh! I love the flower on this one!"

"Yep. And look!" Lia says, pulling an identical purple one from behind her back. "They match!"

"Put it on!"

"You first," Lia counters.

"Same time?"

Lia slips hers onto her head as Olivia does over skin.

"We're twins!" Lia exclaims.

They wrap an arm around each other and pull in close, cheek to cheek. I chuckle at the girliness of it all.

Behind them, the door to the chemo room opens, and Leslie stands there. When she sees the girls making silly faces at each other like they're in a photo booth, she laughs.

"All right, you two," she says. "Olivia needs to start her treatment."

Olivia frowns. "Rats."

"Lia, she'll meet you in The Commons in five minutes," the nurse instructs.

Lia shoots me a pouty face.

I shrug. "Nurse Leslie's a hard knock."

Lia's expression shifts to confusion.

"It means she likes the rules," I clarify.

"Can Lia come in with me, please?" Olivia asks Leslie, and it seems my daughter has taught her friend the benefits of batting eyelashes.

Leslie glances between the girls, who are both giving her their very best. The nurse's eyes flick up to me, and I hold my hands up in surrender.

"Okay," Leslie relents. "But you have to be quiet. There's another patient in there, and she's not feeling well."

The little girls hold hands and start running in place with excitement. "Yay!"

Again, Leslie looks at me.

I grin. "Sucker."

~*~

Lia has officially broken me.

I slide the bowl of macaroni and cheese with cut up hot dogs in front of her. She beams at the fake cheese and processed meat, and I inwardly groan. I can't believe Ellie feeds her this shit.

Dylan swings around the corner. "Dude, did you cook?"

"Yeah, garbage," I say, holding up the empty box.

"Any leftovers?"

I point to the pan. "Have at it, man."

"Sweet!"

Dylan grabs a bowl from the cupboard, loads it up with the exact same thing Lia wanted, and wanders back to the living room. My mother would be rolling over in her grave if she knew I served this stuff to her granddaughter. And here Dylan is, finishing it off.

Whatever.

Before I stride over to the fridge to get myself something to eat, I check my phone. Ellie should be calling any minute now, and I've found my thoughts straying to her throughout the day. This afternoon, I smiled when a memory of Ellie and me in our swimming pool surfaced. We had fun that day. Played for a while before I decided she needed to lose that little bikini she had on. It was the first time I ever fucked her in the pool.

I collect sandwich fixings and carry them to the counter. Lia's got a cute chocolate milk mustache going on, and I laugh when she flashes me her goofy grin.

"Do I have something on my face?" she asks.

I shake my head. "Nope. Nothing."

She giggles and slurps down another gulp of milk. "Now do I?"

"Much better," I say, nodding my approval. As I do, my finger hits the edge of my phone, and I get this total dad idea. I pick it up and find the camera app. "Hey, Lia. Say 'banana monkey'!" It's what Dad used to tell Liam and me when we were kids.

Lia snickers, then tilts her head to the side and smiles—literally—from ear to ear, flashing me her milk clad mouth and set of dimples.

"Can I see?" she asks as soon as I snap the picture. Already, she's pushing her chair back and climbing off it. She runs over to me, the braided pigtails Leslie put in earlier swaying back and forth.

I crouch down beside her, holding the screen out. Lia's eyes light up, and she claps her hands.

"I look *silly*!" she squeals.

I hug her close. Kiss her temple. "You look

adorable."

She skips back to the table to finish her dinner, and I set the picture as my wallpaper image. When I glance up at the real thing, I'm suddenly filled with pride.

Nothing in my fucked-up life merits me having this beautiful little girl, but she's here. She's mine. And she's smiling at me. Right then, my phone rings. It's Ellie, and I can't wait to hear her voice on the other end.

"Hey, Elle," I answer.

I hear a gust blow into the receiver as if she exhaled.

"Elle?" I repeat.

"Hi, Damian. Lia-Kat around?"

Excitement drains out of me. She's back to the same matter-of-fact tone.

"Uh, yeah. Hang on."

I pass off the phone to Lia, and she chats her mom up while I finish making my sandwich. I don't want to dwell on the emptiness that just filled my chest.

Across from me, Lia bursts out in laughter. She tosses her head back, and all I see is Ellie in her place, her long blonde hair stuck to her bare back as water drips from it. Laughing, smiling in the pool like we meant more to each other than we did. In gentle strokes, she runs her fingers through my hair, her pale blue eyes holding something other than pain for once.

With me that day, Ellie was happy.

"I love you too, Mommy," Lia says, bringing me back to reality.

I take the phone from her and press it to my ear. "Hey."

"Lia asked if you'd sent me a picture of her? Something about a milk moustache?"

Lia's beside me, her palms pressed together in front of her and her pouty face on.

"Oh, yeah," I say, giving Lia a playful swat to go eat. "She begged me for chocolate milk when we went to the store today, so I let her have it for supper. She loves that stuff. It was all over her face, and I—"

"Hey, Elizabeth. Do you have any towels?" a voice—a male voice—filters through the phone.

Towels?

"In the basket on the floor beside the shower." Ellie's answer is muffled. She probably tried to cover the phone.

Towels. Shower. Male.

I connect the pieces easily. One—two—three. Blake stayed the night.

He slept over.

Or she slept over with him.

It doesn't matter. All guys are the same, and Blake sure as hell got what he wanted last night.

Fuck.

"Um...uh, Damian..." She trails off because there's nothing to say. She knows I heard.

"You're not alone," I say.

Silence hangs heavy on the other end.

"Damian, it's...he's..."

"Blake?" I finish.

"How did you know?"

"Doesn't matter. I get it." I spin around to avoid

Lia's gaze and lower my voice. "I stay here in celibacy with our daughter, while you have sleepovers with your boyfriend."

"He's not my…" She doesn't finish, and the whole thing is crystal clear.

"Right." I shake my head, close to laying into her. "Like I said, I get it. You know——"

I stop because I don't want Lia to see me lose my cool. "Bye, Ellie," I say, clutching onto the phone. I might break it if I don't hang up.

With outward calm, I set the phone on the counter. What Lia sees is me, acting casual. Inside, though, I'm ready to explode.

And I fucking shouldn't feel this way. Ellie was Liam's girlfriend, not mine. Never mine. When she ditched everything to move south, I couldn't care less. I had my own shit to deal with, and Ellie was of no concern to me. I'd moved on—not that there was anything to move on from.

I was a free agent. As was she.

God-fucking-dammit!

I leave Lia in the kitchen. Go to the living room where Dylan sits with his empty bowl and half a beer.

"I need you to watch Lia tonight for me," I say.

Dylan's eyes peer up from his laptop. "Why? Where're you going?"

"Out."

I don't wait for him to retort before I round the corner to my bedroom. I take off my t-shirt and tug a white button-up from the closet. Then I stuff my wallet into the back pocket of my jeans.

Dylan is standing in the doorway, glaring at me.

The dude's smart and has probably figured out my intentions.

It's what I do.

"Think about this, Damian," he reasons.

"Already did."

He blocks me. "Whatever happened, this isn't the answer, man. What am I supposed to say to Lia when she asks where you went? Remember what happened last time?"

I'm not thinking clearly. Hell, I'm not thinking at all.

"She'll be fine. Get out of my way."

Like an idiot, my roommate stands there and shakes his asshole head. I'll knock it off his damn neck if I have to.

"Move, Dylan," I grind out. I'm trying to contain my anger. I don't want to get loud and attract Lia's attention, but if this dickhead doesn't let me pass, I'm going to fucking detonate.

Dylan must realize I'm serious because he steps aside. I'm halfway to the front door when I spin around, Dylan's words finally registering with me—I can't storm out of here and leave Lia alone. She threw a tantrum and tornadoed my bedroom last time.

But I can't stay either.

All of my muscles tense as I walk into the kitchen. Lia is putting her empty bowl and cup into the sink. My partially-made sandwich sits on the counter.

Her eyebrows narrow, taking me in. "What's wrong, Daddy?"

Three-year-olds shouldn't be this perceptive.

"I'll be right back, Lia, I swear. I…have to go out for a while. Something came up."

"At the hospital?"

I hate what I'm about to do. Lying to my daughter makes me a jackass. "Yeah, babygirl."

"Is it Olivia?"

I crouch down in front of her. "No. It's nothing like that. Olivia is fine."

"Okay. I can watch a movie with Dylan until you come home." She folds her tiny arms around my neck. I hug her back, and suddenly Ellie's face flashes in my mind again. Her stunning blue eyes laughing right along with her smile.

The picture widens. Ellie's in bed, naked, throwing her blonde hair back onto the pillow. The further out the image goes, the more I see, and I realize it's not me making her smile. It's him—a mental rendition of this Blake-guy.

Heat burns through my veins. Anger and hurt—emotions I know too well.

Luckily, I also know how to quench them.

"Be good, all right?" I say, releasing Lia.

"I will. You be good too."

She bounces off to the living room. I don't watch her leave. Instead, I open the back door to the garage.

I've gotta get the hell out of here.

My destination tonight is The Underground. Max's is where I go when I want to unwind. The college hangout is the place to get drunk off my ass and pick up some girl to drown out what the booze doesn't.

The Underground is packed with students

staying for summer term, working in town, or those who went to other colleges and are back home. It doesn't matter that it's a weekday, everyone's here.

I stride up to the bar, flash my ID, and order a whiskey soda. The strong bass pumping through my body does nothing for me. I'm not here to have a good time.

No, I'm on the prowl.

I take the first scan of my options after I suck down my drink and order another. There's a group of three girls dancing at the edge of the stage, going absolutely crazy already. The place just opened for the night, and they're obviously hammered.

They're also a little young to be here, and I wonder if the bouncer is slacking on his door duties. I don't care, but the difference between seventeen and eighteen is huge for what I want to do later. But damn, they look like a good time—wild and willing to do whatever a guy asks.

Right now, the dance floor is low on partiers. People are still working the alcohol into their bloodstream. Soon, though, soon I'll find that perfect lay.

My phone vibrates in my pocket. I pull it out and stare at the screen. Ellie's number and picture flash at me. There's nothing to consider. As I reject the call, I notice I've missed another from her. Whatever. I won't let her ruin my fun.

I finish off my second round and order a third. More girls are making their way to the dance floor, and I study each one. A few are familiar, but I don't recall their names.

On the counter, my phone lights up again. And

again, it's Ellie. I'm keeping it on so Dylan can reach me, but at this point, I shut it off. I don't know why she's calling me, and I don't fucking care.

A few glasses later, I realize I'm beginning to believe it. It's better this way. Fucking my brother's GF to numb my pain is one thing; actually caring about her is another. I'm *not* going there.

After another whiskey soda, I'm good. Relaxed and buzzed, and the chicks in this place all resemble the three teenagers, who have been swallowed up by the now-packed dance floor.

I switch to tequila shots, downing them as fast as the bartender can pour them. She might as well give me the bottle.

I tap the empty glass, browsing my options. A girl with short black hair drags her friend off the dance floor to the bar. Long legs extend from a skirt that barely covers her ass and black boots stop midway up her calves. Her shirt sparkles, dipping into a low V in the front and showing off a full rack.

The friend leans against the counter, back to me, a hand on her hip. She's not as dressed up, wearing jean shorts and looking like the other one begged her to come tonight. The dark-headed one orders for both of them: two rum and cokes.

While they wait, the one I'm checking out glances in my direction and catches me staring. I smile, flash her the dimples girls go crazy over. She winks, cherry lips curving upward.

I know I've got her attention when she keeps peeking around her friend at me. I lift my full shot glass to toast her. She tucks her red lips between her teeth in a flirty grin, eyeing me up and down. I cock my head to the side to invite them over.

Immediately, she grabs her friend and sashays toward me, her hips moving in ways I want to see more of. Behind her, the other girl rolls her eyes.

"Hey," Sweet Ass says loudly so I can hear her over the music. "I'm Cassie, and this is Bree."

"Damian."

"Well, Damian, you look awfully lonely over here all by yourself," she points out. She's got a sexy smirk on her face.

This might be too easy.

"I'm having a great time now."

Bree nudges her friend and whispers something in her ear. Frowning, Cassie shakes her head. Then she steps closer to me. Rests a palm on my knee. "Why don't you tell Bree that it's way too early to go home?"

My gaze slides up to Bree as I check her out, and she blushes an embarrassed grin. "Depends on whose home you want to go to," I say.

Cassie lights up at my line. "Is yours free?"

"Maybe. You interested?"

"Sounds like fun." She twists. "Doesn't it, Bree?"

Bree shoots daggers at Cassie, shaking her head in tiny movements. "We should go, Cassie," she says.

"You go. Damian wants company." Her other hand falls on my thigh. Gently, she pushes my knees apart and slides between them.

Fuck, yes. A feisty one.

To make sure Bree catches her point, Cassie

leans in and goes straight to sticking her tongue in my mouth. Typically, I like to be the one in control, but I have no problems letting this little tiger hold the reins tonight. This is exactly what I need.

When she's done with me, she glances behind her shoulder. Bree's gone, though, and Cassie snickers and turns back to me.

"Let's get out of here, shall we?" she says, curling a short piece of my hair around her finger.

"This way."

I've got to get inside this chick. I need to shed these thoughts of Ellie from my head. When the fuck did they even get there?

In the car, Cassie's all over me. Her hand slides down my inner thigh, making it tough to concentrate on driving. And when she undoes my jeans, damn! This girl doesn't want to wait.

She pulls me out, stroking me, and it's so fucking good. If we weren't in the middle of downtown Ames, I'd pull the car over and let her do whatever the hell she wants.

She peers up at me, a sly grin accenting the glint in her eye. I hold my breath because I know what she's about to do. She breaks away from me and leans down. Trying to keep my focus on the road, I remove a hand from the steering wheel and place it on her head. I press gently, anticipating the warmth and wetness on my dick.

I'm not disappointed.

"Ahhhh," I moan.

She bobs up and down. Lower and lower each time, taking the whole length down her throat.

This girl is going to make me lose my mind.

She's still going at it, licking, sucking, and squeezing when I pull into the garage. Dylan had better have Lia in bed. In *his* room.

"We're here," I say, even though I don't want her to stop. Hell, I might not take the time to lead her inside.

Cassie sits up, pushing the hair out of her face. "Good. Let's go in."

I slip my dick back in my pants. It's freaking uncomfortable, but I'll whip it back out soon enough.

Dylan's in the living room and doesn't acknowledge us when we enter. I take that as Lia is asleep in his room and mine is free and clear. He may hate what I'm doing, but he's not a jackass.

"Your roommate want to join us?" Cassie asks, eyeing Dylan.

"He's not in the mood," I answer quickly for him. Seeing Dylan naked is not on my top million things to do—ever.

"We should set him up with Bree. They'd be cute and lame together." She laughs. "So, where's your room?"

Cassie hooks a finger in my belt loop and follows me around the corner. As soon as I have the door closed and locked, she assaults me against it. Slamming her lips over mine and unzipping my jeans.

I don't even need to kick them off before she's on her knees, her mouth back where it belongs. Pure bliss.

Even so, Blake's voice rings out in my head, asking Ellie for a towel.

The whole thing shouldn't bother me. So why does it?

I push the thought away, lean back, and concentrate on the way Cassie's working me. She moves her tongue over me, knowing exactly what she's doing. She cups my balls and it's fucking amazing.

Too soon, she stands up. She shimmies out of that too-tight black skirt of hers, revealing a black lacy G-string that shouldn't count as underwear. Her bra barely covers her. Boobs that don't fit spill out as she unhooks it from the front.

Nice.

She steps up to me, smashing them against my ribs. Her mouth is close to mine, but they don't touch. With one hand, she rolls on the condom.

"Bed," she orders, grabbing my shirt.

"You're bossy," I say, smiling. "What's that all about?"

She spins me around and shoves me backward onto the mattress. It's not forceful, but I'm a good actor and fall hard on the bed. Cassie steps up on the duvet. Straddles me, then squats down over me, her opening directly above me.

"I just like a good fuck," she says.

Oh. Hell. Yeah.

"A good fuck, huh?" I grip her hips and push her down over me. Warm, soft flesh surrounds me, and it's all I think about.

Exactly how I like it.

Cassie does all the work. She's loud, and I'm too lost in the sensation to care. She thumps on me hard and fast, slowing only to scream out her pleasure as

184

she comes. Then she's back at it—riding, riding— her next climax building with each breathy intake of air and thrust of her body.

She sits up, moves her hips over me, and gives me a nice show as she massages her own breasts. Throwing her head back, she comes again, her wetness dripping all over me.

I'm close, and I can't hold on much longer.

Time to take back control.

I lift her off. She's panting, and I swear I can see her heart beating against her ribs.

"Stomach," I say. She instantly obeys.

I slip back inside. Thrust into her until mind-numbing release sets me free. Gloriously free.

A couple rounds with Cassie and all thoughts of Ellie will be wiped from my mind.

Chapter 17

Ellie

Dammit! Why won't he answer?

And why do I keep calling him? So what if he heard Blake in the background and jumped to conclusions? Even if his conclusions were correct, what I do is none of his business.

I turn my phone off so I won't be tempted to text him, and when Blake steps out of the bathroom fully dressed and smelling like my shampoo, I wrap my arms around his neck.

"I'm sorry about last night," I say.

"Don't be sorry," he repeats. "Last night was one of the best nights of my life. And this morning, waking up with you in my arms, was even better."

I lean back a little to study him. His dark irises smile back at me. I rise on my tip-toes and kiss him. Soft lips separate mine and deepen the kiss.

It's so good, so sweet, so loving. I'm lucky to have Blake in my life and in Lia's.

But—

He's not Damian.

Which is a good thing.

Blake sucks on my lower lip before he lets go. "We'd better head out, babe. That 19-foot hammer won't tag himself."

I sigh. "Yeah. Let's go."

~*~

The next few weeks fly by. We stay out late on the boat, sunrise to sunset, seven days a week, and by the time Blake and I are done for the day, we're exhausted. The experience, though, has been totally worth it. Tagging and collecting blood samples from hammerheads, black tip and white tip reef sharks, and even some tigers. Those catches have been exhilarating!

Because of our new rigorous schedule, I get up extra early to make my daily phone call to Lia, usually while she and Damian are on their way home from the hospital. Apparently Damian taught her how to use his phone because it's her voice I hear when she answers. He doesn't even get on after she says goodbye.

The first couple of times it happened, tears sprung to my eyes at the rejection. Now, though, I realize it's for the best. I have Blake, and he's everything I could ever want.

Most nights, he sleeps in my room, and cuddled up beside him, I sleep better than I have since the nights in Damian's bed. I try not to think about it, and usually I succeed, especially now that he doesn't get on the phone anymore.

I'm beginning to think I can forget him. Move on with my life—be happy with Blake.

After a shower, I snuggle up to Blake following another long day. I'm so sick of takeout that we ran to the grocery store and bought two chef salads and a bottle of red wine for dinner. Most delicious salad I've ever had.

Blake slips an arm around me, pulling me closer. I'm too tired to think, and the alarm is set for the butt-crack of dawn again. Then I'll get ready and call Lia while Blake goes to the gym. Afterwards, he'll shower in his own room and meet me at my door so we can leave together.

That's our routine. In two short weeks, it'll all be over, and we'll be back in the States.

I'm both looking forward to it and dreading it at the same time. On one hand, I miss my little girl so much. On the other, I'll have to see Damian again when I pick her up.

That and Blake and I will have to make a decision about where this relationship is going.

"You're tense," he says. "Sit up."

With a groan, I do what he asks. My muscles scream at me because all they want is for me to lie back down.

Blake scoots up behind me. His palms rest on my bare shoulders for a moment before they massage the tension out of them. I bow my head and close my eyes, letting him work his magic. Warmth flows from his fingertips into my muscles. His thumbs push into the back of my neck, rubbing tiny circles as they move from one knot to the next.

"How's that?" he asks.

I hum out my answer. Words are difficult to form at the moment.

"Good," he murmurs against my ear.

His legs stretch out on either side of mine. He squeezes them, encompassing me with his body. Surrounded by him, I'm all warmth and relaxation.

Blake gathers my hair, twists it, and drapes it over my shoulder. Then his lips press against my neck. Soft, gentle kisses trail over my skin, spreading warmth down the length of my back.

His palms glide down my arms, then circle to my lower back. They dip under my cami and work up my spine, massaging, caressing. Higher and higher, pressing into my flesh, and loosening the muscles with each touch.

I'm in heaven, not thinking about anything except Blake and what he's doing to me. For once, I'm enjoying this moment without letting my brain get in the way.

I raise my arms above my head and Blake takes the hint. Slowly, he lifts my top up, over my outstretched fingers. He tosses it away, then laces his fingers with mine, bringing my arms down and crossing them in front of my chest with his own.

Breath tickles the nape of my neck. Soft, hot air burns into my skin as it rushes over me, sending desire flowing thick through my veins.

My body responds to him, my breathing coming faster, my heart pounding.

We haven't done anything like this since the last time, when I told him I wasn't ready. Now, though, my resolve is paper-thin. Weeks of the two of us spending twenty-four-seven together has worn me down.

I lean back against him, resting my head on his shoulder. Blake dips down, his tongue gliding over my neck, my jaw, finding its way to my mouth. In a gentle motion, he guides my face to meet him.

"Elizabeth," he murmurs.

He's asking permission to continue. Oh, I want to, but—

What reason do I have to decline? None, really. I mean, this is what I want, right? To be with Blake.

To embrace all that I once had when Liam was alive.

So, why am I hesitating? *No* is on the tip of my tongue, but it refuses to be released. I can't make myself nod, either.

I'm stuck.

Stuck between someone I can have—who's here and wants me—and the phantom of the man I love, whom I can't seem to let go of.

"Yes," I hear myself say, and I sound so far away. So *not* me.

"I don't want to push you," Blake says.

He grips my hips and turns my body to face him. I wrap my legs around him, pushing myself against him, my core grazing his arousal.

I circle my arms around his neck, drawing him closer. Lips to lips, I answer, "I want you too."

And I do.

Because I'm tired. Tired of loving Damian, tired of thinking about him, tired of knowing I'll never let anything happen between us yet still hanging onto him. He's a distraction I don't need. A mental game I play only with myself.

And I'm done playing.

It's time to let him go.

"I'm ready now," I say, easing Blake's mouth to mine.

With those words, I light the fuse. Fire rolls through both of us, passion igniting the flame. I'm all thirst. All desire.

For Blake, it's years of want. Even so, he moves with delicate craving. Holding, kissing, caressing as if I am the most precious thing in the world. It reminds me of my first time—with Liam.

So unlike Damian, who rushed, pulsed, and took with heated hunger. A small sob catches in my throat at the reminder of what I was to Damian—a way to control his pain. During all that time, it was all I ever was.

Tight in Blake's embrace, I cling to him. He lays me on the mattress, sits up, and takes off his t-shirt. Then his arms circle under me again. My bra gets unhooked, his kisses moving down my jaw and between my breasts.

He slips the straps off my shoulders until the purple lace falls away. I'm nervous, being this naked in front of him. After Lia was born, I became self-conscious of my post-baby body.

But the soft grin tugging at Blake's lips as his eyes drift over me washes the fear away.

"God, Elizabeth, you're beautiful," he murmurs.

I swallow. I should value the words more than I do. He's giving me the confirmation that I have nothing to worry about. With him, I'm safe.

Then why don't I *feel* safe?

I push through, molding my lips to his. Willing

myself to feel for him the way I want. To reciprocate his affection.

Blake's palms cover my breasts, and I arch into them. My eyelids fall, giving myself over to him.

I squeeze my eyes closed as he works down my stomach. He slides a finger under the elastic of my pants, and I'm trying hard to relax and not think. On instinct, I raise my hips so he can glide the rest of my clothing down my legs.

I'm completely naked now. I open my eyes to study his expression. His gaze sweeps over me, and I see nothing but reverent appreciation.

I love it and hate it. Want it and despise it for all the wrong reasons.

I prop myself up on my elbows to watch as Blake runs his palms up my legs, pausing at my knees. My breath hitches when he gently pushes them apart.

I'm so cold, so vulnerable, so exposed.

Blake undoes his belt and the sound has me aching for him. Damn my indecisive body and mind!

I stare at him, taking in each move, each ripple of muscle as he steps out of his jeans and boxers. He rolls on a condom and gets back on the mattress. On his knees between mine, Blake grabs a hold of my hips and scoots me closer. Touching as much skin as he can, he moves down my legs and tucks them behind him.

Fingertips skim over my stomach, his warmth absorbing into me and lighting me on fire. His thumbs flick the tips of my nipples. At the sensation, my elbows give out and I lay down flat on the mattress. He kisses each one before working his way up.

I'm panting with anticipation. All of my most sensitive parts are on high alert, blood filling the crevices in my body until they're swollen and scream out with eager pleas.

I can feel Blake between me, his head teasing my opening. I want so badly to rise up and meet him, but he presses his weight down on me, pinning me to the mattress.

"Blake," I whimper.

"Baby," he breathes.

He lifts up a little, and as he does, I spread my legs wider. God, I want him. Need him. I bite my lip, eyes locking onto his coffee-colored ones. They're alive with a passion my body longs to satisfy.

And maybe it's not just my body.

Maybe it's me?

Blake pushes into me, and I don't hold back the moan that spills out of me. O.M.G. Amazing.

I circle my arms around him, my fingers digging into the taut muscles of his back. I cling to him, trusting him all the way. Blake's mouth finds mine again, the scent of wine still on his breath.

I'm in the moment. Not thinking about the past or the future. Only right here, right now.

Blake makes love to me. He knows it's been awhile, so he doesn't rush. He takes his time, building me higher and higher. Gathers me in his arms and holds me through it.

Oh God, I'm close. So close.

I squeeze my thighs against him, rising, rising.

I can't breathe. My lips quiver.

Blake senses where I am. He presses me closer as he thrusts faster.

Faster.

Faster.

And I can't take it anymore.

My whole body shakes as I let go, clinging so tightly to him. I bury my face in the nape of his neck.

"Oh baby," Blake murmurs into my ear as he releases.

I'm still coming down off the high, so I don't respond. Still on top of me, Blake holds me close, both of us winded. A few minutes later, Blake pulls out and gets up. He kisses me on the forehead. "I'll be right back."

A moment later, I hear the shower turn on.

That's when the haze lifts.

Oh no. What did I do?

In a daze, I swing my legs over the side of the bed. I'm not sure how I feel, but it's definitely not what I'd expected. I should be happy—elated even. But I'm not.

I'm—

Empty.

I dig out a pair of shorts and a tank top from the dresser, throw them on, and crawl under the covers. My gaze floats to my cell phone sitting on the nightstand.

Damian.

This wasn't how it was supposed to work. Oh God, my heart hurts. The gaping hole is wider, not smaller.

Not gone.

I grab my phone to view my last call—to Damian's cell. His picture lights up on the screen, deep blue irises looking back at me and a sexy little grin teasing his lips. I snapped this a long time ago on one of those rare occasions when he seemed happy.

We were outside in his backyard. We'd just gone swimming—actually, we'd just had sex in the pool—and decided to sun dry on the deck. His hair stuck straight up, and it was damn adorable.

Under the hot sun, though, I'd shivered.

"You cold?" he asked.

"No, I—don't know," I answered. Then I shivered again.

"Come here," he said.

In my black two-piece, I laid down beside him on the lawn chair that definitely hadn't been designed for two people. But I didn't care. The closer I was to him, the better.

My back to his stomach, I didn't notice when he stuck his hand in the pitcher of ice tea behind him then slid it under my bottoms. He grabbed my ass, an ice cube tucked into his palm.

Oh boy!

"Cold. Cold. Cold!" I jumped up and danced around, digging the ice out of my swimsuit. "Damian!"

"*Now* you're cold," he said, laughing.

I glared at him, considering a sweet payback.

Smiling seductively, I sauntered toward him, making sure to work my hips the way he liked. "You are so naughty."

He shrugged, sitting up in the chair. "Whatcha going to do about it?"

I straddled his lap and leaned down to kiss that smirk off his face. His fingertips trailed the neckline of my swimsuit until he found the clasp at the back of my neck. But by that time, I already had the pitcher of ice tea.

"This," I answered, and poured the whole thing on his head as I gracefully dismounted from his lap. I stood back giggling.

Damian sat there, wiping ice tea from his arms and bare chest. He flashed me a devilish grin before he leaped up and tackled me to the grass.

On top of me, he slid the hair from my face. "I'm impressed, Elle. I didn't realize you were *that* cold."

Even now, under the blankets, the memory sends little shivers up my spine. I lived for those moments. For those little tastes of true happiness.

The shower shuts off, and I set the phone back on the nightstand. Wearing only a towel, Blake walks back in, grinning at me. I smile back because it's what people do.

Naked, Blake joins me under the sheets and holds his arms out for me. I slide in beside him, letting his warm skin cover mine.

His lips press against my temple. "I love you, Elizabeth," he whispers.

I have no reply.

Chapter 18

Damian

The sound of high-pitched screaming jolts me awake. Ripped from my sleep, I throw back the blankets and jump out of bed, searching for the source. It takes me a second, but I recognize the little voice piercing my ears.

I jog the few the steps to Lia's bed. She's sitting up, her favorite blanket clutched to her chest.

I kneel down and reach for her. "Hey. Shhhh. It's okay. It's okay."

Cuddled up against me, she nods, but she's crying. "I—I—I—"

"Shhh," I say again to soothe her. It's what my mother did whenever Liam or I had a nightmare.

"I had—a—a bad—dream," she sobs.

"It's all right. You're all right."

"I dreamed Mommy came back and took me away, and I never saw you again."

Her words cut through me. The last few weeks have gone by so fast, and the only times Lia's not with me is when I visit the cemetery. I kept Cassie's phone number, but I haven't called. I've been wrapped up in my time with Lia—I haven't needed to call her.

I don't talk to Ellie at all when she calls anymore. I taught Lia how to answer my cell and how to hang up, cutting out the middleman between her and her mother. Lia's never said Ellie's asked to speak me, so the arrangement works well.

Back to the way it was between Liam's old girlfriend and me after she left—other than the fact I sleep restlessly because I'm wondering what she's doing and with whom.

I guess Cassie didn't completely fuck Ellie out of my head.

"Lia, Lia. That won't happen, okay? I won't let that happen," I tell her.

She glances up at me, the nightlight brightening her eyes. "Can I sleep with you?"

I don't even stop to consider. "Come on."

I kiss her head before I pick her up. She cradles her blanket and sticks her thumb back in her mouth. As I carry her to my bed, she leans her head against me. She nestles in, and I hold her closer.

I lay her down on the mattress, her thick blonde hair spilling out over the pillow and tiny bare feet sticking out from under the sheet. While I tuck her in, her eyes fall closed and stay closed.

I round the bed and get back in, facing her. Both of her hands are by her face, her blanket held in her fists. Moonlight flows over her. She's so precious, so innocent.

She reminds me of Ellie when she sleeps, except

for the thumb. I smile as a memory rolls through my mind. I don't recall why I woke that night, but when I did, Ellie had her head on my chest and one leg woven around mine. Blonde hair tickled my nose.

At first, I wanted to push her away. We had sex, period. Cuddling afterward wasn't part of our deal.

Yet I didn't make an effort to move.

She sighed in her sleep, snuggling closer to me, then her arm draped over me and rested against her face, like Lia's is now.

"Damian," she murmured.

"Yeah?" I answered.

She didn't reply.

For a long time after Mom and Liam's accident, neither of us slept well except when we were together, so I decided not to disturb her. She looked so peaceful, and sprawled out over me, she even kept me warm.

After that, whenever she turned to me in her sleep, I let her. By the time morning rolled around, she'd always be on the other side of the bed.

I'm still staring at my daughter when her thumb pops out. Her lips twitch, and her dimples expose themselves.

It's crazy to think how Ellie and I did this. Together.

Two broken people created this amazing, special little person.

I scoot closer to her, fold my arm around her tiny body, and sleep better than I have in a long time.

~*~

Leslie has the week off, so Lia's hair has been a tangled disaster every day, which sucks because tomorrow is Thursday, and we're meeting Dad for dinner. Lia can't go to a nice downtown restaurant with bird's nest hair.

"How the fuck?" I pause the YouTube video and rub my temples.

"Daddy!" Lia says.

"Sorry. How the...crap?" I correct myself.

I study the picture, wondering how it's the twenty-first century and YouTube still hasn't given me the option to play these tutorials in slow motion. I slide the cursor back ten seconds and watch again.

And again.

"Daddy!" Lia whines, impatient.

"One more time," I say, analyzing the way the chick's fingers hold three pieces of hair at the same time.

"How's it going, man?" Dylan asks, walking into living room. He peers over my shoulder. "Dude, what are you watching?"

"I'm trying to figure out how to braid hair," I say.

"I didn't peg you for the cosmetology type, but whatever floats your boat."

"You're an asshole," I mutter.

"Daddy!" Lia exclaims.

Oh right.

"Sorry, I meant..." *Asswipe? Dickhead? Fucktard?* "Fart face."

Lia giggles, so the ridiculous insult is good enough for me.

"Come here and make yourself useful," I tell my

lingering roommate. Then I say to Lia, "Turn around."

She happily obeys and gives me her pink brush. Even though she's gotten some of the tangles out by herself, it's still ratty. She holds her head to keep it steady as I tug the brush through her hair. I swear, she has as much as Ellie does now.

"Why don't you take her to a salon tomorrow?" Dylan suggests.

"Don't have time. As soon as I get off work, I have to buy her a dress and be at the restaurant at 6:15 sharp. Now, hold this." I pass him a small chunk of hair and check the YouTube video again.

I cross my two strands. Trade one for Dylan's. Then repeat.

"Okay, okay. I think I get it," I say.

"What about the rest of the hair?" Dylan asks, pointing to my laptop. "See how she's adding it as she goes?"

"Shit."

"Da—"

"Crud," I say.

She nods smugly.

I brush out what I had and start over, consulting the tutorial after each move I make. This time, I add sections of hair to the strands Dylan and I hold.

"This is witchcraft," I conclude.

One hour and ten braids later, I think I've done a halfway decent job. It doesn't quite match the one in the tutorial, but it's better than what Lia previously had. Dylan barely helped on the last one. My daughter's exhausted though, slumped in her chair with her hands over her head.

"Are we done yet?" she asks through a yawn.

"Yep, babygirl. Go put on a swimming suit and let's get you in the tub."

Lia skips off to dress for her bath, and I head to the bathroom to run the water. I scoot the toys away from the drain. Weeks ago, I gave up putting the things in the box under the sink. It's easier to just shove them all to one side when I shower than deal with a tired Lia whining about picking them up every night.

I dump a third of the bottle of bubble bath in. She loves her bubbles, and I figure the more soap, the cleaner she gets, so it's a win-win situation. Except we go through a bottle every three days.

She dances in, carrying a couple of ponies. Tonight's suit has a tutu, so she stops and does a ballerina twirl.

I applaud her and she beams. She does another one before she climbs into the bathtub.

"Here, Daddy," she says, giving me a pony.

"Rainbow Dash," I say. I'm not asking because I know them all now. She's the fastest flying pony in all of Equestria. Holding the pony in the air, I make her whizz back and forth over Lia's head.

I can't believe I'm doing this.

I do though, because this is great. Better than I ever imagined.

"Rainbow Dash!" Lia makes Pinky Pie say. "Come down! It's party time!"

Our eight weeks together are almost over, and I have no idea what I'm going to do after that.

This little girl has changed my life.

~*~

Ellie

I have nine days left in the land down under, and I can't look Blake in the eye. Not after last night when he told me he loved me. The silence was deafening.

But how could I answer that?

I've been in love twice in my life: with Liam and Damian.

And what I feel for Blake isn't love.

I wanted to love him. God, I wanted to so badly. Stupidly, I thought last night would throw me overboard from like to love. Except all it did was strike me with guilt.

I couldn't sleep, thinking about the way I used Blake. How I just did the same thing Damian did to me!

I'm such an idiot.

I shouldn't have agreed to this relationship with Blake until I knew for sure I was over Damian.

The wind whips through my hair. I left it down for this very reason. We're going farther offshore than we've ever been, and I'm grateful for this time to think. Most everyone else, including Blake, is in the lab below deck. Only a few of us remain to catch the scenery and fresh ocean breeze.

Miles and miles of water stretch out in every direction. The huge expanse between sea and sky is so distinguishable out here. It's like the universe is reminding me how big it is and how little I am.

I sigh, tucking hair behind my ear. It comes free

a split second later.

"Elizabeth?"

My head snaps in the direction of my name. Blake's standing there, hands in his pockets. He pulls them out and motions to the spot beside me. "May I?"

"Yeah, of course."

This morning when he woke up, he didn't kiss me before he headed to the gym. In fact, this is the first time he's spoken to me since his admission.

He sits and gazes out over the ocean. In total Blake-style, he cuts straight to the chase. "I didn't mean to put you on the spot last night. It was too fast, and I'm sorry. I've had some time to think, and I, uh, don't want this to get in the way of what we have. I can't take back what I said, but I'm glad you know, even if you're not there yet. I respect that." He reaches out and brushes the back of his hand down my cheek. "I've waited this long. I can wait longer."

The sudden urge to be honest with him overcomes me. "What if I never get there, Blake? What if…" I can't finish. We're in too deep, and I don't want to hurt him.

Blake frowns, still caressing my face. "I'm here for you, Elizabeth. Whatever happens, I'll be here."

I nod. Something tells me I'll be putting Blake's promise to the test.

Chapter 19

Damian

I've never paid attention to the little girls' stores at the mall, but holy fucking hell! I've never seen so many frills and shit in my life.

After a long day at the hospital, Lia's dragging behind me. Olivia was there today, and the girls played all morning.

To add to her exhaustion, Lia woke up last night with another nightmare, the same sort of thing as before except in this one, Ellie never came back from Australia. And like last time, I let her sleep in my bed.

I sift through the dresses and find a pretty off-the-shoulder blue one with sparkly stuff. Girls like that, right? I turn around to show Lia. She's sitting on the floor, moving her legs like she's making half a snow angel.

"Get up," I say.

"But I'm sooooooo tired," she whines. Then she freaking lies down.

I pick her up. "Off the floor, Lia."

She lands on her feet and hunches over. "My legs hurt."

I scan the store and find an armchair not far from us where I still have the perfect view of her. It's better than the damn floor. I carry her over and she slumps into the seat.

"Do you like this one?" I ask, holding up the blue dress.

"I don't like blue."

In the short time we've been together, I've learned two things about my daughter. Number one: she's cranky when she's tired, like Ellie warned me about. Number two: hell hath no fury like a sassy three-year-old when she's dissatisfied.

"What color do you want then?"

"Pink," she states.

"That's it? Only a pink one?"

"Yep."

I shoot a glance over my shoulder and do a quick inventory. "I don't see any pink ones. How about one with pink on it?" I ask, even though I'm not seeing any that meet that criteria either.

"All pink!"

I hate shopping.

"Okay, stay right here. Don't move. I'll see what I can find."

I go back over to the dresses, checking behind me to where Lia sits. She has her head on the arm of the chair, watching everyone in the mall pass by the store.

My plan is to gather a couple of options, let her pick one, and get the hell out of here. I'll have to braid her hair again too it looks like.

I plow through the racks, yanking off anything with any amount of pink on it. Lia's on her stomach now. Her feet are crossed at the ankles, dirty flip-flops sticking up as she people-watches.

Shit. She's gonna need shoes too.

I'm about to give up, say "screw this," and buy the blue one when, hanging up on a hook above my head, I spot a row of dresses covered in silver roses. In the very back, there's one with a pink bow.

The perfect dress for my little princess.

I'm fucking excited over a dress. How is this my life?

I drop the few I have in my arms so I can figure out how to reach the one I want. Thankfully, a saleslady walks by.

"Ma'am, I'd like that dress up there," I say, pointing.

"Sure." She grabs a hook on a pole leaning against the wall. Extends it upward. "Pink or white?"

"Pink. Size, uh, four," I tell her, remembering what Ellie told me weeks ago.

Balancing the hanger on the hook, the lady brings it down. "There you go. Can I get you anything else?"

"This is good. Thanks," I say.

I shove the reject dresses on a random rack, then twist to show Lia. But the chair is empty.

She's not there.

I walk forward, thinking she's out of my line of sight. The area in front of me widens, and I can see all the way from the store entrance to the cashier at the back. People are everywhere.

Just not the one I care about.

"Lia?" I say, searching the armchair for any sign of her.

There's nothing. *Nothing.*

Panic is rising in my chest. Pulsing through my veins. Within seconds, it's shaking me to the core.

"Lia?"

I drop the dress and run to the store entrance that leads into the mall. Shoppers crowd the hallways for Independence Day sales. My eyes dart around. Left. Right. Left. Right.

I don't see her anywhere. "Lia. Lia."

I don't know what to do next. I'm frozen in place, waiting for something to come to me or for something to happen—for Lia to grab a hold of my leg and say, "Here I am, Daddy!"

Nothing.

Everything speeds up. Patrons walk faster, some bumping into me as they pass. But I stay rooted.

I lost my daughter. I fucked up again. I fucking fucked up!

My mouth is dry. Precious minutes tick by before I come to my senses. And when I do, I'm a fucking tornado. I spin around and run back into the store. There has to be security cameras somewhere. She can't have gotten far.

There's one woman in line at the cash register. I shove her aside.

"Hey!" she yelps.

"My daughter is missing," I spill to the worker, ignoring the other lady. "I need to see your surveillance."

"I'm sorry, sir, we can't allow you that information, but I can call the police."

"Then what the fuck are you waiting for?"

As she picks up the phone, I scour the store again. I can't sit here doing nothing while my little girl is God knows where. How did this happen? One minute she was there; the next she was gone. I looked away for a second!

Ellie. Oh, God. What am I going to tell Ellie? I can't think straight.

A pair of little flip-flops sticking out of the dressing room catches my attention, and I freaking fly. Rip back the curtain.

"AHHHHH!" the half-dressed girl who isn't Lia shrieks.

"What do you think you're doing?" the woman I assume is the girl's mother screams, hitting me.

"Sorry. I thought…" I back away, but I don't know where I'm going.

"Sir?"

A mall security guard is in front of me now. He's a black, burly guy who looks like he means business.

I point to the dressing room. "I didn't know. I thought my daughter was in there."

"Sir, please, I understand. We have the mall on lockdown. No one in or out until we find your daughter, but I need to ask you a few questions. Is that all right?"

It takes a moment to realize he's not busting me for the dressing room incident. He's here about Lia.

"Yeah, of course."

I follow him to the front of the store, where two

police officers wait for me. They have notepads, ready to take my statement.

I've calmed down. Reality has sunk in, and I'm helpless. So fucking helpless.

I had one job: protect my own flesh and blood.

"Uh, Damian Lowell," I answer the first question. "Her name is Lia. Lia Kathryn Van Zee."

"Do you have a recent photograph?" one of them asks.

I pull out my wallet and give them the only picture I have. The one that fell out of Ellie's purse the day she told me about Lia.

"How old is she?" the other officer asks.

"Three and a half."

"And where was the last place you saw her?"

I point to the armchair. "She was sitting right there, then I turned around and she was gone."

"About how long ago was this?"

"I don't—I don't know," I answer. "Maybe twenty minutes?"

"We're going to find her, okay?" the female officer assures me.

An hour later, the mall opens back up and no one knows where Lia is. I called Dad half an hour ago, and he's on his way. My mistakes of the night are stacking high, so I'm glad he'll be here soon.

But I haven't called Ellie. I can't bring myself to make *that* phone call. Not yet, not until I know something solid.

The female officer—Officer Kane—strides up to me. "Come with me, please. We think we may have found your daughter in the parking lot surveillance."

Relief and panic slam into me. *The parking lot?*

The small security office is crowded, but everyone's focus is on the one screen. Pointing, Officer Kane shows me the tiny image of a little girl, barely in the shot. She's holding someone's hand.

The girl is clearly Lia.

"Who's she with?" I ask. "Is there anything else?"

"No, it seems they cut through here and started for the street. We're checking traffic cameras in the area now."

A replay shows Lia's not scared. In fact, she's smiling.

"Is there anyone she'd willingly go with? Anyone at all?" Officer Kane asks.

Only three people come to mind, and none of them seem plausible. Dylan, Ellie's mom, and my dad.

I shake my head. "No, no one."

"Most kidnappings happen with people the child knows and is comfortable with. Are you sure?"

"The only family she has in town is my dad and her other grandparents, but due to illness, they rarely leave the house."

"How about friends? Anyone who may want to hurt you?"

I think back to Toby Stanton and our brawl. He saw Lia with me. Would he go so far as to kidnap a child all because I fingered his girl?

"There's a guy I go to school with. Toby Stanton. We got into it a few weeks back. Lia was there."

"Do you have an address?"

"He lives off campus up in Ames, but I don't think Lia would go with him."

She writes down the information anyway. "Anyone else?"

"No, no that's all."

"We're going to look into this guy. There's nothing else we can do here, so why don't you come down to the police station."

"Can we issue an Amber Alert or something?"

"Not until we have sufficient cause to think she is at risk of being injured. Don't worry, the majority of child abductions end in the safe return of the child. I have no reason to believe this won't be the case with your daughter. We are doing everything we can to find her."

"Thank you," I say, but I don't hear myself.

Out in the main mall, Dad rushes toward me. He says a bunch of shit that sounds like he's talking underwater. I barely hear him, because right now, I'm drowning. In fear. In pain. In guilt.

I should have never let her sit there, so far away from me. Should have gone with one of the other dresses. Should have fucking let her lie on the goddamn floor!

I'm outside, getting into Dad's car, but I don't remember walking out here. I pull out my phone. The screen lights up with Lia's chocolate mustache face.

I failed her.

Just like I failed Mom. And Liam. And Kate…and Ellie.

I thumb through my contacts until I find her

name. I don't want to call because I don't want to disappoint her. I don't want to prove to her that she was right about me—that I can't do this.

Still, she deserves to know.

I swipe a finger over the screen, put the phone up to my ear, and hold my breath.

Chapter 20

Ellie

I can't suck in air. I'm suffocating.

My heart is pounding so fast, and I barely feel my legs give way.

I'm falling.

Strong arms circle around me from behind, guiding me gently down. They don't let go.

I sit on the floor, clutching onto the phone. Damian's explaining, explaining, but I don't give *a fuck* about his explanation.

He lost Lia. He lost my daughter!

I'm hyperventilating. Blake gathers me to him. Even though his lips are moving, I don't hear anything coming out of them.

All I hear is Damian's bullshit.

When I saw the number belonged to him, my heart skipped three beats. Oh, how I longed to hear his voice.

I should have known better. I should have known that after avoiding me these last weeks, the only

214

reason he'd call would be because he royally fucked up.

I don't want to hear anything else from him. I'm done listening. "I'm booking a flight immediately," I say and hang up.

"Elizabeth?" Blake holds me closer.

"No," I say. "Stop. I have to—"

I Google the phone number to the airport. Call it and buy the first available flight out of Cairns. Now, I have less than three hours to get back to shore.

Without a word to Blake, I unhook his arms from around me. Jump to my feet and dart up to the top deck. The lead researcher is also a mother, so I hope to God she'll understand and turn this boat around. If not, I have no problems diving overboard and swimming back to shore.

"Hannah," I say when I reach the top deck. "I have an emergency situation, and I need to get back to Cairns immediately."

Her eyebrows perk up. If what's inside me shows on the outside, in front of her, she sees a desperate woman. One on the verge of breaking down and going on a rampage.

Neither will help, so I hold myself in check.

Hannah nods, jumps up, and dashes past me to do what I asked. I stay put because I assume she'll have questions.

Blake's on the top deck now too. He comes toward me, arms outstretched. I know I'll crumble if I accept his embrace, but seeing him standing there, his brow furrowed, I realize he wants comfort from me as much as he wants to comfort me.

Blake was at the hospital the day Lia was born.

In fact, he's who I called when my water broke. It was his hand I squeezed through the contractions. His ears that listened to every scream and shout of profanity that flew out of my mouth.

And it was Blake's arms that held her after mine.

On Lia's first birthday, Blake shot all the pictures, edited them, and created the collage that hangs in the living room. Blake who was there to witness her first steps, her first words, her first trip to the ER for two stitches on her forehead.

Blake loves her as much as I do.

I press myself into him, and he cocoons me in his arms. His cheek lies against my head. The first tear I'll cry over this whole situation falls from my eye, slides down my face, and absorbs into Blake's t-shirt.

That one is followed by the next. And the next until I can't hold myself together anymore.

Together, Blake and I shift as the boat does a U-turn. We cling to each other, needing one another like we never have before. Both of us are living a nightmare we're helpless to control.

It's the worst feeling in the world to realize the depths of how powerless we really are. How a moment, a tiny instant, can completely shatter us to an unrecognizable heap of who we once were.

This is not my first time.

I'm empty. So empty.

I don't remember sitting on the bench. Or letting go of Blake to give Hannah the minimal details I know.

"If there's anything I can do, Elizabeth, please don't hesitate," Hannah says, patting my hand.

Ten minutes offshore, tears fill my eyes again. I've received nothing from Damian in phone call or text. I don't have the slightest clue how these situations are handled, but what I do know is that I don't trust Damian to handle them. I need to be there.

I need time to stop.

"I'll take you to the airport," Blake says as we pull up to the dock. "I'll buy a ticket, pack your bags, and be right behind you."

"No." The word is off my tongue lightning fast. At first, I'm not sure why I don't want him with me. I'm traveling back to Iowa—to Damian—and I could use the support.

But…

"No," I repeat, less stern than before. "Thank you for the offer, Blake, but you should finish this study. I need some time alone to think about things. I swear, I'll call and update you as often as I can. I just…I need time."

He understands I'm talking about us. After I get my Lia-Kat back—and I *will* get her back—we'll go home to Florida where I can sort out all this crap clogging my head.

Blake frowns, and it's clear I've hurt him. But I can't think about that right now.

I dig in my purse and hand him my apartment key. "Here. If you want to bring my stuff when you're done, that's fine. If not, I don't care about any of it."

Because my heart and soul is somewhere in Iowa, lost to me.

At the airport, Blake pulls into the drop-off lane.

He parks the car, then peers over at me.

"If you hear anything—"

"I'll call you right away," I finish.

He nods, the muscles in his jaw clenching. "If you change your mind, Elizabeth, I'll be there."

"I know, Blake. Thank you."

I reach for the door at the same time his hand grabs mine. I glance back at him. Vulnerability coats his gaze and strikes me in the chest. He holds his stare a moment, his lips parting in a breath. The words "I love you" are probably on the tip of his tongue, but he holds them back.

"Have a safe trip," he finally says.

"I will. See you in two weeks."

I slip away from him, open the door, and walk into the airport without looking back.

~*~

Damian

I sip on shitty police station coffee.

Dad and I have been here for three hours. Traffic cams couldn't get a facial recognition on Lia's abductor, but we know she's a woman. An older woman.

Officer Kane keeps telling me it's highly unlikely that Lia's in danger. Female abductors tend to be motherly-types, not sexual predators.

But I don't feel any better.

Some strange old woman will probably be able to take better care of my daughter than I ever could. Feed her macaroni and cheese with cut up hot dogs and give her a cookie afterwards. Know how to braid her hair without the help of YouTube. Not run out on her to get drunk and laid when the shit hits the fan. She'd take her to the mall and not take an eye off her for even a fraction of a second.

I finish off my coffee and wander over to the counter to pour another cup. I don't want any more, but drinking it passes the time. What I really want is a bottle of rum. Or whiskey. Or straight-up moonshine.

More than that though, I want my Lia back.

God, she must be terrified by now. Plus, she doesn't have her ponies or the book we read from every night. What if she has a nightmare?

Hands on the counter, I lean over. The sound of the clock ticking off minutes pounds in my ears like the subs in my car. They vibrate through me, each one reminding me I'm running out of time.

I grip the handle of the mug. I'd love to hurl it against a wall. Waiting around is killing me.

I should be *doing* something. Helping somehow. But Officer Kane instructed me to stay here in case they needed additional information.

Like identifying a body?

At the thought, the ceramic in my palm cracks. I hear myself inhale and exhale, each breath coming faster than the one before. It's been eight of the longest hours of my life. Like sitting around Kate's bed, watching her die.

"Damian?"

I spin around at the sound of Dad's voice.

"They just informed me they found Toby Stanton and brought him in for questioning."

"Did they find Lia? Was she with him?"

"No, son. They searched his apartment and didn't find anything."

"Where is he?" I ask, straightening.

Dad nods in the direction of a door on the east wall. "There's a room in there with a one-way window."

I don't bother with the coffee. Even though the police didn't find anything at his apartment, that doesn't mean he might not have her somewhere else. Had someone lackey grab her from the mall for him.

I make a mad dash for the door, throw it open, and stop before I barrel through the glass pane. Toby sits at one end of the table, alone, hands in front of him.

"He's cuffed. Are they charging him for something?" I ask Dad, who followed me in. Officer Kane is right behind him.

"He had three vials of an illegal steroid on him," Dad answers.

Stanton's lips are turned down in a scowl. Sweat drips from his forehead, and even from here, I can see his biceps twitching, probably from a recent injection. It's the off-season for him, which is when they bulk up.

An officer walks in and sits opposite him. He pushes a picture across the table. "Have you seen this little girl before?"

Toby's eyes dip down for a second then back up. "No."

"Why don't you look closer?"

Toby stares the officer down before he finally

picks up the photo. He studies it, puts it down, and shrugs. "I don't know. Kids are all the same."

I cross my arms in front of my chest, studying the boxer for signs he's lying. If he did this, if he kidnapped Lia, I'm going rip his fucking head off.

"Where were you this evening around five-thirty?"

"Hell if I know. The gym?"

"Which gym?"

"The one on campus." Toby leans forward, his elbows resting on the table. "What the fuck does this have to do with anything?"

The officer ignores him. "Where'd you go after that?"

"Home for a shower."

"And what time was that?"

"Nine o'clock, maybe."

"Where were you going when we picked you up?"

Toby pauses and rests back in his chair. "To see my girlfriend. Are you going to tell me what this is about?"

Beside me, Officer Kane pulls out her cell. "I'll be right back," she says and exits, leaving Dad and I to watch.

"This little girl was abducted from the mall today," the officer with Toby says, pointing to the picture.

He huffs. "So?"

"Tell me about Damian Lowell."

Toby chuckles. "You're shittin' me, right? What's he got to do with this?"

"I understand the two of you had an issue not

long ago," the officer says, his eyebrows lifting in question.

"What? Are you charging me for that too?"

"Tell me what happened."

"The little dick finger-fucked my girl, so I did what I needed to do."

"Then what happened?"

"I left the son-of-a-bitch crying on the ground. Fucking pussy. He deserved what he got."

The officer nods slowly. "So, to rub salt in the wound, you kidnapped his kid?"

Toby's eyes go wide. "Hell no, man. What is this? I didn't kidnap no kid, all right?"

His face slackens as he shakes his head. "I didn't have anything to do with his kid, I swear."

Toby Stanton is an asshole, but it's obvious he's telling the truth. He knows nothing.

I let out a breath and push through the door. Cold coffee waits for me.

Fuck.

I sit back down, the cracked coffee mug between my knees. I draw a palm down my face and bow my head. Another dead end.

God, I can't deal with this. The familiar emptiness spreads, racing into my stomach. Only this time it might be worse because there'd been hope involved.

And hope changes things.

Chapter 21

Ellie

I'm dying to check my phone.

When I boarded the plane, I had nothing. No missed calls, no texts. Not a single update, and it had been three hours since Damian told me.

Now, I'm halfway through this sixteen-hour flight from Cairns to San Francisco, and I've never been more anxious. Everyone around me is asleep or dozing, but I'm wide awake, my knee bouncing in a nervous habit, and my nails tapping anything they can hit: my teeth, the window, the armrest.

"Is there anything I can get you, ma'am?" a flight attendant asks as she works her way down the aisle.

"No. No, I'm fine. Thanks," I answer.

She opens her mouth to say something else, then decides against it and offers a small smile instead.

I don't reciprocate.

~*~

Damian

"Toby doesn't have her," Officer Kane confirms. "We're confident we'll find her, though."

She's been missing for ten hours and they haven't issued a fucking Amber Alert because they're "confident." What a crock.

"Thank you," my dad answers when I don't.

I'm close to losing my goddamn mind. There's only so long I can sit doing nothing. I can't imagine what Ellie's going through right now. What I'm *putting* her through.

Even though there's no news, I shoot her a text. There's nothing comforting in it, except at the end, I tell her again how sorry I am. It won't do any good, though. I deserve all the fury she'll throw at me when she arrives.

Dad and I sit in silence, waiting.

Waiting.

Waiting.

I go back and forth blaming myself, being pissed at myself, and praying to God they'll find her soon.

Because now, hope is all I have.

Ellie

I check my phone as soon as the overhead lights flash off. My heart races when I see a new text from Damian.

Please have found her. Let her be safe, I think before I open it.

I slide my trembling finger over the screen.

Police are still looking. Officer Kane says she's confident they'll find Lia soon. Elle, I'm really sorry. I hope you're doing okay.

Tears blur my vision as I stare at the words that tell me nothing. I don't even think about his lame apology. He lost our daughter. Apologies for that shit don't count.

I'm in San Francisco. So nothing yet?

I stand up and grab my purse, the only thing I brought with me. Squeezing my way through the crowd, I keep my phone in my hand in case he replies. Hopefully with something useful.

I'm cold. I glance back down at his text and this time the only thing I notice is how he's concerned about me. He knows how far from okay I am, and the crazy thing is, I needed him to ask.

I want so bad for him to hold me, comfort me. It's irrational, because it's Damian's fault that Lia's gone, but I might even need him more now than after Liam died. Being wrapped up in Damian's arms is where I know I can lose control...and gain it at the same time.

I'm jogging up the ramp when my phone vibrates in my palm. I stop dead, my heart racing. I've never been this scared in my life. Part of me wishes he didn't respond because then I could assume there was no new information.

But this text came too quickly for it to be

nothing.

They're readying the dogs to see if they can track her scent.

I swallow.
*Does that mean Lia's...*I stop there because I can't allow the thought to finish.

~*~

Damian

"Do you have something that smells like Lia? A shoe, an article of clothing, a doll she sleeps with?" Officer Kane asks.

Officer Kane has been at the station all night, giving me regular reports. I'm sure her shift ended hours ago.

"Uh, at home. Wait. Her blanket is my car," I realize.

She'd thrown a fit, but I made her leave it in the backseat while we were in the mall.

"That's perfect," Officer Kane says. "The K-9 units are on their way here. We're going to let them catch her scent off the blanket, take them back to the mall, and see if they can't track her from there. I'll warn you, it might be a long shot since there may not be much of a trail to go after."

"Why didn't we do this earlier, then?" I ask, a little pissed that it's a "long shot" because we waited and the trail went cold.

"It would have been a long shot earlier too," she

says as if she read my mind. "We had decent leads before, and well, now this is what we have left."

I'm not sure what all this means, but I need to know—for mine and Ellie's sake.

"Are you looking for a b—" I can't finish my thought, but Officer Kane picks up where I'm going.

"No, we're looking for a girl—alive and well. And we're going to find her," she assures me again.

God, I hope she's right.

I run out to my car. The sun is already hot on my neck, and I wonder how Lia got through the night without her favorite blanket.

I grab it and slam the door shut. The thing probably used to be soft and silky, but now the threads mat together and strings hang from the slick backed material. It's been well loved by my little girl, like mine had been by me.

I hold it to my nose and inhale. The blanket holds her scent, all right. It smells exactly like her: bubble gum bubble bath and baby powder.

Right then, I realize I won't be able to live with myself if they don't find her.

~*~

Ellie

In the customs line, I search my phone for the first available flight out of San Francisco. I don't care where to as long it's east of here.

I zero in on an available one to Denver that leaves in less than an hour. Since I have nothing with me, hopefully I can make it through customs quickly. The question is how fast can I make it to the next boarding gate?

I wait a few minutes to see how fast this line moves. Not too bad, so I book the flight, and get ready to run like hell.

~*~

Damian

They won't let me go because my scent might throw the dogs off. I fucking hate this waiting around. I should be out there!

I've lost track of how many cups of shitty coffee I've drank. Earlier, Dad did a breakfast run to McDonalds, and I couldn't help but smile. Lia would have approved of our restaurant selection. Hell, she asks to eat there almost every night.

"Can you get something for Lia?" I asked him. "You know, just in case."

"Of course, son," he said.

It was a dumb suggestion because her food will be cold Styrofoam garbage twenty minutes after he returns, but I need something to do. Something to delude myself that I'm taking care of her.

"Oh, and even though it's not a Happy Meal, see if you can get her a pony."

"I'm on it."

Now, her breakfast sandwich and hash browns sit untouched in the bag. I stare at it, tap my fingers against the desk, and grit my teeth.

I consider texting Ellie again. Ask her how she

is, but I'm not sure I want her response.

The K-9 units left an hour ago and I haven't heard a damn thing. I don't know how much longer I can sit here without breaking.

~*~

Ellie

Boarding pass in hand, I make it to the gate just in time.

"Wait! Wait for me!" I call out.

The flight attendant stops and widens the door she was closing. She checks my boarding pass and ushers me inside.

"Thank you," I breathe.

"You seem like you're in a hurry," she says.

"Yeah...uh, family emergency."

"I'm glad you made it, then."

I find my seat in 13B and settle in. I scan through my phone one last time before I put it in airplane mode.

Nothing.

For some reason, seeing the blank screen sends a knife through my heart. Two thoughts cross my mind, and I hate them both.

One: There's no good news to report, which could mean anything.

Two: Damian has nothing comforting to say to me when I need to hear from him so bad.

The second one hits me on a completely different level than the first, but they both hold onto me and refuse to let go.

Now I have two and a half hours to bite my nails.

~*~

Damian

Some dayshift officer walks in, and by the expression on his face, he has news. I stand up at the same time as my father.

"They found her. She's safe," the officer says.

Relief hits me like a hurricane. Hard and consuming, it devours me. Takes everything I am and changes it into something soft and palpable.

I'm broken in an all new way.

Lia's okay. She's okay, I repeat to myself over and over again.

My jaw trembles as tears brim in the corners of my eyes. I'm not a crier, but I don't have the wherewithal to hold these back. I allow them to flow in blissful reprieve.

I look up as soon as I pull myself together. "Where is she?"

"They're bringing her in now."

"And she's fine?" I ask, even though he already told me.

The officer smiles. "Not a scratch on her."

I rest my head in my palms, whiskers scratching against them. If what he said is true…I have to see her for myself. Touch her. Hug her.

Have solid proof in my arms.

Then, I'll call Ellie.

~*~

Ellie

Time is a funny thing. We spend most of our lives believing it goes by too fast. But then we have moments like these. Moments when seconds feel like hours and hours feel like days.

A lifetime is made up of innumerable of minutes, seemingly small things we don't care much about. Each minute melts into the busyness of our lives, and we don't think twice about them until they start to run out.

Or until they become the longest and most important minutes of our lives.

Then we notice them. Then we care.

Still, time moves at the same pace regardless of what's happening. One second at a time, minute by minute, hour by hour.

It's these moments, the ones that test us, that define who we are.

I have at least six hours remaining until I can get to my little girl. And if I'm being honest with myself, to the one man who can make my pain bearable. But until then, I'm struggling to hold it together.

Chapter 22

Damian

Dad squeezes my shoulder. He doesn't say anything. He's a parent and knows too well what I'm going through—except Liam didn't come home safe.

I hear Lia's voice through the closed door before I see her. "Where's my daddy? You said he'd be here."

The sound of her little chipmunk voice causes the dam of emotion to collapse in my chest. I never knew I could feel this way: absolute elation mixed with relief and guilt. I'm the reason she went missing in the first place. If it weren't for my carelessness, she would have been safe with me all of last night, and Ellie would still be in Australia working on the study.

I hate that I've pulled her away from something she cared so much about. I both dread and long to see her again. She's going to be more pissed than I've ever seen her, and I'm betting she'll pack Lia up in a heartbeat. Hell, she probably already bought their tickets back to Florida, and the plane leaves tonight. Neither Ellie nor I are good at handling pain and anger.

We're the type who run away.

"He's right through there," someone says.

I run to the door, but what Lia says next stops me in my tracks.

"Will Olivia's grandma be okay? She's so sad."

Olivia's grandma?

"The police are going to talk with her for a little while," the lady answers.

"Then they're going to take her back home, right?" Lia asks.

Whoever is with her deflects the question. "Your dad is waiting for you."

On cue, I throw the door open.

There she is, my little girl. Same clothes as yesterday, dirty flip-flops on her feet, hair surprisingly brushed smooth, and a smile brighter than Venus on her pink-cheeked face.

"Daddy!" she squeals and races to me.

I act on instinct alone, crouch low to the ground and collect her in my arms. I squeeze her tight against me. Letting go is not an option.

"Lia," I breathe, overwhelmed. "Lia, are you all right?"

A kiss lands on my cheek. "Yes, but I missed you. I didn't mean to fall asleep there. I'm so sorry, Daddy."

"No, Lia. *I'm* sorry. I never should have let you out of my sight."

I study her, those bright blue eyes of hers shining

back at me. Three months ago, I didn't know she existed. Two months ago I almost allowed her to walk out of my life without a second thought. Now, though—

Now I can't imagine my life without her.

I kiss her forehead and pull her close again. Ellie will most likely be at my doorstep late this afternoon, which doesn't give me much time left with her.

I won't fight Ellie when she arrives. I decided that earlier. Everything she spews at me will be completely true. I have no excuses, no defense. Nothing except a bread-crumb trail of mistakes that have led me here.

"Daddy?" Lia asks, her voice so small.

"Yeah?"

"Is Olivia okay?"

"As far as I know she is. Why?"

Lia puffs out her lower lip, causing her little dimples to reveal themselves. "Because her grandma said she was sick. She said Olivia wanted to see me."

I frown. "I don't know Olivia's grandma. Who is she?"

"That woman I stayed with last night. The one who's here talking with that police lady. Are they going to take her to see Olivia?"

I'm confused. I have no clue what to tell her, so I pick her up and take her to the desk where Dad and Officer Kane are waiting for us.

Dad reaches out and hugs Lia. "I'm so happy you're safe."

"I messed up our dinner, Grandpa. I'm sor—"

"No apologies," Dad interrupts. "There'll be other dinners."

I don't ruin the moment between them by pointing out there probably won't be. At least not for a long, long time.

"Okay, Lia," Officer Kane says. "Tell me what happened at the mall."

Lia slinks her arms around my neck again. "Daddy told me to stay where I was and he'd be right back. He went to find me a pink dress. I watched everyone out in the mall, and a lady stopped and held out a cookie to me. I love cookies, especially peanut butter ones, so I went to her. She told me she was Olivia's grandma, and that Olivia was sick and wanted to see me."

I rake a hand through my hair and shift my gaze from my father to Officer Kane. "Is that woman really Olivia's grandmother?" I ask.

Officer Kane sighs. "From what we've gathered, she had a granddaughter named Olivia who passed away fifteen years ago."

"Fifteen years ago?" I ask, because *what the hell*?

"Go on, Lia," Officer Kane prompts. "What happened next?"

"I thought she was taking me to Grandpa's hospital. If Olivia was there sick, Grandpa would be there too, taking care of her and he'd call my daddy. Olivia's grandma doesn't drive, so we walked to her house. She said Olivia's mommy would be there soon to pick us up. I watched cartoons and ate a ham sandwich and a piece of cherry pie. It was sooooo good, Daddy. Olivia's grandma makes the best cherry pies."

I smile. "I'll bet she does."

"Then she fell asleep on the couch, and I was tired too. I found a pillow and blanket and thought when Olivia's mommy got there, she'd wake me up. But in the morning, Olivia's grandma didn't know who I was or why I was there." Lia's eyebrows furrow. "That's when I got scared."

I hold her closer. Dammit! Lia should never have to be scared and alone. Never.

"Hey, I'm here now," I say. "Are you still scared?"

She shakes her head, blonde hair falling into her eyes. I push it away and kiss her nose. "Good."

"What happened after that, Lia?" Officer Kane asks.

Lia shrugs. "She made me eggs and you showed up. Where is she now? Can I see her?"

"She's speaking with the other officers."

I catch Officer Kane's eye, and she holds my gaze for a second. There's more she's not telling Lia.

I clear my throat. "Dad? Could you check over Lia for me? Make sure she's okay?"

"Of course."

I set Lia on the desk even though I don't want to. "I'll be right over there," I say, pointing to the far corner of the same room.

Lia nods, and I follow Officer Kane to where I'd indicated. I overhear Dad assuring Lia that Olivia is fine and *not* in the hospital. Finally, she grins as though she believes him.

Officer pulls out a notepad and lowers her voice.

236

"Her name is Margaret Harper. She's a widow, living by herself. We called her daughter, and she's on her way. After speaking to the daughter, we found out, like I said earlier, Margaret had a granddaughter named Olivia who fell ill when she was Lia's age and passed away. Margaret is in the early stages of Alzheimer's and it seems as though she had an episode, either thinking Lia was her granddaughter or a friend of her granddaughter's."

My eyes wander over to Dad and Lia. She's giggling and wiggling her bare toes, and I wonder how much the experience has fazed her. She seems concerned for Olivia and Margaret, but that's all. She's not hurt.

"Would you like to press charges?" Officer Kane asks.

Keeping my focus on Lia, I shake my head. "No," I say. "Just get her some help."

The officer nods.

"Are we free to go?" I ask.

"You're free to go," she affirms.

I walk over and scoop my little Lia back up in my arms. Then I squeeze her against me again. At best, I have six hours before Ellie arrives and pulls her out of my life, and I'm not wasting another minute.

Ellie

The plane lands in Denver, and before I even stand up, I check my phone.

They found her. She's safe.

I read it again to be sure. Then my hand flies to my mouth as I let out an uncontrollable sob. I clench the phone into my palm and hug it against my chest. Tears of relief stream down my face as I gasp for air. I'm falling apart, and I barely notice the other passengers staring and whispering until a lady sits down beside me.

"Are you all right, dear?" she asks

I smile at her through the tears. "Yes, thank you. I'm great."

She must see I'm happy and not upset, because she smiles back at me. "Good news, then."

"Very."

After she leaves, I take a deep breath and exit the plane. In the lobby, I'm focused again. Dead set on finding the next flight out of Denver—hopefully direct to Des Moines.

Skimming through my options, I find exactly what I'm looking for. And only one gate over, leaving in forty minutes. I smile as I hit "Purchase tickets."

Then I search again—for two one-way tickets to Florida.

Chapter 23

Damian

Lia and I drove to Dad's house as soon as we left the police station. The day belonged to Lia, and she wanted to race speedboats in the swimming pool. We'd done it once before. During a Thursday night dinner, Dad surprised her with three remote controlled boats. Hers, of course, was pink.

"Grandpa, you cheated!" Lia says, pointing at Dad's green boat in the middle of the pool.

"How is that cheating?"

Lia rolls her eyes Ellie-style. "Because I said the rules were you can't cut through the middle."

Dad over exaggerates a confused expression. Then he peers over at me. "I don't remember those rules. Do you?" he asks me.

I shrug. "This is between you two."

"See, I thought you said we couldn't cut up a fiddle. And I haven't cut up any fiddles in this race," Dad says, working to keep a straight face.

"Grandpa!" Lia giggles. "There are no fiddles in

the pool!"

He scratches his head. "Hmm. I thought the rule seemed strange."

"*Middle*," she says, drawing out the word. "You can't cut through the *middle*."

"The middle?"

"Yes-yes."

"Oh, okay. I think I understand now."

I laugh when Dad winks at her.

"She's a smart little thing, isn't she?" Dad says to me.

"She's a Lowell," I confirm.

"She sure is."

"Start over," Lia directs, and we all steer our boats to the east corner of the pool where we'd set up a checkered flag. "Ready? Set? Go!"

We zoom around the edge of the pool, and each time Dad's boat wanders too far into the middle, Lia would call him back in line.

Half a NASCAR race around the pool, Lia's attention span runs out. Completely unexpected, she jumps in the pool—the shallow end—fully-dressed. Maybe this little girl has some of me in her.

I don't have to think twice about this. I cannonball in after her. Scoop her up and throw her in the air. Lia squeals in delight.

"Oh, what the hell?" Dad says, and dives in.

The last time I remember Dad being in the pool was before Mom and Liam died. We'd had a two-on-two basketball game: Liam and Ellie versus Dad and me. Mom reffed.

Good times.

I haven't thought much about Ellie since we left

the station. Okay, that's a lie. I've done nothing *except* think about her.

About what she'll say when she arrives.

About whether or not Blake is with her.

About how I can't wait to see her, even if she's pissed at me.

I feel myself grin as a memory of Ellie in one of her rare lose-control-moments surfaces in my mind. She'd recently started college at Drake University in Des Moines and someone who knew Liam came up to her, gave his condolences, then hit on her.

Damn, I never knew that girl to breathe fire, but when she showed up in my bedroom that night, smoke was swirling around her.

The way her eyes widened when she told me what happened was fucking adorable. Her lips puckered, and I tried to hide my smirk. It didn't make me happy this douche bag came onto her, but whatever he said made her come *alive*.

The spark had been lit, and even though it didn't last, I was glad to see it could still burn. Her fire gave me hope that someday I'd be okay too.

Tonight, I'll see it again, but this time it will be different. *I'm* the douche bag in this story, not the hero she'll run to for comfort.

Even though I'm pretty sure I hate her knight in shining armor, I won't interfere.

~*~

I should be packing Lia's bags, but I can't make myself put a single thing into the new suitcases I bought her. I wonder if she even realizes what's

241

happening.

My eyes flick to her. She's lying on my bed, her little feet taking turns pounding on the mattress and bouncing back up again as she watches a *My Little Pony* video on my tablet.

When we got home, she'd asked me to braid her hair. The end hangs over her shoulder, and she's playing with it.

I may never see this again.

I get up off the floor and go to the dresser. Pull open the top drawer. The little black box has its own corner now. I lift it out and slide off the lid. Inside is the trinity heart necklace I gave to Kate, the one Lia found when she destroyed my room.

I touch my chest, where the symbol is inked into my skin, over my heart. Then I glance at the clock.

I have time.

I put the necklace in the pocket of my jeans and face my daughter. "Hey, Lia. Come on, there's some people I want you to meet."

"Where are we going?" she asks from the backseat.

"A place I should have taken you a long time ago," I answer.

This is so overdue. Not only because I want her to meet Kate, either. Mom and Liam are her family, and she has a right to know them.

Maybe it's stupid, and she might not understand. Even so, this excursion is for me as well as for her.

I turn my car into the cemetery. Behind me, I

hear Lia's sharp intake of air. It's more from surprise than fear.

"Daddy?" she says.

I don't answer right away. Instead, I park first and twist around to her. "You know every week when I leave you with Dylan for a few hours?"

She bobs her head slowly, her eyes focused on me.

"This is where I go." I open the door and get out. Lia does the same, and I meet her on her side of the car. "This way," I say, taking her hand.

Together, we walk toward the elder tree. It's in full blossom with small white flowers scattered along the leaves. A light gust of wind brushes past us, a faint hint of lilac carried among the breeze. Lia's face tilts up at me, and I smile down at her.

I lead her under the tree where we can see all three stones, and they can see us. Beside me, Lia squeezes my hand.

I lower myself to my knees to be closer to my daughter. The plan is to move down the line in the same order I do all the time—saving the best for last.

"Mom, I'd like you to meet your granddaughter, Lia. Lia, this is your grandma. Her name is Nora."

"Like the lady in the picture at Grandpa's house?" she asks.

"Yeah, this is her."

Lia smiles. "Hi, Grandma."

"And this"—I motion to Liam's stone—"is your uncle Liam."

"Look." She chuckles softly. "That's my name without the 'm.'"

"Because your mother named you after him."

Lia studies Liam's headstone for a second, then she lifts the sleeve of my t-shirt. "That's the same," she notices. "And...Mommy has one too."

I hesitate, wondering what I'm supposed to tell her. If she knows anything about Liam.

"It's the Celtic symbol for brothers. Liam was my brother, and your mom loved him very much."

Her blue irises flash up at me. "I thought she loved you."

I smile. "No, Liam has always held her heart," I say, and as I do, I wish it wasn't the truth. "Liam was a good guy, Lia. You would have liked him."

She wiggles tiny fingers at him. "Hi, Uncle Liam."

Her voice is so cute when she says it, and I hope, wherever he is, he can hear her.

I guide Lia to the next stone. I stare at it before I say anything. This cold piece of granite doesn't even come close to representing the person Kate was. The strong, beautiful, caring human being that cancer stole away.

Kate is everything I hope Lia will become.

In my pocket, the necklace weighs me down. For months after Kate died, I wore it around my neck to feel closer to her. The only reason I took it off and kept it off was because some girl asked me about it as I stripped her down. I hated the reminder, so I put it in a box and kept it on my dresser.

I clutch the charm. Kate made me a promise the night she gave it back that she would always be with me. Kate never went back on a promise, but I've never understood this one. Because she's not with me.

Maybe one broken promise in a lifetime isn't all that bad.

From beside me, Lia steps forward. Then she takes another, and another, until she's standing right in front of Kate's headstone.

She falls to her knees and cocks her head to the side. With outstretched fingers, she traces the heart symbol.

"This is her, isn't it?" Lia asks. "The girl who got sick, like Olivia."

I'm not surprised she remembers. After these last weeks with Lia, it seems she's inherited her mother's memory for important details.

I close the distance between us and kneel on the ground next to her. "This is Kate," I say.

Lia nods. "From the picture."

"Yes."

She points the symbol engraved in the granite. "That's her necklace."

I squeeze the gold tighter. "Do you remember what it stands for?"

She pauses, thinking. "Hope."

"Hope," I repeat. "Kate held onto that until her last breath. She never gave up. She fought to the end. Do you know why?"

Lia shakes her head.

"Because of love. Because she loved her family, and she wanted to give them the best of her."

"And you," Lia says.

"What?" I ask, not following her.

"And you. She loved you too, right?"

The bottom of the heart digs into my palm.

Slowly, I release it, and it sinks low into my pocket. I can't let it go.

"Yeah, baby. She loved me too."

Again, Lia's fingers glide over the stone. I watch as she traces over the K-A-T-H-R-Y-N of Kate's name.

"That's my name. Lia Kathryn." Lia peers up at me. "Am I named after her too?"

"You were."

"Why?"

"Because you were named after the two people your mom and I loved most," I say.

My whole world is right here with me, and as I gaze over the three headstones and the little girl at my side, I realize I'm only concerned with one of them. The one who is the culmination of the other three.

The one who's still with me.

Mom, Liam, and Kate—they've all moved on, and I'm the only one who hasn't. I've had seven weeks with Lia, and tonight, when Ellie arrives, I'll have to let her go.

On our way back to Ames, I receive a text from Ellie.

Just landed.

That's it. Two words that rip me to shreds because I know what they mean. I glance in the rearview mirror. Lia's reflection guts me even more.

I speed up to make it home faster. I want to make Lia an ice cream sundae and plan a party with her and Pinkie Pie. God, I want more time. There's not enough.

I park my car in the garage. Dylan's at work and probably won't be home until late, after Lia and Ellie are long gone.

Like a prince with his princess, I open the door for Lia and give her a bow. She giggles and skips inside.

"Go grab all your ponies, and bring them to the table," I say after her.

"Okay!" she hollers back.

As she gathers them, I scoop out vanilla ice cream into two bowls. Add strawberries and sprinkles like my mother used to do, and I set them on the table.

Lia hops up and down in delight when she re-enters, ponies overflowing in her arms.

"It's a party," I say.

She picks up Pinkie Pie, the party pony, and makes her dance across the table. "A party? Yay!"

I don't tell her it's a goodbye party. Goodbyes are never happy occasions.

With Twilight Sparkle, I follow Lia's Pinkie Pie around the table to the party hall. One by one, each pony arrives. They "eat" ice cream from our bowls and open pretend presents. The best part is seeing Lia's face light up when I try to talk in a girly-pony voice.

I laugh. "The apples from my orchard are the best tasting apples in Ponyville," I say in a horrible rendition of Apple Jack.

"They sure are," Lia's Rainbow Dash says. "There's no worms or anything!"

"No, siree. Not in *my* apples," my Apple Jack agrees.

I hear a car roll into the driveway. It's too early to be Dylan, which means it's Ellie, and my time with Lia is over. I set my pony down and collect our empty bowls, avoiding the frown on my daughter's face.

"What's wrong, Daddy?"

"Nothing, babygirl," I answer with my back to her. Lying seems like a better option than telling her the truth and breaking her heart.

Knock. Knock. Knock.

I turn away from the sink. Lia says something to me, but I don't hear her. I'm focused on the front door.

Knock. Knock. Knock.

The sound is louder this time.

I have to face Ellie. Already, though, I can sense the disappointment clouding those gorgeous pale blues of hers, and that might break me more than what she has to say.

I swallow as I reach for the door.

I swing it open. Ellie's standing there, eyes red from tears, no makeup, and blonde hair oily from running her fingers through it over the last 24 hours. She stares at me, mouth trembling, like she wants me to say something first. As if somehow I have the power to erase the last couple of days with the right words.

I can't, though. I can't even make my lips move,

because the only thing I'm thinking is how much I want to pull her into my arms and hold her against me. Take all the tears I've made her cry and bury them where they can no longer hurt her.

That's why I don't say anything. Why her pleading gaze slowly morphs into the one thing I feared that twists the knife, leaving me to nothing.

"Where is she?" Ellie asks, her voice small yet tough at the same time.

I'm about to answer when, from behind me, I hear Lia cry out, "Mommy!"

She zips past me and straight into her mother's open arms.

"Lia-Kat. Oh, baby," Ellie murmurs, clutching Lia against her. "Sweetheart, I love you so much. So very much."

"I love you too, Mommy. I missed you," Lia answers.

Fresh tears stream down Ellie's cheeks as she holds Lia tighter. I take a step backward, further away, distancing myself from them. Mother and daughter—the way it was before me.

The way it's supposed to be.

I back up a little more. Neither of them watch me. They're wrapped up in each other, Ellie clinging onto Lia for life.

Even in her state, Ellie is gorgeous. Motherhood suits her well, and she's good at it. Lia is safe with her.

I tear my gaze off them. Emptiness spreads throughout me even though they're still here. Ellie hasn't yelled at me, and I think I need that punishment from her in order to feel again.

Fuck knows I deserve it.

Finally, Ellie's eyes lift to mine. There's pain in them. Pain I've seen a thousand times, but at this moment, it shoots into the pit of my stomach. Because this time, I caused it.

And I can't do shit about it.

Again, Ellie holds my gaze, begging me to say something, but all I have is "I'm sorry," and that doesn't seem to cut it.

Another tear slips down her cheek, and it kills me to not rush over and brush it away. Together, we've put this distance between us, and both of us are better off moving on.

Besides, she has Blake, and I have...

Lia looks at me, and slowly her smile fades as if she realizes what's happening.

"Daddy?" she says.

I'm at the entrance to the kitchen now. I shoot a quick glance over my shoulder, pin-pointing her favorite blanket, the one the K-9 unit used to find her. She'll want that on the way home.

I catch Ellie's stare again, but I duck into the kitchen before I break down and go to her. I grab Lia's blanket from her chair and make my way back out to the living room. Ellie's standing, both hands on Lia's shoulders. I stop a few feet from my daughter and hold out the blanket to her.

"You'll want this," I say.

"I don't want to go," she whispers. She understands now. Her eyes glisten with moisture, and I'll be damned if I stick around to see anything fall from them.

"You belong with your mom," I tell her, refusing

to look at Ellie. "Go."

Lia shakes her head. "Come with us."

"I can't, Lia."

Her lower lip juts out, and she breaks free of Ellie's hold, running to me. She throws her tiny arms around my leg.

"You said you wouldn't leave me," she cries. "You promised!"

I reach down and smooth my hand over her head. A bullet rips through my chest as she turns those pretty blue eyes on me.

"I'm not the one leaving, Lia. You are."

I'm an asshole.

"But…"

"Lia," Ellie says. "Come on, our plane leaves in two hours."

Little arms release me, and I've never been more alone. Lia remains focused on me, though. Ellie puts an arm around her shoulders and leads her toward my front door. Lia's brows pinch together, waiting for me to come get her. But I don't move.

Ellie opens the door, and Lia steps out onto the porch. That's when she finally looks away, putting a gaping hole in my heart.

"Wait there," Ellie tells her, then she faces me. "Damian, I—"

I cut her off. "I'll mail you her things."

"Thank you," she murmurs.

She reaches for the door again. "Damian, about…everything, I…"

"I know, Elle. Just go."

Ellie's gaze pierces into me, and if she doesn't leave soon, I'm going to do something I'll regret.

251

"Go," I say again.

"Goodbye, Damian." Ellie's voice is barely above a whisper, but it rings loud in my head. Two words I loathe, grating in my mind.

The door clicks shut behind her. A minute later, headlights filter in through the windows. I ball my hands into fists, squeeze my eyes shut so I don't see them leave.

For once in my shitty-ass existence, I'm doing the right thing. So why the hell does it hurt so bad?

I head to my room so I don't hear the car back out of the driveway. Lia's bed sits unmade against the wall, her pink My Little Pony jammies spread out on her pillow. The book she picked out for tonight lays at the foot of my own bed.

I even smell the faint scent of her in the air—bubble bath and baby powder.

Death stole Mom, Liam, and Kate away from me. Now, life has taken Lia and Ellie.

This—right here, right now—is why loving someone is hell. Becoming attached to someone isn't worth the pain you suffer when they're gone.

Goddammit!

I pull Kate's necklace from my pocket without looking at it. The reminder of times lost isn't something I want to deal with tonight. I drop it back in the box, shove it in my dresser drawer, and slam the drawer closed. The picture of Brennan with Mickey falls forward, and Twilight Sparkle tumbles to the floor.

Fuck. It. All.

Chapter 24

Ellie

It's hard to ignore the fact that Lia cried herself to sleep in the seat beside me. Each quiet sob stabbed me through the heart because I know whom they're for.

God, a part of me wanted so bad to lay into him. Scream and yell and make him realize what he put me through. What he could have put *Lia* through. Did he know she could have died?

I couldn't, though.

When he opened the door, I froze. The fear written all over his face paralyzed me, and I realized he'd been through the same hell I had the last two days. The way he stared at me...it took all my will-power not to fall into his arms where I could drop this strong-mother façade and let him hold me up like he used to.

We were good for each other that way. Together, we could break down safely in our own pain, clinging onto the one person who understood what we were going through.

Running to Damian is a bad idea, which is why I stood my ground. Still, all I wanted was for him to say something.

Something to confirm I'm not crazy for leaving Lia with him in the first place. That somewhere under that cool exterior is the man I fell in love with.

I glance at the daughter we created together. She's curled up on the seat, sleeping like only a child can do with her body twisted in an awkward position. My neck aches looking at her. The tail of her French braid lies over one shoulder, and I wonder if the old lady who abducted her did that. Damian assured me in a long text she took good care of Lia.

Oh, Damian.

I slide both hands through my greasy hair. I can't stop thinking about him. I hope he's not drowning himself in booze and girls.

The thought sends a ripple of tremors into the pit of my stomach. I shouldn't have taken Lia and left him to his misery.

This is so messed up!

There is nothing—*nothing*—that makes sense here. He freaking left Lia unattended in a mall and someone took her. Talk about irresponsible. Not to mention the expanding list of faults that keeps knocking on my brain, playing peak-a-boo with me.

Yeah, I see them. Each line of mistakes he's made gets clearer and clearer, yet…

I peer out the window, watch the clouds pass by, and bite the inside of my cheek to remind myself of the pain Damian's caused me.

It doesn't work, though. I can't seem to help myself when it comes to him, and I've tried so damn hard to get him out of my head.

Blind love. That's what I have for him, because there's no other explanation.

I lean my head against the plastic pane. I wish somehow I could turn back time and either stop myself from ever finding comfort in Damian's bed, or recognize that I was falling for him in the first place. Then I could have cut off our arrangement before it was too late.

Maybe if I figured out a way to hurt him before he hurt me, I'd be able to move on with my life without seeing his face every time I close my eyes. It's a stupid thought, though, because I know I'd never hurt him on purpose. Not only because I hate seeing him in pain, but because that would mean assuming he's in love with me.

God, I can't keep doing this to myself. Or to Lia.

I pull out my phone and scroll through my contacts, bypassing Damian's picture. When I get home, I'll replace it with a big, bright, stop sign, and pray I can summon the wherewithal not to answer it if he calls. Instead, I tap on Blake's photo. It's one I took the first day out on the boat with the ocean in the background.

Black hair rustles in the breeze, and gorgeous chocolate eyes flirt with me from the picture. This man, this responsible, amazing, caring man loves me. So why can't I love him back? Blake should be easy to love, and Damian should be easy to let go.

Unfortunately, "should" isn't on my side.

~*~

The fasten seatbelt sign lights up with a ding, and soon, a flight attendant is telling us we're making our descent. It's currently eighty-eight degrees in Tallahassee with dropping barometric pressure and fifty-three percent humidity.

"We will be landing at gate forty-four. Thank you for flying with us, and have a great evening," she says.

My head falls back against the seat and I sigh. Home sweet home.

Both Damian and Blake are miles away, and for the next two weeks it will just be Lia and me. Maybe I can figure out my life before fall semester starts.

I don't wake Lia until the plane lands.

"Hey, sweetie," I say, gliding my fingertips over her cheek. "We're at the airport now."

Her eyelids open and those bright blues that are as expressive and beautiful as Damian's blaze into me. He definitely taught her something during her stay, because wow, that gaze mirrors his perfectly. If it was on his face, I'd lose my senses, but on our daughter's, I can stand my ground—I think.

She twists back to me in a sassy huff, her arms crossed over her chest, butt cemented to the seat. I've witnessed this move plenty of times before today, and I'm not surprised to see it at the moment.

"You don't have to like me right now, Lia," I say, "but you *are* getting off this plane with me if I have to drag you out."

Her shoulders hunch forward. We've been

through this enough times that she knows I'm not joking. If she kicks and screams, I hold on tighter. I've survived worse than a tantrum by a three-year-old.

The plane slows to a stop at our gate, and a minute later, the fasten seat belt light switches off. Passengers begin to collect their things from under their seats and the overhead compartments, but Lia and I have nothing except my purse and her blanket. Lia wads up the worn pink material without looking at me and stands up. She stomps her way into the aisle, her nose in the air.

I shake my head. It's going to be a long few days.

I follow her off the plane. She refuses to hold my hand, but I grab it anyway. After what we just went through, I'm not letting her walk around the airport with me simply trailing after her. At my touch, her eyes narrow and her lips pucker in an angry face only she could pull off. It's cute and annoying at the same time.

Since Blake drove the two of us here, his car is in the long-term parking garage, and I don't have access to it. So, a taxi it is.

Several are lined up outside. I pull Lia behind me to one of them, then I put her in the backseat first. I don't think she'd run from me, but with this mood she's in, I'm not taking chances. Lia's more like her father than I'd like to admit.

The silent treatment continues when we arrive at our apartment. Without a word, she storms into her bedroom and slams the door, another one of Damian's traits shining through.

I don't bother going in after her. She'll cool off by tomorrow, and hopefully, I will too. I doubt I'd be able to hold myself together if we talked tonight anyway.

I dig out my phone and collapse on the sofa. Blake will be out in the boat since it's afternoon there, but he's been expecting something from me, and really, he deserves to know what's going on. I should have done this earlier, but with Damian, it slipped my mind.

Lia's safe. We're back home now. Everything went fine.

I don't expect an immediate reply, and I don't receive one. Instead, my phone rings. Blake's picture lights up my screen, the little smirk on his face making me smile for the first time today.

"Hey," I answer.

"God, Elizabeth. I've been waiting forever for you to call me. I was going crazy, here," he says, relief coating his voice. "How's she doing?"

"Well, in terms of the kidnapping, she's great. Doesn't seem fazed by it at all."

"But…?"

"But"—I breathe out—"she hates me for taking her away from Damian."

"Elizabeth, you did what you had to do. Give her some time, she'll get over it." He pauses. "I'm, uh, sorry for pushing you into making her stay with him. I should have listened to you and supported you. I…"

"It's not your fault, Blake. I wanted him to keep

her too." Even if that had less to do with the trip and more to do with my own guilt for never telling him about her. "I'd really hoped he had changed."

"That's not your fault, either, babe," Blake says, his tone soft and soothing. "I can hop on a plane in two hours if you want me to."

I love his offer, even though I won't accept it. I close my eyes to allow the words to sink in and fill me up like he's here with me, but the lips I see speaking to me aren't Blake's. And in my mind, I'm quick to nod my answer to the man whose arms I long to have around me.

Warmth caresses my skin, and I swear I can smell the scent of Damian's body wash and deodorant. It's so good I inhale again, deeper, imagining that when I open my eyes he'll be here.

"Elizabeth?"

At the sound of Blake's voice, my eyelids fly open. I'm disappointed. My empty living room, quiet and dark, stares me down for a second before I push the thought of Damian away.

"No, Blake, it's okay. Finish the study. We'll be here when you get back," I say.

"I'm a phone call away, all right? Any time."

"I know."

Silence drops in on us, and I shift on the cushion. I sense "I love you" is on the tip of his tongue, and I hope he doesn't say it. The words are beautiful, but there's only one person I want to hear them from.

And earlier today, I chose to walk out of his life…again.

"Bye, Blake," I whisper because the painful memories are taking over my whole being.

He hesitates.

I know I'm hurting him with my brush-off…and I'm sorry.

"Good night, babe," he finally says.

I hang up first, then slowly make my way to my bedroom right before a scene plays out in my head. I'd gone to Damian's house the day before Kate's funeral to tell him goodbye and to fully lay Liam's ghost to rest. Damian caught me in Liam's bedroom, anger blazing in his eyes. I see them clearly even now, how they bored into me like he hated my being there.

It tore me up. He was hurting so badly, and I would have given anything to take it away. The bottle of whiskey in his grasp cut me to the core, because he was spiraling when finally I wasn't.

I couldn't return to where he was, broken in so much pain there's no room for rational thought. The whole world's a blur and completely against you, and when you're that far gone, you're desperate.

Damian was desperate that night, and I hated seeing him hurt like that. The way I'd been after Liam's funeral when he'd numbed my pain. I owed him.

A part of me died that day, when I left Damian broken in his bedroom.

The rest of me died today.

I can't hold myself together anymore. Face-first, I fall onto my bed and shatter.

Chapter 25

Damian

It's been two days since I let Ellie and Lia go. Two long days where I've thought of nothing else, but I've got to get my shit together. So, today I'm packing up Lia's things to ship back to her. Having them around is messing with my head.

I grab a box and empty the drawers I'd cleared out for her clothes. As I go, I'm reminded of this same scene at Kate's house, only in reverse. Then, I was moving in because I didn't want to miss a single second with her.

I lift out the My Little Pony jammies I bought Lia on our first day. *"Can I get two?"* she'd asked, and I couldn't say no. I look down and pull out the second, identical nightgown. Since I don't do much laundry, I'd insisted on her picking out a couple more pairs, but I don't remember her wearing anything else to bed except these.

I fold them up and set them in the box. Soon, there's nothing left in the drawers. I close the box flaps, tape it up, and move on to the next box. This one I fill with books, movies, and her collection of ponies. The only thing left when I'm finished is her bed.

That I doubt Ellie wants. Maybe I'll give it to Goodwill.

I label the boxes with the address Ellie texted me. Then I carry them to my car. With the last one in my arms, I peer over the room to make sure I have everything. It's empty. My gaze lands on the Twilight Sparkle Lia gave me, sitting back on top of my dresser. I stare at it for a second, recalling the day she gave it to me.

My chest tightens, and I have to get away.

I shake the memory away, flip off the light, and close the door behind me.

I'm glad I kept Cassie's phone number. She's been a useful distraction since Lia left. What makes it better is that I don't have to think when she's here. She and the liquor do all the work until I'm nice and numb.

Then I wake up, and the familiar pang of emptiness engulfs me again. I guess it's better than pain.

A million times I've thought about calling Ellie and Lia to check up, but each time I go to do it, I back out. If Ellie wanted to talk to me, she would have called by now. She hasn't. I royally fucked up, and I don't deserve to be forgiven by either of them.

Even at my weekly visits to the cemetery, I have

nothing to say. I stare at Kate's headstone, and all I can think about is Ellie and Lia and how I've disappointed them. There are no comforting words I can give them for what I've done.

I avoid Dylan as much as I can. I swear, the dude watches me like a stalker and it's fucking creepy. My guess is that my Dad put him up to it, since he's all too familiar with my track record with this shit. I guess I can't blame him for trying.

"Look, man, I'm okay," I tell Dylan one night as I pour myself a tumbler of Captain. "Go to The Underground or something. Live it up."

Classes start up again tomorrow, and the club is where everyone will be. Everyone except me—I'm not in the mood tonight. It's lame, but my plan is to have a few drinks and crash early. Cassie's not even coming over.

"Nah. I'm staying in. I have an eight o'clock in the morning," he says and slumps onto the sofa. Kicks his feet up on the coffee table. "*Assassin's Creed?*"

I can't think of anything better to do. "Sure, let's do it."

A few hours and the rest of the rum later, I jump in the shower. I stand there, letting the water rush over my back, and suddenly Ellie's in front of me. Like she used to be the mornings after she stayed all night. Her hair is tangled, lips full and pink, and her nipples erect. She steps toward me, her gaze shifting from my eyes down my body and back up.

"I had fun last night," she hints. "I have some extra time before class this morning."

Damn, I must have drunk more than I thought.

I'm quick to catch on. And with how awesomely tight her thighs wrap around me, the slippery shower wall will be no match for how I'll use it.

I grab her hips and yank her into me. I lean down as she tilts her head to the side, giving me better access to that succulent neck I've always loved to devour. Her arms circle me, fingers trailing over my bare skin and making me want her even more.

Cassie has nothing on Ellie. My mind-number is pure pleasure, whereas Ellie is a craving you can't get enough of, even after you've had it.

I don't think when I pin her up against the wall and drink her in. There's more than raw desire there, and it's not the first time I've seen it in Ellie's eyes. I just didn't recognize what it was back then.

I swallow, studying her. Delicate fingertips work their way to my chest and trace over the Trinity heart tat. I love how she touches me with gentle strokes, as if I mean something to her.

Has she always done that?

I press my forehead against hers and tip up her chin. She blinks, confused, probably because I usually don't take this kind of time. Normally, I dive in and take what I need from her. But I don't want to do that right now. No, now I want to taste her. Hold her.

Love her.

Closing my eyes, I lean down to kiss her. Suck her lip into my mouth and keep it there because it's so good I don't want to let it go. I do, though, and open my eyes to see what I've missed in the last few seconds.

Ellie's pale blue irises peer back at me.

"Damian? Are you okay?"

I shake my head. I'm so far from being okay. I'm in the shower with a memory of her, and I want so fucking bad for it to be real.

"Hey," she says, her fingers twisting through my hair. "Letting someone go doesn't mean you forget them. It means you love them from here and move on with your life like they would have wanted."

My throat goes dry at Ellie's familiar words. The ones she spoke to me the morning of Kate's burial.

Kate.

I squeeze my eyelids shut again. I've had enough of this shit, and I need Ellie out of my head. This is what I have Cassie for, but she's fucking out of town tonight.

"Damian," a voice says, but it's not Ellie's this time.

It's Kate's.

"Damian," she repeats, and I'm close to breaking down. "Please."

Palms as soft as I remember caress my face, coaxing my eyes open. She's there, light auburn hair falling in and framing her face like when I first met her. God, she's beautiful.

"Katie," I breathe out, not sure whether or not to believe this.

She smiles at me, a fingertip gliding over my lips.

"Katie, I—"

"Shh," she says. "Damian, listen to me. You need to move on."

"I can't," I murmur.

"Yes, you can. You have to."

I'm done trying to hold myself together. The shower's spray mingles with the tears burning in my eyes. "I miss you so, so much, Katie. I'm sorry. Sorry that I couldn't save you," I sob.

"Oh, baby. Don't put that on yourself. Besides, you did save me."

I shake my head while she nods.

"You did," she says. "The months I spent with you were the best of my life, and I wouldn't change them for even *one more day* if that day didn't include you. You were my ray of sunshine, Damian. My shining star."

Something is lodged in my throat, and I can't respond.

Her hand slips down my chest and covers my heart, over the tattoo. "This no longer belongs to me. It's time, Damian." She rises up on her tip-toes and lightly presses her lips against mine. "Let me go."

And then she's gone, and I'm alone.

I don't have a clue what just happened, nor do I want to think about it. I shut off the shower and shake the loose water from my hair. Then, I step out on the mat, reaching for a towel that's not hanging up on the bar.

"Shit," I mumble.

I open the linen closet to get a clean one, but I stop dead in my tracks. Because directly in front of me, arranged in the shape of a heart, are Lia's bottles of bubble bath.

~*~

I couldn't stay home. That was some messed-up shit fucking with my head. I consider heading to Max's Place to unwind, but halfway there, I decide I don't want the demons that manifest themselves in the quiet. So, I do a U-turn and go in the opposite direction—to pounding subs and loose women.

At the counter of The Underground, I order a beer and a shot. I've only been here for an hour, and I'm pretty sure it's obvious I'm over the limit. But Chris doesn't care and loads me up.

It doesn't take long for me to spot tonight's pain-reliever. She's a busty brunette, sitting a few stools over. Two empty shot glasses sit in front of her, and Chris gives her another.

Dressed in jeans and a simple black top, she's clearly not the party-girl type I enjoy picking up, but something about her draws me in. She stares forward, and I catch her expression through the reflection of the mirror lining the back wall of the bar. Her eyes are glossed over, and she's not wearing the layers of makeup the other chicks in the joint sport.

This girl is here for one reason and one reason only.

I signal to Chris to bring me my next round, then I get up and slide in beside her. She doesn't look at me, though, as she knocks her shot back.

"Another fireball," she says.

Chris pops the cap off my next beer, and I take a deep swig.

"Hey," I say.

She ignores me until her next shot is in her hand. Then she gives me a small glance before she downs it.

"Another." She buries her face in her palms for a second before she pushes her fingers through her hair.

"On me," I offer.

She cocks her head to the side, her dark hair falling over a shoulder, and studies me. Probably wondering if it's a line.

I hold up my beer. "I get it."

Her gaze drops for a second then lifts back up to me. "Thanks."

"No problem."

With a finger, she rounds the rim of her new glass, staring at it.

"You don't want to drink it," I say, my eyes flitting up to her.

She doesn't look at me. "Don't I?"

"Nah. It won't fix anything."

"Really?" She nods at my bottle. "And that will?

I shake my head. "Nope. It's not magical."

"If that's true, why're you here?"

"Because sometimes being numb is the best answer I've got. Better than feeling the pain."

"Does that work?"

"For a little while. Until it wears off."

A little smirk appears on her face. "And then what?

I inhale deeply. Blow it out slow. "Then you have to face reality and hope it doesn't kill you."

Quiet, she finally shifts her eyes to meet my gaze. "You seem to have lived."

I reach across her and pick up her drink. "This, baby, isn't living. This is surviving," I say, repeating Kate. I down it, no longer feeling the burn as it coats my throat. "What I do know is that it's easier when you're not alone."

"That's good, because you owe me another drink."

I laugh. "How about we skip the drink and move on to other activities."

The girl's eyebrows shoot up. "You asking if you can take me home with you?"

"Misery loves company."

"You've done this before," she says, and it's not a question.

"What can I say? I'm a survivor."

She sighs, considering my offer. By the looks of her bloodshot eyes, she's a lightweight and probably a good girl. My guess is that she's never done anything like this before.

"All right," she says, picking up her purse. "Show me how to survive this."

I lead her through the club, my hand on the small of her back. We move slow since she's having a hard time walking. Five fireballs, to my knowledge, is all she's had. But she knocked 'em back one after the other.

I get her to my car, and she slides in. I shouldn't be driving, but when's that ever stopped me? Except when I was with Kate. Her pleading eyes when she asked me not to drink and drive always, always guts me when I leave the bar.

And tonight, Ellie's disappointed gaze joins Kate's in my mind. All those times, though, Ellie never said a word about it. Until our last night together.

That's the look I see in my mind now. The tortured one I didn't notice then because I was too busy drowning in my own sorrow to notice hers.

On the way to my house, the girl beside me says nothing. She fidgets with her hands in her lap as she watches the world pass by out the window. I wonder if she'll renege on her decision to come with me.

In the garage, I open the door for her. She never offered her name, and I'm not going to ask. Names make shit personal.

She stumbles over the step. I wrap an arm around her and walk with her into the kitchen, then to my bedroom.

I don't bother with the light. The girl follows me in, and I lock the door behind her. In the glow of the moonlight creeping in through the window, I see her purse her lips. She stares at my bed, probably thinking that if she's going to back out, now is the time.

I stand behind her. Smooth my palms over her shoulders. Her purse falls to the floor, and her whole upper body lifts as she inhales. Slowly, she faces me, and I half expect her to ask me to take her home.

She doesn't say anything, though. Instead, her fingers fumble with the buttons of my shirt. Usually, I don't let girls do this, but for some reason I let her. One at a time, they pop free, and I roll my shoulders back so the shirt falls to the floor.

"My turn," I say.

I skim up her sides until I have her arms above her head. Then I work my way down, grazing the

270

sides of her breasts as I go. I don't pause to enjoy them. That's not what tonight is about.

At the bottom, I grab the hem and pull the shirt off her. I toss it behind me. Her skin is cool under my touch, and I feel the goosebumps poking up all over it.

I circle my arms around her and unfasten her bra. She shivers against me, but doesn't lean in. Warm breath pours over my chest as she exhales.

I back her up to the edge of the bed. Finally, her eyes open and they lock onto mine. Even in the dark, they're familiar because they're the same eyes I see when I look into the mirror. The same ones I peered into for two years with Ellie.

Pain-filled, hurt, and desperate.

Hers is new pain. Fresh. And it's breaking her down. Soon, it will tear her up and leave a gaping hole in her heart that nothing, *nothing*, will ever be able to fill.

Even drunk off my ass, it doesn't feel right to take advantage of her. It never does, but I push through it like the asshole I am. I lower her onto the mattress and slide the black bottoms and panties off her hips. She doesn't move as I step out of my jeans. Hell, she doesn't even look at me. When her head turns to the side to avoid me, I know I should stop.

But then, she opens her legs wide for me. Inviting me inside to merge our pain and extinguish it until morning.

I glide my fingertips up the insides of her thighs. She lifts up a little to meet me. A puff of air leaves her lungs and exits with a soft gasp.

I'd rather not spend the time on foreplay, and I don't know if she expects it. I just want to get inside her and be done. Still, I can't do just *nothing*. It's better for me if her desire rises and releases with mine.

Between her legs, I caress, massage, and tease. There's no laughter or giggles or breathless bursts of passion. Only small movements of her hips as her body gets ready for me.

I position myself on top of her. I'm not thinking about how this isn't what I'd pictured for tonight. Or that this girl really doesn't want to be here. Or even that the whole reason I'm doing this isn't to wipe away Kate's voice from my head like is standard for me. I want the last eight weeks gone.

My gaze wanders over the girl under me. She's staring at me now, her lips parted and puffy.

"Please?" she begs, a tear dripping from an eye. "I don't want to feel anymore."

That's when it punches me in the stomach and knocks the wind out of me.

This girl isn't me—she's Ellie. After Liam died.

It's why I chose this girl. I'm not thinking about Kate. I'm thinking about Ellie!

I push my fingers through my hair. "This isn't what you want."

"You said—"

"I was wrong," I cut her off. "Truth is, you'll wake up tomorrow with another layer of pain to add to the one you already carry."

I hand her the clothes from the floor, turn away from her, and flip on the light.

"Sometimes it just has to hurt," I say.

Behind me, I can hear her get dressed. It takes her a while, and when there's no more noise I spin around. She's on her knees beside Lia's bed, smoothing her hand over the blanket.

"You have a daughter?" she asks.

I definitely don't want to go there, but the way her voice cracks does something to me, and I answer, "Yes. But she's gone with her mother. I don't know if I'll ever see her again."

The girl lifts her face to me, tears streaming like rain. "Why?"

"Because I messed up."

"Every parent messes up. Don't let that stop you. If you love her, fix things. Before it's too late."

I close the distance between us and kneel down beside her. "What happened to you?"

"Today, I buried my little girl. She was riding her bike outside. I told her a thousand times not to cross that road, but…but she did. And…" She sobs, dropping her head into her hands. "I should have…done something. She was only four years old, and now…" She looks up at me. "Don't lose her. Do whatever it takes, because you may never get another chance."

After I take her home and give her the number to a good therapist, I lie on my bed and stare at the ceiling.

I'm a fucking disaster, and I don't know what else to do. I typically only cave on the anniversary of her death, but tonight it's calling to me.

I dig out Kate's diary from under my bed. The box I keep it in also contains her hospital wristband, a lock of her hair, and the letter she wrote me.

I'm not looking for anything specific, just something from her. Something to keep her in my head and Ellie out.

January 27
Dear Diary,

This is crazy. I'm crazy. Not five minutes ago, I overheard Dad talking with Damian outside. He told Damian that he's part of the family now, which is great. Awesome. Spectacular. I mean, I love having him with me, beside me. I don't know how I'd make it through this without him, but...

What if I choose to not take the drug? I'm leaning toward that decision, and each time I think about it I can't wrap my mind around how this will affect Damian long-term. With everything he's already been through, how can I add to it?

Even so, he has to let go of his mother and Liam. Move on from the past. Make amends with his father, regardless of my decision. Because all the hurt, all the pain, all the anger he carries will kill him.

And I'm not sure he sees that.

But peace and healing can only come with forgiveness, and I have a feeling the person he needs to forgive the most is himself.

Only then can he move on. Find himself and where his heart truly lies.

Again, I may be insane—off my rocker, Grandma would say—but I think I can give him that. At least lead him to the pool. I can't make him drink.

This drug isn't a guarantee. I'm living on borrowed time if I take it. I'm living on borrowed time if I don't.

I love Damian too much for him to destroy himself after I'm gone. It's going to hurt, I can't stop that. It's the price we pay when we love someone.

We'll take baby steps, though, in the form of five wishes.

And then...

Then he'll have what he needs to let me go.

I close her diary and focus on the wall. That entry was her end game. Because she loved me. Because she knew someday I'd have to live without her.

"Oh God, Katie," I say out loud as I finally realize what she'd been telling me.

Those five wishes? They were Kate's gift. Her promise of always being with me is wrapped up in those five little wishes, and now I finally see them for what they are.

One: A visit to Mom and Liam's graves to drive

me out of the anger stage of my grief.

Two: Golfing in order to begin the process of fixing my relationship with my father.

Three: Watching the sunrises with her not only because she wanted to see them, but to remind me of what she said. That no matter how dark it gets, the sun always rises and starts a new day. The darkness is forgotten.

Four: Me graduating from high school, the first step in moving forward without her.

Five: To let her go.

These are what Kate left behind.

With me for always.

Chapter 26

Ellie

I can't sleep. Damian clouds my head, and my mind keeps sending me flashbacks of moments long gone and words I've tried to forget.

As I close my eyes, all I can see is his smile, both dimples pinching inward as those gorgeous blues I love sparkle in the glow of orange, yellow, and red flames. The memory overwhelms me:

Dr. Lowell had some charity event, and because they were giving him a special award in honor of Liam's service, he expected Damian to go—and Damian had asked me to go with him.

I did—reluctantly—but neither of us lasted an hour among all those people who kept telling us what a wonderful person Liam was. It had been a year since his death, and the condolences still weighed on us. Those people didn't know Liam like we did.

"They're just trying to be nice," I said, prying Damian's fist open and replacing it with my palm. I led him to a secluded corner of the ballroom before he could lash out on some unsuspecting member of the city council.

"It's pissing you off too." His gaze sliced into me, and I suddenly felt small under his scrutiny. "You know he would have hated this circus, all these shitty decorations, and the fucking award. He didn't give a rat's ass about this stuff. The only thing he wanted was to help people, not spend thousands of dollars to have these people parade about and pat each other on the backs on a job well done. This is bullshit, Ellie."

I glanced at my shoes, then looked up at him. "You're right, it does piss me off, but Damian, there's nothing we can do about it. The money is spent. The people are here. The award will be given."

He twisted and scanned the room of tuxedos, evening gowns, and champagne. When he faced me again, there was a mischievous spark in his eyes.

"Maybe there is something we can do," he mused. "See the penguin with the beard and yellow tie over there?" He held me against him and I followed to where he nodded. "He's the organizer, and earlier I saw him put a trophy thing behind the podium."

"For Liam?" I asked, even though it was a stupid question.

"That's why we're here, right?"

"Okay, so then what?"

Damian smirked. "Then you and I can honor him the way he would have wanted."

"How?"

He leaned into me until his lips were at my ear and his warm breath was hot on my neck. The motion sent a chill through me. "You'll see." He slipped the valet ticket in my hand. "Get the car. Meet me at the front."

I immediately knew that whatever he had planned, I was on board. Sticking it to the man for Liam made me feel a little rebellious, and it felt good.

I did as Damian asked, and just as the valet rolled his black BMW to a stop at the curb, Damian was behind me and opening the passenger side door. His grin was devilish, and I couldn't help the excitement bubbling under my skin at whatever happened next.

He slid behind the wheel, closed the door, and pulled a glass trophy from under his jacket. "Piece of cake."

"Your Dad's going to know it was us," I pointed out, setting the award on my lap.

Damian shrugged. "Good. He also should know this whole shindig is a massive waste of time."

I wasn't surprised when we pulled into Damian's driveway. Or that he led me around the back instead of taking me inside. We were doing this for Liam, so of course our private event would happen outside in one of his favorite places in the world.

"Want to get your hands dirty?" Damian asked as he opened the door to the shed.

"I'm game."

"You might ruin your dress." Damian's brow quirked, and his sly grin returned. Clearly, he already knew my answer. And the way his eyes roamed over me, head to toe, I knew he had something else on his mind too.

"Do you care?"

His dimples deepened. "Not as long as it ends up on my floor tonight."

"I'm sure it will," I flirted back, and it was the first time I realized I *wanted* to be with him. Not because I needed to numb the pain or forget about Liam, but being with him, having his body against mine had my heart racing.

Damian disappeared into the shed and came back with an armload of firewood. "It's bonfire time."

I laughed. "Perfect."

I helped carry wood to the pit Liam built a few years ago. He even created log benches that circle the stone ring in the center. The two of us spent so many nights out here I'd lost track.

When we finished, my sleek mint-green gown was filthy and covered with snags. I wiped my hands on the satin while Damian placed the award on top of the pile. He stepped back and stood next to me, admiring our work.

He picked up the can of lighter fluid. "Ready?"

"Light her up," I said.

Damian soaked the wood all the way around and tossed the empty can on the ground. Then he lit a match and held it up in the air. "To Liam."

I smiled, took a step closer to Damian, and threaded my fingers with his. "To Liam."

Damian threw the match. Flames erupted, reaching higher and higher into the sky. After a few minutes, I glanced up at Damian. The smile on his face was gorgeous, and I'd have loved to know what he was thinking. I didn't ask, though, because that moment was perfect.

Alone in my Florida bedroom, I open my eyes and the memory fades away. It isn't until now that I realize that was the night I let go of Liam and started to fall for Damian.

I pull the blankets to my neck. My bed has never felt lonelier.

My mother's words come back to haunt me. *"You can't give the two of them this time, rip it away, and expect him to be okay with that."*

There is nothing about this mess that has worked out like I wanted. I didn't intend to "rip Lia away" from him. I knew that once she was in his life, we'd have to figure out a way to keep her there, even from a thousand miles away. But now?

Now things are different. The mall fiasco screwed everything up, and I don't know what to do. I should probably stick to the plan. I moved to Florida to get away from Damian, move on with my life, and fall out of love with him.

Still, the knots in my stomach tighten as I consider the very real possibility that Damian is spending the day drunk off his ass with an equally drunk girl under him. Or on top of him.

I roll onto my stomach and slide an extra pillow over my head to block out the image. It's one I've seen too often, and each time my mind replays it, it tears me apart. I'm not sure if it's the thought of the girls who've replaced me or that I feel cheated on even though we were never together.

I can't lay here any longer, thinking about him. I get up, grab my robe, and stand outside Lia's bedroom door. Quietly, I open it and peek in. She has her favorite My Little Pony pajamas on. As usual, her blanket is tucked up close to her, but her thumb has fallen from her mouth. The duvet only half covers her, so I widen the door and tip-toe across the floor. I pull it up to her shoulders and kiss her forehead.

My little princess sleeps peacefully. She's already been through more in the last forty-eight hours than anyone her age should, and I'm so grateful to have her safe and home where she belongs.

I turn back the blanket I just put over her and slide in behind her. I fold an arm around her.

"I love you, Lia," I whisper, then snuggle up against her and fall asleep.

In the morning, I usher Lia into the tub. God only knows the last time she had a bath.

"Who did your hair?" I ask, untwisting the rubber band and combing through the tangled braid with my fingers.

"Daddy."

"Your dad did this?" I repeat, unsure if I believe that.

She heaves a sigh so loud it makes me giggle. She even adds a little eye roll to drive home her point. "Yes. He made me stand up for a million hours while he watched a YouTube video. My neck hurt real bad, and my head hurt too."

"Well…" I'm speechless.

"Do I have to put on a swimming suit?" she asks with her hands on her hips, her head tilted to one side.

Okay, I'm officially confused. "Lia, you're taking a bath. We're not going to the beach."

"Duh, Mom. I know. But Daddy always made me wear a swimming suit in the bathtub."

"That's...weird," I say, but in the back of mind I think it's kinda cute. "No swimming suit, Lia-Kat. Come on, get in before the bubbles deflate."

"Can we go to the beach later? Daddy bought me this swimming suit with a tutu on it, and I want to—" She stops suddenly, her lips pucker into a frown.

"You want to what?" I ask.

"To show you, but all my stuff is at his house." Lia plops down in the pool of bubbles.

"He said he'd mail your things to you," I inform her.

"Mail them?" she pouts. "Why can't he bring them to me?"

God, I hate this.

"Honey...I don't think that's going to happen."

She cocks her head to the side. "Why not?"

"Because he said he'd mail them," I repeat, and it's clear from her expression that she doesn't like my answer.

"I want to call him."

I figured she'd want to talk with him eventually, so I'm not surprised. I'm just not ready.

"Let's give it at least few days, okay? All of us need some time to settle down."

"I don't," she clips out.

"I do," I say.

She responds with a glare. Then she stretches out until the water covers her ears and she can't hear me.

Chapter 27

Damian

"See that little phone icon, there? You tap it to make a call to the person you're staring at," Dylan says from behind me.

"Thanks, dickhead. Now go mind your own damn business."

"Going to work. Later, man."

I stand up as soon as I hear the backdoor close. I toss my cell on the sofa, then grab a beer from the fridge.

At the cemetery a couple of days ago, I'd decided Ellie and I have to talk. Lia is my daughter too, and I don't want to lose her. I won't. And I need to hear Ellie's voice again.

When we spoke earlier this summer, I could hear her smile as she went on about her trip and the sharks. God, she sounded so happy. She even fucking laughed, and that's what I can't get out of my head. I don't want to either; I want more.

I take a drink and lean back against the cushions.

As far as I know, she's with that Blake guy, though, and I've done too much shit that can't be undone.

You see, when you're in the pit, the only pain you see is your own, and it's easy to project it on others. It blinds you as much as it rips you apart and isolates you.

I guess that's why they call it hell.

I pick up Lia's Twilight Sparkle from the end table. This little McDonald's toy bridged the gap between Lia and me, and I haven't been the same since.

After my daughter arrived, staying sober was no big deal. Hell, I went weeks without getting laid and I hardly thought twice about it.

My little girl filled my time, and I loved listening to the sound of Ellie's voice when she called and actually talked to me.

I was happy.

It's been almost two weeks since they left, and now I finally know what I want. I take another swig of beer and reach for my phone. It rings four times before Ellie answers.

"Hello?" She's quiet and acts like she doesn't know it's me.

"Hey, Elle."

She pauses, and I hear her bed creak as she sits down. "Hey."

"How's Lia?" I start. It's late and she's probably in bed.

"She's fine. She's in bed right now," Ellie confirms, and I smile, thinking about my daughter holding her blanket and sucking her thumb.

"Did you get the boxes I sent?"

"Yes. Thank you."

The small talk is killing me, but hearing her voice again is so worth it. Still, I need something more before we move on because I'm longing for it. "Good. Could you do something for me?"

"Depends. What?"

"Laugh."

Silence fills the phone line. "What?" she finally repeats.

"I want to hear you laugh," I say again. The request is strange and probably confusing for her, and her hesitation tells me she won't do it.

She sighs. "Is that why you called? Because there's nothing funny to laugh at."

I can't help notice the tone of her voice has the same studded edge she carried after Liam died. "Yeah, I guess not. Listen, um, I realize I fucked up this summer, Elle."

"Fucked up, huh?" She breathes out a scoff. "That's putting it lightly, don't you think?"

"I think everyone makes mistakes."

"Not everyone's *mistakes* puts their kid in danger, Damian. What would have happened if—"

"You don't think that's all I've thought about?" I say, my voice growing at her accusation. "I didn't think about anything else while she was gone, Ellie. Not a goddamn thing. I fucking sat at the police station doing nothing except worry about her safety and think about the fact I put her life in danger. So yeah. I know."

"You got lucky she wasn't hurt, Damian. You never should have turned your back on her for a second!" she fires back.

I lean forward on the sofa. "You're telling me you have an eye on her twenty-four-seven? That you don't glance away ever? Because I'm calling bullshit on that."

"I told you when you wanted to keep her that she was a handful, and you had to watch her."

I shoot to my feet. "If you didn't think I was qualified, then why the fuck did you let her stay?"

"Because I thought maybe it would be good for you."

I push a hand through my hair and lower my voice. "It *was* good for me, Ellie. That's what I wanted to tell you if you'd stop screaming at me for a minute. Yes, I messed up big time—I know that. But will you please give me a second chance? I can do better. I *want* to do better."

"You can't be serious. Damian, what the hell? Are you drunk?" The disdain in her voice stabs me in the gut.

"No, I'm not," I say calmly because she has to understand. "But yeah, I'm serious. Look, let me fly you both up here for Christmas break. We can talk, sort shit out, and—and—Lia can play in the indoor pool at Dad's."

The silence on the other end is deafening, and I hope to God she's considering my offer. It's far enough down the road for me to do what I have to do—show Ellie I'm responsible and can be a good father to Lia.

When she doesn't answer, I add, "I want to see my daughter again."

"You got Lia kidnapped, Damian. *Kidnapped*! What makes you think you deserve to see her again?" she snaps, and I lose it.

"She's my *daughter*, dammit! That's why!"

"You want to be a father *now*, Damian? After everything?"

"If we're going to play that game, what category do you think you'd fall under? You *hid* her from me for four years." It surprises me that I threw that in her face, but that shit needs to be dealt with.

"I *protected* her."

"No. You protected yourself."

"So what if I did? Isn't that all you're doing with the girls and the drinking and the visits to the cemetery? Sounds like the same song, different verse."

"Songs end, Elle. Give me another shot."

She doesn't answer, and I can guess by her muffled breaths that she's crying. It's like mental torture for me, so I try to explain another way.

"I want to be Lia's father, and not the kind that calls once in a while, sends a birthday card, and sees her every other weekend and half the holidays. I want to do it right, and if you give me the chance I'm asking for, I want to do it with you, Elle. The three of us—together."

Ellie sniffles on the other end, but still doesn't say anything.

"I can do this, Ellie. Please."

Finally, she sighs heavy into the receiver. "I'm only going to say this once, okay? I transferred to Florida to get away from everything there. To leave all that stuff in my past where it belongs." Her voice cracks as she continues. "And that includes you. I think it's best if…"

Fuck.

"You don't mean that," I say, and I know I'm right because she doesn't sound like this when she's confident. "Give me until Christmas, Ellie. I'll prove to both of you I can change—that I *have* changed. I've got a plan, and I want both of you to be a part of it."

"Because you love Lia?" she whispers, her voice breathy and heavy at the same time.

"Yes, Elle. I love her so much," I say, half-smiling because maybe I've convinced her.

A few silent moments pass before she says, "Thank you for the offer. It sounds beautiful, Damian, really. And a few years ago I would have accepted it in a heartbeat, but…"

I know what's coming; I can hear it in her voice. I back up against a wall. "No, Elle. Don't do this."

She takes a deep breath to hide how upset she is. "I'll send you pictures. Maybe after things settle down…you can call her sometime."

I'm shaking my head as she talks. "Don't cut me off, Elle. I'm begging you."

"I'm sorry. I have to," she murmurs.

"You don't, Elle. I can make this right, I swear to you."

"Damian." The way she says my name makes me wish I were there to hold her and make her understand. "It's too late."

"Don't say that. It's never too late," I plead, my own voice on the edge of a knife.

"I'm sorry," she repeats. Her voice is barely above a whisper, letting me know she doesn't really want to say what she says next. "Goodbye,

Damian."

"Ell—"

But she's already hung up.

I bow my head, gather the hair on top, and pull.

"Goddammit!" I yell.

Because, fuck—

I missed my shot.

Ellie

I end the call, hug the phone to my chest, and squeeze my eyes shut. I hold my breath to push down the urge to cry. I'd imagined him saying he wanted to be with us for so long, and I had to fight myself to not scream yes. He loves Lia, and I love that he does, but he's irresponsible. Loving her just isn't good enough, no matter how much I want it to be.

Still, I don't want to let him go. It hurt so much, but I had to do it. Hanging on to him was killing both of us.

I finally suck in air only to blow it out slowly. I've waited so long for him to become the man I know deep down he is. Now, it's time to let go.

The smart thing to do is move on with Blake. With time, I can learn to love him the way I want to, because he loves Lia *and* me, and he's already proven himself to be responsible.

I roll to my side and pull a pillow into my arms.

I did the right thing—

Right?

Chapter 28

Ellie

I feel a little better in the morning. Fantastic, actually.

Because I've made up my mind. I'm sticking to the plan—I'm moving on. I've tortured myself enough when it comes to Damian, and I refuse to do it any longer.

I'm ready to be happy, dammit. Past experience has taught me I don't find happiness with Damian, and I'm tired of living in those long-gone shadows. He needs to face his ghosts and fight his demons before he'll ever be able drop the weight he carries. Forgive himself.

Stop going to the cemetery.

And until that happens, I'm done putting myself and my daughter in his self-destructive path. I gave him a shot when I left Lia with him; he fired in the dark, and he missed. End of story.

"Mommy? Are you okay?" my Lia-Kat asks.

I look up to see her standing in the doorway to

my bedroom. Escaped hair pokes out from the French braid I put in last night.

"I am now. Come here," I say, holding my arms out to her.

She shuffles over to me, frowning. Then she stops just out of my reach.

"What's wrong?" I ask.

Blue eyes pour into me like honey, sweet and thick. "Do you think Daddy will come for us?"

"What do you mean? Like drive here to see you?"

"No, like come here and take us back home with him. So we can be a family." Her pouty face slices into me, and I hate the way it makes me feel.

"Oh, sweetie." I lean forward to scoop her up onto my lap. "Your dad...he, uh..." I trail off because I have no idea what to tell her. Anything having to do with Damian is complicated.

"He what?" Lia asks, blinking. Her long lashes partially conceal her irises the same way Damian's do.

"He's had a lot of hard years. You see, a long time ago—"

"Grandma and Uncle Liam died. Yeah, I know," she says, and the corner of her lips pulls to the side, revealing a dimple.

I don't even try to hide my surprise. "Oh. How did you know that?"

"He took me to visit them—and Kate."

"He did?"

She nods. "Hmm-hmm. He told me about the symbols on the gravestones, and Kate had a necklace he keeps on his dresser that matches hers.

293

He said it stands for hope, and when she got sick, she never gave up hope because she loved her family. She didn't give up on the people she loved."

"He told you all that?" I ask, amazed she remembers. Then again, I shouldn't be. She remembers everything.

"He loves us, Mommy."

"Baby, I—"

"We're his family," she says. "Like that girl, he won't give up on us."

I'm at a loss for what to say. That may have been what Kate was like, but Damian? Maybe that was true before he lost everyone.

But that was then and this is now. And now, Damian's going to break her little heart when he sinks into his same old pattern of letting pain control him.

~*~

I tuck Lia in and read her a story. One she's heard a thousand times but loves just as much as the first.

"Mommy?" she says after a yawn.

"Yeah?"

"I love you."

I lean down and kiss her forehead. "I love you too, sweet girl. Good night."

"Mommy?"

"Yes?"

"Did you ever love Daddy?"

I smooth a palm over her blankets. "I used to," I finally say. Then I stand up and walk toward the door, hoping our Q and A is finished.

It's not.

"Mommy?"

I turn around. "Hmm-hmm?"

"Will you again?"

I reach for her doorknob to buy myself a few extra seconds. "I don't know."

"Think about it, okay?" she says, and I smile at her grown-up tone.

"Okay. I'll think about it. Good night," I repeat and close the door.

After a quick shower, I lie in bed and skim through my missed calls. There's a handful of them, but none from Damian.

Since he called last night, I've thought about nothing else. Just hearing his ringtone and knowing his voice would greet me has my resolve shaking.

This moment reminds me of that one life-changing scene in the movies where the girl is at a crossroads. It's one road or the other; it can't be both.

Blake or Damian.

The regrets will be there, they always are. That's life. You live with them, learn from them, and get on.

And the funny thing is, I already made my choice, so it's ridiculous that I'm sitting here swaying once again. In fact, I made my decision a long, long time ago.

I tap on his picture and hold the phone to my ear. He answers right away.

"Hey, babe."

I smile at the sound of his voice. The sound of

Lia's and my future.

"Hey, Blake."

Damian

The first week of senior classes kicked my ass, and the second week wasn't any better. For the first time since Liam died, I actually have to study—sober.

It's a bitch too, because Ellie's in my head nonstop. I even sent Cassie packing a couple of weeks ago.

My efforts may be futile, but I'm not giving up yet. If Kate taught me anything, it's that there's always hope, and that little moment of hesitation when Ellie said goodbye gives me the sliver I need to hang on.

I know Ellie, maybe better than anyone, and I know when there's more she doesn't say. I used to wake up to her sobs, and a few times, they didn't come from beside me—they came from Liam's room. I never went in there, though.

I think of the time I caught her standing by the window in my bedroom.

Moonlight burst through the crack in the curtains as she peered outside. She crossed her arms over her chest and hugged herself. Wearing nothing except the white button-up shirt I had on earlier, she looked so sexy, and I was an asshole for wanting to take it off her and lead her back to my bed while she was crying.

She reached up and wiped a tear from her face. With the light coming in, I saw her bite her lip to hold back another sob. It didn't quite work, though, and she buried her face in her palms.

I promised Liam I'd take care of his girl, so I threw on a pair of boxers and walked over to her.

"Thinking about Liam?" I asked, because I didn't know of any other reason why she'd be upset.

Her attention snapped to me like I startled her. "Did I wake you?"

"Yeah. What's wrong?"

She hugged herself tighter, and part of me wanted to pull her against me. I didn't though, because that was too intimate for the relationship we shared.

"Nothing. I couldn't sleep." She didn't look at me when she said it.

"Right. Well, I'm awake now," I said, and reached out to unbutton her shirt. "I can help you sleep."

On instinct, she stepped back a little. Then stopped herself. "I'm not sure if it will."

"Oh yeah? It always has before."

Her lips trembled, and she averted her gaze from me. Her hair covered her face as she wiped her eyes. When she returned to me, she gave me a tiny smile.

"Maybe I should just go."

I shook my head. "Not until you tell me what that was all about."

She stared at me, not saying anything. Pain flashed in her eyes, and I was close to walking away from her so I didn't have to see it.

"What are we even doing, Damian?" she finally said.

"Being there for each other," I said, not sure where she was going.

"No, not right now. This whole thing, this...relationship between us."

"You want out?"

She hesitated. "No."

"Then I don't know why we're having this conversation." I slipped my hands under her shirt and glided them up her waist. She shivered under my touch, so I undid the rest of the buttons and slid the material off her shoulders. Circled my arms around her and brought her into me, skin on skin.

I kissed the nape of her neck, and she tilted her head to let me. She swallowed against my mouth.

I cupped her face in my palms. "Close your eyes," I instructed, and she obeyed. Slowly, I brought her lips to mine and kissed them. "If you need a reason, Elle, it's because we understand each other. Because when we're together, we're whole."

I pull a hand through my hair and gaze over the pile of textbooks on my bed. Somehow, I need to get cracking. I have a ten page paper due at nine in the morning, and if by any miracle my plan to get Ellie and Lia back in my life is going to work, I can't fail this class.

Chapter 29

Ellie

Blake didn't push me when he returned. In fact, on the outside, life seemed to go back to normal as if the summer never happened.

Blake takes Lia to the park or to the beach while I work, and the three of us fall back into our standing Friday night dates at our favorite pizza parlor, the one that serves the most amazing ham and pineapple pizza.

Other than stolen glances in each other's directions, we slipped into a semi-platonic relationship. Not what we had before Australia, though, because after sex, there's no going back to being "just friends."

It works because I'm not ready to dive headfirst back into things with him even though I made up my mind that Blake's the one. Not while Lia's hung up on Damian.

My professor let me do a short stint with another research group studying the migration of bull sharks off the coast of the Gulf of Mexico. Between the two, she gave me full credit, and I have enough notes to finish my thesis.

So, at the start of fall semester, I keep my mind busy, working non-stop on the paper that's bound to take up most of my life. Blake holes himself up in the library or in his apartment writing his as well, and we only emerge during the weekends or for three a.m. Starbucks runs to compare notes.

It's a decent distraction, except I'm not sure how long it will hold.

Talk of what happened between us at Cairns, for now, has been drowned out by statistics, graphs, and temperature patterns. Talk of Damian, however, resumes each night when I tuck Lia in.

"Did he call today?" she asks.

I lift the covers up to her chin. "No, sweetie. He didn't."

"Do you think he lost our phone number?"

"I don't know," I answer, and the thought of him deleting it leaves a pang of emptiness in the pit of my stomach.

"I want to call him tomorrow," she decides, crossing her arms over her chest.

"Lia…" I've run out of excuses for why we can't, and I'd prefer not to lie. Cutting him off cold turkey like I did last time is the best option. We'll both get over him quicker.

Besides, I told him goodbye, and he seems to have actually listened—which is a first for Damian. It's strange since he wants so badly to be a part of Lia's life, but I haven't heard a peep from him since.

And I can't decide if I'm okay with that or not.

"Lia," I say again, sliding two fingers down a tendril of her hair. "Damian's back in school right now too. He's busy."

She blinks, thinking. "Then I'll leave a message, and he can call back when he's not busy."

I smile at her rationality. "We'll see, all right?"

"All right, Mommy," she concedes.

"Story time?"

Lia gives me a My Little Pony book Damian bought her over the summer. He'd packed it at the very top of one of the boxes he shipped to us. She squealed in delight when she saw it, and we've been reading from it every night since.

"Again?" I ask her.

"Yes, please. It reminds me of Daddy."

I lie down beside her and read. Lia's head rests against my shoulder, and when I say "The end," she's already asleep. I close the book, slowly sneak out from under her, and make sure the blankets are in place. She shifts a little before settling into her pillow.

I kiss her forehead and switch off the lamp. "Good night, my Lia-Kat."

Softly, I shut her door behind me. I'm exhausted, but I should stay up for a few hours to work on my paper. I grab the laptop off my bed and sit in the kitchen with a cup of hot tea. Notebooks, reference books, and loose paper clutter the table in no time.

I have six internet tabs, two Word docs, and a spreadsheet open on my computer. I switch back and forth between them and reach for the hard copies to cross-reference.

But after an hour, I've only typed half a sentence, and I'm not even sure it's accurate information. I can't concentrate with thoughts of Damian rolling through my mind. Without thinking, I grab my phone and find his number. Then I stare at it like the digits themselves will tell me what he's doing and who he's with.

"You made this bed, Ellie, now lie in it," I tell myself out loud.

Da, dum. Da dum. Da dum. Da dum, dadum, dadum, dadum.

The theme from *Jaws* sounds from my phone, startling me. Before it grows in intensity, I answer it.

"Hi, Blake," I say.

"Lia in bed?"

"Yeah, an hour ago."

"Working, then?"

"Trying to," I reply, picking up a notebook and flipping through it as if I'd been hard at work when he called.

"Want some company? I'll bring Starbucks," he sweet talks in my ear.

Ah, Starbucks.

"Extra foam?"

"Double shot, just how you like it."

"You've got a deal," I say.

"Great. See you in twenty."

Twenty minutes later, Blake knocks on the door. "I come bearing gifts."

"I love you," I breathe out and take the latté from him. Not until after I've taken a sip and he's staring at me do I realize what I said. I swallow and

302

nervously lick my lips. "Thanks for this," I clarify.

"Anytime," he says, his eyes drifting over me the way they did in Cairns.

"So," I say to break the tension, "how's yours coming along?"

"Blood sample comparisons were a bitch, but I managed. You?"

"Slow," I admit. "I don't have the final reports for the Reef Study, and I need them to analyze body and water temperatures."

Blake nods. "Yeah, uh, Hannah said she'd send them by the end of this month, so…"

"Oh, good." I shift my weight and avoid meeting his gaze. As I do, I realize the only thing he brought with him was my coffee. "No laptop tonight? Makes it kind of difficult to work."

"Yeah, about that. I was hoping we could talk."

"Right," I say, nervous because my guess is he doesn't want to talk about school. "Um, let's sit on the sofa."

Blake follows me to the tiny living room. I curl up on one end of the sofa, legs tucked under me, and Blake sits beside me. With both hands cupped around the warm Starbucks cardboard, I take another drink to calm my growing anxiety.

"When you left Cairns, you said you wanted time," he says. "It's been three months, Elizabeth."

"I know," I answer. I let out a breath before I continue. "Look, Blake, I…I *have* thought about things. And for a while, I thought I had it all figured out, but then…I don't know. Lia grew pretty attached to Damian, and…"

"Are you in love with him?"

"What?" I say too loudly. "Sorry, I…why would you ask that?"

Blake leans forward, his elbows sitting on his knees. "Lia."

"Lia? What do you mean?"

"She said that Damian loves you."

"That's ridiculous, Blake," I say, waving it off.

"Is it?"

"Yes, of course. We have a history, but that's all."

"I'm not blind, Elizabeth. I've watched you tense up every time Lia mentions him, and I've seen you get that happy little puppy-love gleam in your eyes when you answer. That 'history' you have seems to run deeper than you let on. To be fair, I think I deserve to know what's going on. What was there between the two of you?"

I lift my face to the ceiling, push a hand through my hair, and sweep the loose strands to one side. The past is the last place I want to go again tonight.

I drop my arm and peer over at Blake. "What was between us? Pain. A lot of pain."

Blake clenches his jaw. "And what? Lia was born from the tears?"

I hesitate. "Actually, yes. Damian's tears, not mine. Because by that time, mine had run dry."

Blake is quiet, carefully studying me. Waiting.

"Before Damian, there was Liam—Damian's brother. We were together for all four years of high school, had plans of getting married. But then he was killed in a car accident, and I ran to Damian, the only other person I knew who shared my pain. He starting drinking and doing other things, but together, we mourned, we cried—we survived.

"And then Damian found someone. A girl who had cancer. He eventually lost her too, and we conceived Lia the night of Kate's funeral when Damian was at his most broken."

I take a deep breath before I continue. "I left Iowa because of Damian, Blake. Because I couldn't stay there and watch him destroy himself again. Because…" I break our connection when the sting of emotion burns my eyes.

Blake brushes the hair away from my face in time to see a tear slide down my cheek. With a thumb, he wipes it off, but I can't face him.

"Because you loved him?" Blake asks.

All I can do is nod.

"And now? Do you still?"

I don't want to answer this question. If I say it out loud, I can't take it back.

I bite my lip, squeeze my eyelids shut.

Blake is on his knees in front of me. He cups my face, forcing me to look at him. "Do you love him, Elizabeth?"

Slowly, I feel myself nod. "Yes. Yes, I love him." Hearing myself say the words makes them more real than the pain illuminating Blake's eyes. "I'm sorry, Blake. I'm so sorry."

Blake leans back, his touch falling away from me.

"Blake," I repeat when he doesn't say anything.

Silence stretches out the distance between us, and that earlier emptiness in my stomach expands. Suddenly, I'm cold.

I don't know how long we sit there, avoiding

each other. Time always lies in these situations.

Finally, Blake eases up off the floor. His gaze meets mine again, his brilliant brown irises duller than I've ever seen them. He slides his hands in his pockets like he's holding himself back from touching me. "I'll pick Lia up in the morning and take her to the beach so you can catch up."

"Blake," I start. "I don't want—"

"Is ten o'clock okay? Then we'll meet you for pizza at six?"

"Yeah, sure. Thank you."

"See you tomorrow, Elizabeth," he says, walks around the sofa, and lets himself out.

Chapter 30

Damian

I'm swamped. Between homework, prep-classes, and upcoming finals, I don't go to the cemetery this week. I don't meet Dad for dinner, either. Hell, I haven't seen Dylan in three days because I've been camped up in my room and the damn library. But if I'm going to ace the MCAT exam next week, show Ellie I've changed, I've got to keep my head in the game.

"Another?" Daphne, the waitress asks, nodding toward my empty glass of whiskey.

"Nah, I'm good. Thanks," I say.

She doesn't leave though. Instead, she slides closer to me and wraps an arm around my shoulder. "Whatcha working on?"

I'm at Max's for a change in scenery. And with Daphne taking care of me tonight, I must say, the scenery is nice.

Her shirt is unbuttoned low enough to show her D-cup rack, and she's all over me. Oddly enough,

I've only tapped this girl once, and that was a year ago. After that she got herself a boyfriend and has been off the market—until now, apparently.

I float my gaze up her body, enjoying every curve, dip, and show of bare skin.

"I have a big exam tomorrow morning," I say, unable to keep my eyes on hers with those sweet-ass tits—one hundred percent natural, by the way—in my face.

"Oh yeah?" Daphne sits down beside me and crosses a leg over mine. Her short skirt rides up her thigh as she does it. "Is that why you're a one-drink man tonight?"

I can't help myself; I graze my fingers over the inner thigh that's on top of me. Soft. Smooth. Hot.

"Something like that," I say.

Daphne grins and tucks her lower lip between her teeth in a moan.

I watch her eyelids close as I move further in between her legs. She rolls her hips toward me so she can open herself up more. It's not much, but it's enough to find out that she's wearing crotchless panties.

And she's already wet.

I glance at my laptop. Organic chemistry or Daphne?

Uncomfortable, I reach down to adjust my hard-as-granite dick, but Daphne's hand makes it there first.

"I can take care of that for you, Damian. However you'd like me to," she whispers in my ear, her breath warm on my neck.

Holy fuck.

308

I've been so focused on school—on Ellie—I haven't been laid in forever. Last time, I was with Cassie for three days straight after Ellie and Lia left. In an effort to earn Ellie and my daughter back, though, I've taken more cold showers than any man should have to.

Right now, I'm dying for a good fuck, so it surprises me when I say, "Not tonight, Daphne."

In response, she cups me a little harder. "You sure about that? 'Cause I can make it worth your while."

"Oh, trust me, I know. But I can't." I pull away so I'm no longer touching her.

"Daphne!" Max hollers from the bar.

"Duty calls," she says. Then she licks my neck up to my jaw. "You know where to find me if you change your mind."

"Sure thing."

Daphne flashes me a seductive grin, swings her leg off me, and stands up so her ass slides up to my elbow. She slithers her skirt down to cover her cheeks before she walks away.

I watch as her hips sway side to side until she disappears behind the bar—and wonder what the hell I'm doing.

I reach for my phone to remind myself. Turn it on and stare at the goofy chocolate milk smile grinning back at me. Then I swipe through until Ellie's picture fills the screen.

Yeah, I gotta get out of here before Daphne comes back and breaks me. I gather my stuff and dump it in my bag.

I need a good night's sleep. Tomorrow is a big

day.

~*~

"Cheers, dude," Dylan says, holding up his cheap beer. "It's over."

I do the same. "That was one helluva a test."

"Damn straight."

I'm beat. The exam robbed me of all the brain energy I own, and then some.

"How long until our scores arrive?" Dylan asks.

"Four weeks, give or take," I answer, killing half the bottle in one swig. "Until then, we have finals to keep our asses busy."

Dylan grins at me in fatherly sort of way. I cringe, thinking he's going to go all Freud on me again.

"What?" I ask.

"I'm proud of you, man."

"Oh shit. Don't lay down an estrogen blast on me, dude."

Dylan laughs. "Wouldn't dream of it. Just—"

"Yeah, I know," I say. "Bottoms up."

We knock back our beers and grab another.

"I can't think tonight," Dylan admits and tosses me an Xbox remote. "We've earned it."

"I couldn't agree more."

~*~

Ellie

I'm drowning, and I don't know how to come up for air. Since admitting to Blake I'm in love with Damian, the emotions I worked so hard to control have barreled to the surface. Damian fills my every waking thought. Memories sideswipe me, overtaking me until I break down.

But I fight it.

I have to. Damian was right—he's not cut out to be a father. No matter how much my heart longs for him, I have to do what's best for Lia. Even so, I'm dying to call him. I won't, of course.

Besides, what would I even say? I screamed at him last time, blamed him for everything and conveniently ignored how I carry some guilt too. Maybe if I'd have told him about Lia in the first place, none of this would have happened.

I look up at the pictures of her on the wall. In a straight line, there's eight total—one taken every six months of her life, starting the day she was born. God, she was such a tiny thing, just over six pounds. I remember when the nurse gave her to me how worried I was that I'd break her.

I didn't know anything about being a mom back then. I called my own more often than I'd like to admit because I didn't have a clue what I was doing. But I grew up. Learned how to be a parent by experiencing it, and I realize now that I robbed Damian of the same opportunities over the years. Technically, his unrefined parenting skills are on me.

I stare at the Christmas tree box in the corner.

Blake's going to help put it up this weekend. I take a sip of chardonnay. *Home for the Holidays* plays from the iPod, and it crosses my mind how nice that would be. There's nothing like a white Iowa Christmas.

Damian's offer to fly us up rings loud in my ears. What's the worst that can happen if I say yes?

Either way, I need to get control of myself first. The sooner, the better too. Because if I don't, I'll sink to the bottom of this whole mess I created.

Chapter 31

Ellie

"Can we put a star on top instead of the angel?" Lia asks.

"Let me see what I can find," Blake says, rummaging through the one tote of Christmas decorations I own. "All I see is an angel."

Lia's shoulders slump. "An angel is fine, I guess."

Blake grins at me and I toss him a shrug. "How about I find a star for next year?" he asks her.

She places an index finger over her lips. "Hmmm. Deal." She sticks out her hand, and Blake shakes it.

"Okay, let's get this angel on top, and I think we're done," he tells her.

The tension between Blake and me has eased in the last weeks. It's had its repercussions, though. Blake spends less time here. He doesn't call unless it has something to do with Lia. When he comes over, he actually knocks on the door, and he never

313

falls asleep on my sofa anymore. When it comes to me, you could fit three couples between us most of the time.

"You staying for a movie tonight?" I ask. It's been tradition that when we put up the tree, we drink hot chocolate and watch *Miracle on 34th Street*.

Blake glances at Lia, then back at me. "I actually can't. I have other plans."

"Oh," I say, and I'm sure I'm not hiding my surprise well. "It's okay."

"No, it's not," Lia says, stepping closer to him.

"Lia," I warn.

"No, Mommy. Blake *always* stays with us tonight."

"Sweetie," I start, but Blake interrupts, reaching out to Lia. "I'm sorry, little Lia. I kind of forgot that we were doing this tonight."

"Then cancel your plans," she says with a pout.

"I can't, but I'll see you tomorrow, all right?"

"At the art center?"

"If you still want to go."

Lia studies him, her long lashes slowly coming together as she averts her gaze then brings it back up to him. "Yes, I want to go," she finally says.

Blake laughs. "Okay, then we have a date."

"Is that where you're going tonight? On a date?" Lia asks.

"Lia," I breathe out, and I'm not sure why her question bothers me the way it does.

Blake twists his head to me. He holds my attention a second before facing Lia again. "Yes, actually I am."

I'm not sure what I expected, but this definitely wasn't it. Four years of Blake hanging out with me, seeing only me, and now he's dating. I shouldn't be surprised, really. Just...it happened so...fast.

Blake kisses Lia's forehead. "I have to go pick her up now."

His eyes meet mine, but only for a split second. "Have a good night, Elizabeth," he says.

"You too," I murmur, but he's already at the door.

Lia wanders over and wraps her arms around my legs. "Mommy?"

"Yeah, sweetie?"

"I guess it's just you and me now, huh?"

"What do you mean?" I ask, even though I already know.

"Daddy left us. Blake left us. We're all alone."

I lower myself to the floor, pull her against me, and kiss her head. I don't say anything because there's nothing to say. I pushed Damian away. I pushed Blake away. So Lia's right—we're all alone.

Damian

The Underground is the place to be tonight. The parking lot is near full already. Finals are over, and it's time to break loose, knock back some shots, and lose control. Hell, I deserve it.

I've worked my ass off this semester, harder than I ever have. Not to mention the lack of drinking and sex. These last few months, I became my brother with all the studying.

Already buzzed from the liquor at home, I hit the bar first. Slide onto a stool and scan the crowd.

"What'll it be tonight, Damian?" Chris asks.

"Give me the hard stuff, man. Death wish."

Chris's eyebrows shoot up. "Are you serious? Do you *have* one?"

I smirk. "Play hard or go home."

Chris shakes his head. "You got it, man."

"Damian," a familiar voice wafts up from behind me. I grin as her arms circle my waist, one hand taking a slight detour a little further south. "Long time."

I grab her wrist and press her palm into me. She breathes out a laugh in my ear.

I spin around to face her. Cassie's hair is half up with strands falling around her face. She's wearing a strapless top and skintight black pants. I squeeze her ass, bringing her closer to me.

"Got any plans tonight?" she asks.

Cassie wasn't exactly what I had in mind when I came here, but I'm game. As far as I'm concerned, I'm a free agent, and Cassie is all sorts of fun.

"I do now," I say.

Her cherry lips curve up in sexy little smile. "Your place, three a.m."

"Can't wait."

Cassie shoots me a wink, and I watch that sweet ass sway as it walks away.

"Death wish," Chris says.

I take a drink, and it's damn good. The burn is exactly what I needed.

"Mix me another, man," I say.

"Dude!"

"Hey, I'm in it to win it."

"Or die."

I snicker. "Nah. Load me up."

~*~

Ellie

I'm doing it.

I realize this makes me absolutely insane. Straitjacket crazy, probably, but I can't take it anymore. I have to talk to him even if it means I'm crying myself to sleep tonight.

Lia's in bed, and I don't have much to lose because he's on my mind constantly anyway.

I can't believe I'm actually considering taking him up on his offer to fly Lia and me to Iowa for Christmas. I mean, that's why I'm calling him, right? To accept?

When he first pitched the idea, he said something about proving himself to us. Maybe he realizes he needs to let go of the past. Whatever it is, I'm ready to talk. Work some crap out and tell him to his face that I'm sorry for keeping Lia from him. Ease his conscience over Lia's kidnapping. I never should have put all that on him—it could have happened to anyone. Plus, if I go, I could spend the holidays with my parents for the first time since Lia's been born.

The last six years have been hard on everyone, and it would be nice to have a taste of what "normal" is like again. Back when things were simple and easy, and what I looked forward to most was Liam's white Mercedes MI 350 parked outside my house, waiting for me. Before life as I knew it shattered right in front of me, leaving me a shambled mess of the girl I used to be.

Damian's the same way, and the fact is, I don't blame him for the path he chose. Mostly because I chose it too, only in a watered-down form. But I also don't carry the weight he does.

I still remember the night he broke down and told me, though I doubt he remembers any of it. It was late, and he'd been drinking—a lot—when he told me.

Rain pelted against his bedroom window, the wind howling and shaking the panes. Hail knocked on the glass, but I barely heard it.

On his bed, Damian thrust into me again and again and again. Harder than he ever had. Sweat dripped from his brow, and his eyelids squeezed shut.

"Damian," I whimpered. "Please."

In answer, he gripped my butt to raise me a little higher so he could plunge deeper inside me. I stretched my arms over my head and clung onto his headboard for leverage. Planted my feet on the mattress and held my breath.

Panting, I turned my head to the side. Empty bottles of booze littered the surface of his nightstand. More lay scattered on the floor that I didn't see earlier when I arrived. Not that it would have mattered; I needed to forget tonight as much as he did.

I glanced back up at him. Bloodshot eyes peered

at me before they closed again. Pain was what we both knew, and Damian held onto his like he was afraid to let go. I got it, though, because I was there too—in that place where you struggled against every second wanting to be free and to be sucked in deeper at the same time. It was why I allowed what he was doing to me.

Thunder boomed outside, and a crack of lightning lit up the room. Damian's whole body glistened with new moisture. His fingers dug into my flesh as he dipped down to bite at my neck.

"Damian, please. You're hurting me," I said, but he didn't hear me.

Another bolt of lightning cracked above us, the first big storm we'd had since the accident two weeks before that took Liam's life. It was the reason I went there—so I wouldn't have to bear it alone.

Damian's groans told me he was close to the edge, so I tightened my grip on the headboard, holding myself steady. Right then, I decided when we were finished, I'd grab my clothes and crash in Liam's bed until the storm passes. Clearly, Damian was too drunk for me to get the comfort I needed from him.

His body tensed, and he pushed himself deep, deep inside me.

"Ohhh," I cried out in pain.

His moan drowned me out, though. Still on top of me, he breathed hard for a minute. He didn't look at me, and I didn't look at him. Then, without a word, he lifted himself up and got off the bed.

I pried my grip from the headboard and curled my hands into a ball. My arms and legs hurt, too, and I wondered if I could even stand.

I bit the inside of my cheek, searching the floor for my clothes. When Damian ripped them off earlier, he'd flung them everywhere. I should have known then that something was off.

I located my shirt and panties—one on a chair, the other at the foot of the bed.

Then I found Damian.

He was at the window, gazing out. Slowly, I sat up, careful to not disturb him. I preferred to make my exit without him noticing.

But as I went to stand, my legs gave out and I fell back on the bed. Damian's attention swung to me. Tears streamed down his face, and his eyes roamed over me for a second before he made his way to the bed.

"I'm sorry, Ellie. I didn't..." He brushed over the teeth marks on my neck. Then he gathered me in his arms, something he'd never done before. "I should have taken care of you like I promised. I should have..." He dropped to his knees and buried his head between my breasts.

I wasn't sure what came over me. Maybe it was his brokenness or that he was Liam's little brother, but I held him against me and let his tears drip down my stomach.

"It should have been me that night," he said. Even though he hadn't talked about Liam since before the funeral, I instinctively knew what he meant.

"It's not your fault, Damian," I said, running my fingers through his hair. "The storm. The roads were slick, and..."

"No, Ellie. You don't understand." He lifted his head, and all I could see was the overwhelming guilt in his eyes. "Mom didn't want to go out by herself, and Liam was studying for an exam, so I told her I'd go. But then…then Dad called to say he was with a patient and wouldn't be home until late. I was pissed at him. I said he didn't deserve a stupid cake for a birthday he didn't even show up for. I told Mom I didn't want to go with her."

Damian's palms slid down my body as he swallowed. "Liam didn't want her to drive alone. He didn't say anything to me when he left. All he did was turn his back and walk her out.

"Elle. They're both dead because of me."

Chapter 32

Ellie

I stayed in Damian's room that night. Holding him, comforting him until he fell asleep in my arms. He didn't mention it after that, and I never brought it up, but it's not something that's easily forgotten. However he dealt with the guilt, he never hurt me like that again.

I hug the blankets to my chest and bury my face in them. So much time has passed, and I've worked so hard to convince myself how much I don't need him.

These last years, I thought I was building a wall to shield myself. Each time I stopped thinking about him, and for every memory I pushed back, I stacked the bricks higher and stronger—impenetrable.

But walls crumble. Break down and leave what's behind exposed. I don't know how much longer I can hold my resolve.

Because right now, at this moment, I don't want to be without him.

~*~

Damian

I'm so fucking drunk and it's great. I shoot back tequila shots one after the other. By eleven o'clock, I've lost track of how much booze I've downed.

Tonight, I'm not thinking. I'm tired of that shit. Tired of the last six months with my mind on nothing except Ellie and Lia. I've been walking the line for them, but right now, I'm off the beaten path and loving the freedom a shit-load of alcohol can give.

The Kappa girl is working me over good in the furthest stall in the men's bathroom, but I'm considering bending her over the toilet because that would be even better.

I watch her because it's fucking hot what she's doing—her tongue gliding and licking all over me. Her eyes flick up and catch me staring. I grin, flashing my dimples to reward her efforts. With a mouth full of me, she does her best to counter.

I gulp down a swash of beer to keep my buzz strong.

"Want a drink?" I offer.

The chick pulls away from me, and I tip up the bottle for her. She sucks it down like a pro, leaving me dry.

She wipes her mouth with the back of her hand. "Thanks."

Oh hell yes.

"I can have a condom on in two seconds flat if you want a little extra fun," I offer.

Her finger circles my length, and she shakes her head. "Sorry. I'm already taken."

Before I can respond, she has me in her mouth again, moving faster and faster. She grabs my hips and pushes me into her.

I ride the sensation higher and don't even try to hold back when I'm at the top. I tip my head back as I release into her mouth, and Ellie's face flashes in my mind. Pale blue irises pierce into me.

My eyes fly open because I don't want to think about Ellie. She's the number one reason I found my way into this bathroom.

The moment's over. I zip up my jeans and walk out.

"Tequila. Double," I say when I get to the bar.

I shoot back the drink, but I know it won't do any good. Not if Ellie keeps making appearances in my head.

Suddenly, I'm not in the mood to party anymore. I pay my tab and go out to my car. Grab my phone from under the seat. I don't look at it, though. Ellie's thinking about my offer to fly them up for Christmas, she said, but she doesn't respond whenever I text her.

I'm not sure what I'll find, and neither option sits right with me. If the screen is blank, I might punch the window out. If it's not and she called while I was inside, then what the hell am I supposed to do with that?

I want Lia back. I want Ellie. But I hurt them both, and Ellie may never forgive me. Then again, after tonight…

Fuck, I don't know what I'm doing.

I turn on my phone and see two missed calls—both from Ellie.

Shit.

I'm wasted now, and she's probably already asleep.

I drive home, even though I should have called Dylan for a ride. I bypass the liquor cabinet and make a cup of coffee to sober up. Then I head to my room. Fall on the mattress and stare at the ceiling. My phone is still clutched in my hand.

Against my better judgment, the alcohol eggs me on, and I dial Ellie's number. I listen to it ring, hoping she won't pick up. But she does.

"Damian?" Her voice sounds tired, like I woke her up. Even so, it's the most beautiful thing I've ever heard.

"Hey, Elle," I say.

"It's, um…almost three in the morning. Everything okay?"

I laugh. "Yeah, I'm returning your call."

As soon as I say it, I realize how slurred it sounds. Ellie notices too.

"Right. Are you drunk?"

I shake my head even though she can't see me, giving myself a second to concentrate on what to tell her. "Had a few at The Underground is all."

"Oh, well I've been thinking about your offer to fly us up for Christmas, and…"

My bedroom door swings open, and I don't hear the rest of Ellie's sentence. Cassie stands there, wearing a floor length coat. I'd completely forgotten she was coming. Slowly, she unties the belt, and the coat falls off her shoulders.

Son of a bitch.

A fire-red lace bra accentuates her perky nipples and full breasts; it's paired with matching panties that give everything away. In red heels, Cassie saunters toward me, her hips swaying as she moves.

Her knees hit the edge of my bed, and the mattress sinks as she climbs up. On all fours now, she prowls up my legs. She straddles me, and the swell of her tits squeeze together in front of my face.

I'm instantly hard.

"Damian? Did you hear me?" Ellie asks.

Her voice brings me back, but I don't have a fucking clue what she said. I close my eyes to focus on her instead of Cassie.

Cassie unzips my jeans and starts dry humping me. "That...that sounds great, Elle," I stutter out.

Next thing I know, Cassie's sucking on my neck, and I let out moan.

"Damian?" Elle says, and I register the crack in her voice. "You're not alone, are you?"

I don't reply, and she's quiet for a second.

"Of course not. Why would you be?" Ellie answers herself with a sarcastic chortle.

Cassie giggles, her laugh slicing through me because I know Ellie heard her.

"Ellie—" I breathe out.

"Stop, Damian. Just...stop, okay?"

She's crying, and it's fucking tearing me apart. I shove Cassie off me and retreat to the living room.

"Ellie, listen," I try again.

"No. I'm done listening, Damian. I can't believe I thought..."

326

"Thought what?"

"It doesn't matter."

"It *does* matter, Elle. It matters to me." I'm forceful because I have to get through to her.

Cassie walks in and leans against the doorjamb and watches me. I turn my back to her.

"Stop calling me that," she half cries half shouts. "It doesn't matter because nothing has changed and nothing ever *will* change. Shit, Damian. You called me drunk and with some girl all over you. Who does that?"

"Why do you care so much about what I do?" I throw back.

She hesitates, and I imagine her biting her lip. "Because Lia—"

"No," I interrupt. "Enough hiding behind Lia. You've done that for four years now, and I'm not buying it. We didn't go through all the shit we've gone through without getting to know each other. So, I'll say it again: why do you care what I do?"

I hear her breathe on the other end, and with how long it's taking her to answer, my guess is she won't. Not honestly, anyway, because she's pissed at me.

"I don't," she says, and I know she's lying by the low tone of her voice.

I lower mine to match hers. We're opposites like that; when I speak softly it's because I'm being brutally honest. "She doesn't mean anything to me, Elle. I swear to you."

"She doesn't mean anything to you? Oh, that makes it all better."

"I haven't heard from you in months. What the

fuck did you want me to do? Besides, nothing happened, and nothing's going to happen because I'm sending her home."

Ellie sobs on the other end, and I'd do anything to take back this whole shitty night.

"Elle?" I say, still quiet.

No answer. I can still hear her breathing, though, and I'm surprised she hasn't hung up.

"Elle, please." I pause. The next words I'm about to say scare the hell out of me, but it's now or never. "I'm flying you up so we can talk. Because, Elle...I love y—"

Click.

I stand in the middle of the room and stare at the phone. Why do I keep fucking up?

Goddammit!

I squeeze the cell until I hear a crack, then I chuck it across the room at the door. I'm so pissed at myself, all I see in front of me is a haze of red. I walk over to retrieve my broken phone so I can throw it again. Instead, though, I slam my fist through the drywall.

Once.

Twice.

I get three hits before someone grabs me.

I don't think; I react on instinct. I spin around and land my fourth punch on whoever's behind me.

The haze clears, and I see Dylan hunched over and glaring back at me.

"Shit, Damian," he says, wiping the blood from his lip. "What is your problem, man?"

I glance over at Cassie, who's leaning against the doorjamb like she's bored, and back to Dylan. "I don't know."

"You need to figure it out, dude," he shoots back.

Cassie pushes out of the doorway and starts over like the whole thing was for her entertainment. She slinks her arms around my neck. "Come on, baby. That girl on the phone doesn't know what she's missing."

I bite my teeth together, my gaze locking with hers. She wears a seductive smirk and licks her lips as if to show me what I'm in for. But I already know.

"Yeah, I'm pretty sure she does, and I don't blame her," I say. I unhook Cassie's arms and step away. "It's time for you to go."

"Are you serious?" she asks, her eyes skimming over me.

"I'll get your coat."

She grimaces. "If I leave, I am *not* coming back."

As I brush past her, she huffs. Whatever.

Back in the living room, I toss her the coat. "You know your way out?"

She rolls her eyes. I don't watch her leave. Instead, I go back to my room and collapse on my bed.

Dylan's right. If I don't figure shit out soon, I'll lose Ellie and Lia for good.

Chapter 33

Ellie

I receive an email the next day, confirming two tickets with American Airlines to Des Moines in five days. Damian also arranged for a rental car. Too bad it's for nothing.

God, I was so stupid! I let my guard down for a minute, and Damian took the opportunity to rip my heart out. That's not even the worst part, though. The worst part is how bad I wanted to tell him how I felt. Because right before I hung up, he started to say the words I've only dreamed of hearing from him. Except, I don't believe him.

"Elizabeth? Are you okay?"

Blake's words pull me back into my living room. My eyes flick up to him.

He motions to the tape and scissors I'm holding. "You've been wrapping that one present for a half an hour now," he says.

I look down, and suddenly I remember what I was doing—wrapping Lia's Christmas presents.

"Yeah, I'm good. Just tired," I say, waving off my distraction. "I didn't sleep well last night."

Blake tosses me a glittery pink bow that matches the paper I'm using. He watches me, and I squirm under his gaze.

"I haven't wanted to pry, but uh, what's going on between you and Damian?" he asks.

I shrug. "Nothing."

He quirks a brow.

"I don't want to talk about it," I mutter.

Blake rubs his chin and sighs before he finishes wrapping his box.

Ten minutes later, I've done nothing but stare at the wall. Blake scoots beside me, puts an arm around my shoulder, and hugs me to him.

And I fall apart.

~*~

Damian

I haven't heard from Ellie. I've called a few times, but she won't pick up. Nor has she answered my texts.

Their plane is supposed to land at noon in two days, and I'm praying they're on it. Even if they don't see me, I want my babygirl to have a white Christmas like the ones I remember when I was a kid with snowmen, snow angels, and ice-skating. She'll for sure have it too, since the ground is already covered, and a fresh blanket is due to roll in tomorrow night.

I went overboard with gifts for her, all under the

tree at Dad's house. I bought Ellie a few things too.

"Damian?" Leslie says, rounding the corner into the nurses' station. "Your dad's in his office. He wants to see you."

I make my way down the hall. His door is open, so I let myself in.

He wasn't around when I arrived this morning for work, and one of the nurses said he'd been called down to emergency—that was a couple of hours ago.

He lifts his head when I enter. His eyes are bloodshot from lack of sleep, I guess. "Have a seat."

I do.

Dad peers at me for a second before he takes off his glasses and squeezes the bridge of his nose. I've known my father long enough to understand what this means.

"I don't know how to tell you this, son, but you're going to find out, and I'd rather it be from me," he starts.

I readjust myself in my seat as chills race over my skin, though I have no idea what he's talking about.

"Have you heard if Lia and Ellie will be up for Christmas?" he asks, and I'm confused because surely what he wants to tell me doesn't have to do with Lia.

"No, I haven't yet."

He nods, pushes a hand through his hair. "I admitted Olivia today."

"Why? I thought she was doing well. Chemo was working."

"It is." He hesitates. "Cancer is tricky, and I wish

we had something other than chemotherapy to treat it. Chemo comes with its own set of complications. As you know, it weakens the immune system, and—"

"Get to the point," I interrupt because I have a feeling I know what's coming, and I don't need the back story.

"Pneumonia."

Kate's voice slams into my head with Dad's diagnosis. She once told me cancer wouldn't be the disease that killed her. That more than likely it would be something a healthy immune system could have fought off.

And pneumonia? That's what killed my Katie.

"What are you going to do? Knock her out?" I ask, recalling his treatment for Kate when she had a virus.

"I hope it doesn't have to come to that. Olivia is young and on chemo for the first time. As of now, we're going to push the antibiotics and wait it out."

"So, what are her chances for recovery?" I ask.

Dad rubs his chin. "At this stage, fifty-fifty."

~*~

I have to see Olivia for myself.

I wander down the hall. Room 324 is at the far end of the corridor. Her parents are probably in there, and I'm not sure what I'll say. I knock, though, and wait.

The door opens, and a tiny woman with bags under her eyes opens the door. She squints at me.

"Hi. Uh, I wanted to check on Olivia," I say.

"How is she?"

The woman opens the door wider. "She's asleep right now. The nurse was just in here, though, and took her vitals."

"Oh, I'm not a nurse. I—" I stop myself and take a different approach. "Did Olivia ever mention a little girl she played with during treatments here? Lia?"

Recognition lights her face, and she smiles. "Yes. Olivia talks about Lia all the time."

"I'm Lia's dad." Funny how that came out so easily.

"Dr. Lowell's son, right?" she says. "The one who suggested Olivia keep a picture journal?"

I scratch my head, impressed. "Spot on."

"Thank you for that. The journal has helped my daughter so much. And I appreciate Lia's friendship as well. Olivia was upset when she didn't get a chance to say goodbye."

"There was a family emergency, and she had to go back to Florida with her mother." It's not a lie, but I hate the situation so much the truth feels like lead in my mouth.

"That's too bad. I hope everything's all right."

"Yeah," I respond so it's not awkward.

"Well, Olivia's been waking up every few hours. I'm sure she'd like to see you."

"I'll be back. Thanks."

When I leave, I don't go back to work, to the list of stuff Leslie has for me today. I have too much on my mind. I need to get away for a few minutes and figure out my next move.

The cafeteria downstairs is dead at this time of

day. The breakfast crowd is gone, and it's too early for lunch. There're only a few hospital personnel scattered throughout the room. I pour myself some coffee and sit as far from people as I can.

I dig out my phone and stare at the picture of Lia wallpapered on the screen. Her big chocolate milk grin never fails to make me smile. I hate that I haven't seen the real thing in over five months. Hell, I haven't even talked to her.

In my contacts, I find Ellie's number—it's at the top of the list. Ellie's coy little smile teases me, and I'd give anything to feel those lips on mine. Somehow, I have to get through to her.

My finger hovers over the green button. She hung up on me last time, so my guess is she won't answer if I call. I decide to shoot her a text.

> Lia's friend, Olivia, is in the hospital. She has pneumonia. Thought you'd want to know.

I wait, sipping on my coffee, for fifteen minutes. Ellie doesn't text back.

~*~

On my way back to the third floor, I pick up a bouquet of flowers from the gift shop. It's been a long time since I've done that, and I hope I never have to do it again. Not from a hospital. Not for this reason.

I check in on Olivia again a couple hours later. She's awake. Though her eyes are heavy with sleep, she offers a smile when I set the lilies next to her

335

bed. The resemblance between her pale skin and Kate's at this stage is striking, and I have to force back the image.

"Hey, kiddo," I say.

Olivia points to the corkboard behind me. "There," she says. "For Lia." Her voice is weak, and it's probably taking a lot of energy for her to speak.

Pinned in the center is a picture of Lia's favorite pony. Multi-colored, hand-drawn hearts circle Twilight Sparkle, filling up the page. A message to Lia is scrawled out on the bottom.

"This is beautiful, Olivia," I tell her.

"Mom...helped," she answers. "With the words. Tell her thank...you for me." Olivia nods at the notebook I bought her, laying on the table at her head. "Open it."

I flip through the pictures. The first is of a house. A big sun in the sky, birds in the trees, flowers in the beds out front, a swing set, and Olivia and two friends with huge smiles on their faces. I turn the page. Storm clouds roll in and cover the sun. Rain falls in around the house, and Olivia now lies on the grass, curled into the fetal position. Her friends are kneeling beside her.

On the next page, the sky is colored black. The house is on fire. Olivia is alone, her friends' feet are barely on the edge of the paper.

A lump forms in my throat, and I look at Olivia on the hospital bed. She nods for me to continue, so I do.

This picture is of a doctor's office. Dad stands in front of Olivia, frowning. Tears spill from Olivia's eyes.

The next is Olivia sitting alone in The Commons, her arms over her head. The walls are red with yellow eyes drawn on them.

"You're scared?" I ask, showing the drawing to Olivia.

She nods. "All the time."

Olivia drew her parents on the adjacent page. Her mother has a puddle of tears at her feet, and Olivia's dad is yelling. A large bolt of lightning rips down between them.

The next picture, I recognize because I'm in it. She drew The Commons again, but the red walls aren't as red, and there are fewer angry yellow eyes. It's the day we first met.

And then I turn the page and see Lia giving one of her ponies to Olivia. It's the only picture since the first that Olivia drew herself with a smile. That's not all I notice, though. In this one, the walls are a dull pink with only one set of eyes.

"And here? You're not scared anymore?" I ask.

Olivia takes a second before she answers. "I was always scared then. But less when I wasn't alone."

"Your mom was here," I remind her.

"Yes, but..." Olivia shrugs, and I think I understand. Kate said once that those around her could support her, but they're not the ones who have to fight.

"Cancer isolates you, makes you feel you're alone, right?" I say, and Olivia nods. "You're not alone, okay? Don't ever think you're alone."

Olivia nods again, but she doesn't look at me. I set the notebook back on the table.

"I'll make sure Lia gets this," I say, holding up the picture of Twilight Sparkle.

"Thank you."

Her eyelids drop, signaling her meds kicking in. I walk backwards to the door as I watch her doze off, her little bald head falling to one side.

I watch her for a full minute. Half of that time I don't see Olivia lying there; I see Kate. How even in this state, she radiated courage, strength, and hope.

Back when I took Lia to the cemetery, I'd thought about how much I wanted Lia to be like that too—to have those same qualities. But now, I realize she already does. My little girl gave Olivia compassion when she needed it most. And she didn't get that from me. No—

That came from her mother.

Chapter 34

Damian

Ellie and Lia weren't on the flight. I waited for over an hour, spoke with the airline—and called Ellie's cell.

No answer.

I drive home, pull out a bottle of whiskey, and don't bother with a glass. I uncork the cap and knock some back. Behind me, the door opens, but I have to look to know it's Dylan.

"You're here," he says, and I can't decide if it's a question or not.

"Yep."

"They didn't show." Again, I'm not sure if he's asking, but I answer like he did.

"Nope," I say, and gulp down a large swash of amber.

"Dude, I'm sorry."

"Yeah, whatever."

"Here." Dylan tosses today's mail in front of me. On top is an envelope with my name on it, from the

AAMC.

"MCAT scores," Dylan says, grinning like an idiot.

"You opened yours?"

Dylan's big-ass grin widens. "Thirty-three, man. Eighty-fifth percentile."

I pick mine up and rip it open. I could use some good news today, and a high score coupled with my almost perfect GPA would mean I could enroll in any medical school in the country...which is good, because I have one in mind—south of here.

Oh, and, a higher score than Dylan's would wipe that too-happy smile right off his face.

I flip the paper over. Stare at the score and about shit myself. I throw back another drink and look again to be sure.

Son of a bitch.

Impatient, Dylan yanks the mail from me and examines it. Then it registers. "Holy. Fuck. Dude. Thirty-nine? That's top one percent, man!"

I'm speechless.

"Oh come on, Damian. This calls for a celebration," Dylan says.

I agree with him. Except I'd hoped to be celebrating with someone who's not my roommate. Had Ellie boarded that plan like she was supposed to, this moment would belong to the two of us. Hell, the three of us, including Lia.

Now, though, I'm not in the mood.

"You go ahead," I say.

"A kick-ass score like that and you want to mope around?"

"Who said anything about moping?"

Dylan holds up the bottle of T. Rye. "I know you. Besides, tomorrow is Christmas Eve, so The Underground will be packed tonight. Let's go, have a few drinks—"

"And get laid?" I finish, smirking.

"Yeah, that worked out real well last time, right?"

I'd meant him since he never brings home chicks, but I can see how he'd boomerang that back at me. Fair enough.

"Do you want Ellie or not?" he asks.

"Dude, I don't know what more I can do. I hate to give up, but what other option do I have? She won't even talk to me."

"You know you deserve her silence."

"Not the point."

Dylan crosses his arms. The damn therapist is about to emerge again, though I guess I asked for it. "Quick question—you don't even have to answer—then we get out of here. Deal?"

"Ask away, Doc."

"Have you considered what all this has cost Ellie? 'Cause from where I'm standing, man, there's so much shit going on, even I'm dizzy. I get that you're pissed because Ellie's leaving you high and dry, but put yourself in her shoes. Lia is all she has and leaving her here with you for eight weeks was probably the hardest thing she's ever done. I'm not going to sugarcoat it: you're reckless, Damian, and Ellie knows you as well as I do. Maybe better. What she did—putting her trust in you for the summer with the most important thing she has— took a lot of fucking faith. And then you go and lose

Lia at a mall. If I were her, I'd be asking myself why the hell I agreed to let her stay. Mix that in with the history you two share, it's no wonder she's giving you the cold shoulder, dude. It's clear you guys share a whole lot more than just a daughter. So, now ask yourself: What are you going to do about it?"

Dylan's brows lift as if he's waiting for the light to flip on in my head.

It doesn't, though, because I have no answers.

I grab my keys from the counter. "That was more than one question, Dr. Phil. Let's go."

The Underground is alive. Partiers are dressed for spring break in Cancun instead of Iowa in the dead of winter. I'm cool with that. The more skin, the better, and the ladies tonight are showing a lot of it.

Dylan's on the dance floor, living it up. I gotta give him credit, the dude has moves, and the girls go crazy over him. He won't bite, though. Not until he's sure his ex is out of his head.

That's where we're different.

We've been here a while now, and I realize I haven't drank enough to even notice. Actually, I'm still nursing the beer I ordered an hour ago.

"Hey, baby," some girl says, leaning up against the counter. Dark hair falls across her eyes, and she sweeps it away. "You look lonely. Want some company?"

Pouty red lips curve up in a sexy little smirk. She

rolls the tip of her tongue over the bottom one as her gaze drifts over me, and she moves closer.

Normally this sort of thing turns me on so fast I'm ready to usher her out the door before she even finishes her line. I mean, the round swell of her breasts over the top of the strapless corset thing she's wearing is enough to drive any sane man crazy, but I'm not feeling it tonight. I only came because of Dylan.

I shake my head. "Nah, I'm good."

"Ah, come on. One dance and one drink?" As she says it, she walks two fingers up my thigh. "I'll make sure you don't regret it."

"Not interested."

I snicker to myself. I have no doubt she'd do what she promises; I'm just surprised *I'm* saying no.

She backs away, scoffing. "Your loss."

I don't even watch her walk away. I guess I'm not in the mood to wipe Ellie from my thoughts.

This is nuts and so not me. I'm turning into a fucking celibate here. All for a girl who's a thousand miles away and wants nothing to do with me.

I suck down a drink and sigh.

"What the hell am I doing?" I mutter.

The answer comes easily, and I blame the psycho bullshit Dylan smacked me with before we left. It all happened so fast. Finding out about Lia, her staying with me, feelings for Ellie surfacing, etcetera, etcetera. It was a whirlwind of crap I never expected to deal with, and now I have no choice. They're in front of me, staring me down like the silence in my car on the drive back from the airport earlier today.

It's deafening, and I'm neck deep. If I can't figure everything out soon, I'll suffocate. I need to get out of here. Go for a drive and clear my head.

I leave my half-drunk beer on the counter and push through the crowd. Outside, I slide into my car and take off.

It's not until I'm there that I realize where I am. I've only been out here a few of times, all of them with Liam. The neighborhood is more run down than I remember. All the houses have worn paint, half-hung shutters, and gutters that needed to be replaced fifteen years ago. Rusted vehicles sit in driveways and front yards.

I slow down and stop against the curb. A couple houses down is a tiny white house with crooked green shutters. One strand of red Christmas lights frames the front door, and a wreath hangs in the middle.

It's where Ellie grew up. Where her parents still live.

I'm not sure why I came here. Maybe to see if Ellie took an earlier or later flight and is spending Christmas with her family, but the only car in the driveway is Ellie's mom's twenty year old Dodge, and they don't have a garage.

Dylan's questions circle through my mind again. If Lia weren't part of the picture, would I be sitting here, wishing Ellie was inside?

Funny thing is, I'm upset. And I'm here. Not at the cemetery.

~*~

Ellie

It's Christmas morning, and everything about it feels wrong. Blake's not here like he's been the last four years. He's spending the day with his new girlfriend at her place. But that's not what gets me.

I'm happy for Blake. More than that, *he's* happy. I'm not, though. I'm miserable.

I wanted this year to be different. I wanted to finally be able to leave my past behind and forget it ever happened. Instead, the past is all I've been able to think about.

Damian in bed with some girl—

Who wasn't me.

I should have heard him out at least. He deserved that much from me, right?

But pride and pain got in the way, and I couldn't listen any more. I'm so tired of my own silence, Damian's excuses, and this tornado of bull we created that doesn't matter.

I sip coffee as I watch Lia shovel her breakfast in her mouth and eye the presents under the tree as if at any moment they'll sprout legs and walk away.

"All done," she says, her cheeks stuffed full of cheerios.

"Swallow."

She inhales deep through her nose and chews her cereal the best she can. I'm afraid she's going to choke and everything's going to fly out at top speed.

Finally, she sweeps her sleeve across her face. "Swallowed. Now can we open presents? Pleeeeeeeeease?"

Her adorable pleading eyes don't faze me. Much. But then she bats her eyelashes, and she knows she has me.

"Let's go," I say, standing up and grabbing my coffee.

Lia sprints the ten feet between the table and the Christmas tree. She plops down on the floor and rubs her little hands together like a maniacal super villain.

I get comfortable on the sofa, curl my legs under me. "Have at it, Lia."

"Yessssss!" she hisses out then grabs the package closest to her. The ones I bought her are wrapped in My Little Pony paper. She also has one under there from my parents and a couple from Blake.

When she's finished, she's surrounded by new books, clothes, and toys. Her hoard will keep her busy the rest of the day.

"Mommy?" Lia asks.

"Yeah?"

"There's nothing for you."

"Sure there is," I answer, smiling at the confused expression on her face.

She shakes her head. "Nuh-uh. I opened them all."

"Mine's not wrapped." That confuses her even more, and I laugh out loud. "My present is watching you open yours. There's nothing better than that."

Lia jumps up and throws her tiny arms around me. "Merry Christmas, Mommy. I love you."

I squeeze her. "I love you too, sweetie."

Lia pulls away, and instead of the toothy grin I

expected, she's frowning.

"Hey, what's wrong?" I ask. "No sadness on Christmas."

Lia heaves a sigh bigger than mine and swings her gaze to her stash of gifts. "I guess I thought…maybe Daddy would have sent us both something. I think he forgot about us."

I purposely didn't tell her about the plane tickets since deep down I knew as soon as I received them we wouldn't be using them. Instead of answering, I kiss her forehead, hoping that pacifies her.

It doesn't.

"Can I call him? Wish him Merry Christmas?" she asks.

"Lia—" My voice cracks when I say her name, because I want to hear his voice so bad too. We've made such a mess out of things. "I don't think that's a good idea."

"Why?"

"Lia, it's just not," I say more forcefully than I intended.

"Why, though?"

"Because. Just…because." I don't have a better answer, especially not one I want to give to an almost four-year-old.

"But—"

"I said no, okay?" I snap.

She glares up at me, tears filling her eyes. Then she runs to her room and slams the door.

Lia doesn't stay in her room long, though. Soon, she's back in the living room, playing with her new toys. Then, after a phone call from Blake, she's all smiles again.

Later, we enjoy a Christmas dinner, just the two of us.

"Can we watch my new movie?" Lia asks.

"Sure," I say. "Let me finish cleaning this up first."

When I'm done, I check the living room for her, but she isn't there. On my way to her room, I notice my bedroom door cracked open. I widen it and find Lia sitting on my bed, my phone to her ear.

"Daddy?"

Chapter 35

Damian

I avoid the den when I walk into the foyer at Dad's house. The room is decked out in Christmas decorations, and gifts brim out from under the tree for the first time in years.

I toss my coat on the chair in the corner and head to the kitchen. Dad ordered a feast from a local restaurant, but it'll only be the two of us for dinner.

"Guess we'd better eat before this gets cold," Dad says.

His eye catches mine for a second before I break the connection. I don't want his sympathy or an episode of *Wisdom from the Old Man*. All I want is to eat and go home. In silence, I help uncover the food. We fill our plates, pour a couple glasses of red wine, and sit in the breakfast nook instead of the formal dining room.

I take a drink of wine. It doesn't have much of a kick, but it's only for show anyway. I stuff a piece of ham and slice of pineapple in my mouth, thinking about how both Lia and Ellie probably would have preferred them on a pizza. I wouldn't care. In fact, I'd fucking enjoy it if they were here.

The sound of silverware hitting the china fills the room. We sip our wine, and when our plates are empty, we rinse them off and stick them in the dishwasher.

"You know, Damian," Dad starts, pouring himself more wine, "I'm not going to sweeten it for you—you lost Lia at the mall, and Ellie has every right to be pissed."

"Oh great. Thanks for the pep talk."

"But we're not perfect," he continues, ignoring me. "Things happen, Damian, and sometimes they're out of our control. Ninety-nine percent of the time when parents turn their backs, the kid is fine. You screwed up and got the short end of the stick. It could have been anyone, son."

"It wasn't anyone, though. It was me. It was Lia. And it was Ellie." I bow my head, not wanting to continue this conversation. But I go on. "It's not only that. I've put Ellie through so much, caused her so much pain."

"Damian, you and Ellie have been through more than anyone should ever have to at your age. After Liam died, you bent, and bent, and bent, but together, you never snapped. That's more than most people can say."

"Dad," I say, topping off my wine. "I fucked up too many times. I don't deserve—"

"Oh stop it. You think I deserved your mother? Because I didn't. The fact is no man merits the love of a good woman. Not me. Not you. Not anyone."

350

"Liam did."

Dad's quiet for a moment. "Maybe. But you know what I think your brother would say if he were here?"

"Stay the hell away from my girl?"

Dad snickers. "Let me rephrase that. What the *ghost* of your brother would say?" He doesn't wait for my answer. "He'd say if you love her, go get her."

I stare at the wine, thinking about how obvious I must be for my father to see through me.

"Do you love her, Damian?" Dad prompts.

"She's all I think about," I murmur.

"That's not what I asked. Do you love Ellie?" he repeats.

I ball my hands into fists, squeeze as hard as I can, then let the tension drain out of them. "Doesn't matter."

~*~

The nurses did one helluva job putting on a Christmas party in The Commons for the kids who had to spend the day here.

Dad needed to wrap up a few things in his office, so I volunteered to help with clean up after everyone had cleared out.

"Perfect." Leslie shoves a garbage sack into my chest. "Have at it."

"Wait. Where are you going?"

She winks. "Santa had a long night. Time to get him home and unwind with Mrs. Claus."

"Right. Merry Christmas to you too."

Leslie laughs as she walks out, leaving me with the after-party mess. I swipe up the wrapping paper, ribbons, and bows. Plastic cups and plates from off the tables and chunks of food from the floor.

I work my way around the room. At the windowsill, there's an unopened package with Olivia's name on it. Earlier, I'd asked Dad about her, and he said she wasn't any better. I guess that meant no Christmas party.

I tie up the sack, lean it against the wall, and grab Olivia's present. The hallways are empty now that all the kids are back in their rooms.

I knock softly on Olivia's door. When no one answers, I quietly push it open and step inside.

Olivia's alone, sleeping. I walk up to her bed, and her eyes open. A small smile spreads across her paled lips before she yawns.

"Santa left you something at the party," I say, holding up the gift.

"Open it for me?" she asks, her voice weaker than I remember.

"Of course." I pull a finger under the tape, snapping it. I'm not sure why, but I carefully remove the rest of the tape to avoid ripping the paper.

"What are you, a girl?" Olivia asks, and I chuckle.

"Okay," I relent. Then I tear the package open like I'm six again. I show Olivia the box.

"Shutterfly," Olivia says. "My favorite pony."

"Where are your parents?" I ask, even though it's none of my business.

"Work."

"On Christmas?"

Olivia nods. "Christmas is busy at the hotel."

"Oh."

"It's okay. They were here this morning. Did Lia come back?"

The day after Ellie took Lia back to Florida, Olivia had a chemo treatment. When she asked where Lia was, I told her that her mother had returned early and took her home.

"No," I say. Then to chance the subject, I point to her empty glass. "Can I get you anything before I go?"

"Yes," Olivia says, "I want to write on the wall. You know, in case I don't have another chance."

Everything in me screams to tell her she'll have plenty of chances, but experience keeps my mouth shut.

"Will you help me?" she asks.

"Sure."

I hold onto her as she eases her legs over the side of the bed. She's weak, and I doubt she's even supposed to leave her room. But she wants this, and I have no problem breaking rules.

She sits, catching her breath. Even the smallest movements exhaust her.

"Let me carry you," I suggest.

Olivia nods and points to the IV pole. "Don't forget that."

I pick her up, and she wraps her arms around my neck. I barely feel them, though. She weighs nothing. Olivia's slippered feet dangle off my elbow as I reach for her metal lifeline.

"You good?" I ask.

She nods again.

I walk her down the corridor. A few nurses stop to watch, but no one says anything. The Commons is empty when we arrive, and I switch the light on.

"Which wall?" I ask so I know where to take her.

"That one."

I follow her gaze to the one wall that's completely void of writing. The one with all the windows.

"You sure you're allowed to color on that one?" I ask.

"I think so. Someone else did."

I skim over the bare walls again and see nothing. "Where?"

"Behind the chair. In the corner," Olivia says.

It's the same area I first noticed Olivia last summer. Scooting the IV pole in front of us, I make for the chair. Slide it out of the way.

"Down there. I want to put mine next to it."

"Hang on," I say, staring at the familiar handwriting. I'd know this delicate script anywhere; I have a diary full of it.

I set Olivia down in the chair I just pulled out, then crouch down at the wall. I touch the words, imagining Kate in this very spot, probably in the middle of the night, leaving her mark in the same manner she did everything—subtle, quiet, beautiful. How did I miss this?

The stars never stop shining, but we only see them at night. The same holds true with us. It often takes the darkest moments in our lives before we can

354

glimpse the most beautiful light. And it's in that place, that instant, where hope is born. ~Kate Browdy

"I remember the night she crept in here to write that."

I don't turn around because I'm not surprised he's here. Something tells me one of the nurses ratted Olivia and me out to him.

"She'd stopped treatments, and her symptoms were beginning to weigh on her," Dad says. "I'm not sure how she got up here, but she did.

"I asked what she was doing, and she said she finally figured out what she wanted to contribute to the Hope Wall."

He pauses. "I wondered why she wanted it way down there, where no one would be able to see it, and she told me 'because it fits.' I'm not sure what she meant by that."

"I do," I say without thinking. "Kate said something like this once. That in our lowest times, when we're down in the pit, that's when we realize what we have."

Dad's hand lands on my shoulder. "She said she found light in you."

My phone ringing interrupts us. I pull it out and check the screen. Ellie's beautiful face peers back at me, and Kate's words on the wall swell inside me. In all of my darkest hours, there's been light, even if I was too damn blind to see it.

I close my eyes. Kate's holding my hand, and I hear her voice in my head, encouraging me. "It's in this place, this moment, where hope is born."

She smiles at me, and I pull away from her because I'm finally ready. Opening my eyes, I slide my finger across the screen and place the phone against my ear. "Hello?"

"Daddy?"

Chapter 36

Damian

"Lia," I breathe out, the sound of her little voice shooting into my chest.

"Merry Christmas, Daddy," she says.

Behind me, Dad helps Olivia write her message on the wall. I stand up and push a hand through my hair before I walk to the middle of the room. "Merry Christmas, babygirl. How are you?"

"Okay. Me and Mommy had turkey and cookies."

I snicker. "That sounds pretty amazing. I wish I was there."

"So, why aren't you?" she asks, and I can picture the look on her face as she says it. Those big blues digging in deep.

"Um, I—" Ellie probably didn't tell her about the tickets, and since I can't come up with a good answer, I change the subject. "What did Santa bring you?"

Lia doesn't answer me though.

"Lia? You still there?" I ask. I don't want her to hang up.

"Yes. But I asked you first."

I nod, amused. "Yeah, I guess you did." I pause. "Is your mom around?"

"Uhhhhhhh…" She hums into the phone like she's doing something she shouldn't. "Hi, Mommy," she says, clearly not talking to me.

"Who are you on the phone with, Lia?" Ellie asks.

"Daddy?" She says it like it's a question. "He wants to talk to you."

"You called your dad?"

"Yeah, here." Lia's voice sounds further away, and my guess is she's holding the phone out.

"Elle?" I say, in case she can hear me through the phone.

"Not now, sweetie. You talk to him," Ellie says, and a piece of me breaks.

Lia huffs when she gets back on the. "She said no."

"It's okay," I say. "Tell her I understand."

My daughter mutters the words to her mother, then to me she says, "Are you going to answer my question?"

I have to admit, I kind of love her persistence.

"Family is important, right?" Lia says, surprising me. "You said that girl—Kate—loved her family and wanted to give them the best. *We're* your family. Daddies aren't supposed to leave, remember? You promised-promised." She sniffles before she murmurs, "You promised."

Air is sucked out of me, and it takes me a few

moments to respond. "Yeah, I remember."

~*~

I help Dad take Olivia back to her room. She's whiter now than half an hour ago, and she seems to struggle with each breath.

"I should stay here tonight," Dad says, checking her over.

"Yeah, okay."

Dad presses the nurse call button. "She needs oxygen."

After that, everything happens fast. Olivia's eyes roll back into her skull, and her head slumps to one side. The monitor tracking Olivia's vitals goes off. The screen flashes, dropping numbers. Dad lays her down and unwraps the oxygen cord from the machine. One of the nurses runs in, and Dad barks out a medication order as he places the mask over Olivia's nose.

I'm frozen in place, watching it play out. Another nurse rushes in followed by the first. She injects serum into Olivia's IV.

"Come on," Dad mutters, his eyes glued to the monitor.

A moment later, the alarms stop, replaced by the slow, steady beeps of rising blood pressure, oxygen, and heartbeats. Everyone lets out a breath except me. I'm in déjà vu mode. Even so, Kate isn't the one who's on my mind.

I glance over at Olivia's coloring journal, and what she said about fear and being alone drives into me. I can delude myself all I want, but that's the one thing that clutches onto me tighter than anything else. Letting go of Kate, keeping my daughter, loving Ellie—I'm fucking scared. What if I can't live up to their expectations?

I walk behind the nurse and pick up the notebook. Sweep past the pages I already saw to the more recent ones. Olivia's alone, standing in The Commons. The walls are red again with even more eyes than before circling her. They have her backed up against the door.

At the top of the next page are Kate's words Olivia copied from the Hope Wall. Below, is what I guess is Olivia's contribution that Dad helped her with. *Fear is the darkness, and the longer you're there, the bigger it gets. Courage is the light, and light always defeats the dark. Don't let fear win.*

The last picture in the book is Olivia standing by the window, letting in the sunlight. Behind her, the eyes fade into the walls.

I look at Olivia. She has tubes sticking out of her, pumping medicine and oxygen in. And yet—

She doesn't seem afraid. She isn't allowing her fears to control her, and I realize now it's time to quit hiding with my tail between my legs and do what I should have done a long time ago. I slip out of the room and start down the hall.

"Damian?" Dad hollers after me. "Where you going?"

I spin around. "Home."

~*~

Ellie

I lean down and kiss Lia's forehead. "Good night, sweetie."

"Mommy?" she says, staying true to our bedtime routine.

"Yeah?"

"Why didn't you want to talk with Daddy?"

I sigh. "Lia, you're the one who wanted to call."

"Grown-ups are so silly, sometimes. You could have at least said hi," she pouts. "It *is* Christmas."

"It's complicated," I say.

"You love him. He loves you. How's that compicated?"

"Complicated."

"Whatever."

I sweep her hair out of her face. "Baby, it just is."

Lia rolls her eyes, and I laugh.

"It's not funny," she says.

I narrow my eyes into a Mrs. Potato Head version of an angry face. "You're right. Not funny."

Lia puckers her lips the way mine are, giving me a taste of what I must look like. When she does it, though, it's pretty adorable. I glare at her, moving closer, closer, until our noses touch. Then she breaks into a smile, her little dimples pinching inward, and throws her arms around my neck. I hold her against me and kiss her cheek.

When I let go, she waggles a finger at me as if she's my mother. "He wants to speak with you. That's all I'm going to say," she says in her big girl voice.

361

"Noted. Now go to sleep."

Lia shoots me one last dimpled grin before she rolls onto her side and sticks her thumb in her mouth.

I slide under the covers of my own bed and lie awake. I rotate onto my stomach, then to my right side. Left side. To my back again.

I'm slipping. Years of being strong, of holding back, and I can't do it anymore. My train of thought is flirting with danger, but I don't care.

The bed's too big. Too cold. And I realize what I've always known: there's only one person who can make it warm.

I'm tired of breathing without him.

I grab for my phone and dial Damian's number from memory. Voicemail picks up immediately, and my heart sinks.

"You know the drill." *Beep.*

Damian

I'm still on hold, and it's been fifteen minutes. Online, all the flights say they're full for the next two days, and I'm not waiting that long. Fuck, I don't want to wait another minute.

"Sir?" the lady answers.

"Yeah?"

"I can get you on the ten-forty-five in business class, direct to Tallahassee."

I check the clock: nine thirty-six.

"The next available won't be until—"

"I'll take it," I say, cutting her off. I give her my credit card number, hang up, and am out the door in under five.

On the way to the airport, my phone beeps, alerting me to a missed call. My first thought is that it's Dad about Olivia, but when I look, I see it's Ellie's number with a message icon.

I don't hesitate. Her voice sinks through the receiver into my ear.

"Hey, uh, it's me," she says. "I want to talk. So, when you get this, no matter what time, please call me."

I don't know what she wants to say, but I'd give anything to silence her with my mouth. Then I smile to myself because in a few hours, that's exactly what I'll be doing.

Chapter 37

Damian

The sun isn't up yet when I knock on Ellie's apartment door. I don't want to wake Lia, and I hope to God Blake isn't here. The thought that he might be almost makes me sick. This is *my* fucking family, and it's way past time for me to claim them.

I knock again, a little louder this time. Stepping back, I shift my weight, impatient. I'm ready, so ready to be the man they deserve.

I can't be without them for another minute. If Ellie doesn't answer soon, I might resort to breaking down her door. But before I raise my hand again, it swings open. Ellie stands there, hair a mess, sleep heavy in her eyes. She wears a black top with super skinny straps and a tiny pair of pink shorts, and all I can do is stare because even half-asleep, this girl looks amazing.

She blinks. "Damian? What are you—"

"You alone?" I interrupt, glancing around her and into the apartment.

"Uh, Lia's here. What's going on?"

"Only Lia?"

Ellie takes a step back. Peers up at me through long lashes. "There's no one else." Her voice is soft, and I hope I'm right in what it implies—that Blake is out of the picture.

"No one?" I repeat to be sure, moving into her until our bodies barely touch, her breath coming warm and fast from her chest.

Slowly, she shakes her head. "No one, Damian."

As she says it, her gaze lowers to my mouth before it flicks back up again, and I realize she's in as deep as I am. Blake is gone.

I can't take it anymore. For so long I've fought this twist in my stomach, this ache in the depth of my soul, that now, standing here with this gorgeous, incredible woman in front of me, I'm at a loss for words. There's so much I want to say, that I want her to understand. Instead of saying any of it, I cup my palms around her jaw and crush my lips against hers.

"Don't ever answer the door wearing that," I say against her.

She gasps. Stares at me for a second like she's wondering if this is really happening.

"Believe it, Elle," I tell her before I return to kissing her.

I walk her backwards, kicking the door closed behind me. I keep going until I have her pushed up against the kitchen counter.

"Lia asleep?" I ask.

"Yeah." Ellie watches me, the wheels turning in her head. Probably thinking and rethinking what's happened between us and what's going to happen. Analyzing it play by play.

"Elle, baby, stop," I say, calling her out and running my palms under her top and up her stomach. "This—you and me—we make sense. Everything we've been through has led us here, back to each other. We belong together, Elle."

"That's what scares me, Damian—the past," she whispers.

"No," I say, taking her face between my palms again. "The past was our foundation. Yeah, it sucked sometimes, but that doesn't mean our future has to. You said it yourself: it's time to stop hiding. Don't let what's behind us stop what's right in front of us."

I search her eyes. Bring her mouth up to mine. "This is right, Elle," I say against her lips before I kiss them. "You know it!"

I'm right; I know this girl, and all the signs are there—in her gaze, in the way she bites her lip, and how she breathes with her mouth slightly open. I glide two fingers down the side of her neck. She shivers as she closes her eyes to revel in my touch. When they open, she focuses on me.

"Damian," she says. Judging by the tone of her voice, her doubts are reeling her in.

"Elle," I murmur, and taste her again. I won't let her head get in the way of this. "Stop thinking and tell me you love me," I tell her, hoping to make her smile. Maybe even laugh.

Instead, her fingers curl into my hair. "I love you," she whispers.

My heart stops. "Say it again."

She presses her forehead to mine, pauses there for a moment. "I love you, Damian Lowell," she says. "I love you so much."

I push my hands into her hair. Words form on the tip of my tongue, but I can't get them out. I'm too elated. It doesn't matter, though, because all I want to do is show her anyway. Talking is suddenly overrated.

I grab a hold of her ass. She gives a little jump, wrapping her legs around me. We're mentally in sync. Our motions are automatic, like our bodies remember how well we fit together.

Squeezing a butt cheek, I press up against her. Push into her in the same rhythm she has with me. I hold half her weight, the counter accommodates the other. Those tiny shorts she has on ride up her crack, so I'm gripping bare skin and loving every second. I crave each dip and curve of this body, the one that's so familiar to me, but I never fully appreciated. Tonight, I'm going to change that.

Ellie moans into my ear, then she devours my neck, sucking and nibbling like she's never tasted me before. And like this, she hasn't. All of her guards are down. What held her back each time we were together before doesn't hold her back now because she's not doing this to help numb anyone's pain. Right now, she's pure desire. Want. Need.

I lift her arms over her head and hold her wrists with one hand. With the other, I slide her shirt up, enjoying the sight when it goes over her boobs. Fuller than I remember, they bounce a little as I tug the material over her head. I skim my palms over them. Thumb the hard nipples bubbling from the

367

centers.

As I do, I cover her lips with mine and slide my tongue inside to massage hers. She responds with urgency, her arms lowering and circling my neck to pull herself closer.

I've touched Ellie a million times. Kissed her. Felt her. Did all these things, but they've never sent me soaring the way they do now. I want to touch, caress, taste every inch of her, and when I'm done, I want to do it all over again.

Ellie's hips thrust into me, harder each time, and I need to get her to her room and finish stripping her down. With her legs still wrapped around me, I carry her down the hallway to where I assume her bedroom is. I kiss her and try my damnedest to be quiet. The last thing I want is to wake Lia up.

"Here. Left," Ellie pants, her voice breathy. Then she tugs my bottom lip between her teeth.

Inside, I don't want to put her down and stop touching her, but I have to so I can lock the door. Afterward, I toss my shirt on the floor before I get back to her. Topless and on her back, Ellie's so fucking sexy. Large round breasts tempt me, and I slide my knee onto the mattress and crawl up to her.

She shudders under me, and I lower my body over hers to warm her. To protect her. I suckle on her neck, the soft flesh so succulent in my mouth. She holds onto my biceps and turns her head to the side, giving me better access.

I trace a finger over her lips, her chin, and between her breasts. Her lungs expand as she fills them up, anticipating my next move. I don't stop. Down, down, down her body. Lines of silver stretch marks from her pregnancy run down her belly and hips, and they're so beautiful to me. They signify the miracle of life that grew inside her, that she sheltered for nine months and beyond.

I run a fingertip over one of them and peer up at Ellie as I do. She looks me over for a second before she rips her gaze away, suddenly self-conscious.

So I bend down. Kiss them. Glide my palms around her hips and bring her up to me.

"You're perfect, Elle. Beautifully perfect," I say against her skin. I peer back up at her. "I should have been here. I'm sorry."

"I am too," she murmurs. Then, she takes a hold of my wrists and guides them down, trusting me with her. Ellie's not simply giving me permission; she's giving me herself.

And I accept. Hooking my thumbs into the waistband of her shorts, I slide them down her thighs, touching as much skin as I can on my way to her ankles.

I toss them behind me, meet her stare, and smile. She's propped up on her elbows watching me. Her lips red and slightly separated, she's breathing heavy, and I know I'll never get enough of this woman.

I skim the insides of her legs, her thighs, working my way up. Hands first, then my mouth follows. I want to kiss every part of her—finally make her mine.

At her knees, I push them open. She relents easily, letting them fall to the sides. With nothing more than a short graze of my tongue over the tip of her clit, I bypass what will be my taste of heaven so

I can tease her some. Even after all these years, I remember what she likes. She whimpers, her mouth widening in an anticipation I won't fulfill yet.

My dick is aching, but this isn't about me. Too long have I played that game with nothing to show for it except pain and loneliness. So unlike all those times I fucked her to numb myself, I'll make love to her with everything I have.

I round her hips and smooth over her pelvis. The brotherhood tattoo that matches mine is inked into her skin on the right side, on top of the bone. She cried when she got it done, her eyes connecting with mine as I sat beside her.

I sweep my thumb over it, and I'm reminded of the promise I made Liam—I'd take care of Ellie for him. I've done a shitty-ass job so far, and now I don't want to take care of Ellie for him. No, I want to take care of her for *me*.

I lower my head down to her belly and slowly glide my tongue up her stomach. She flattens herself onto the mattress, still taking me in. Then, she cocoons me around the waist with legs that feel as good as they look. Tightens them around me before she brings me up to her mouth.

She giggles at her little trick, and all I can think about is how wonderful the sound is. How I don't even care that she's in the driver's seat right now. That's the thing about Elle, she never took the reins when we were together. She simply followed my lead and never asked or complained about anything.

This Ellie isn't afraid. Isn't hurting.

"Kiss me," she says.

And I do. I suck her bottom lip into my mouth

and slide the tip of my tongue over the smoothness. Letting go, I feel her exhale against me.

"Better?" I ask.

"Much."

"Any more requests?"

She smirks. "I'll let you know."

I smile, tease her mouth with mine before I move down her body again to those plump breasts. I massage them, kneading them, savoring them. Before, I typically went straight for the gold, bypassing these beauties with little more than a short nibble and a squeeze.

Now, her nipples pebble under me. She closes her eyes and arches her back to relish in the sensation. I lick the tops of each. Blow cool air on them before sucking again. Under me, Ellie squirms against my stomach, raising her hips so my skin rubs her where she's dying for me. She's antsy, and I fucking love making her antsy.

Ellie lifts her hips into me, her pelvic bone hitting my arousal in the most perfect way. She props herself up on her elbows again and watches as I dip lower and lower, kissing her as I go.

Even before I get there, her legs are open for me. I can't wait to be inside this woman, filling her the way she fills me. I kick off the rest of my clothes. I'm between her legs, and she sucks in a sharp intake of air.

I glide one finger through her crevice. Then two.

"You're so fucking wet," I murmur, adding another finger and another until I've coated my hand with her. She's so ready for me, and I'm desperate to dive in.

I massage her. Kiss her. Finger her until she comes in my hand.

"Damian," she cries out, her head sinking deeper into the pillow. It's the first time she's called out my name with such pleasure, and I need to hear it again. I belong to her as much as she belongs to me.

"More?" I ask, even though I already know.

"Yes. Yes," she says, still panting from the orgasm I just gave her.

I position myself on top of her because I want to see her as I make love to her. Look into those gorgeous blues and watch every expression on her face as I take her higher and higher.

"Wait. I don't have any condoms, and I— stopped taking the pill," she breathes out.

I lean down and skate a kiss over her lips. "Good. I want to feel you. *Only* you."

Ellie shakes her head. "But, Damian, what if—"

"I'm taking my chances. What's the worst that could happen? That Lia gets a little brother?" I grin, and, slowly, a small smile appears on her face too. "I'm in this for the long haul. This is our family, and I'm going to take care of it."

Her breath hitches, and she stares at me. Pale blue irises connect with mine, and her chest rises as she finally inhales.

"I love you, Elle."

When she'd hung up on me, I'd only gotten the words half out. Still, I knew she heard them. But now, *now*, she believes them.

Eyes search mine, taking me in. Then, one hand caresses my face. A thumb traces over my lips.

"Say it again," she says like I did earlier.

372

"I love you, Elle," I say. Then I make us one.

Chapter 38

Ellie

The world stops spinning. Or it's spinning faster—I don't really know.

When I saw him on my doorstep, I had a major *Jerry McGuire* moment. Though he had me way before "hello." The man who helped pick up the shards of my brokenness and then pieced me back together after Liam died is the only one who can make me whole. And that's exactly what he's doing now—making me whole.

Slow and tender, Damian glides in and out of me, making love to me in a way he's never done before. He cradles me, caresses me, kisses me. Gently strokes my body with a softness I didn't know he had.

I'm not used to this Damian. The one I knew only worked you enough to make his climax better. But now? Now he's owning this. Not only with his body, it seems, but with his heart and soul too. I see it in his eyes—they're brighter than I've ever seen.

And as he stares at me, rocks into me, there's a different kind of desire in his gaze. One that's not focused on deadening the pain. It's focused solely on me.

Through the lungfuls of air I'm heaving, I slip my tongue in his mouth, moving it to the rhythm he's set for us. His thumb slides back and forth over a nipple and the sensation drives straight to my core. Between that, the kiss, and the perfect way he's thrusting into me, I'm close to losing it again.

I tighten around him and dig my fingers into his biceps. It's not until he speaks that I realize I've stopped kissing him.

"Come for me again, Elle. Just let go," he murmurs against me.

I cling to him. My heart pounds against my ribs, and I wonder if he can feel it too. He pumps into me faster, tipping me over the edge. With my face buried into his shoulder, I cry out my pleasure. I raise my hips to meet him as the aftershocks rock my body.

He slows but doesn't stop. Eases himself in and out as I contract around him. He sucks on my neck and I lay back to let him do whatever he wants. I'm putty in his hands.

"That. Was the sexiest thing I've ever heard." He's grinning like an idiot, those dimples I love pinching in deep.

I'm still catching my breath, so I don't answer. He's not waiting for one anyway.

He lifts up on his arms to stare at me. A mischievous grin appears on his face.

"You good?" he asks.

I nod and reach up to lower his mouth to mine again. Our tongues meet in the middle, and he begins to speed up again, and I realize he hasn't finished yet.

As if reading my thoughts, he smirks. "I want to hear you one more time. Louder."

I'm speechless, and the only thing I can think to say is, "Lia-Kat?"

"We gotta talk about that nickname, baby. Don't worry about her. That girl sleeps through anything, and tonight is about us. So lay back and enjoy what I'm doing to you."

I don't respond because his lips are on mine, and I have no choice but to obey. I sink into the mattress, concentrating on his body against mine. Skin against skin. Warmth against warmth.

God, he feels so good.

I run my palms up his arms, devouring him with my touch. I used to cover up the brotherhood tattoo on his arm as if by doing that, it would conceal the guilt I felt for sleeping with him. Like Liam wouldn't see what we were doing.

Now though, I realize it's a piece of Damian—a piece of me—that has led us to this place.

He pushes into me, and I'm so lost in him. I focus on his eyes, those brilliant sapphires I've dreamed of for years, which finally belong to me.

Damian slips a lock of hair behind my ear. "I love you, Elle. You. Only you. Everything about you."

"Damian," I say, just to taste his name on my lips.

He lowers himself over me, covering the length

of my body with his and pushing deeper into me. His breath flows against my neck before he sucks the tender skin between his teeth. But I still need him closer, somehow still afraid that if I let go, he'll disappear.

I wrap my legs around his hips and bring him into me. He groans, causing my desire to build higher. I wind my fingers in his hair to hold myself together for a little longer, because I don't want this to end.

"Elle, you feel so amazing; you're going to make me lose my mind," he murmurs.

"Good. I want you to," I breathe, barely able to get the words out because I'm so close to the edge. My whole body tenses, anticipating the release that will send me soaring again. I can't hold back much longer.

Damian delves into me once.

Twice.

I squirm under him, gripping onto whatever part of him I can.

Three times—

And I lose it.

I hear Damian's moan at my ear as he comes with me. His arms cradle me against him, his lips leaving a trail of kisses as they move from my neck to my mouth.

"Promise that I get to hear you cry out like this every night from now on."

I'm panting, unable to catch my breath as I bathe in the afterglow of our love.

"Promise me," he repeats, tucking my hair behind my ears.

Slowly, my senses return, and I nod.
"I promise."

~*~

Damian

The last traces of moonlight dance over her skin. Her head nestles against my chest. Ellie fell asleep cuddled up like she used to do. Only this time, I want her here because she belongs.

I trail my fingers up and down her bare back, and it's like touching her for the first time. This beautiful woman, the mother of my child, loves me. It's crazy amazing. Especially after all we've been through—pain, loss, more pain.

But I'm ready. I'm so ready to move on. Because after so much darkness, I finally see the light.

I sweep Ellie's hair from her face and kiss her forehead. Her lashes flutter but don't open, and the simple act makes me smile. I hug her closer, press my lips against her, and close my eyes.

Life doesn't get better than this.

Chapter 39

Ellie

I wake up to the smell of bacon. Lia's giggles bubble into my bedroom, followed by Damian's voice.

"Shhh. Mommy's still asleep, and we want to surprise her."

Last night wasn't a dream, but I'm pretty sure I'm living a fairytale.

I stretch my arms above my head while I wait. The blankets slip down, and I realize I'm—

Naked. Crap, I'm naked!

If my nose is correct, they're serving me breakfast in bed…and I'm naked.

I toss off the covers and begin a frantic search for my clothing. I only find half of it, though, before I remember the top part is in the living room.

"You got her coffee?" Damian asks, and my guess is that they're in the hallway.

"Yep-yep!" Lia quips, then she giggles. "We're like spies."

379

Damian laughs. "Tip-toe like this. Very quiet."

I scurry over to my drawers and throw on whatever shirt is on top. I jump back in bed, throw the blankets back over me, and pretend to be asleep because I don't want to ruin their fun.

The door creaks open, and another little giggle escapes Lia. It's silly and adorable, and I have to work not to snicker.

I hear the click of the light switch as it's flipped on.

"Careful," Damian warns in a hushed voice, and I suspect Lia turned on the light while carrying my cup of coffee.

"I got it," she whispers back with some sass. "I'm almost four, you know. Next month."

I inwardly cringe, hoping he didn't give her a *full* cup of coffee to carry. Surely, not...right?

"Well, four-year-olds need to be careful too," he says, and I just know our daughter rolled her eyes at that.

There's movement on the nightstand as Damian rearranges the things on it and sets the tray down.

"Coffee?" he asks, and I assume Lia gives it to him. "Thank you."

Then the mattress sinks beside me and Damian's fingers sweep across my cheek.

"Elle, baby? We made you breakfast," Damian murmurs. The nickname sounds so sweet coming from his lips this morning. In fact, everything seems sweeter this morning.

In answer, I give a little moan to play along. Lia's patience, though, is at its limit, and she has no time for my games. "Mommy, wake up! Look who's here!"

Her little body climbs up on top of mine before she straddles my stomach and bounces on it.

"Mommy!" she repeats.

"I'm up. I'm *so* up," I say, half laughing.

Damian leans down and kisses me. "Best morning of my life." His nose grazes mine, and I glimpse a hint of those dimples that make him so irresistible.

I love you, I mouth, wishing this little moment we're sharing would last longer.

"See, Mom?" Lia interrupts us. "I knew he'd come for us."

I hug her to me and kiss her head. "Yes, you did."

"We made you breakfast," she says. "Daddy even let me crack the eggs!"

I flash Damian a glance. "Brave."

"Maybe, but you're the one eating them," he answers, grinning.

I take it as a challenge. "Whatcha waiting for, then? Bring it on!"

Lia claps her hands as Damian places the tray on my lap. I start with the eggs because Lia's eagerly staring at me with wide eyes.

"You look like a monkey," I tell her before I scoop the eggs into my mouth. "Mmmm." Really, they're not bad. Lacks salt, but at least there's no shells.

"All right, babygirl," Damian says, picking Lia up off the bed. "Big day. Go get dressed and pack a bag."

"Okie dokie!" Lia says and skips out.

"Pack a bag?" I ask, my brows high on my forehead. I'd kind of been hoping our first day together would be uneventful.

"Big day," he repeats.

"Care to elaborate?"

Caribbean blue eyes study me. Melt me into a school-girl puddle of puppy love, and suddenly I don't care as long as he takes me with him.

"There's something I have to do, and I want you with me, Elle."

He's serious as he says it, making me a little worried. I trust him, though. "Anything."

He caresses my face, a thumb smoothing over my mouth, which has become one of his favorite things to do, apparently. "Good. We leave in two hours."

"Damian?" I ask because I need to get this out before we go anywhere. "I'm sorry. I'm sorry for not telling you about Lia. For stealing away all that time the two of could have shared. And I'm sorry for not flying up, and I'm sorry that—"

"Baby, it's okay. I was an asshole."

"Please, Damian, let me say this," I say, but he's shaking his head.

"We can sit here and spend our day apologizing to each other for all the shit we've done, but then what? I'm sorry too, Elle. For a mile long list of crap, but wounds don't heal with words alone. They're just the starting point. Trust and forgiveness takes time. Action. And I'm done screwing around. I'm here for good, and I'd rather spend every second of my life proving *that* to you."

He brushes my tangled hair away from my face.

"We both fucked up. We're both sorry. Now let's move forward. Can you do that?"

Slowly, I feel myself nod. In a way, it's like we're starting over. Not with a new slate, though. With a clean one. One we've scribbled on over and over, black and messy, and now we're wiping it off. Sure, it'll get dirty again, but I smile as I think about repeating this process with the man I love, growing together.

"Good." He kisses me and lowers the blankets from my chest. An eyebrow quirks up when he sees me.

"What in the world are you wearing?"

I look down to see what I threw on. It's the ugly red Christmas t-shirt I made for a party at school. Lia helped, and it very closely resembles elf vomit—glitter, sequins, beads, you name it—splattered all over the material. There's even a glob of glue Lia accidently dumped on it that, covered in gold glitter, hangs from Rudolf's nose like a booger.

"Um, well, what I wore before wasn't exactly appropriate," I say. I need to trash this shirt as soon as possible.

Damian's gaze slides down my body and back up, and I shiver. "No, baby, what you wore before is the *only* thing that's appropriate."

To emphasize his point, warm palms slip under the hideous t-shirt and begin to lift it off.

"Damian," I breathe against his mouth. Nipples hardening, my body is already reacting to him. "Lia."

"Your door has a lock," he says, necking me.

I hold back a moan that's dying to come out.

"Yeah, but that won't do much good since she's standing at the door."

Damian rotates and lets go of me. I snicker at his surprise.

Lia doesn't look impressed. In fact, the little eye roll she gives us clearly indicates she has a timetable we're not sticking to. To prove it, she holds up her suitcase. "All packed. Let's go see Olivia."

~*~

As soon as we land at the airport, the hospital is our first stop. Lia silently takes in the snow outside and the Christmas decorations. Damian threads his fingers with mine and leads the way to the third floor.

"How is Olivia?" I ask now that we're here, lowering my voice so only he hears.

"When I left, not well. Dad was putting her on oxygen."

"Will Lia even be able to see her?"

"I'll make it happen."

We walk down the corridor to a room at the end of the hall. Dr. Lowell steps out and turns to close the door. When he sees us, he stops short though. His gaze lands on his son first. I can't read it, but then he smiles when he peers at Lia and me.

"It's good to see you again, Ellie," he says.

"You too, Dr. Lowell."

"Grandpa?" Lia says from beside me. "Can I see Olivia now?"

He sighs through his nose and glances at Damian

again. "She's weak. Very weak." He looks at Lia again. "Don't stay too long. She needs her rest."

With the way Damian's jaw tenses, I understand what Dr. Lowell is saying: there's nothing more he can do.

"Come on, Lia," Damian says, reaching out to our daughter.

Lia takes his hand in one of hers. She grabs mine in the other, and together we walk inside. When Lia sees Olivia, she lets go of me, silently stepping forward to the bed.

I stay back, giving them the moment. But even from where I stand I can see the ghostly white of Olivia's skin. Her eyes are sunken in, and her lips are the palest of pink. On the pillow, her bald head barely makes an indentation.

"Lia," the little girl rasps out, her mouth turning up in a smile. "You came!"

"Olivia." Lia takes her hand. "I'm so sorry you're sick."

"Me too, but I'm happy you're here." She turns her head and coughs before continuing, "You're my best friend."

"Oh, here," Damian says, pulling out a piece of paper from his back pocket. "I thought you should be the one to give this to her."

Olivia smiles at him. Then she unfolds the paper and gives it to Lia. "I made this…for you. To remember me."

"Thank you," Lia says.

"The bottom…it says…'Thank you, Lia. Friendship *really* *is* magic.'" Olivia pants and coughs again.

Lia looks up at Damian, and I see a tear slip down her cheek. Damian wraps an arm around her shoulders. Lia wipes it away before she faces her friend.

"Don't give up, Olivia," Lia sobs. "Please. There's always hope."

Olivia nods. "I know. I won't."

Chapter 40

Damian

Even though she was quiet in the car, Lia's eyes light up when she sees the tree with presents loaded underneath. A massive stuffed Twilight Sparkle sits in the corner. Her jaw drops open, and she looks up at me.

"Are those for me?" she asks, half timid, half excited.

Ellie's expression is priceless too, and I lean in and kiss her for it. "You didn't..." she murmurs.

I smirk. "Of course I did."

She blushes, and it's the cutest damn thing I've ever seen. I grin as I pick Lia up.

"Tomorrow night we'll do the whole Christmas shebang. Even invite your other grandparents too," I offer, flicking my eyes to Ellie. She smiles.

"Yes! Yes!" Lia exclaims and throws her arms around my neck. "You're the best daddy in the whole wide world!"

I chuckle and kiss her cheek. "Even if I say it's

387

bedtime right now?" I ask.

Excitement drains out of her as if she suddenly realized she'd forgotten her favorite pony toy back in Florida. "Do I have to?" she whines, flopping her weight on me.

"It's late," Ellie helps, and I figure she's less likely to cave than I am at the moment. If it weren't for what I need to do next, I'd let Lia stay up until she dozed off on her own.

"Fiiiiiine," Lia drawls out.

She hugs my neck. Her head rests on my shoulder as we walk up the staircase. We go past my old bedroom and Liam's, to one of the guest bedrooms—the one Mom decorated in purple pastels in hopes that one day her granddaughters would sleep there.

Ellie gets her ready with her favorite My Little Pony jammies, and Lia jumps up in the queen-size bed that's way too big for her. I tuck her in. Ellie and I kiss her goodnight.

"Sleep tight, babygirl," I say.

"I love you, Daddy."

I brush blonde hair away from the face of the little girl who's changed my life.

"I love you too, my Lia."

~*~

I take a deep breath. Grip the box a little tighter. This is it.

"What's up there?" Ellie asks, motioning toward the door we're standing at.

"The attic," I answer.

"I know, but…"

I breathe deep again. Face Ellie. "Something I have to do."

She tilts her head, blonde hair falling over a shoulder. "You have to go to the attic?"

I nod. "Yeah. And I'd like you to come with me."

"If that's what you want," she replies softly.

We walk up the stairs hand in hand. At the top, I flip on the light. I haven't been up here since I was a kid, when Liam and I used it to play hide and seek.

Now, it stores all of his and mom's things—the ones we couldn't get rid of but didn't want to see, either. There's also old furniture and crap. Stuff I'm not sure where it came from.

Ellie squeezes my hand as her gaze lands on something familiar. She lets go and moves toward the wall. On the desk, there's a picture of her and Liam at prom, and Liam's tux hangs on a hat rack beside it. She fingers the sleeves and brushes the lapels.

Then, she picks up a framed certificate, blows off the dust, and smiles. I step up behind her.

"This was so stupid. As seniors, we had to vote on all these dumb categories for each other, and the winners got an award. Liam cleaned up, winning a bunch of different ones: hottest guy, smartest guy, nicest car, best smile, most unavailable. But this one?" She flips it around to show me. "This one he was the most proud of—Messiest Locker."

I snicker. "Probably because it seemed out of character to everyone."

Ellie leans against the desk, facing me. "It's been a long time since I've thought about Liam. I've…" She pauses. "I've spent the last few years thinking about you."

I reach down and touch her cheek, and she turns into my palm and kisses it.

"I spent a lot of time feeling guilty for loving you," she continues. "Because of Liam, but…he was gone. And by the time I began to accept that, you'd found Kate."

"I'm sorry, Elle," I say, because I am. I never meant to hurt her.

"It's okay. It all worked out, right?"

I laugh, shaking my head at the realization that just popped in my head.

"What?" Ellie says, my amusement confusing her.

"Kate used to say that all the time. That everything would work out in the end. I never believed her. I guess I didn't consider that my end and her end were two different things."

Ellie frowns and stares at her feet. "She sounds pretty wonderful."

I lift Ellie's chin so she's looking at me. "She was. But so are you. Kate's part of my past, and you're my future. You and Lia." I cup her face, gaze into those beautiful eyes. "I love you, Elle. Now and always."

"Can I tell you something?"

"Anything."

"I know you blame yourself for Liam's and Nora's death. Maybe Kate's, I'm not sure, but it's not your fault. They loved you no matter what."

I don't remember telling her that, but it's strange. I'm relieved she knows. "Yeah. That's going to take me longer to sort out."

She presses her palm over my heart. "I understand. I just wanted to tell you I'll be there."

I lean down. Kiss her. Feel her soft lips against mine to seal the promise.

~*~

Ellie stands behind me, her knees touching my back as I sit. Her being here while I do this makes it easier. Makes me stronger.

I open the box of Kate's stuff for the last time. All the contents are there, including a rose from her funeral. I pull out her diary. Flip to the very last blank page and write.

Dear Katie,

It took me awhile. Almost five years, but I understand now. Katie, you gave me wings, and I'm finally starting to fly. It's beautiful up here.

There's so much I regret. Words I didn't say. Things I didn't do. I realize now, though, that I can't go back. I'm moving on. Accepting the mistakes I've made because I can't change them.

I've held on to you for a long time. I

thought if I let you go, then what we shared wouldn't be real.

But Katie, I'm ready now. You showed me who I could be. And I want to be that person for the rest of my life.

Someone once told me that letting someone go doesn't mean you forget them. It means you love them from here and move on with your life like they would have wanted.

That's what your fifth wish was about, right?

Katie. I'm finally doing it.

All five wishes are now complete.

Love Always, Damian

Ellie's hand rests on my shoulder. I reach up and squeeze it.

"Here," she says, kneeling beside me. She gives me the picture of Lia I keep in my wallet, the one from the diner when I first found out about her. "So Kate knows how your story ends."

I take the photo, slip it behind the last page, and close Kate's diary. Then I place it back in the box that's been under my bed for almost five years.

I stand up and slap off the dust on my jeans. Scanning the room, I find the perfect spot. I pick up the box. It surprises me how light it seems now that I'm finally doing what she asked.

In the very back corner is my mother's vanity. On top lies her brush, some jewelry, and the Celtic cross she kept on the nightstand, the one I designed my tattoo after.

I can't think of a better place to fulfill Kate's final wish for me. *My last wish, Damian, is that once you've read my diary, you'll put it in a box. Place it in the attic somewhere and leave it there. Let it collect dust.*

I set the box beside the cross and turn around. Taking Ellie's hand, I close my eyes for a moment. Kate's face appears, and she smiles her approval. I open my eyes. Give Ellie's hand a squeeze, and together we leave, closing the door behind us.

That's not all, though. You have a whole life in front of you. Don't waste it. Don't dwell on the past. Move forward.

Damian, my love, my final wish is for you to let me go.

"Tell me, Elle," I ask after we've descended the staircase. "How does my story end?"

Ellie grins and tucks her bottom lip between her teeth. She circles her arms around my waist. Rises up on her tip-toes and kisses me. "It's going to be a happily ever after."

Epilogue

Damian

The ring clenched in my left hand feels like air. Giving it to her today is the easiest decision I've ever made.

The piece of jewelry in my right hand, though, weighs on me. Never in my life have I held something so small and so heavy at the same time. But I have no doubts; I'll give it to her when it's time.

I roll the ring between my index finger and thumb, mostly because I'm nervous. With all the shit I've done and put her through, I can't believe she still wants me.

"Hey, man!" Dylan leans in from around the corner. "You ready?"

I take one last look at the ring and smile. "Yeah. Yeah, let's do this."

Dylan slaps my back on my way past. "Dude, you forgetting something?"

I pause. As soon as I give it to him, there's no

turning back. I take two steps toward him and shake his hand.

He grins. "Me being your best man is still a no, huh? You're a douche-bag."

"Better than being an asshole." We do a quick man-hug. "Where's my dad?"

"With Lia."

"All right. See you in a few."

I take a deep breath as Dylan jogs down the hall. In front of me is the door, and all I have to do is walk through it.

I don't hesitate.

The pianist and violinist play whatever music Ellie picked out. I don't know what it is, but I listen to commit it to memory. I don't want to forget anything about this day.

I scan the sanctuary until I find them. Jason and Marcy Browdy, Kate's parents, sit halfway down on the left side. I'd caught them when they first came in.

"We're so proud of you, Damian," Jason said, referring both to the wedding and finishing my first year of med school at the top of the class.

"Kate would be too," Marcy added.

"Yeah, I know," I said and gave her a hug.

Now, my dad walks down the aisle and is the first one at my side. He embraces me, patting me twice on the back.

"Big day, son. Or should I say Dr. Lowell?"

"Not yet. I still have a few years before that."

"You know you're welcome on my staff when you finish."

I hold out my hand to him. "Here, before I forget."

"I wondered if you were going to trust me with that. I *am* the one who picked it out twenty-six years ago." He laughs, and so do I.

"Technically, it's Liam's job, but I guess you'll do." I wait a second for the sting of what I just said to hit me. It doesn't come. Somewhere above me, my best man is proud.

Dylan fist-bumps me as he takes his place beside my father.

Down the aisle walk our flower girl and ring bearer, both in matching satin gowns that reach the floor. Tiaras in their hair, Lia and Olivia look like the princesses they are, or BFFs, as they refer to themselves. Since Olivia's remission, they've been inseparable. We even flew her down to Florida for Lia's fifth birthday at Disney World this last January.

Lia beams at me, and I think that I've never seen her happier. She's been waiting impatiently for today.

The music changes, signaling go time. In the back, the doors swing open, and my bride stands there, eyes finding me immediately. She laughs, and I'm in awe of the sound even though I can't hear her that far away.

She pushes her father's wheelchair down the center of the church, and I can't take my eyes off her. Nor do hers waver from me.

Her walk seems like it takes forever and no time

at all. Her father gives her away, placing her hand in mine, and I know from this moment on, I'll never let it go. Everything we've been through, the love we share has brought us here. Our past and our future bind us together.

"The rings," the pastor says, holding them up. "Rings are a symbol. They are circular with no beginning and no end. The space inside isn't simply empty space, either. But rather it symbolizes a door, both to the known and the unknown. Whatever may come in your lives, remember these rings signify your love and eternal commitment."

"With this ring, I thee wed. Until death do us part," I say, slipping my mother's ring onto Ellie's finger. Her smile hits me, and I'm so lost in her.

"With this ring, I thee wed. Until death do us part," Ellie repeats and slides my ring into place.

I don't know what's said next. I don't care. All I want is to kiss my wife and make this official.

Ellie can see what I'm thinking. "Not yet," she mouths.

My gaze dips down to her lips, and I wait until she leans in. Then I kiss my wife, the first of the millions of kisses I'll give her.

"And now, Lia, would you please join us?" the pastor says. "Your father has something he'd like to pledge to you."

Lia skips up to us, and I crouch down. I lift the necklace out of my pocket and place the Trinity heart charm in my palm.

"Daddy," Lia says, recognizing it.

"This," I say, circling the chain around her neck, "is the Celtic symbol for hope. Now you'll always know where to find it."

Little fingers touch the silver and gold now lying against her chest. I think of how the symbol is permanently etched over my own heart.

Then I take both of her hands in mine. "Lia, I want to make a vow to you too. From this day forward, I will always be with you. Here." I pat over her heart. "And even when you think you're alone, you won't be."

My daughter peers up at me. "Promise-promise?"

I smile. "I promise-promise."

The End

Acknowledgements

As I went to write this acknowledgements section, I stared at the blank screen for a few moments. I did this for two reasons. Number one: I really don't want to leave anyone out. And number two: I'm in awe. In awe of the number of people who have supported me. In awe of my husband and children who have put up with my craziness. In awe of my author besties who've been there for me. In awe of my amazing readers. In awe of the fact that this is my fifth published novel. How did that happen?

First, foremost, and always, I thank God, my Lord and Savior. Without Him, none of this would be possible.

Next, to my amazing husband, who reads through all of my books and encourages me like no one else. I wouldn't be where I am today without him. I love you, baby!

For my four little minions, number three being a huge inspiration for this story. She's Lia, I swear, in looks and in attitude. My kids put up with me and constantly remind me of the meaning of grace. I love you! I love you! I love you! I love you!

A special shout out to my brother Landon for this book. For the whole series, actually. For allowing me to use his song, "My Hiding Place" in *Love Always, Kate*. And for asking me to put a character look-alike of him into one of my books. Say hello to Dylan Akoi, who not only became a character look-alike of my brother, but somehow got some of my brother's personality traits as well.

Thanks for the suggestion, bro!

To my parents, in-laws, and extended family for all their support. Thanks for being there for me!

Thank you to my beta readers—Tonille Burrows, Temperance Elisabeth, Kim Jackson, and Heather Jelsma. <3 <3 <3

I've been blessed with some awesome author besties, who also dub as CPs, therapists, cheerleaders, editors, pimpers, and friends. This book wouldn't be what it is without them.

Sunniva Dee—did you read the above? Book #5! Can you believe it? We've been in this crazy business, holding hands, since the beginning of our careers. Before the beginning, really. We've shared ups and downs, successes and failures. We've laughed together, supported each other, cried together, growled at each other, and even as I write this, we're diving into our next books together. #herestomanymore

Laura Thalassa—we've come a long way since you found my query letter on AQC, haven't we? Career-wise, writing-wise, and friendship-wise. For all five books now, you've had your awesome eye involved. I can't tell you how grateful I am for that. I'm looking forward to seeing what this year, and many years down the road, brings. #bringiton #hashtagconversations #hashtagawardceremony #weshoulddothat

Angela McPherson—this is the first book you've CP'd/beta read for me, and I'm so very thankful. I love having you as part of our little writing group thingy. I enjoy our #workdates, and since you and I are more of the night owl types than the other two (and we're in the same time zone), we've had many #workdates and gotten to know each other better. I'm so excited to help you tear apart *Gypsy Love* next. #meetuptonighttowrite #youbringthewine

Thank you to my wonderful street team. I love knowing I can bounce ideas off you, and that you'll give me your honest opinions on teasers, art, and author logos. Thanks for your support and for loving my books.

A huge shout out to the bloggers and reviewers who have supported me and this series. I'm too scared to name you all because I'll probably leave someone out, but you know who you are. You've helped get my name out there, loved my books, and welcomed me into the writing community with open arms. You deserve so much more than a simple "thank you." Really, you do.

Toni Rakestraw, my editor, you were wonderful to work with, as always. I get my manuscript back from you and have way too many SMH moments, so thank you so much for catching my errors. And my logical issues. And my punctuation mishaps. And for explaining why. Thank you so very much. ☺

A huge thanks to Wicked by Design for the beautiful cover art. I love it! And thanks also for the new cover art for *Love Always, Kate*. Both covers now match perfectly!

Eternal thanks to Limitless Publishing! Jennifer O'Neill, Jessica Gunhamer, Dixie Matthews, Lori Whitwam, thank you! Thank you! Thank you! It's been a pleasure.

Now to the readers. You guys are the ones who

bring this story to life. Who breathe air into its lungs and make the story something more than just a story. When you read it, Damian, Ellie, Kate, and Lia all become real. You get to know them. Feel for them. Live their lives with them. And grow to love them. They belong to you. Thank you for giving them life.

Love Always,
d.

About the Author

Born and raised in Iowa, d. Nichole King writes her stories close to home. There's nothing like small-town Midwest scenery to create the perfect backdrop for an amazing tale.

She wrote her first book in junior high and loved every second of it. However, she couldn't bring herself to share her passion with anyone. She packed it away until one day, with the encouragement of her husband, she sat down at the computer and began to type. Now, she can't stop.

When not writing, d. is usually curled up with a book, scrapbooking, or doing yet another load of laundry.

Along with her incredible husband, she lives in small-town Iowa with her four adorable children and their dog, Peaches.

Facebook:
www.facebook.com/authordnicholeking

Twitter:
www.twitter.com/dnicholeking

Website:
www.dnicholeking.com

Pinterest:
www.pinterest.com/dnicholek

Goodreads:
www.goodreads.com/author/show/7762889.D_Nich
ole_King

Made in the USA
Monee, IL
22 January 2022

89572789R00239